BOOK 2

WARLORD
OF THE NIGHTMARE REALM

DOC SPEARS

WARGATE

An imprint of Galaxy's Edge Press
PO BOX 534
Puyallup, Washington 98371
Copyright © 2022 by Doc Spears
All rights reserved.

Paperback ISBN: 978-1-949731-81-1
Hardcover ISBN: 978-1-949731-82-8

www.wargatebooks.com

✦ ✦ ✦

THE WAR IS PAUSED, BUT NOWHERE NEAR OVER. BENJAMIN COLT AND his team have done the impossible. With Talis Darmon seated on the Spectral Throne, the Red Army gathers strength before their Warlord leads them to one last battle and total victory.

Long held apart from the kingdom, the far western city of Pyreenia is home to a people alienated from the rest of Mihdradahl, and the last holdout of the barbaric army led by Ben's former teammates.

But festering in the remote city is an evil greater than any horde of four-armed savages. And like the many mysteries of Vistara, it awaits discovery not only by the Green Berets stranded there, but by the very natives of the red planet, descendants of civilizations and histories known to them all only by myth.

With the help of new allies and old enemies, Benjamin Colt and his friends explore realms lost to time and sanity, all to keep a promise. By his life or his death, he'll use everything learned as a Special Forces operator to win his queen her kingdom.

The atmosphere is depleted. His army is rife with infiltrators bent on murderous revenge. His queen's council is riddled with conspirators who plot his demise. And if that isn't enough, the queen questions if he's the champion she'd hoped for.

Evil has a name as well as a sanctuary, leaving Benjamin Colt no choice but to take the path he knows best—to walk the gauntlet of combat. He'll wield his brand of destruction to prove himself the true inheritor to the title, chosen by the ghost of the only other to bear the name. Until everyone, including the greatest threat in this or any universe—the slumbering leviathan god, Anso-Kylon—proclaims the truth.

The name Warlord exists to describe one man. And his name is Deacon Benjamin Colt.

01

"ONE GOOD HIT BEHIND THE FRONT SHOULDER SHOULD ANCHOR them. Don't kill the riders. I want every one of them." Like so many of the creatures on Mars, the horses had four pairs of shoulders. But like most any critter, the boiler room sat right up front. With arkall, it just happened to be between the first and second shoulder. I trusted my companion like almost no other person from Earth or Mars—Red, Green, or otherwise—but I had a tiny bit of apprehension about his ability to put the 230-grain copper death pills where they'd do the job. What he was about to attempt was easy only in the movies.

"There is a cursed rock under my chest." He broke position to scoot himself and the gun laterally a few inches and recomposed his prone position. With his extra set of upper limbs, his anatomy was somewhere between mine and the arkall he was about to drop. "I do not perceive myself performing with the same ease you demonstrate," he fretted. This would be the first time Khraal Kahlees had actually pressed the trigger on a living, moving target at such a distance. I'd never seen him so anxious.

"You're doing fine. Settle in and get ready for a wind call."

"To any but you, I would not admit my apprehension, Benjamin Colt. I have not felt such since I was little more than hatched and beside my clansmen for my first mounted charge into battle. Why is that? We are in no danger."

"It's like we talked about. Don't think about the consequences of missing, think about the act. Get your head in the game, brother."

It was cool to be excited by the anticipation, but it was not cool to let it affect your performance. He was in the throes of buck fever. I grew up in Appalachia where deer hunting was more necessity than hobby, more religion than diversion, where putting meat on the table was a measure of competence and considered as gravely as any quality that spoke to your character. That you hit what you aimed at was as important as telling the truth, working hard, and holding your hat over your heart when you pledged the flag. Say what you will, it made me who I am today.

You can judge whether that's a good or a bad thing.

"If it were easy, anyone could do it, Double-K. Check your cant." I could see out of the corner of my eye the level indicator was off. At some point, you have to take the training wheels off and let junior ride down the concrete street in shorts. Experience is a valuable teacher and knowledge trickles down, not up. It takes generations to influence how an army goes to war, but with more threats on the horizon than we had bullets or ray guns to counter, our army didn't have that kind of time. If the general of our army could do this, it would send a message through the ranks—the Thulians have a better way, and we can learn it.

And I was the one to make it happen—the last sniper on Mars. Just because I was Warlord didn't mean I had to let everyone else have all the fun. Lying here on the killing floor with my friend was a better place than most to be when the alternative was another dull day in the palace.

Double-K made a tiny adjustment to the side-focus knob. "It seems an adage in the making that whichever of the enemy holds the information you desire is the one inadvertently killed in the ambush, wouldn't you agree, Benjamin Colt?"

I did. "So don't screw the pooch. Give me a one-mil lead and send it." I held off making my own shot and prepared to follow the hazy trail of his bullet's wake.

I'd found out quickly after the first time I broke the trigger here on Mars that because of the low gravity and thin atmosphere, dropping anything within 1500 meters was child's play. Not to take away from my Tarn brother's talent at his newfound passion, but between the environmental conditions that made a bullet fly better than anywhere on Earth and his extra set of arms spread wide to make him especially stable, I needn't have worried.

My MK 22 sniper rifle barked obediently for him as though she were his. The lead arkall lumbered along, asleep on its many feet, droning through the desert like a sleep-deprived Ranger student on an endless patrol. The red Martian sun glinted off the bullet until it became an elastic hole in the sweet spot just behind the front shoulder blade, a handsbreadth high. Like a house of cards hit by a gale, the beast collapsed. Double-K hadn't just put a pill into the pump and pipes; he'd spined it. The Tarn rider was launched off, caught in the drowsy semiconsciousness of a night watchman with no coffee on board.

I was a proud papa.

An ambush is the greatest practical joke in the universe. A good mechanical ambush is the best. Claymore mines pelting thousands of steel balls to turn a patrol into so much hamburger is the dependable cheap laugh of combat comedy. A sniper initiated interdiction is more akin to an ensemble cast that brings the laughs slowly. Precisely planned and quirky bits building until the pieces connect at the end of the story to produce the more sophisticated ironic chuckle of totality. It was the difference in how the two guys in *Stepbrothers* brought the yucks versus the *Curb Your Enthusiasm* kind of comedy.

Both of those gems now lived only in our memories, but ambushes remained. It was time for me to have some fun.

"You're dialed in, Double-K. Keeping sending them."

I settled in behind my M-110. The .308 was no slouch but, compared to the MK 22, it deprived enough in the velocity department that I needed twice the lead. I pressed the trigger, and while the result wasn't as lightning-strike profound, it got the job done. Ten shots between us, ten of the eight-legged horses were down. The Tarns reacted predictably. With no indication of which direction death had come from, chaos gripped them. Some hid behind their felled beasts. Others fled.

I opened my wrist link. "Roll them up, Dave."

"We're moving, brah." Dave might have been a career Special Forces operator, but the boy from Oahu never lost his pride in being a native Hawaiian. Even on Mars. I'd always assumed it was part of why he'd made the Ranger Regiment a visit rather than the permanent destination of his Army career. Had he not gravitated to a place like SF, where informality was part of the culture, he'd never have survived in the army.

Everyone came to SF for their own reasons. I'd come to get the juice of action I'd always wanted and a sense of self-respect I craved. And for whatever sins I'd committed, I'd wound up on Mars. Now, my remaining friends and I warred with a world of desert savages. We were sworn in loyalty to green death-dealers who swung two swords in upper arms while running a ray gun in the other set. But I'm a veritable superman in the lower gravity of Mars. I'm also betrothed to a queen, the most beautiful woman in the universe. All in all, a pretty good trade-off for being thrust into a situation as fantastic to us as it would be for a penguin abducted off his iceberg then charged with operating a sno-cone machine. Yeah, the penguin is down with the cold like we're down with violence, but damn! With no friends and a whole planet trying to kill us, that penguin had a better chance at those stubby wings winning him Dairy Queen employee of the month than we had of surviving those first months.

But we made it. Some of us.

Before you think I slipped in a pigsty and came up dangling diamonds instead of dripping shit, you should know… Mars—Vistara— is dying. The atmosphere is almost depleted and the technology that makes it is failing. Enemies within and without my queen's kingdom want to destroy us, enabled by the man I've sworn to kill. My former teammate—though he never earned the title to my satisfaction— Brandon Bryant.

And to top it all off, I'm expected to save the day.

Enter Warlord Deacon Benjamin Colt.

I've no one to blame but myself. After all, I did promise. And whenever I look into her eyes, it reminds me it wasn't an idle promise. I mean every word I've ever said to her. Because for my Talis Darmon, I'd fight a world. Which again brings us to me behind a semiauto sniper rifle. Because when the problem's overwhelming, do what you do best.

And bring friends to help.

Double-K and I stayed fixed to our scopes, and Dave and the Tarn riders of the Korund Mountains surrounded the dismounted Mydreen. Ever see a cop on horseback break up a riot? Imagine an eight-legged horse the size of a Clydesdale crashing into a crowd. The Korundi made flying tackles from horseback onto the dazed Tarns and hog-tied them while a few blasts from low power fizzle guns stunned the ones who'd tried hightailing it out of the ambush. Those greenies would be singed a little, but otherwise none the worse for wear for a little tactical questioning, a.k.a. battlefield interrogation.

"Dave, it's a still-life oil painting as far as I can see in every direction around you. We'll bring the reserve up in the flitters to take charge of the prisoners. Good to go?"

"Sure thing, brah. Hey, you let Double-K take the first shot?"

"That he did."

"Nice! What was the range?"

"1477."

"He's gonna beat you, Ben-dog." My record being nearly a thousand meters beyond that, he wouldn't do so anytime soon. "First sniper kill. Tell him he's buying. See you in a few."

My four-armed battle buddy had taken to sniping like a duck to water—though there were neither ducks nor water for them to take to. Khraal Kahlees was dutifully returning my most prized possession to its soft case. She was *my* girl, but she was quite literally the last of her kind. You learn to be flexible about your possessive jealousies in a situation like ours. I had to share. When Karlo could make the time for Baby Blue to crank out enough MK 22s to outfit a sniper section for every Tarn unit, I wanted the new general of our army to be an advocate for his people to learn yet another one of our ways.

Double-K's fighting prowess was a legend among his own people. For knocking him from the top spot among Vistara's warriors, he'd never shown jealousy toward me. "Khraal Kahlees, I'm going back to the ORP to send up the flyers. I'll be back shortly." I could bound back to our rally point a few klicks behind the rolling dunes, send the rest of the patrol on to the objective, and be back to retrieve him and our gear in our own flitter before he could've made it halfway back to the staging point.

"No argument, Benjamin Colt. As you say, have at it."

By the time we set down on the objective, the Korundi had dispatched the last of the wounded and dying arkall. Leaning over a map spread across the deck of an air car, Dave was supervising the hooding and segregation of the captures, giving last instructions to the men, and handing out the accolades.

"That's how it's done, Aldar Tak. It's not every day you get to show off in front of your Warlord. Good job. Take time and assemble your men for your patrol back to the forward operating base."

"Thank you, David Masamuni. Capturing Mydreen is not as satisfying as killing them, but all understand the necessity of it." The Tarn patrol leader crossed four arms and made a curt dipping bow to Dave, then to me, but waited for Khraal Kahlees to take his leave. It was a subtle moment. Looking to the senior Tarn for final approval was just one indication that we were still far from being the integrated fighting force I meant us to be. Double-K took the opportunity to use some of the interpersonal skills we'd discussed.

"As Queen Talis Darmon has said, if we are to succeed against our enemies, we must learn new ways, Aldar Tak. Carry on as ordered."

Now the Tarn took his leave.

"Were my words 'subordinate development oriented' enough to satisfy you, Benjamin Colt?"

"Constant but gentle reminders of the big picture are better than a thousand memos no one reads, Khraal Kahlees."

"I do not compose memos, Warlord. I lead warriors and crush our enemies to dust."

"That you do, my friend."

The Korundi were the bulk of our army. The old Red Army—not that it'd been much of one—had been all but destroyed by the Mydreen. Our human/Tarn army was still finding a rhythm to the style of music we DJ'd. Not only was it things like adapting to air travel—the Tarns had a natural dislike of it—it was both Vistaran races having to adapt to what us Thulians brought to the mix.

Red troops were so far exclusively our corps of pilots, and they waited on the decks of the grounded flitters as Green ground troops loaded the prisoners. While we were far from a cohesive fighting force, this had been a good step forward. Even if the prisoners brought us no good intel.

My Tarn friend was fixated on the nearest prisoner being loaded. "Do we yet know that this group has come from Pyreenia?"

I'd suffered at the hands of the Mydreen, as had those closest to me. But Khraal Kahlees had reason as good or better to hate them. And like me, he'd also made a promise. Mine was to secure my queen her kingdom. His was to wipe the Mydreen race from Vistara.

Dave grunted. "Can't get much of an answer out of any of them. None of them are looking too good. See how stringy they are? Like they haven't eaten in weeks. But it's more than just that."

"Whatcha mean, Davey-Dave?"

"Their surfboards don't float, brah. They act like they've sucked too much salt water."

Unlike their allies from the mountains of the Korund, the Mydreen were nomads spread across the wastes of Mars. When their tribal leader Domeel Doreen called all his clans to war against the Red Kingdom, it had taken months for word to reach all the lands of their range. We'd beaten their army soundly and taken back all the major cities they'd raided. All but two. Maleska Mal, the crumbling remnants of a once great Red metropolis that the Mydreen called their capital, and Pyreenia—the mystical city isolated in the farthest domain of the kingdom of Mihdradahl.

It was to Pyreenia where Domeel Doreen and his army retreated. The city from where an evil rot had grown to threaten our adopted kingdom. And where Brandon Bryant and Chuck Simpson hid, the last two living enemies from my old A-Team. It was their craven desires that had catapulted the instability of a war that swept across the Red Kingdom in their hopes to become kings of Mars.

In the weeks since we'd recaptured the capital of Shansara and seated my Talis Darmon on the throne as queen, bands of Mydreen continued to filter across the vast deserts, headed for Pyreenia, answering the call of their tribe. Bryant, Chuck, and their puppet Domeel Doreen weren't yet defeated. We'd beaten their army, slaughtered them wholesale with superior weapons and tactics. And yes, I'd led the mass extermination of an entire battlefield of our foes with chemical weapons. And still, a new army aimed at our destruction was building in Pyreenia.

The problem was this: to get where we were now, we'd used every bullet and blaster we had. The race was on to rebuild our army before they could rebuild theirs, while as yet another potential threat rose from the southern hemisphere of Mars—the Yellow Kingdom of Annameria.

Mars—Vistara, as it was properly called—was a contrast in ironies. An ancient world full of wonder and incredible technologies, mired in decay and lost knowledge as their civilization died with the planet. The technology for long-distance communication on Vistara had been all but lost, and our radio communication was feeble and practically useless in the poor ionosphere. In that respect, it was no different from the prehistory of Earth until near the twentieth century, where word could travel no faster than the conveyance used by the messenger. The handful of grand cities of my queen's people—the Red human race of Vistara—was spread across the northern hemisphere of the planet.

As a result, our ability to anticipate and carry out combat operations was a game of crisis response played by catch-up. My least favorite game. But we were overcoming that handicap. Our crotchety ace-in-the-hole, the hermit Cynar of the reclusive cult of the water priests, had saved our bacon from the fire once again with his scientific prowess.

We now had enough of the wristlets that all our forces spread across the kingdom could communicate with each other. Despite his constant insults, I'd developed an affection for the kooky wizard. He was like a crazy uncle who could fix anything, but one I hesitated to invite to my Labor Day barbecue for fear he'd ruin it with one of his rants about airliner chemtrails or lizard people running the government.

So, when our first real-time intel came from a patrol sighting Mydreen coming *from* the direction of Pyreenia rather than toward it, I left the hallowed halls of the palace to get in on the action.

Khraal Kahlees moved to a Mydreen being loaded to a flitter. "Halt, Korundi." The two troopers obeyed while maintaining grips on the hooded prisoner. He snatched the sack off and grasped the prisoner by the throat. Khraal Kahlees was everything the costumed and impotent Red generals were not, which is why the queen had bumped him to lead the new Red-Green armed forces. His lower hand grasped a dagger.

"From where do you come, Mydreen vermin? Speak or be ready to ride the River Blix."

Just when I thought my friend was growing into his role as exemplar to our new army, he was proving my new axiom…

You can take the Tarn out of the Korund, but you can't take the homicidal impulse out of the Tarn.

This was a custom that had to stop. As Warlord and his boss, I moved to restrain him, but Dave beat me to the punch.

"Double-K, brah, we talked about this. No executing prisoners. Especially ones we went through all this trouble to snatch."

Tusks jutted forward. The dagger went away, but the grip on the prisoner's neck remained. "Such pain as you have never imagined awaits you," he continued to growl. "Best tell me now and save your suffering. From where do you travel?"

I know the Mydreen well. While different from my Korundi clansmen, the Mydreen aren't cowards. They're fierce fighters. Courageous. And cruel. Mydreen balk at the threat of torture with grim laughter. I've seen them defy a captor with deadly determination to resume the fight, ready to pounce at the first sign of inattention. They don't accept parole. They prefer an honorable death on their feet.

This one dribbled saliva. His eyes were wide, black globes darting as if looking for the predator that would tear his flesh asunder if it caught him. His tremors and buckling knees made the Guard's grip tighter to keep him standing.

"Speak!"

The prisoner made a pitiful gurgling sound.

Khraal Kahlees returned the hood and motioned the Guards to take him. "Just our luck. We've captured a mute."

But I didn't think so.

Dave sidled closer to me. "Ben-dog, you ever see a Mydreen act like that?"

"No. Double-K could make even a Mydreen piss their loincloth, but there's something else going on here. Let's get these prisoners to Kleeve Hartus and let him figure it out."

"Yeah, and you've been off the leash too long, brah. Time to get you home to mama before she starts worrying."

I winced. It wasn't because he was wrong. It's because I hadn't told the queen what I was doing today. Fun time was over. Now it was time to pay the piper.

"Want me to come with? I can tell her it was my fault. That I made you do it."

"Bro, give me a break. Talis Darmon's been through a lot, you know. She's just stressed to the max trying to save the kingdom. Not to mention her father being murdered, two captivities by the Mydreen, almost dying in the mountains, having to kill her brother, surviving the assassination attempt. Cut her some slack, man. And the separation anxiety thing's getting better."

"Sorry, brah, not trying to bust your shells. It's just that your girl-friend—" he didn't finish the thought. Dave was my closest friend. We'd been through the war together. Literally. He was holding back.

"What? Out with it, brother."

"Brah, I'm just saying, you fell for a wildcat. We may be on Mars, but women are women. The more beautiful they are, the more high-strung. Not to mention, she's a royal. Ben-dog, even without all this other stuff, I'm betting on a regular day she's as touchy as an old electric blasting cap."

Some of what he said was true. Just like what I threw back at him.

"Is that some kind of transference on me? I see you getting pretty chummy with a beauty yourself, bro."

I made a show of giving a good-natured laugh because I didn't want Dave to think I was taking his ribbing badly. I didn't have another friend like him and never would. I needed him to always speak plainly to me.

A Warlord needs to be grounded. And who better than Dave to keep my head from getting too big? His compound expletives, malapropisms, and unflinching bravery made him the best comrade ever. He'd helped me weather the worst storms on a world that, though it had no clouds, had done everything it could to kill me a dozen times over.

"You don't have to worry about me, Ben-dog. I'm not settling down anytime soon. Besides, *my* girlfriend isn't a witch. Sometimes Karlo and I wonder if Talis Darmon didn't put a spell on you, brah. Like that song."

He started singing. Badly.

"I put a spell on you, 'cause you're miiiiine."

With anyone else, I would've denied it. But he was right.

"She did, bro. And I'm the better man for it."

02

FROM THE AIR, SHANSARA WAS A SIGHT THAT ASTOUNDED EACH AND every time. It was a Frazetta painting on steroids. Not like everything else on Vistara wasn't, but the architecture and the colors of the capital were something that had never existed in even the wildest imagination of the greatest fantasy artist that ever lived. We had a *Death Dealer* print on the old team room wall. I had the image saved on my MacBook. If it was in one piece somewhere on Vistara and Karlo could get it running, I'd find an artist to paint a giant mural of it above the training grounds. It always motivated me to try to be as big a badass as I could. If that didn't inspire the new Red recruits, I was at a loss to think of anything that would.

By day, her towers and spires shimmered in a pearlescence that shifted between purples, blues, and whites, depending on the angle viewed. By night, the surfaces reflected the moons in an otherworldly green. Constructs which bulged and expanded the higher they rose were joined by translucent bridges of incredible spans, designs that should not have been capable of defying any gravity, not even that of Mars's lesser pull.

First Shield Kleeve Hartus and a contingent of Guards waited for us at the LZ. I took a hand off the controls to return his salute as I made a sweeping descent before spiraling to a touchdown. I'd become pretty confident as a pilot. Truth be told, the flitters weren't really that hard to fly. But neither were they the high performance craft a helicopter was. For sure, they were no jet fighters. The way they floated and turned with the radius of a tractor trailer made them more like Grandad's ancient Oldsmobile.

Waiting for me was an anxiously twitching Apache. My gadron was the size of an African lion, but every bit the puppy he acted like. His stubby tail wagged and his hind quarters collided against his minder at the sight of me. Kleeve Hartus released the big baby and I braced myself for the collision that was about to come.

"Oof. Down, boy, down."

If Apache was mad at me for leaving him behind on this trip, he was over it after a few good pats that would have been cruel abuse to a real dog. Dave gave him some attention and received a lick of appreciation. Khraal Kahlees brought him to a cautious freeze until the gadron gingerly sniffed the proffered hand and allowed the Tarn to scratch his head. Apache had been raised amongst the Mydreen, who were as cruel to animals as they were to each other. He was still gun-shy around all but a few Tarns.

"I see you had good hunting, Benjamin Colt." Kleeve Hartus was another valued friend and new appointee to the queen's administration. Gold-cloaked Guards took charge of our prisoners and herded them away. The Gucci gladiator costumes still caused me to shake my head. Change took time, and on my list of important things to do was to get the Guards and the Army outfitted in uniforms more useful for something other than showing off physiques. But it was an item far down the list. I wasn't any kind of stickler about uniforms or that kind of thing—in SF you could roll out for a fight in a baseball cap and Slayer T-shirt under your armor. But running around mostly naked—covered by tiny bits of armor and in capes—was a deal breaker.

The last of the prisoners off-loaded, he joined us as we walked.

"That we did," I told him. "They were headed from the direction of Pyreenia. Get everything out of them you can, especially about what's happening there." I lowered my voice. "Still no word?"

He shook his head grimly.

"No. I would have immediately informed you. It's been too long. I've held off hailing Avril Mysteen for fear of compromising him. Not a single contact since he signaled going silent to infiltrate the city. I fear the worst."

The young Guardsmen Avril Mysteen had been selected by the first shield and I to lead the secret reconnaissance into the enemy stronghold. As a pilot, cop, and willing fighter, he was uniquely suited to the task and the best of what remained of the Guards contingent from Clymaira.

The Guardsmen were not the army. Each city was protected by the combination constabulary and border patrol, performing functions of civil law enforcement as well as acting as a paramilitary force for protection against threats like the Mydreen, whose banditry plagued the Red Kingdom.

Under my old A-Team, the Mydreen evolved from Bedouin raiders to a tribal army. They nearly toppled the whole kingdom. The poorly led Red army had been a token force, small and ill-equipped for real war. We were rebuilding it as fast as we could, and it was the Korundi who'd willingly stepped into service to aid us rather than return to their mountain domain.

But with the mission to Pyreenia producing only grim doubts about its success, I felt guilty for sending them to do what may have been better done by the army. Avril Mysteen was a protégé to both me and Kleeve Hartus. Unspoken between us was the dread that we'd sentenced him to death.

Double-K also spoke in secretive tones. "Warlord, is it not time we considered a new mission to infiltrate Pyreenia? What transpires there is critical knowledge."

"In our next closed council, we'll discuss that very thing with the queen." I checked my watch and knew I couldn't hold off any longer. "All good things, brothers. I have to split. Talis Darmon's undoubtedly getting ready for whatever official function's on her calendar. I better go fess up before she leaves."

Finding quiet moments was often difficult. Our private life had been anything but. After long days of council meetings with petty administrators came endless dinner meetings with visits by the Shansara elite.

Dave made a sheepish grin. "Brah, my offer stands."

"Thanks, Davey-Dave, but not necessary. See you for morning PT?"

"You know it. I'll check in on Karlo and see if he can peel some time away from all his science-y stuff to join us."

"On the flip side then, bro. C'mon, Apache."

My puppy trotted happily along with me as we wove through the polished corridors of the palace until we arrived at our private chambers where he had to be content to remain outside. Apache could gas out a ballroom. The usual attendants were present as I dropped my gear in the outer room. Beraal exited the bedchamber, closing the doors behind her.

"Benjamin Colt, you appear none the worse for your day's adventure," she greeted me. My princess's confidante was as close to my heart as Talis Darmon's. The three of us had endured hardship and danger, and it was together we'd survived. But Beraal and I shared a special connection. Our psyche-shattering ordeal in the maw of an ancient monster left us bonded closer than siblings. She was the sister I'd never had, and I called her that in every private moment.

"And another day of court life doesn't seem to have taken too much of a toll on you either, sister."

"No, my brother. It has not."

She shooed away the staff before she let me give her a quick embrace, her four arms surrounding me like a blanket. What can I say? I'm a hugger by nature. It's just how I grew up. The human gesture that had once embarrassed her, she'd grown fond of. As long as we were alone.

"Which Talis Darmon am I going to find on the other side of that door, sis? My betrothed, glad to see her hero return, or the queen, ready to scold me for being the bad boy?"

That brought a Tarn chuckle, which sounded more like a wolf rending a wet kill. "You must discover for yourself, Benjamin Colt. I depart."

I'd decided to not be the shrinking violet and pushed the chamber doors open.

"Princess, I'm home."

My perfect girl was at her dressing table. Her glorious smile and radiance told me I wasn't in trouble. Yet.

"Welcome home, my hero."

An armful of her and a kiss and I knew I truly was home.

She lay in my arms a short while later, and I chose that moment to apologize. "I'm sorry I didn't tell you where I was going today. It was a matter of urgency and I had to act quickly."

"No less than I would expect of my Warlord. But it is I who must apologize, Benjamin Colt. Forgive me if you've thought me too controlling of you. My fears and worries are great and not a reflection of my confidence in your skills as a warrior. It's just—"

If anyone had a justified anxiety about being vulnerable without her protector close by, she rightly did.

"No need to explain more, my princess. And love means never having to say you're sorry."

"It is a nice aphorism, betrothed, but don't you also always say that the things that go without saying bear repeating over and over?"

"That I do, Talis Darmon. Like I'm the luckiest man on Vistara or anywhere else. Now tell me, what's on the agenda tonight? Dinner with the minister of such and such? After that welcome home, I'm restored and replete with enough *tell me mores* and *that's so fascinating!* to make you proud."

"I'm always proud, my coarse soldier, but no. Tonight is reserved for just us. After you've scrubbed the sands of Vistara off you, a private dinner here, and then just you and I until dawn."

There was still much I longed to ask her, so much I didn't know about her, and about Vistara. It just seemed that since those first days together in Maleska Mal—she and Beraal prisoners of Domeel Doreen,

16

paroled to me for my early education, followed by the months of our long march across the Korund—that the right time never came to learn more about who my Talis Darmon was. Since then, the days had been punctuated by crisis after crisis, with little real time to just *be*. To have what any couple should have. Time alone.

She'd made this Herculean adjustment to her schedule just for us. It wasn't the right time to plumb the depths of her past. As crushing was the weight she carried as regent, I knew she needed this as much as I did. Time to just *be*. Together. Whenever she wanted to tell me something, she would.

Above all, a sniper knows patience.

"Baby, you just made all my dreams come true."

✳ ✳ ✳

A sword edge nicked my shoulder, accompanied by the grunt of someone expending all effort to kill me. I instinctively twisted and closed with a short hop to drive a fist into the Red soldier, more than a little surprised that'd I'd been attacked without warning. He was no expert, overextending his swing, no doubt hurried in his attempt. I hadn't landed a fight-ender, as the Red soldier was still on his feet, but my rushed blow knocked him away and bought me time to make an instant assessment.

"Stand fast! I'll deal with this!" It was just the one and I wanted him alive. I let him make a return swing. Still off balance, his next attempt was also poor as I slipped outside and let his blade slice empty air. With my left, I trapped his sword arm above the elbow and drove down, settling his weight to glue him in place. I owned him. With the full force of my rear leg behind my punch, I drove my right cross square onto his chest plate. The Red recruit flew onto the sand a few meters away, sword still in hand, but limp and out of the fight.

Had I landed one on his chin, he'd be DRT. Dead right there.

Three more Red recruits flew from out of the ranks, swords drawn. Mine came out, too. Play time was over. Sword in hand, Dave landed beside me, the compact sand of the training grounds fracturing under his touchdown. I met the one on my right as Dave handled the other two. A simple parry and I drove the pommel of my blade onto this one's helmet. He folded like a house of cards and I found myself surrounded by mountains of Tarns, bringing the chaos to a close.

It was over nearly as quickly as it had begun.

Garlak Ranz took control. "Hold fast in the ranks. Any recruit who twitches is dead."

Dave's sword dripped blood. "You good, Ben? All I saw was that Red try to Pearl Harbor you, and I jumped."

The man who'd almost split me from shoulder to ass was still on his back. Two lay butchered by Dave's quick hand, and the one I'd buffaloed was out for the count. We needed space and time to piece this together.

"Warmaster Garlak Ranz, move these troops out. Continue with your exercises," I ordered. The Tarn commanded and the training company marched off, broke into a double time, and were out the gates, their Tarn drill sergeants in charge again.

Garlak Ranz had stayed behind. "Warlord, are you sure it is wise to proceed? If there are more traitors in the ranks of the recruits—"

I pointed at the bodies. "Do you recognize these men?"

"Thorian recruits, Warlord."

Dave wiped his sword on the cape of one of the dead before sheathing it. "Shit. We've got dozens of volunteers from Thoria in this latest company."

Rebuilding was slow. Our Tarn cadre were training new recruits as rapidly as possible. Mass graves outside Shansara told us that any Red soldiers who'd been loyal to King Osric Darmon had been purged under the new regime of his son, Carolinus. Add those dead to the number who'd fallen fighting the Mydreen hordes plus the rest we'd cleaned up taking back Shansara left us few Red soldiers with which to fill the ranks of our army.

But this attack hadn't been against the Korundi, who were now the majority in the new Red/Green army of Mihdradahl. It had been aimed at me.

"Let's get these two to the infirmary. This interrogation I'm handling myself."

In the infirmary, the Red medic shook his head, pointing. "He will not recover, Warlord." The one I'd taken down with my pommel had a fractured skull. On the pallet beside him the one with the caved in chest plate groaned. He winced and wheezed, cracked ribs grating with each strained effort to take a breath.

"Thulian monster. I almost had you. Revenge for Thoria. Your demon powers won't save you forever." He succumbed to his pain and was unconscious, on the way to join his conspirators in death.

The medic attended. "Shall I revive him, Warlord?"

"No. I've got my answers."

Dave was at my side in the harsh sun. "Brah, you should let the doc patch you up."

"Just a scratch. For real. I'm more pissed about my shirt." The tip had sliced a gash in the shoulder of my Crye shirt. I only had two more.

"Yeah right, brah. You almost got filleted. Did you get any of your spidey-sense warnings about them being, you know, one of *them*?" Dave was among a handful who knew about my connection to the evil that had awakened on Vistara.

"No. This was straight up Red-on-Red. You heard him. Revenge for Thoria."

Dave scrunched his face. "You weren't even there when the Chief had us invade Thoria. I *was*. If anyone, that assassin should've gone for me."

"Spilled milk."

"Not all Thorians are artists and hippy types, I guess, huh, brah?"

"I guess having your city laid waste by murderous savages trained by Thulians can do that to you."

"So now we've got yet one more thing to worry about, brah. Can we turn our backs on our own troops?"

03

KARLO HADN'T MADE IT TO JOIN DAVE AND ME FOR THE MORNING smoke session and assassination attempt. Looking at him across the council table, I could tell why. He had raccoon eyes, and the densely muscled athlete looked as though he'd been skipping meals. Busy as we all were, we hadn't seen much of each other. Since he'd asked for release from the army to concentrate on running the Baby Blue and to work on solving as many of our technical problems as possible, he'd thrown himself into his task like a one-man R&D section.

Of course, his partner in crime, the irrepressible Cynar the Magnificent, didn't need sleep like a normal human. Talis Darmon thought the wizard was over a thousand years old. His scientific mastery and incredible inventions were transformational to our success. But he was crazy, of that I was certain. The mystic regularly bathed himself in the healing rays of a device that was not only responsible for his long life but, along with his more than ten centuries living as a recluse, had unhinged him.

Not even the decorum of his appointment by the queen had attenuated his joy in peppering me with insults whenever possible. It was a small burden to bear. I loved the old coot. But there was only one person who brought him more joy to taunt than me. And unlike the good-natured barbs he threw at me, right now that person was the focus of all the former hermit's ire and venom.

"You colossal ass! The queen has ordered you to permit me full access to the atmosphere works. Why must I be forced to berate you in her presence to see you comply? Not that I care one whit for your discomfiture, dullard. I should plead with her to execute you and the whole lot of the Atmosphere Guild and rid Vistara of your imbecility once and for all."

Supreme Guild Master Tyreen Sorell turned the same beet-red of his dyed goatee as he choked out, "Queen Talis Darmon, what the madman says is not true. I have permitted him more access than has ever been allowed into our inner sanctum."

"Liar. Liar and nincompoop. Once since her decree have you allowed us into the atmosphere works—though there's little evidence of *work* occurring there. I've taken measurement of the products of the flux from your factory. You produce not enough air to benefit the lowliest worm."

When I was at her side in these councils, I tried to act like a good warlord and spare the queen having to run the meeting. It was time for order. "Cynar, calm down."

"And you, Warlord!" He was just getting started on his list of grievances, like Festivus fully arrived. "I petitioned the first shield to enforce the queen's order. Nothing. Am I not scientist supreme? If all you muscle-bound ruffians can't do your only chore and facilitate the important work of your intellectual betters, what good are you? Is that why the first shield is absent, avoiding my condemnation before the queen? Tyreen Sorell is a pretender, but at least he's not a coward."

"ENOUGH!" the queen said, firmly taking back the reins.

She fixed the old man in her squint. I'd been there. It carried the same gravitas as a dagger to the throat.

"Cynar the Magnificent, I've learned that I must permit you at least one outburst per meeting. We make allowance for your eccentricities, good friend, but that is all I will allow for this month. And do not malign a person of honor, especially in their absence. Apologize to the council for your remarks about the first shield."

Cynar's cadaverous body slumped, gray beard puffed against his chest. His wild eyes cleared. "Forgive me, Queen Talis Darmon. I did not mean to impugn the character of the first shield. It is difficult to cope with others. It is a thing far more burdensome than I had permitted myself to consider. But I accepted the oath and I swear to fulfill it. There is so much to be done, and the obstacles continue, despite your stated desires."

"Apology accepted, Scientist Supreme. Karlo Columbo, can you provide an objective perspective on these matters?"

My friend, former teammate, and all around amazing human, obeyed. "Yes, ma'am. Our inspection was anything but open. We were rushed through the peripherals then obstructed from seeing more until we were finally herded out of the facility by the supreme guild master and his brethren. Without resorting to force, we couldn't have begun any kind of true assessment."

Cynar expanded, his chastisement over. "Ha! As I said."

All eyes on him, the henna-bearded wizard defended himself. "You were shown more than any not a member of the guild itself. And portraying to the queen what I exposed as peripheral is untrue."

Karlo was always a study in control. In the middle of a firefight, he never flustered, his voice never harried, and I bet his pulse never raised more than a few beats per minute. In his fatigue, the reserve of his stoicism broke. He swung to the wizard. "You forget that I've inspected the works in Clymaira. You didn't allow us anywhere near the heart of the factory or its controls." He turned to me.

"Ben, I'm sorry I haven't had the chance to bring this up to you before. They're acting as evasive as Iraqis in a WMD inspection."

Then he addressed the queen.

"Ma'am, Cynar is correct. We're being deceived and stonewalled by the air wizards. Your directives are not being complied with."

There was an increase in the heat in the room. My princess radiated anger and her skin flushed a brighter red than I'd seen since she'd accused the leader of the Korund of duplicity in his own throne room.

"I need hear no more. Tyreen Sorell, I charge you with treachery against your queen. Take him into custody."

Two Tarns stepped out of the queen's ring of bodyguards to take the wizard. Protests blurted from around the table. One of the ministers spoke loudly above the shocked buzz coming from everywhere but our end of the table.

"Queen Talis Darmon, please reconsider! The supreme guild master has ever been a loyal steward and served your father and the kingdom well. Such a charge is unwarranted. I would not accuse the regent of tyranny, but there is a process of law in Mihdradahl!"

Talis Darmon's resolve was the same with which an executioner wielded the axe. "Our diminishing atmosphere is an existential matter. The Atmosphere Guild has wantonly disregarded my command to further a resolution of this issue. I have exercised my powers with restraint, Terran Dullmar. I did not command Tyreen Sorell to take the walk north, though perhaps I should have. Do you wish to further debate the point?"

The minister of works took his chastisement with visible umbrage. "No, Queen Talis Darmon."

Another minister stood. "Queen, would it not then be most proper to allow the supreme guild master opportunity to demonstrate his renewed attention to the matter?"

She rightly ignored them. "Warlord, please instruct the Guards to occupy the atmosphere works. If it can be accomplished with as little harm as possible to the structure and the wizards, that is my desire."

"I'll lead the raid myself."

"No, Warlord. Please delegate. We have other matters to attend to."

I gave Dave the nod, who was only too ready to take charge.

"Bring him along." Dave pointed to the wizard in the custody of two towering Tarns. "I'll give you a chance to open up and call out your men before I enter by force. The Clymaira chapter of your club has no doubt told you what happens when we come knocking and you don't answer."

The queen gave her last command on the subject. "Your cooperation is ordered, Tyreen Sorell. Am I clear?"

The wizard quaked. "Yes, Queen Talis Darmon."

She waved them away.

"Hehehe! Soldiers arresting the buffoons of the atmosphere guild! Hauling them away in chains! Hehehe." Cynar gleefully rubbed his hands together as if anticipating a sumptuous feast.

Karlo nudged the old hermit. "Internal monologue, Cynar."

The din of outrage by the councilors and ministers—the elite of Shansara—had died to grumbles. I hadn't forgotten the disdain with which this same gentility had reacted to the queen's reordering of her kingdom's top tier, nor especially how they'd responded to my appointment to power. To ease my betrothed's anxieties, I'd lately silenced my suspicions that her father's fall had been assisted from within by these very people. No more. I leaned closer to my princess.

"Shall I dismiss the general council? We're not going to get much else accomplished with them today. Or ever, unless we flush out the other traitors still hiding in their ranks."

She frowned at my renewed reference to that problem, but gave me the high sign to send the functionaries away.

"The queen's inner council will continue. The general council is dismissed."

Beraal moved from her seat on the wall to attend. "Please take tea, Talis Darmon. You need to refresh yourself."

"Thank you, dear Beraal. My commitment to maintain the stability and tenor of our aging kingdom fatigues beneath my impulse to ignite progress."

Soon the room cleared. Khraal Kahlees, Karlo, Cynar, and Beraal drew seats close to the queen and me. The Tarn bodyguard remained near, but relaxed at my command.

Talis Darmon sighed.

"Someone, please give me some good news."

04

Karlo brightened. "Cynar and I back-engineered the accelerator weapons."

The fizzle guns were the secondary armament of Vistara. The weapons were weak—which is why we'd dubbed the Buck Rogers's ray-guns so—until Karlo figured out how to increase their effectiveness. Produced only in Shansara, like so much of the native tech, it was on its last legs. Edged weapons predominated a lot of the combat because the fizzle guns had such limited effect and shot capacity.

My relief was the crumbling dam holding back a river. "Hallelujah, Karlo! That's great."

Karlo was always humble out of proportion to his talents, but he beamed satisfaction with his new assurances. "Baby Blue's producing them now, but the better news is that the arms factory is up and running again. With help troubleshooting the inevitable problems while the engineers relearn the process, it'll stand on its own soon enough. Once they do, I'll have Baby Blue back to other priorities."

"What was the problem that shut down their fizzle-gun production to begin with, Karlo?"

My friend was not just brilliant, he had the education to match his talents. One of the many things I always admired about him was that when he was out of his element, he was the first to admit it. Head tilted, eyebrows raised, lips pursed, he said, "I don't have the background in organizational psychology to say for sure, but I do understand techno-logic history. It seems like there's a societal inertia that's developed—or devolved, really—and it's affected most every institution. The essential knowledge is there, but it's been allowed to founder."

Cynar spoke. "Karlo Columbo and I have discussed this. Lack of demand, excess, stability, malaise… Many named are the elements. In my time sequestered from the world performing my guild's work to save her, much has deteriorated."

Despite appearing physically fatigued, Karlo was energized. "Getting to know the people who work in the Golden Hub, I've found a lot of underutilized potential." The Hub was the center of industrial production and innovation in the kingdom, a sprawling borough within Shansara. "A cultural anthropologist would better be able to unravel it all. Trade guilds predominate, and they're very familial. There's a kind of artificial limit on production and productivity. It's like a mesh of hundreds of gears gummed up from disuse. I'm not an economist either, so it's hard for me to analyze the root causes, but all I can say is, I'm very encouraged. I think the Golden Hub as a whole will rise to the occasion of the challenge."

Cynar was focused and eager. "Where there are shortfalls in technical ability and knowledge, we can solve their deficiencies. Of that I am certain." Karlo had won Cynar's respect almost immediately, and the attitude of cooperation from the cantankerous old fart meant his respect had only grown in their short association together.

And then there was Baby Blue. The horn of plenty which had intrigued even the master inventor that Cynar was.

Khraal Kahlees growled in Tarnish approval. "If we no longer need have concern that the army is Winchester, our greatest deficiency is soon behind us."

Karlo and I shared a grin. Both Double-K and Kleeve Hartus had adopted a lot of our old-school U.S. of A. military jargon like it was their own. Using the term *Winchester* to mean out of ammo was one of them. But a grim shadow replaced Karlo's brief lapse into amusement.

"Ma'am, I'm reluctant to ask this, but I'm afraid I must. I request a resignation from my position as head of production."

The queen had immediately appointed Karlo at my recommendation. "But why, Karlo Rinaldo? Your work is exemplary and without fault. Phenomenal, even."

"Thank you, ma'am, but I'm under water. I can't be an administrator *and* be the one working on all the technical problems. My strength's in the shop. At the lab bench. Troubleshooting. Running Baby Blue. I'm falling behind on everything."

I stepped in before he felt he had to explain further. "My fault. Outside of this room, there are only a half-dozen people I'm confident aren't actively seeking to undermine us. I asked the queen to appoint you without even asking if that's the job you wanted. Sorry, buddy."

Karlo nodded. "Which is why I feel so disloyal by asking. But I've come to know Perrin Halser." The former minister of production had taken his demotion without protest, and continued to serve as Karlo's second.

"Perrin Halser's more than a member of the aristocracy. He's technically minded and a good engineer. He's a good administrator, as well. He's shown me he cares deeply about supporting the queen and treats every task with serious determination. I think he deserves to return to the post. Anyway, that's my recommendation."

I turned my full attention to Talis Darmon while she considered.

"You have my full confidence, Karlo Columbo. If that is your recommendation, I would be foolish to discount it. But ability, authority, and responsibility must be linked. The dissolution of those virtues has caused so much of our paralysis. Hmm. My decision is that you will remain titular head of production, but that you may delegate all authority to Perrin Halser in my name. He must keep you informed on all matters, but I respect your need to cease the day-to-day administration and frequent attendance at council. Does that satisfy?"

Karlo dipped his head. "Yes, ma'am. Thank you."

The queen looked to Beraal who'd been typing on a lit scroll the whole time.

"I've composed the directive for your approval, Talis Darmon."

"Excellent. We progress."

Dave came into the room a short while later.

"It's done. No muss, no fuss. Well, not much of one, anyway. Kleeve Hartus's people hold the atmosphere works, and all the air wizards are in detention."

Cynar stood. "Then, by your leave, Queen, I depart to solve yet another crisis as only I can."

That brought the first smile to her lips I'd seen since last night.

"In a moment, Scientist Supreme. We have another matter to discuss."

Only one? I thought.

Her mood turned dark. "The evil that permeates Pyreenia."

It was only among those in this room that the haunting threat had been openly discussed. The evidence that black witches and a foul power existed in the remote city was undeniable. Talis Darmon was certain of it, as were Beraal and I. My chosen sister and I had experienced the depths of that evil—we needed no further proof. The queen's brother, the Prince Carolinus Darmon, had been under the influence of one of their cult. At Talis Darmon's command, I'd shot the witch in mid-spell-casting, and witnessed my beautiful princess become a ruthless avenging angel and empty her brother of his blood with brutal efficiency atop the very Spectral Throne to which she ascended.

My Talis Darmon was a queen of many talents.

"What news from the mission to investigate what transpires there?"

I answered, "Nothing. Our agents are so deep they can't risk making contact, or they've been discovered and the worst's happened." Avril Mysteen was a newly promoted buck sergeant when we'd selected him to lead the mission, full of the confidence and gusto that only a young warrior could muster for a task so dangerous. Now it seemed certain I'd sent an unexperienced man and the select team he led to their deaths.

We all sat in silent consideration.

Beraal broke us from our trance. "Talis Darmon, what is your sense of things there?"

She closed her eyes. "I sense it rests. It gathers strength. It waits."

"Maybe they've shot their wad at us," Dave said. "There've been no more of the witches trying to do the queen in. They gave it their best and spent their hocus-pocus power." Since the attempt on her life in our quarters, both Beraal and I had been attentive for the presence of that evil. Both of us could feel its malevolence when near, a remnant of our time trapped in the soul-eater. Everywhere I went in the city, I tried to heighten my awareness for the sensation, for some tingling to come to life within me as an early warning. That eerie scratching at the base of my spine that reminded me of the hopeless void.

"No, David Masamuni. We have wounded them, but they conserve their strength. They are not gone. Sleeping, is my ken of it."

"I have greater unease about the remaining Thulians and the Mydreen scum that harbor there," Khraal Kahlees said. He was not entirely skeptical about the dark power we discussed, but was concrete in his concerns, like a good general should be.

Dave nodded. "It would be good to know what their dispositions are. Bryant and Chuck have laid low since the one comm. If I know them, they haven't abandoned their intent to do us harm. Bryant's on a mission to see Ben dead."

"Tell me something I don't know, bro." It was with satisfaction I pictured the surprise in Bryant's face when he learned I was alive, and that I'd engineered his defeat. Chuck's scarred face and wheezing cough from being caught in the mustard gas attack gave me no pleasure, but neither did it bum me out.

As much as they might want me dead, I wanted them dead more.

Karlo brought up the other sword hanging over our heads. "Any further moves by the Yellows?"

Khraal Kahlees unfolded his arms on the table. "Our eyes over the Furrow of the Creator have sighted no activity in the air or in the depths of the great chasm. Our superior communication system gives us a decided advantage over both our enemies in Pyreenia and Yellow foes in the kingdom of Annameria."

"There have been no further diplomatic communications from them either," the queen added. "But I do not believe that no news is good news in this case."

Our Tarn general was thoughtful. "That I am at last able to fully arm us to potential far superior to that of our adversaries should be comforting, Queen Talis Darmon. Overmatch is one of our many strengths. But, Warlord, as Karlo Columbo has himself admitted, I too am overtasked. David Masamuni and I have need to spend even greater time away to ensure our army is ready. Too many meetings, Warlord."

"I agree," I said, "and I have some ideas about how to alleviate some of that and get you more competent help."

Dave cocked an eyebrow. He knew who I meant.

"I recommend we adjourn, Queen."

"Yes. I have alliances and loyalties to reinforce after today's events in council. Let's adjourn."

I gave her my hand to stand and stole a close moment before she and Beraal departed with her guard. "See, my princess? Everything's going to be alright. You have the best and the brightest working on all the kingdom's problems. We're going to be okay." I gave her the most glowing smile of reassurance I had.

"Oh, Benjamin Colt, how I pray it is true."

"See you tonight."

"Benjamin Colt. One thing more." Her countenance changed. From vulnerable anxiety to passionate reproach. She was mad. At me.

"I named you Warlord. It is time you acted so." She turned on her heels and was gone. The others couldn't help but have heard. Karlo nudged Cynar to spare me embarrassment.

"Ready to make an air factory obey?"

He cackled. "Hehehe. It will be child's play."

I motioned Dave and Double-K to close on me. Before Dave could prod me about the minor ass-chewing I'd taken, I said, "Before you two get back to the troops, do you want to see what intel Kleeve Hartus has been able to pry out our prisoners?"

Khraal Kahlees thumbed his dagger.

"If he has not loosed their tongues, I am eager to bring encouragement that he would not."

✳ ✳ ✳

Kleeve Hartus was there to meet us. "I regret I missed such an interesting council. I would like to have seen Tyreen Sorell's shock for myself."

The first shield begged us to follow. Kleeve Hartus ardently despised the air wizards, almost as much as Cynar did. With the dawning revelations about the long-con the air wizards had run, allowing the world to believe that they were able stewards of the atmosphere factories instead of the incompetent charlatans of Cynar's prejudice, the first shield was among the first to want to punish them. "I think the move well justified by the queen. They've stalled discovery of their deception for too long. Her patience in the matter has been prolonged."

I gave him a quiet side-mouthed, "I'll fill you in on the rest later, when we're alone."

He took the hint. "Per your command, I have been dedicated to nothing save the captured subjects, Warlord."

We followed him to a part of the headquarters that reminded me of the same layout as a TV detective bureau. Cells with tiny windows lined the hall, and in the center stood a pair of interrogation rooms with one-way glass. In each, a Mydreen sat restrained, a Guard questioning.

"We've worked them without rest. Fatigue has reduced all but these two subjects as incommunicative for further interrogation. The others were already dulled. In some stupor. They are less useful now even than when I took custody of them." He touched a faceted stone near the window and the voices within became dimly audible.

The investigator was working the subject. "For how many days had you been on the plains of Mak Sar? Your pace was quite feeble. Where you were picked up, it would be a journey of two weeks from Shansara, at least. Where was your band traveling to?"

The prisoner's lower arms were shackled in front at the wrists. He cupped a thin vessel of water. A Tarn used the "sky hands" for eating and fine motor tasks, though the lower set of "driving hands" with which they controlled their mounts—their upper arms free to hold weapons—were no less capable. This was how you cuffed a Tarn long-term, allowing them to do necessary things like feed themselves without having to risk removing any portion of their restraints. We'd learned that lesson from the Guards, and it was a good one.

The Mydreen took a sip. "When will you kill me and allow me peace, Red fool? There is no understanding you can come to that will save you."

I was once the intelligence specialist on my A-Team. I wasn't an interrogator, but I understood the basics. Separate the prisoners. Get them to corroborate their timelines. Find the inconsistencies in accounts. And when differences in even the mundane appeared, they were the big flashing red signs that became the picks you used to break the lock on the treasure chest of their secrets.

I wandered over to the other interview room and touched the crystal.

"What do you mean, you do not know your destination?"

This prisoner had the same agitated eye movement his comrade displayed during Double-K's spot questioning at the interdiction site. It was how a dog cowered in a cage, waiting its turn to be put down.

"Away. We had to get away."

"You had to get away from Pyreenia?"

The Mydreen's eyes darted around the room. He spoke in low mumbles. "The light is good. The light keeps them away. Do not put me in the dark again."

Khraal Kahlees was listening as well. "This one is maddened. The other is in possession of what few faculties a Mydreen possesses, but has never been visited by the wisdom spirit. If this represents the far-clans who answer Domeel Doreen's call, we have little to worry about from his army."

The investigator persisted with the agitated subject. "What is in the dark? Your people roam the night deserts of Vistara. You act is if you fear the dark. What kind of Mydreen warrior are you?"

It was a good tactic. Insults often provoked an unguarded response. He responded.

With a scream, the Tarn rose to his feet, chains strained, thick skin tearing beneath the cuffs to make blood seep. "The darkness comes for Vistara! The White lords are powerless to stop them. The River Blix floods and Temple Farnest crumbles. A new underworld rises to the surface. Anso-Kylon. Anso-Kylon. ANSO-KYLON."

Guards rushed in to restrain the prisoner.

Kleeve Hartus sighed. "This one's finished, Warlord. We'll start again on the others. They've had a few hours of sleep. It may render them more useful now."

"Somehow, I don't think so, First Shield, but keep trying."

The agitated prisoner collapsed into a catatonic plank and was carried to a cell by four large Guards.

Dave stroked his stubble. "This whole group of Mydreen is nutty. What the hell's going on? Double-K, my decipher didn't help me there at the end. What was he saying?"

My Tarn comrade thrust tusks forward in contemplation. "Nor did mine. Meaningless babble from a desert vereen. The mission to capture these vermin was a worthy effort, if only for the opportunity to exercise, but the hunt has produced little meat. It is time we hunt harder, Warlord."

"It hasn't been a kill big enough to feast on, but there's value here— our enemy isn't in great shape, whatever the cause. What say you, Davey-Dave?"

My brown brother gave my Green brother a grunt. "Double-K and I've been kicking this around, brah. When Karlo gets us fully kitted, the best move is to go for it. Leaving Chuck and his pack of Elviras and Mydreen feeling like they're in a safe space needs to stop, Ben-dog."

I thought about what Talis Darmon had said to me.

"I'm also about through waiting. We're at war. And it's time a Warlord starts acting like one."

05

Jodal Jark and Sarkan Sell stood guard in the anteroom.

Walking up, I said, "Hail, Korundi. Been a while since you stood watch together."

The Korundi pair were battle buddies of mine, and now remained close by as part of the queen's bodyguard. Though I saw them often, there was rarely time for comradely banter.

The younger bowed. "Yes, Warlord. And always warmed with memories of fury in combat at your side."

"What's the matter, Jodal Jark? PSD getting boring?"

"No, Warlord! It is an honor to serve."

"It's okay. There's hardly a duller duty. Especially since we've vetted anyone allowed in the palace three times over. There's not much of a chance of another assassin making it close to the queen. If either of you decide you want to return to the army, I'll approve the request. There are abundant warriors who can rotate to the duty."

The older Sarkan Sell dipped his head. "Is there a move to war, Benjamin Colt?"

I shrugged. "Just remember what I said."

I was surprised to see a table set for three in our private quarters. I expected the queen to be in one of her political jousts disguised as a dinner function. Beraal entered from the kitchen. "Clean yourself and dress for dinner, Benjamin Colt."

"What's the occasion, sister? Just the three of us, like old times? I thought the queen was anxious to mend fences after today."

Beraal cast a glance to our closed bedroom. "It is her intention. The trade minister sent a message that she and her husband could not attend, with no further explanation. Talis Darmon correctly perceives the slight."

The repercussions of her bold action against the air wizards were already being felt.

"She's been patient, but the old fools have been slow-walking all her directives," I noted. "She's the queen. What she says is law."

"If only things were so simple, brother. Go give her ease."

Talis Darmon sat at her desk over a lit scroll. She barely looked up as I gave her a peck on the cheek.

"Anything you want to talk about?" I asked.

Her posture went from rigid to soft. "I don't know where to begin, other than to apologize."

"I've told you about feeling like you have to say sorry to me."

"I am frustrated. For having spent a lifetime perfecting empathy and communication, I seem to be the least diplomatic with you, Benjamin Colt."

"It's fine. I'm no brittle figurine. What did you mean, though? Do you want me to step it up? Wield more of the power you gave me? I've been trying to be deferential and restrict myself to what I know best. I don't exactly have a role model to follow. The last Warlord died so long ago, his history is more legend than blueprint."

I'd seen some of Vistara's past in a kind of vision. It was once a world rich with an ocean, and war raged between all its peoples.

"The Warlord Jawn Kurz was real. He unified what became Mihdradahl and defeated all her enemies. He established the prosperity we have lived in since. Now we are in a sand vortex that chokes the thin air from every lung. I have growing doubts I am equal to the task before us."

"You are, and you're not alone. C'mon. Take a break. I understand we're on our own tonight?"

She frowned. "We are."

"Twice in as many nights. Let's make the best of it. The three of us. No business of the kingdom. I'm up for more language lessons."

I'd been studying. The deciphers were amazing in their ability to telepathically translate. The silver arm band also served to drive some of the language into my subconscious. But I never again wanted to be in a situation where my function was impaired without one.

She smiled approval. "Your ease in speaking improves."

I could understand the majority of what was said to me in Mihdra without the device, and also a lot of the Korundi tongue. From my time with the Mydreen, I also knew some of their speech. I still made a lot of mistakes and had to think carefully to construct my sentences.

"Why does everyone wear a decipher? There's so little intercourse between the races except here in Shansara."

"It is a habit. You must admit, it is a great convenience."

After dinner, I removed the decipher and tried out some of my Mihdra. I asked the ladies questions about their day. About the weather. Inquired about their health. All the usual vague discourse and pleasantries you first drill when studying a new language. My next effort made both ladies giggle. I didn't take offense. I'd grown up holding the flashlight for my dad. I was immune to ridicule. And bringing mirth to my closest companions by any means was a good thing, even at my expense. That's something you learn in the army.

"What?" I asked with a grin.

Talis Darmon giggled some more. "You asked for sweets the way a child would. The intonation was adorable. Which brings me to this. We need to set a firm date for our—"

I missed the word.

I opened the English/Mihdra dictionary Karlo had started compiling.

Yup. *Wedding.*

Our nuptials had been in the early stages of planning when we'd had to set it aside for more important matters. And what hadn't been more important? The looming wars had eclipsed most everything.

Married. Shansara society was not particularly sensitive to marriage as a prerequisite for much. Before I'd moved into the palace with Talis Darmon, I'd incorrectly assumed I had to conceal our living together.

"It is not because I am regent or subject to different standards of conduct, Benjamin Colt. If anything, I am judged by a higher standard. But no, by our mutual declaration of commitment, our cohabitating does not violate any of our customs. Clymaira is perhaps more conservative in many regards. Thoria—well, I find their attitudes a bit too relaxed when it comes to relations, but it's no matter for the queen to judge. For its beauty, grand Pyreenia—if it has not changed—has an air of impersonality. Observances of etiquette and social convention are stifling there."

I'm far from prudish, but there were times when dinner conversation between my betrothed and her guests made my ears burn hot. In a society where they ran around with skin exposed like a bunch of Scandinavian sun worshippers, there weren't many topics off-limits.

"I'm ready any time, my princess. But does it have to be such a production? I know you're the queen, but would it make things easier to arrange if it were a smaller, private affair?"

Beraal skewed her jaw and tusks to the side. "You said *production*, which in that case refers to goods. Not a correct usage. *Spectacle* or *display* would be the correct word, but I understand the confusion of equivalence from Thulian. And no, Benjamin Colt. Condensing the event would not be acceptable. The marriage ceremony is also a declaration that the union will produce continuity of the queen's line."

I hadn't forgotten about that one. Not by a long shot. Not once since the day she announced to the planet that there would be "issue" from her body. I wasn't sure I was ready to be a dad. But like joining the army, you didn't get to pick and choose what you did and didn't want to do. Pulling guard duty, marching in formation, carrying obscene amounts of weight on your back, sleeping in a room full of men—it was a parcel deal that came with being able to parachute, break expensive things, and kill bad guys. Not that marrying Talis Darmon was a term of enlistment.

My princess's hand found mine on the table. "It is more than that, my hero. I very much *want* a child with you. And it is proper that we be wed first."

"Then the sooner we wed, the better. What do I have to do?"

Beraal coughed a Tarn laugh. "If you are wise, brother, what you are told."

While the women happily through scrolled images of decorations and fashion, I mused over what it was going to be like to be married. I thought about the last wedding I'd been to, and the cute flower girl and ring bearer. Both were barely out of diapers and brought chuckles of amusement at being the center of attention as they stumbled up the aisle. An oddity occurred to me.

"Talis Darmon, may I ask a question?"

"Of course, my love."

"Where are all the children?"

She was taken aback. "What do you mean? There are many children about."

In Maleska Mal, the streets were full of Mydreen children, herded to-and-fro by attentive mothers. In the Korund, I'd seen the same. By firsthand observation, all the Tarn were big on kids. But in three Red cities, I'd rarely seen more than a single Red child in one place. Suddenly the contrast struck me as very odd. I'd just assumed that because of the war, kids had been out of sight, but now I wondered. I explained how I perceived the difference among the Tarn compared to here.

"Their way of life is frequently brutal and short, even amongst those of the Korund, my betrothed. And as we've discussed, the Tarn biology drives them to… reproduce regularly." While much about sexual relations wasn't a sensitive topic, the same hesitancy she displayed reminded me of the way she seemed to hold the topic of births a taboo when I'd asked her and Beraal about it in the Korund.

"And among humans?"

This she seemed at ease about. "We don't have those pressures. It's not that children are not valued, but our cities are full. Position and fruitful employment are balanced so there is no idleness of purpose or lack of fulfillment. We have nowhere near the prodigious numbers of offspring as the Tarn."

There was something I wasn't getting.

"But why?"

That brought another frown of concentration.

"I suppose it's because we are so long-lived."

I was getting closer. Maybe I misunderstood the word. "What do you mean by *pressure*, Talis Darmon?"

"Well, take the example of someone in the trades. Say, a builder. Only so many are needed for their services. Repair and maintenance are constants, but we do not expand our borders, nor do we reimagine parts of the city. It is already a paragon of perfection. That we have suffered the damage of war will no doubt tax their roles, and I fully anticipate there being many births among all our citizens as an indirect result, though of course, it will do nothing to alleviate any current shortages in the demands of skills and labor. Is that not a natural phe-nomenon on Thulia?"

"Sure. Post-war, there's usually a population growth." But my ques-tion hadn't been answered to my satisfaction. If people were long-lived, wouldn't that mean more children over a lifetime? Maybe I didn't un-derstand what she meant by long-lived? "How long does the average person live here?"

She made the "ah-ha" look. "I forget sometimes that in so many ways, you are a stranger here, my love. Among the many worlds of our mutual kind—yours of Thulia, Hyboria, Sarkasia—the races of Vistara live the longest."

I'd never asked, it was never important, but I'd always assumed she and I were about the same age. I'd seen her at her most strained and taxed. Without any makeup or finery, she was a smooth-skinned wom-an of no more than thirty.

"How old are you, Talis Darmon?"

"Oh."

My question startled her. Maybe it was a universal thing, asking a woman her age. Oops.

"By measure of the number of journeys by Vistara around the sun, I have seen more than two hundred revolutions."

I had trouble with the numbering system in the Mihdra language. I tried to sort it out and was about to use my fingers when I gave up and put my decipher back on.

"Once more, darling. How old are you?"

"I don't keep count but—"

Beraal chimed in, "Two hundred and eleven."

My pulse raced.

Talis Darmon smiled. "That's right."

I'd heard her correctly. I gulped.

"Don't worry, my love. It will be many years before I have to resort to the cosmetic improvements to which many must subject themselves in order to remain youthful. My family is very blessed in that regard."

My stomach had butterflies like the first time I shuffled to the jump door of a C-130. There was something else amiss about the population of Vistara I'd noticed.

"Darling, I rarely see any elderly. Where are all the old folks?"

"I suppose it depends upon what you mean by old. It is true that many tire of their existence and choose to journey to the River Blix to begin the next life in the underworld."

Beraal seemed eager to help explain. "It is not as common among Tarn, brother. We pass into the underworld most frequently by other means, but it is not unheard of."

My head was spinning.

"Two hundred and eleven years old," I murmured, shocked. Another thought popped into my head.

"Sweetheart, I need to ask. In a life so long, have you been married before?"

My beautiful princess took her hand from mine.

"Is this important to you?"

Beraal sucked air through her tusks. "Talis Darmon, have you not told him?"

My princess made a sour face. "Hold your tongue, Dosenie."

Beraal growled. "I am more than that, hatchling. Queen or no, I do not deserve your scolding. You know I am right."

My stomach graduated from butterflies to flip-flops.

She didn't look away, but neither would she meet my eyes. "Yes, Benjamin Colt. I have been married before. Twice."

I suppose it shouldn't have surprised me, but right now, everything was just that.

"Children?"

She did not answer.

Without consciously meaning to, I rose and stumbled from the table. The room closed in on me and I felt a vertigo as if I'd opened my eyes to find myself on some steep precipice.

"Where are you going, my love?"

"I need some air. I don't know where I'm going. Just out."

I raced to the outer door.

"Benjamin Colt!" I left her calling my name and burst through the doors, out of our apartment, and past the Guards without explanation. Apache aroused from his snores in the outer hall to join me to wander the dark streets of a quiet Shansara. I lost track of time until I found myself at my friends' apartment. A drowsy Dave answered with M17 in hand.

"Whazzup, brah? Everything all right?"

"Can we come in?"

Karlo stuck his head out of his room, a lit scroll in one hand, and his own pistol in the other. It wasn't habit. It was no different for us than the functions of our heart and lungs. Automatic. Because if you need a gun and don't have one, it's too late to get one.

"Ben! What brings you by?" he said.

I plopped onto their sofa. Apache made himself at home, grinding into the rug to make a comfy spot from where to return to sleep.

"This isn't a work thing, is it, Warlord? You guys have a fight, brah?"

I shook my head. "Dudes, I've got something to tell you. I just learned why things are the way they are, and you're not going to believe it."

06

At first light, Karlo and Dave were on the move with me to a new destination. Dave tried to console me as we flew.

"Relationships are like helicopters. I have no idea how to operate a helicopter."

I sighed. "Thanks."

"Why do you care if she's been married before, brah?"

"I guess I don't. But all that other stuff? About being two hundred years old? I mean, doesn't that freak you out?"

Dave was as plain as an unbuttered bagel. "Nope."

"How come?"

"Nothing I can do about it. Doesn't affect me. So what?"

Karlo joined in. "It does explain a lot, though. The malaise that affects this society, the constant references by the ministers to stability and consistency. All the conjecture by social scientists about what extreme longevity would do to a society, it's all right here for the study. It even sounds as though some people commit suicide from weariness at such a long life."

"We're here." Dave landed us and, in a moment, I was knocking on his door. The sight of us on his threshold made Doug Knoblock give a grin as big as the man.

"Ben! Bros! What a surprise!" He stepped aside and waved us in. "The girls are still conked out, but don't worry about them. They're sound sleepers. Make yourselves at home."

Music played in the background.

Dave tested the air. "Is that the Wu-Tang?"

Smooth shaven, hair cropped, our teammate looked fit again. He was dressed in a lavalava sort of wrap that wouldn't have been out of place at a beach party. He was sweaty like he'd been working out. "From the slums of the Shaolin, homie. Been missing you guys. How's tricks?"

Dougie's suffering at the hands of Bryant and his cohorts was different from mine, but had affected him worse. When we'd found him in Thoria, he was in a deep funk and was numbing his pain in a haze of drugs and debauchery. He'd admitted he was on his way to killing himself. The realization that our Earth and everything he'd ever known was gone—made yet more unbearable by Bryant's mad plan and Doug's forced part in it—had left him isolated and desperate.

I once knew the feeling, but I had someone to help me. Dougie'd had no one.

"I'm sorry I haven't been around to check on you. Karlo's kept me in the loop, but that's no excuse." Karlo hadn't relinquished his role as team medic and on top of everything else, was carrying that responsibility, too. No wonder he was so spent.

"Ah, fuhgeddaboudit. Warlord's got things to do. And I'm fine, Ben-dog. Better than ever."

"You look it! Has, uh, has treatment been good?" Broaching the subject of his therapy was touchy in my mind. It just wasn't the kind of personal thing you asked even a close friend about. Worse than bringing up hemorrhoids over dinner. But unlike the futility of seeing an army psychologist, the Vistarans had means of healing unknown to Earth science. And unlike much of their science and technology, what they did with the mind was not failing. I asked Talis Darmon to help him as she'd helped me, but she begged off.

"It would not be proper. But I am not alone in such ability. We will get your friend help."

Whoever had been treating Dougie, it looked like they were doing him a good service.

"Yeah, man. I mean it. I feel good. I'm focused. Strong. And I'm optimistic for the first time since we got here. Mostly."

Dave pointed to the room beyond. "How are things with the, ah, wives, brah?" It was another potentially touchy subject.

Doug chuckled. He'd insisted the three women accompany him to Shansara. Karlo had been first to agree with me that whatever was likely to bring our brother comfort should not be denied him. "It ain't like that, bro. The girls are free spirits. They've had a bad time of it too, you know? Thoria was a bad scene. Things here are—better. For me and for them."

"'Better' is a big improvement from when we found you, brah," Dave said. "What would help get you the rest of the way there?"

Doug motioned us to sit with him. "I need to make amends, bros. Healer Shalees Parn's got me seeing things in a new light. I feel guilty about a lot of things. Some of them I can forgive myself for. Some of them…"

Karlo waved him off. "Every one of us but Ben's got blood on their hands for Thoria, Dougie."

I had many weights on my own conscience. No one was free of the stain. I jumped in. "You're blameless, Doug. I hold no one but Bryant and Chuck accountable, and neither does the queen."

Dougie met my eyes. "I heard you settled with Marky-Mark."

"And I'm going to finish settling up."

"I would be down with that."

I was hoping to hear him say exactly that. "That's what I came to ask you. You feel ready to go back to work?"

Doug was on his feet, pumping his fist with each syllable. "Yes! I! Am!"

"Good enough for me, Dougie. Then as Warlord, I declare you fit for duty."

Dave smacked his fist against palm. "Thor's back!"

Doug traded bro hugs with us. "I should tell you, that's your laptop, Ben-dog."

Now I recognized it. The tunes cranking out of the small speakers continued.

"It was with my stuff. Been meaning to give it to you when I saw you."

"No sweat, amigo. Mine's yours, bro. Hang on to it. There's nothing important on it I haven't been living without just fine." I remembered the Death Dealer photo. Other than that, there was nothing I cared about.

"Nothing important! Ben-dog, that playlist's been a life saver. My stuff crapped out. I was in a hurry and didn't plug my laptop into the surge protector back at the C-17 and it fried."

"Great work, engineer. And they say weapons men are dumb."

I shot Dave a look that should have frozen him. There was a time for busting shells, and this wasn't it. But then again, tiptoeing around like he was wounded was a special treatment not appropriate for a teammate going back to war.

Doug roared in laughter. "No kidding, right? They'll take my MOS away."

I relaxed. He was the old Doug.

"When you're ready, your mission—should you choose to accept it—is to get us ready for war."

"My specialty. Thanks, Ben. I won't let you down."

Dave humphed. "Be careful what you wish for, brah. Khraal Kahlees and I have a list of about a hundred things we need help with. You ain't gonna have a lot of time for playing house. I'll send someone to bring you around later. How much time you need?"

"I don't have much to get together. All I've got are some uniforms. You have all my kit?"

Karlo nodded. "All your stuff's safe in the locker with Baby Blue. Weapons lubed, breaching tools rust free."

He looked over his shoulder to the bedroom door. "Noon time, then. I need to tell everyone there's going to be some changes. Daddy's going back to work."

✶ ✶ ✶

We left Doug to clean house. "I wasn't kidding about there being a hundred things I need help with, Ben. I'm getting ready to throw him in the deep end, if that's all right?"

"Then that's great for all of us. We get the help we need; Doug gets himself right doing what he loves."

I knew a pilot who'd been a POW. Immediately after he was released, barely cleaned and rested, his Navy brothers put him in a flight suit and in the right seat of a helicopter and told him, "Your aircraft." Their trust in their brother was absolute. And they let him know it not by words, but by deeds. I choke up when I think about it.

But like most things in the military, there's a funny part to the story. He'd literally been grounded for seven years in the Hanoi Hilton. His first time behind the stick wasn't brilliant. A difficult landing concluded with the chopper coasting down the runway—not a thing of beauty for a helicopter, even if it did have wheels. His IP didn't let it go.

"We're the Navy, not the Air Force. No more rolling landings."

My point is this—his fellow aviators knew how to restore a warrior's dignity and bring him back home.

Doug was ready to come home.

There was a buzz on my wristlet. Kleeve Hartus came to life in the cloud. I'd told him to comm me at any time if something useful came from the Mydreen prisoners.

"Warlord, it is Avril Mysteen! He has been found in the Mak Sar Desert."

"He's alive?"

"He is, Warlord, but in grim condition. He is being flown to Shansara as we speak and will arrive within the hour."

Karlo made to spring away. "I'm going to grab my aid bag. Meet you there." Two bounds and he was deep into the forest of city spires.

"Get Double-K on the move, Dave. He needs to be in on this."

Talis Darmon had refused one of the wristlets. "I am never alone," she'd said. "If there were yet one more means to disturb me at any time, I should die of the exposure."

So I commed Beraal.

"Benjamin Colt! I have restrained myself from hailing you. Talis Darmon has been—" in the background I heard her voice.

"*Is that him?*"

I stayed on topic. "Bring the queen and meet us. Quietly and low-key. We have word arriving from the west." Abruptly, I extinguished the cloud. "I'll fly us. Let's go."

✷ ✷ ✷

We crowded around until Karlo and the Red medic repelled us back with equally annoyed body language. Avril Mysteen was weak. His lips were cracked and he was thin, his face the deepest red from long exposure to the harsh Martian sun. He was dressed in black, from high collar to boots, more clothing than I'd ever seen on a Vistaran. Karlo had one IV started and was working on another. The Red medic opened the shirt and placed a pad on his chest, the colored lights of the gemstones meaningless to me. Were they monitors? A healing ray?

The young Guard raised his head and took a ratcheted breath. "Warlord, Guardsman Avril Mysteen presents with report."

The first shield stepped forward. "Soon enough. Rest for now, Guardsman, and listen to your physicians. We will remain. You are surrounded in the armor of your comrades."

The patient relaxed back.

A Tarn preceded into the hospital room ahead of Talis Darmon, Beraal a step behind. I dismissed her Guard and took bold steps to meet her at a quiet speaking distance. Though her beauty always struck me like a rising sun, for the first time I could recall, I did not smile because of it. Her lips parted to speak, but I cut her off by motioning Beraal close.

"Thank you for coming so quickly without an explanation. Avril Mysteen is back."

As though he heard me whisper his name, the Guardsman spoke.

"I will not be prevented from completing my mission. Warlord, I wish to make my report."

Karlo was a warrior as well as a doc. "This man's all soldier. Let's sit you up. But I'll stop and send everyone out if it gets to be too much." Karlo looked at me, making sure I understood that his word on the matter would be final.

Avril Mysteen took an offered sip of an orange fluid, then with sudden recognition stiffened. "Queen Talis Darmon, forgive me. I must rise."

"No, Avril Mysteen. Be at ease."

She overruled his effort by placing a hand on his forehead. Like a sick child comforted by a mother's touch, he obeyed. I wondered how many times she'd done just that to her own, whoever they were. I'd never been a father, but felt like one now.

"I'm listening, Avril Mysteen. We're all listening. Take your time. There's no hurry."

His distress rose and with it, my own worry, as the tiniest of scratches teased my bones.

"But there is, Warlord," he said. "I do not know efficiently how to tell what I have seen. I've tried these many days in the desert to form a concise report, but it has eluded me."

Concerned but flushed with pride, the first shield said, "Then tell us as you are best able, Guardsman. Start at the beginning."

He closed his eyes and, as if reciting a movie from memory for the benefit of the blind, he began.

"The light of the two sisters had not yet risen when Guardsmen Kal Trantar, Park Stellen, and I grounded the flyer just outside the aurora of Pyreenia's glow…"

07

WE PASSED OVER BANDS OF MYDREEN MANY TIMES AS WE FLEW TOWARD Pyreenia. Disguised as we were in the cloak and uniform of the Red Army, it was Park Stellen who thought we should risk making contact. He was most correct that if we remained confident in our guises, we stood a good chance of gaining valuable intelligence.

With quick recognition at our hail and no suspicion on their part, my story was accepted that we'd fled the fall of Shansara and had taken great care and been long engaged evading Korund army patrols to join the rest of our army in Pyreenia.

These travelers had not been in the battle for Shansara. They were fresh, come from the farthest East on a circuitous route to join Domeel Doreen's call. The Mydreen have a language of signs they leave in the desert for others of their tribe to read. They'd been told to avoid all Red cities until they arrived in Pyreenia, where it would be safe for them. They told us that this far into the Mak Sar Plains, there were no Korundi patrols and we should be able to make direct flight without concern.

They knew little else but that their chieftain called them to glory for all Mydreen everywhere, and that the Red Army and theirs were joined under Domeel Doreen to take what belonged to them.

We did the same a day later, learning little more, except to expect that Pyreenia was no longer only a Red city, but was in its way to becoming as Shansara, a place where Mydreen could live equal to the Reds. The Tarns were fierce in their joy at this prospect, and bragged how we would no longer be their tormentors but instead be the same in obedience to Domeel Doreen and his war council, in a place grander than Maleska Mal with much treasure to pillage.

We asked who sat on this council. The nomads repeated the same tale. The Whites from another world.

I had never been in Pyreenia, but from the many portraits of its skyline and great beauty, I thought I knew what to anticipate. Kal Trantar knew the city well, his maternal line long established there. It was he who raised our concerns at the sight of her.

"It is not well there," he cautioned. "The spectrum of her colors at night is as a prism. But lo, I behold naught but dull emanations. Where is the joyful cast and flags that inspire awe, even in the darkest night?"

And indeed, the pall over the city was not as I'd remembered from pictures. We traveled cautiously, expecting to encounter patrols around her borders, but the sands were still and empty. We waited. Eventually a band of Mydreen loped by on mounts and we followed at a distance. We observed them admitted into the city by human guards and without challenge.

"It is time to commit, Guardsmen," I said. "A kingdom depends on us." I offered to go ahead alone, but my two brave companions rejected my offer. Their courage made mine all the greater.

The sentries gave us no challenge either, much to my surprise.

"We are just arrived. To where do we report?" I asked them.

The sentries were dulled and uninterested. They did not salute. I was about to play my role as officer and dress them down for such slackness in their duties when one of them answered.

"Those uniforms won't do." The sentries were not in the dress of the Red Army, but in black covering all but their faces. "Get them some covers until they can get theirs. I s'pose us Reds have to stick together. There ain't many of us left." One of the men returned with three black robes. "You'll find the garrison near the governance square."

Kal Trantar assured them we knew the way.

But before we moved on, I had to know. "Security seems relaxed," I told them. "Don't we prepare to repel an attack?"

The same sentry shrugged. "Our orders are to keep anyone from leaving, not from entering."

We put on the robes and started off. "Pyreenia's not as grand as she once was, is she?" he said to our backs as we departed. It was not to report for duty where we aimed. We followed Kal Trantar and made our way to where he still had family from whom we would seek shelter and a place to make our base of operations. So far, the infiltration into the enemy-held Pyreenia had been little effort.

It was late and the streets were deserted. We crossed paths with foot patrols of both Red and Green soldiers, but none challenged us. Again, everyone seemed dull and uninterested. The boisterous anticipation of plunder of the Mydreen we'd encountered on their way to Pyreenia wasn't present among the Greens roaming the city. After several hours taking turn after turn through the maze of the city familiar only to Kal Trantar, we arrived at a residence.

There were no lights from within and after many firm knocks and no response, my companion entered a keycode and gently parted the entrance. It was dark inside, and the odor of human uncleanliness filled my nostrils. A frightened voice pierced the dark. "Who is there? I have nothing to hide, nothing to give. Begone."

"Grandmother, it is Kal Trantar. These are friends. Why do you not light a stone?"

We pushed into the darkness and when the entrance was sealed, she lit the tiniest of stones to reveal herself. The woman was dressed from head to toe in black. She pushed back a hood to reveal her face. "Grandwean, how come you to be here? What madness fills you?"

She checked the tapestries on all the windows and bade us sit. "I have nothing to offer you. Daily I must go to stand in line to receive the day's ration of food and water."

"Rations?" I asked in disbelief. Even more so than Shansara, there were many grand fountains as a result of the great reserve of groundwater that made Pyreenia the envy of the kingdom. "Is there no running water?"

"They shut off service to the entire city." She produced a necklace. "If you don't have one of these, you can't get a drop. Or food. And what they give is barely enough to survive on. I've never known hunger in my life except by choice. Now, it is a constant." She put the necklace away as quickly, but even in the dark, I spied the symbols on it, ones strange and unfamiliar.

"Who's done this?" we asked.

She told us that it had begun under Prince Carolinus Darmon. At first, it had been little things. The shelves had become sparse with goods. The prince blamed excessive consumption by the people and told them it was their fault, and that he had to adjust the economy to balance the demands. People grumbled, but many more agreed with him that they had to reject the ways of the rest of the kingdom, that their waste was responsible for hastening the downfall of all Vistara.

Kal Trantar had been raised in Pyreenia, and told us that it was true they were a culture of strict behavior. People dressed modestly. Kept to themselves. Did not complain. He'd moved to Clymaira while young, but had never forgotten the contrasts between the physical beauty of the city and how reserved life there seemed. The freedom and sense of well-being in Clymaira had convinced him never to return to the land of his mother.

His grandmother explained more. "We thought when the prince took the army to aid the king in Shansara that things might improve. But things worsened under the prince's ministers. The Whites came and went as they pleased with their Tarn minions. There were the other strangers. The women of the black mist. Even the common folk like myself heard rumors about what went on in the mansions of governance. Things that would make a Thorian blush."

I knew by the Whites she meant the Thulians. I asked who the strange women were. She didn't know. A trio of them accompanied the prince at public events, but then the prince departed, and soon the populace was ordered to stay at home except to retrieve the daily ration and for business deemed vital.

It was certain we could not remain there. There was no way to support ourselves with even basic sustenance and if discovered, it would surely bring fearful harm to the woman. We decided the best course of action was to report to the garrison and be integrated into the occupation forces. First, we chose to sleep, for it had been some time.

"Sleep if you can," she told us. "I try not to."

I dreamed such visions as I had never known I possessed. I saw creatures of grotesque shapes, wings and fangs, fat appendages without bone but with scales and blazing red eyes. I awoke more fatigued than when I closed my eyes. It was then that the song in my head began. Whispered words too faint to comprehend, and behind the chorus, the hint of an orchestra of snapping bones and breaking glass. I kept my dread visions to myself, certain it was a lack of courage and repressed it all, determined to be as brave as the men I led.

We found the garrison. The officer of the day eyed us suspiciously. There were a few hundred of the army who'd escaped and trickled in to Pyreenia, but we were the first to appear in weeks. Our units of origin accepted, our covers seemingly solid, we'd crossed yet another hurdle.

We were told, "For now, we wait. With King Carolinus Darmon dead, we occupy Pyreenia while our army rebuilds. The Mydreen are filled with bloodlust to retake all the Red cities. The Thulians lost some status with Domeel Doreen after the many defeats, but his White generals are busy with new plans."

We would be placed into a new cohort assigned to the Thulians for special duty. Our weapons, we kept. Our old uniforms were taken from us, and we now wore the black of the Gazraal Select. But the prized wristlet I could not conceal. It was taken with all our old trappings.

The three of us were separated and sent to different squadrons, which likely aided our covers. As a junior officer, I was placed in charge of a subsection and we went to work on the task of soldiery.

My men were similarly grave and taciturn as all the inhabitants of Pyreenia, but deadly serious about returning to fight the Korundi. Like the Mydreen, they lusted after the blood of any Red who was not with us. My subtle queries of my fellow soldiers as to why they wanted their fellow Mihdra dead were met with odd disbelief and suspicion. I had to halt all attempts at investigation—and suspend trying to act with fellowship toward my fellow soldiers. Comradeship was out of place amongst those in the Gazraal Select. In secret, Kal Trantar, Park Stellen, and I met.

Park Stellen felt as I did. "These men are not men. It's as if they are under the influence of some drug. We eat the same food and drink the same water, but it has not affected any of us. How their minds are poisoned, I cannot discover."

Kal Trantar had been assigned to a section that worked with the Mydreen. "The nomads number five thousand, with as many arkall. Their army is large enough to crush us if they march on Shansara. We must get the warning to them."

"If there's more to learn here, I don't know what it could be," I told my companions. "One of us must reach Shansara." We were unanimous. We would leave as soon as possible.

I regret we did not make our escape that very night.

A formation was called the next morning. We were to be inspected by the general himself. I had not seen either of the Thulians since we'd infiltrated. It was said that only one remained while the other sought allies elsewhere in the war to own Mihdradahl. The Thulian was scarred and moved stiffly. I knew him to be Charles Simpson, the one maimed by the weapon used to destroy the Mydreen trying to raze my sweet Clymaira. Deformed and cruel of face, I did not fear him. Though a Thulian, he was still just a man—one defeated by Benjamin Colt. I formed a rash plan to exchange my life for his and kill him there and now, where he felt most secure and when none would expect it.

My hand was stayed by the black-clad thing at his side. She seemed a woman, but was too terrible to be made of a flesh and blood capable of nurturing life.

The witch froze me with but a single wave and the maddening music in my head grew louder, and before I could react, a dozen hands restrained me. I was pummeled until I lost consciousness. When I awoke, it was to her dark aura. She laid hands on me and a foul mist enveloped me in a cloud so thick, the light of day vanished. I was no longer on Vistara.

I was transported to a land of night. Sticky soil pulled at my feet and my legs were as heavy as the stone of the Korund. I was on the shore of a vast ocean that smelled like a hundred open graves. Risen from the waters were giant pillars, structures of abnormal geometries and acute angles, graven with symbols and characters of no language.

From out of the risen city, a thousand foul beasts on four legs, slithering bellies, and skittering claws appeared. On the horizon, the waters churned and bubbled, and from it a thing so massive rose, and my insignificance in its presence condensed my being into a tiny fleck of sand.

The music grew louder yet, the beaks and maws of the singing creatures grew to a force in its own right. The words they sang carved terror in what remained of my soul.

"ANSO-KYLON."

08

"THAT'S ENOUGH, HE NEEDS REST." KARLO INFLATED THE CUFF AROUND the patient's arm but I didn't need to see the numbers to know what the ashen pallor meant.

The youngster fought back. "No! I must complete my report. The Warlord must hear."

I sat on the side of his bed. "I'm listening, Avril Mysteen. What happened next?"

His eyes cleared and he seemed to take comfort.

"Little else after my time in that place is as certain in my memory. For an eternity, I dreamed of dark and horrible things until one night I awoke. Kal Trantar and Park Stellen had come to my rescue. They carried me through the city. A fight broke out. Kal Trantar remained behind as Park Stellen rushed me into the desert. Our flyer was still hidden. He placed me in it and sent me off, chased by the bolts of a hundred weapons. How long it flew on its own, I do not know. I did not wake until it crashed, and I was thrown onto the hot sands. I marched for days until the patrol found me."

He said no more.

The first shield stepped closer yet. "Your mission is complete, Guardsman. The sacrifice of Kal Trantar and Park Stellen will be honored. You have the thanks of your kingdom. Now rest."

Avril Mysteen became agitated again. "You must send me away! You may think my tale is but fevered dream, but I carry proof. It burns me without respite." Tears streamed as he pulled aside the remnants of the stained black tunic. Between his shoulders, a brand scarred his flesh, the skin waxy and hateful. A symbol. A sickly animal of all parts from which barbed tentacles menaced.

"She put her mark upon me."

Tiny claws scratched at the base of my spine.

✳ ✳ ✳

I was grateful for the end of his tale. We left Avril Mysteen to sleep, now thankfully sedated by the medic. My head reeled, picturing the horrible things he described. We stood together in silence, consumed by the dread images of things not describable.

Khraal Kahlees brought us out of our trance. "Your trust was not misplaced, Benjamin Colt. His perseverance was great, but what he describes is a product of his torture. Yet within those delusions is information of military value for us to consider."

There was nothing further I needed to deliberate.

"It's time for action. Gentlemen, this is your warning order. Begin the final planning for the siege of Pyreenia. By morning, I want an accurate order of battle, unit statuses, and shortfalls. The mission is this. We *will* destroy all opposition in Pyreenia. We *will* take the city. We *will* use all means at our disposal. And we will not cease until we have achieved total victory. Whether we are as prepared as we would like to be or not, the moment is now. Dismissed. I'll join you later."

All came to attention and saluted—even Karlo, who no longer wore the uniform. I was alone with Talis Darmon.

"Is that Warlord enough for you, my queen?"

Her face became stone. When she finally spoke, her voice was a whisper.

"Do not be so cruel to me. I regret my words to you every moment since speaking them. I was frustrated. And scared. The throne I thought so firm beneath me seems to fade. I cannot bear to continue if, like it, I in turn become a phantom in your heart."

Tears ran from the corner of her eyes, but she did not move.

And neither did I.

"Talis Darmon, you will never be from my heart. You are why it beats."

I held her gaze.

"Which is why I deserved better."

I knew that, of all people, she understood. I'd committed to her mind, body, and soul. She'd kept things from me that would matter to anyone, be they Vistaran royalty or a simple soldier from Earth. Her hand wiped the wetness on her cheeks.

"Your worth is great, Benjamin Colt. If ever you doubted, I'd hoped it long erased. But you are correct, you deserved better. I can and I will explain. I will tell you anything you wish to know, but please, come home."

There was nothing I wanted more than to take her in my arms and carry her home.

"I will, Talis Darmon. But your Warlord cannot be your betrothed just now. I serve you best by finishing the last of your enemies in Mihdradahl. I will come to you tonight. And we'll talk. But our bed is too soft a place for a soldier to rest his head just now."

I called to the next room, "Dosenie Beraal. Come and take the queen."

✿ ✿ ✿

The breezeway was unoccupied as I passed column after column of flowering crystal trees and the gems that dangled from them like fruits. I had no idea how to find what I was looking for. A librarian appeared from somewhere unseen, and I reflexively put my hand on my pistol, then relaxed. Interruption was exactly what I sought.

"How may I be of service to our Warlord?" The man wore a gossamer drape, common as an overgarment in the dark hours and fading heat. His head was clean shaven and around its crown rested a silver band not unlike the decipher worn around his arm.

"I need your assistance locating historical records."

"Of course. Can you be more specific? What is your interest?"

"I'm looking for anything about Warlord Jawn Kurz."

The librarian frowned. "'The Song of the Amethyst Sea'?"

"What's that?"

He was not judgmental of my ignorance. "The prehistory of the Fall is contained in collections of poems, such as 'The Song of the Amethyst Sea.' There are many analyses of the works that delve into their construction that are very worthwhile for any student of the classics to peruse."

"I was looking for something historical. Anything by the man himself, or anything about him or the geopolitics of the time."

"I see. Please follow me, Warlord." He led me to a spiral staircase of the same crystal construction where on the floor above, another grove of willows pulsed as though the gentle light coursing through their thin branches was part of a life-sustaining circulatory system. The librarian turned into a recess where a tower held more of the gems. He picked one up, returned it, then selected a dark green one and placed it on a small box. The connection glowed and rows of symbols appeared above.

"This collection contains much from the period. There is one work attributed to Jawn Kurz, though it has been unauthenticated by many scholars. It contains no references to the events of the period in which it was purportedly written—one of the elements contributing to its criticism—a treatise on strategy titled, 'Meditations on the Path of Disruption.' There are several contemporary works of fictional adventure that use the character of Jawn Kurz, but they have no historical value."

He scrolled to a new group of symbols.

"There are many works concerning the period of turmoil that characterized the pre-Fall history. I think you would find this one the least cumbersome." He hurried to correct himself. "Forgive me, Warlord. By that, I only meant to say that to anyone not a specialist, the numerous citations with which one historian invalidates the observation of another can be tedious."

"You understand my needs then, thank you."

He took the gem and led me to a reading room, set the volume on a reader, and told me to chime if I had any other needs.

I don't know what I was looking for, but after an hour scanning pages, whatever inspiration I hoped to get, it wasn't here. Maybe I'd have been better served by reading one of the Mack Bolan treatments of the first and only Warlord before I was so named. I chimed and the librarian returned.

"This isn't it what I had in mind. I wonder—I've visited the library of Clymaira. I saw a part of it not meant for the public. It was a hall of mirrors."

The librarian tried to conceal his surprise. He was good. Calm. Controlled, the way a good poker player let that last card drop into his hand that gave him three of a kind like it was nothing. But he failed. His recovery from the smallest wrinkle on his forehead back to smooth wasn't quick enough to evade my detection. He began to make noises of ignorance. I was through being the retired detective trying to appeal and coerce his way into working the unsolved case he obsessed about long after retirement.

You're a Warlord; it's time you act like it, echoed in my brain.

"Stop. You've been very professional. Don't change my opinion of you by lying. It will displease your Warlord if you persist."

He paled.

"Please come with me, Warlord."

We descended and descended again. Another subterranean collection in the library led to a hidden sally port. He used a code on the gems, and the door parted to reveal yet more stairs. The atmosphere works were many klicks away, so I thought it unlikely that this led to their works as had the library in Clymaira. At the last tread, a door waited, another code, and beyond that, a room. The same rough crystal frameworks and giant mirrors that had shown me living history formed the walls.

"Warlord, to best serve you, I should inquire if you're familiar with the Mists of All Past."

"I've never had time to learn."

His reverently glided towards the mirror deepest into the room. "The Wars of the Oceania Kingdoms are saved here. The vistas are sometimes quite random, rarely chronologic, and often difficult to navigate for historic accuracy. Many have tried. Some ancestor of ours toiled to capture what exists here. If only they had done a better job organizing it! Many have tried, but it was a time of legend and chaos, and it is all but impossible to do so with the fealty it deserves. The decision has always been above all to preserve it and let scholars of our guild use it as a tool, with the understanding that it is not an encyclopedia."

He waved a hand across the mirror. "May I remain, Warlord? I will not disturb your reverence, and I may be able to answer any questions."

"That would be welcome, thank you."

The mists formed and cleared, and the librarian was true to his word and remained silent as the past came to life. The images had depth and a taste to them; the air I breathed held the flavor of ozone and rain during a thunderstorm, the mint chill of the Amethyst Sea in winter, the coppery blood and gangrenous death over yesterday's battlefield, the butcher's bill paid in meat revealed the same beneath Red and Yellow skin.

Without having to ask, I knew him when he appeared. Not because Jawn Kurz was a god. But because he was a soldier. He cut a fine figure of a Red man. He swung a two-handed sword as thick as his thigh. Carried a rifle that spat red bolts of hate. He charged from the front, ten thousand behind him. Up steep cliffs and across grassy fields of blue thickets. Rode ships with golden sails and on great airborne carriers, energy weapons toppling green towers in a city larger than all those of Mihdradahl combined.

Interspersed were other vignettes—non sequiturs and, above all, dull. Gone were the battlefields, and in their place the mundane stuff of civilizations building and growing. I saw him again for a brief moment. He stood tall, in glittering armor, rifle slung across his back. Seated on a throne beside him was a queen with lavender hair instead of Talis Darmon's raven black. When the images shifted again to farmers tending a field, I checked my watch.

"I think I got what I came for. Thank you."

Outside, I was alone with my thoughts. I hadn't learned a single word of advice from my predecessor. I still knew nothing about the strategy he used or the challenges he faced. But I'd always believed that what one man could do, so could another. Without that belief, I would never have been able to do what I'd done to join the ranks of those who wore the green beret. If all I knew was to lead from the front, then it seemed like I already had the most important lesson Jawn Kurz would've given me.

I'd promised Talis Darmon I would return to our home. My rectitude to not lay my head on our bed fought at me, and I felt guilty about my intentional cruelty to the person I loved above all. I was about to bound off when a cloaked figure stepped from the shadows.

"Warlord, how does this evening find you?"

He was no longer in the uniform of the Red army, but the pencil-thin goatee and the slurpy thickness of his baritone had not changed.

"General Marviel Lanconin! I didn't expect to run into you." His brief tenure as commanding general had been halted by the queen's appointment of Khraal Kahlees.

I never heard them. I scarcely saw the hand that darted beneath the edge of my vision. The taste of whatever was sprayed at me was sweet, and before I could sink my hips and drive an elbow into the abdomen behind me, the horizon tilted and I dropped. I fought to stay on my hands and knees, but the stone walk seemed irresistible, and all I wanted to do was lay my face against its cool smooth surface.

"Be quick."

Hands were on me, the whir of an air car was in my ears, and then came the brief inertia of flying before I was on the deck of a ship riding the waves of a purple sea.

09

I WAS WARM AS THOUGH WRAPPED IN A BIG FUZZY BLANKET. TETHERS bit into my skin from my chest to my feet, but the ground was pleasantly comfortable and I didn't care. I knew I should try to open my eyes, but the lids were heavy as pig iron and when I did, the effort mocked me. My eyes were covered. I shed my guilt and let them close again.

Whatever I'd been given reminded me of the same thing I'd had before they took my appendix out. One minute I was uncomfortable and a little anxious about the surgery. The nurse put something in the IV, and the next minute, I didn't have a care in the world. I was smiling at everyone in the OR and felt like I was on a cloud.

I'm a cheap date, by the way. One drink and I'm slurring words.

"Take the stone. Help me roll the brute."

"He's getting a light sentence."

"It is poetic justice. Not since the seas dried has one been executed this way."

"Far less cruel than the deaths he's dealt to others."

Were they talking about me? Cruel? I was a pussycat. Why didn't they like me? What had I ever done to them? I was pretty certain one of the voices belonged to Terran Dullmar, the minister of works. We'd dined together several times. I even liked his wife. Hands pushed me from face onto back onto face, then—expecting another thud onto my back again—I fell off the edge of the cliff. For the briefest second. My legs hit water and I rushed a deep breath just before my head went under.

They meant to drown me.

The cold water stole the fleece blanket feeling and instead left me irritated. I'd gone from the deep bliss of sleeping in late on Sunday morning to my nirvana being abruptly ruined by a loud pound at the door and yells that I was late for CQ duty.

In a lucid moment, I asked myself, *Where on Vistara is there a lake big enough to drown me?* Just as I began to wonder how deep it could be, I hit bottom.

As I floated on the rocky floor, I tried to focus. Three voices in addition to Marviel Lanconin's gave away their numbers. Like him, they were confident. Not particularly strong. It took all of them to manhandle me. They'd most certainly hang around to make sure the job was done. I had no urge to breathe yet, and the drug still made me as anxiety-free as a nursing baby.

Eventually, the first burn of oxygen starvation started to gnaw. I let it build to an acid burning in my blood, got my legs under me, and gave a gentle push off the bottom. A few dolphin kicks as I stretched my lips to lead the way up, I reentered the world of air. I sucked a silent breath, and held. I heard nothing during my split second just above the surface, and partly exhaled to sink.

I repeated this a few times as I tried to work out my options. Testing my bonds, they didn't budge. My wrists were secured behind my back, bindings across my chest pinned my arms to my sides, and my thighs and legs were tied together. I could leap over a small building in a single bound, generate fantastic forces to break a sternum like it was brittle clay, but tensile strengths were a different matter. The edge of the pool was in front of me. If I could propel myself up to the lip I'd been pushed from, I could get out of the water and find the exit.

Then there would be hell to pay.

The water thought differently of my plan. All that resulted from my most powerful spring off the bottom were scrapes and contusions against the rocks as I fought to worm my way up and onto dry land. I sank again.

My drug-induced sense of humor had worn off.

Taking a few more abrasions by rubbing the side of my head on the rough wall, I was able to lower the blindfold. On my next bob to the surface, I was disappointed to find that the world was just as black as it'd been with the blindfold on—the bottom of a well at midnight.

I could bob all day. I hadn't had to since scuba school and honestly, hadn't spent much time in the water since. For a skill that was deemed so important in Special Operations—other than the pride that came with having the diver helmet badge—it hadn't done much for me. One thing for sure, I doubted there were any Vistarans who knew how to do what I was doing. There were some men I'd like to give a taste of Key West pool week right now.

It was time to play blind man's bluff and probe the borders of my watery cage. I aimed myself away from the wall. A few bobs out, it deepened. Then, trying to do a one-eighty and go back in the other direction, I got disoriented and had a mini-panic when I couldn't find the edge again.

The cavern—or whatever it was—was big. Too big for me to sound out in this manner and I was fatiguing. I hate having to eat my words. Maybe I couldn't actually do this all day.

I had no sense of time, and it was hard to keep a bearing in complete darkness. I thought about those isolation chamber experiments where guys said after floating in the complete absence of light they began to hallucinate. No thanks. I'd about shaken off the drugged euphoria of whatever they'd sedated me with and didn't want any other kind of impediment to my brain working. Tripping like it was the end of *2001: A Space Odyssey* wouldn't help me find the way out.

And when I found it, someone was going to be sorry. Several some-ones. And at the top of that list was Marviel Lanconin.

I changed tactics and started a shallow swim, a half chest of air letting me hang just below the surface, more dolphin kicking propelling me very inefficiently ahead. Swimming without arms sucked. I anticipated I'd crack my noggin on something at any moment. When I did, the head bonk was as welcome as a love pat. I returned to bobbing again, keeping the edge on my left, and mentally constructed a top-down view of my prison as I took the tour, one bob at a time. I was just about to give up for a while and rest in a dead-man float, when I came to an abrupt incline and soon enough, was standing with my nose just above water.

"About friggin' time," I said loudly. If it drew someone's attention, so much the better. Nothing had changed about the ambient light situation, though. Still as dark as the inside of a coffin.

I did find a consolation prize. Right about waist height was a projection from the rock face. To work my bindings against the small edge, I had to simulate a crank shaft with my whole body, and at one thousand repetitions, I stopped. It just wasn't working. In a fit of frustration, I pulled my wrists apart and the band snapped with glorious freedom.

Exhausted, I celebrated by breathing. Divine, unhampered breathing, my chin buoyantly rising and dipping below the surface with my breaths. I was able to snake my elbows in front of me and from there, the bands around my upper arms became slack. After another interminable amount of time, I had my arms free. With the use of them again, one more strong push off the bottom and I easily reached up to the edge and vaulted out. This dry spot had just become my most favorite place on all of Vistara.

I hadn't meant to sleep. My shivering woke me, and immediately I went back to working on the knots of the bands lashing my legs. Finally released, I massaged my quads until I could stand.

I do not recommend this workout routine. Zero stars.

The ledge I'd ended up on was an isolated landing, little more than a tiny indent into what I pictured as the walls of a cave. Back in the water, I continued my search for new points of egress. I found more ledges, all of them blind ends. Standing on each dry recess, I put hands over every square inch of surface vertical and horizontal, probing and pushing at the rough rock faces, and finding nothing. If any of these places had been the entry where my abductors had brought me, the portal was so well concealed I couldn't find it. Many hours passed.

It was no coincidence that it was the voice of the minister of works that I heard with Marviel Lanconin. This had to be a cistern beneath the city. Some kind of hidden entrance protected the sanctuary, and it was eluding my ability to find it in my blind condition. But, I had to hand it to them. The way the guilds and trades protected secrets—like jealous office workers with their favorite staplers—there might not be anyone besides the four who put me here who knew where this was.

I found a few small stones and tried my next plan. The first I threw to my left.

Plunk.

Straight ahead and even harder this time, I hurled. A few seconds of flight was ended by a solid *thwack* and I involuntarily cheered. To my right, another splash.

In my mental map, I was in the middle of a big oval, and straight across from me was the other side of the pool. Maybe I'd been dumped in from there and in my drugged, disoriented, and bound state, I'd gotten all the way to the other side.

What else was I going to do? Wait for help to arrive? The choice seemed obvious. I was somewhere beneath Shansara. I'd once infiltrated into the city through the subterranean aqueduct and seen the strange works beneath the fountain plaza of the Waters of Persidia. Water was a rare resource in the kingdom. It made sense to me that somehow, this was all connected. It was time to swim again.

I imagined the far side was two hundred yards away and broke into a breaststroke, not wanting to bang my head into anything hard again. The sound of splashing water returned and I slowed. As I did, I caught a tiny glimpse of a flicker of light from the depths below. I squeezed my eyes tight several times and with each opening, the refracted light was still there, shifting beneath the swells. It was not me having some weird sensory deprivation episode. Filtered through the water and no brighter than a firefly in a deep mist was the first light I'd seen in many hours.

I took a few more strokes, found the far side and an edge, and explored the dry landing as I'd done the others. Nada. By a factor of one thousand, this was worse than the land nav course for SF selection. Finding a series of three-foot-tall green stakes in the North Carolina woods at night, separated from each other by ten kilometers, was a piece of cake. A man alone with only his mind, a map, and a compass was one of the best tests of resilience and coping that there was. If I ever got out of this, I had a whole new selection challenge to inflict on someone.

I sat and hugged my knees and shivered. This was a predicament. I wasn't being ransomed—this was a clumsy assassination attempt. My captors thought they'd drowned me. No one could possibly know where I was. Talis Darmon was safe in the shield of her bodyguards, but my abduction was nonetheless a stab at her. Who knew what these conspirators' next move would be? I had to keep trying.

I looked out on the waters for the light. It was gone.

I eased back in, took a few strokes, and turned back. The light was there again, in the deep. It couldn't be daylight; it had to be artificial. How hadn't I seen it before if I'd been deposited in my watery grave from somewhere over here? My mental map was worthless as tears to the tax man. I went under.

Now I understood. The deeper I went, the angle increased, exposing the source of the light. A jagged gap of a cleavage, just wide enough for a man, was exposed by the dim light from within. A couple more trips up for air—and conversations with myself about how stupid it would be to drown in some tunnel—and finally it was time to go for it.

I made one trip to what I thought was about the halfway point—a midway where I could turn around and not die—and did so. Just where I'd paused to turn back, the light ahead seemed like it was getting brighter.

I calmed my breathing. Contrary to common wisdom, it was a rule to not hyperventilate before going under—you blew out too much CO_2—which was a sure way to go into blackout on a prolonged breath-hold dive. After a few normal breaths, I took a deep lung-full and dived.

Staying calm was the key.

I kicked and pulled with my arms, and imagined I was bounding in my superman strides across the deserts of Mars. The need to breathe tickled, and I stroked harder. I fixed on the brightening light ahead and fought the urgency to draw air into my lungs. The acid burn of oxygen starvation was past the level of inducing panic, and I fought the battle that any second I would take that gulp of water into my lungs and meet my end. I came out of the tunnel into a sheltering sky of light penetrating the mercury above and pulled hard to the surface.

In every military school that tries to prepare you for the adversity of combat, you're told that no matter how hard it is, it's never as tough as what you'll someday have to endure for real.

They were right.

As I broke the surface—not caring if there were a low ceiling of sharpened spikes waiting for me—every difficult thing I'd ever done became a memory of a sweet walk on a primrose path. I sucked in dry Martian air.

Had I said that dive school hadn't done much for me? Today would go down in history for two things: coming as close to death as I ever had, and for eating more of my words like Halloween candy than ever before.

"Scree!"

I was in a cave of white crystalline light, rat-like vereen on hind legs cheering my entrance. I paddled weakly to an obvious shore and lay there as a stampede of eight-legged vermin scurried over the glowing rocks, creating a disco ball effect, with a little anoxia thrown in for good measure. It all made for a theme park light show, just for me.

"Thanks for the grand welcome, guys. When I catch my breath, how about showing me the way out of here?"

10

I'D SEEN THESE KINDS OF CRYSTAL FORMATIONS BEFORE—IN CYNAR'S hideout. The occasional rat brushing past me on the rocky path didn't bother me in the slightest. I was wet, cold, and tired, but I could see. Light was at the top of the list of morale builders, right up there with fire and a good Wi-Fi signal.

A few false starts on paths that led to blind ends didn't discourage me. Like all vermin, the vereen would only be here if they had a way to the surface and food sources from the refuse and castoffs of people. I was below Shansara, I was certain. Where they scurried, I followed.

It was slow going. Just when a passage became so narrow that anxiety gripped me, the trail opened again and I was able to continue. I didn't want to be the guy who bitched because the rope they hung him with was too new, but I was thirsty and wished for water. One minute drowning, the next dying of thirst. There's no pleasing some people. I trudged on.

"Warlord."

I froze. It was just the echo of my footfalls.

Then I heard it again. The faintest whisper ahead.

"Warlord."

"Down here," I called, and picked up my pace, shouting at the top of my lungs to my search party as I tried to achieve a trot through the sharp rocky passage. I stopped, calmed my breathing, and strained my ears.

It was silent for the longest time.

I shrugged it off. "Don't go bonkers, Ben. You're just hearing things, dumbass." There was nothing to do but go forward.

I didn't have my watch, my folding knife, or even a ball of lint. Things that had been part of my daily pocket check for years were all gone. They'd thoroughly stripped me of everything. It was as my mind wandered to where my M17 and my sword would be when I reached a flat spot on the trail and fatigue took over. Just a nap. It was the only way I had to refresh myself. I'd marched for so long that I was dry, inside and out. On my side, I curled into a ball and was immediately asleep.

I knew I was dreaming. An amber stone radiated brighter with the advancing steps of the one who held it. From out of the narrow passage ahead of me stepped Jawn Kurz. His dazzling armor reflected the light back like the sequins of a million stars from a sea of velvet blackness. He smiled and beckoned to me.

"Rise, Warlord. Rise and follow."

I did.

I trailed behind him through the caves without question. His long stride carried him farther and farther away until I could no longer keep up and he disappeared. Out of breath, I struggled to catch him. I came to a great hall where seated on a pair of thrones, there was Jawn Kurz next to his queen. She smiled brightly and dipped her head to me in recognition. She looked much like my princess, save instead of Talis Darmon's bounteous raven locks, this lovely face was framed in tresses of amethyst. Her Warlord rose.

"Come find me, Warlord. You have need of my gifts to battle the evil to come."

I awoke on my side, my ribs and other bony prominences talking to me in unkind terms.

"If only, dude."

It was time to get going again.

For many hours, I plodded. It couldn't use my natural ability to bound in these tight spaces and tried a pace count but abandoned the effort as useless. Just as I felt every muscle in my body beg for another nap, I broke into a widening part of the trail. I felt a new energy and picked up the pace. The way ahead grew wider until suddenly, I broke into a cathedral of many colors and gasped.

Stalactites and stalagmites of purple and white crystals filled the giant cavern, but it was not that which stunned me. In the middle of the natural sanctuary was the focus of many rays of light from the hanging formations, as though grown there for the specific purpose of honoring the creation beneath. It was a monument. A throne carved from crystal and on it, a man. A king.

A Warlord.

Jawn Kurz.

Not a sculpture. The man. Turned to stone. Not stone, but mummified. Dead skin stretched over the skull, the eyes empty sockets yet a frown of command still there. I touched the armor and wiped away a scale of decay to reveal the chest plate that held the Milky Way on its surface. I took it all, from the helmet to the arm bands, and dressed. It warmed to my touch and fit me as though made for me. His two-handed sword went to the scabbard on my side, and the rifle came into my hands as effortlessly as picking up my M4. I swung it onto my back and took a last look at the Warlord I'd stripped.

"I answered your call. I'll keep your faith. You can depend on me."

On the path again, my steps were light. Dressed for battle once more, I felt neither thirst nor hunger, neither fatigue nor fear. The journey was a blur until I came to a smooth floor and a passage lit by amber stones. A curving way broke into a room and there with his back to me was a gray man in rags. He spun at my entrance, saw me, and screeched in fright.

"Hold, water priest, it is only your Warlord. Do not fear, for I bring you glad tidings." I drew the sword and held it over head. "Our peril is over, for I have the blessings of the protector of our land. Give call to the world above and let them know I have returned, born again."

"Aiyeee!" the old priest howled and ran off.

I looked at my raised arm. There was no sword in it. I put hands to my chest. I wore no armor. I was dressed in my frayed fatigues. I shook my head like a wet dog. Everything else was real—the amber lights, the workbench, the old hermit, and especially his panting escape.

"Hey! Dipshit! Don't run off. Get on the horn and call Cynar. Tell him Benjamin Colt's on the other end. Tell him to come get me. And tell him I want Marviel Lanconin's balls in a jar."

✳ ✳ ✳

"Lemuel the Novice, isn't it?"

The water priest cowered but didn't run off again.

"We need to call Cynar. Can you do that?"

The hermit nodded, and I followed him through his maze to a jeweled terminal. A cloud materialized and resolved into Cynar's face. He scowled at me.

"Benjamin Colt! Why do you waste time with Lemuel? What could he do for you that I could not do a hundred times better? At least it was not to some brothel to which you disappeared. Most irresponsible, you clot."

There were some constants in the universe.

"Shut it, Cynar. I was kidnapped."

"Kidnapped? Hmm. You look like you fought a gazraal."

"Been there, done that, but thanks, Cynar. You look like death warmed over, too. What's the quickest way out of here?"

"Your path out you already know. It leads beneath the Waters of Persidia."

"Get the gang together and come meet me."

"Are you aware the entirety of the kingdom searches for you? Your disappearance has brought great strife to the city."

"I'll tell you about it soon enough. I assume junior here has another set of keys to get me through the barrier?"

On cue, Lemuel produced a shining orb that was the key to opening the way.

"I don't want all of Shansara to know I'm back. We have a chance to roll up the conspirators who attempted to murder me, maybe the whole lot of them."

"Murder, Benjamin Colt?"

"I'll explain later. Word of mouth, Cynar. I'll see you at the fountain." I closed the link. "C'mon, Lemuel, you look like you could use a little exercise. On the way, how about something to eat and drink? I feel like you look, buddy."

The way out was a climb up many switchbacks of rough carved stairs to a concealed exit near the fountains—a piece of cake after my trek. In the secreted foyer was a small crowd and at its center, my princess. My heart jumped and I dried her tears as soon as she brought her head from my chest.

"When Cynar brought word you were alive, I nearly collapsed. It's been three days, Benjamin Colt. Where have you been?"

Three days? I'd lost all sense of time while on my inadvertent adventure.

"It's okay, Talis Darmon. I screwed up. My stupid pride almost got me killed." I told her my story.

Khraal Kahlees seethed, "Marviel Lanconin! Who would have thought the oaf more than empty armor? I will peel his skin off and make a cape of him for you, Warlord."

"If I hadn't been off on my own, they never could have gotten the drop on me. Apache would have chewed them to bits. Where is he?"

Talis Darmon clung to me. "After you did not come home that night, the next day we searched. He led us to the library but lost your scent from there. He is inconsolable and refuses beckon and wanders the city."

Kleeve Hartus put his hand on my shoulder to join the many others. "I've questioned the librarian. Only his sincerity has kept me from locking him up. Am I wrong that he had no part in this?"

"No. I went to the library on a spur-of-the-moment kind of thing. They must have had me under surveillance. They waited to make their move until I was alone. I'm never leaving Apache behind again."

Dave was not his usual happy-go-lucky self. He'd aged a decade in days. Ten miles of bad road looked better. "Brah, we've tossed the city day and night looking for you. You disappeared without a trace. I couldn't begin to think what we were going to do if..."

"No worries, brother. It won't happen again. And I'll tell you what we're going to do—where does Marviel Lanconin lay his fat head to sleep?"

✹ ✹ ✹

"How many ways out of there?" The ex-general's digs were in the lone tower sprouting from the middle of a plaza. The sun was setting, and the city adopted the iridescent green glow of its night palette. Foot traffic was dwindling as people made their way home.

"Let us handle this, Ben-dog." Dougie patted the M4 on his chest.

"Fat chance." I pointed to the roof. "There's a flitter parked up there. Top-down and bottom-up. Quietly. The fewer of us the better. They don't know they weren't successful." I couldn't wait to see the look on Marviel Lanconin's face. "I'm taking up. You with me, Dougie?"

Dougie was like me. He didn't mind climbing. "Someone's full of piss and vinegar. Yeah, alright. You're a little light in the bang-bang department." He took off his war belt and pistol and offered it.

"He better know where my stuff is. I want my M17 back."

"Karlo'll make you a new one, bro."

Talis Darmon put hands to her temples. "No, Benjamin Colt. Why must it be you who goes?"

Beraal did similar with sky hands. "Brother, is this wise?"

Khraal Kahlees bared his tusks. "No warrior would have it differently." As if he'd settled the issue, he continued. "Kleeve Hartus, David Masamuni, and I will await your signal and make ascent to his door. Enjoy your trek, friends."

Doug and I took a path in the shadow of a wide building and paused to assess. I charted our path up the outside of the high rise. "There's a balcony on every level. He's on the top floor."

"Let's do it, Ben-dog. When you're a superhero, it's easy-peasy."

"Lemon-squeezy. Follow me."

A slow, casual walk across the plaza. I ignored the people in the square, not caring what their reaction would be to the show we were about to give them. I sprang. It was an easy series of hops from the edge of each balcony, barely pausing to get a new grip and vault on to the top of the wide railing before springing over and up again, hitting one after another like a pachinko ball in reverse. On the roof, I moved aside to make room for Doug, a second behind me.

"That was quick, bro," Doug whispered. He pointed. "Staircase down." It was the rooftop entrance to the penthouse suite.

I touched the bracelet and whispered, "We're set. Take the ascenders. We're going in." I didn't wait for a reply. "Let's do it, Dougie."

Dougie pointed with his muzzle and pumped it ahead twice. We padded down the stairs, to the landing and the door. I kept my pistol up while Doug assessed. He pulled a pry off his back and set the edge into the jamb. I gave him the sign, he seated it, and levered. The thin door slid open a crack, Doug thrust both hands in and heaved. A tone sounded within.

We poured in to a service area and on into a kitchen, where a pair of surprised servants gasped in shock at the appearance of two armed men. We rolled through and divided to cover the room. Dropped platters clanged. We interrupted a feast—the dining table seated four men.

"Hands up, don't move!"

Marviel Lanconin leaped to his feet and before I could, Doug's giant fist hammered him to the ground.

"Don't understand Mihdra? He said don't move."

Khraal Kahlees burst in from the other side of the room with Dave and Kleeve Hartus. The first shield lowered his K-spec. "The minister of works. The vice minister of the purse. And the master of lights. All residents of the Sinasian Towers. Great thanks for saving us the effort of collecting each of you from your apartments. Warlord, four together I think is no coincidence. We may have rounded up all your abductors in one step." He spoke into his wristlet and Guard flitters levitated into view outside.

I holstered and with a single fistful of collar, hoisted Marviel Lanconin's feet off the ground to meet my eyes.

"Surprised to see me? Here's a tip, buddy—drown proofing is how a combat diver relaxes. You shoulda cut my throat. Better luck next time."

11

Talis Darmon clung to me as we flew to the investigation center. "Betrothed, must you always take such risks?"

I pulled her close to put my lips to her ear. "I am Warlord first. And a Warlord leads. Jawn Kurz was always at the front."

The movies I'd seen in the library had made an impression. So much so, that in my fatigue, they were the seeds for the visions I'd had of him. Subconscious images breaking to the surface like my ascent through black waters for air. The answer to my desperate wish for a role model I'd felt I needed as badly as I'd needed oxygen.

Because, what else could explain why I'd imagined what I did?

"Jawn Kurz is as much legend as real. You need not copy a myth. Is that what you were doing at the library?"

"It was."

"When you disappeared, I briefly entertained that you punished me in some petty way. As quickly, I discounted that. No matter what injury I had done to you, you would not do something so hurtful and childish. It could only be because you met with foul encounter."

"That I did, my princess." I didn't want to admit how close I'd come to dying. "With me gone, their next move would've been against you—unless you started taking steps backward to let them back into power. But now we have them, Talis Darmon. And we're going to find out what they know."

"Whatever Kleeve Hartus learns, can you please permit others to act next on the product of his work? Not only for my sake, but for that of all who depend on you. You are not the only capable arm of my will.

You cannot imagine how desperate was our thinking when we could not find you."

"I promise." But in my mind, I saw a man in velvet black armor charging a hill with an army behind him.

When we arrived, the captured conspirators were already in the interrogation rooms. I played back in my head the curses my captors cast as they sought to drown me. The minister of works's squeaky voice was distinctive.

"Terran Dullmar was one of them."

Kleeve Hartus stroked his chin. "And few but the minister of works would know the full extent of what lies beneath our city."

"I can't say with complete certainty that these others were there."

Khraal Kahlees was only too happy to volunteer his services. "First Shield, you already know my mind on these matters. I would rest their secrets from them with the first digit cleaved."

Talis Darmon flared. "I am of a heart to allow just that, General, but the queen is the guarantor of all rights. Yet, there are other means." She burst through the door to where Marviel Lanconin sat chained, startling the interrogator to his feet. Kleeve Hartus groaned at her abrupt disturbance of their process and started after her. I caught his arm and as quickly released him at his frown.

"My investigators can do this, Benjamin Colt. They have not yet begun to apply pressure. These weak men will turn on each other to save themselves."

"Time is against us," Khraal Kahlees grunted. "What say you, Benjamin Colt? In all matters existential to the kingdom, only the queen is above you."

I thought I knew what she had in mind. "Brothers, let's let her work."

The interrogator stepped out as his queen ordered, but blocked the door, pausing to let Kleeve Hartus give a nod of approval before closing it behind him. I admired the detective. How hard was it to resist a queen? Few of us knew. For sure, it was a move fraught with more peril than ignoring a command sergeant major's order to trim that mustache. We gathered at the window and the dismissed interrogator joined us.

"He's a stone, First Shield. He will not answer, not even to admit his own name. It will take time with this one." Then he saw what I did through the glass, only he gasped, "Twin Sisters above!"

Talis Darmon radiated gold.

"Look at me, Marviel Lanconin."

The defiant ex-general opened his mouth as if to hurl insult from wrinkled lips. His eyes widened and the sneer left his face. She spoke in a hypnotic language of syllables that did not pause and which my decipher lent no translation. The bound man wilted, and his stubbornness with him.

Eyes fixed, Khraal Kahlees reverently said, "We forget Talis Darmon is a sorceress. I have not seen her wield her craft save the day she took the Spectral Throne, but I know the presence of power when it is exercised."

She reached into the space between them with open palms, her aura converging on him. "Who joins you in this plot to harm the Warlord?"

He named the three men in the other rooms. "Cravon Tahl, Dumar Sifan, Terran Dullmar."

"And who else?"

He named others I didn't recognize. The first shield whispered to me, "I am sending men now to arrest them. They are within the elite of Shansara, but of lesser position. All are known to me. There will be others below them."

She held his gaze. "Was this conspiracy of your making, Marviel Lanconin, or are you directed by another?"

There was a moment of hesitation, until her aura changed to the glow of iron taken from the forge. Her subject did not blink as the light brought tears. He was fixed like a bug pinned to a board.

"Tyreen Sorell's displeasure joined ours, but was jailed before I completed the plan."

Double-K seethed. "The serpent! The air wizard deserves a Mydreen fire for his many crimes."

Dave spoke for the first time. "How about it, Intel Sergeant? Are you drawing up your organizational chart of their cells yet? Talis Darmon's quite the interrogator, brah. Many's the time we could've used her in Venezuela."

The fire in the queen's voice dimmed. She lowered her hands, the light relaxed, as did the man. "Why have you done this thing, Marviel Lanconin? Was your pride wounded by your demotion? It was your decision to retire rather than assist Khraal Kahlees in service to the kingdom."

At the peak of her intense eminence, there had been fear in his eyes. Now as she dimmed her light, he regained some of his defiance.

"You plot a course for Mihdradahl that brings a foul change, Talis Darmon. You ignore long established tradition. It was your doing that loosed these Thulians on Vistara. Tarn savages have overrun Shansara. You and they must be removed for the good of all."

Her aura grew intense again as she asked the question I wanted to hear. "Was your next plot against me?"

Grim, he answered, "With Benjamin Colt at your side, your reign would continue."

Dave humphed. "That's a big 'yes' in my book."

Talis Darmon pursued. "How is it you think that I brought the Thulians to Vistara?"

Marviel Lanconin squinted in accusation. "In your hunger for the throne, you used your Sylah sorcery to summon the off-worlders. It is too much of a coincidence to be anything else. Only you and they have benefitted since their arrival."

She slapped the table with both hands. "Weak-minded fool! Is this what Tyreen Sorell has told you?"

He nodded.

"Who advised my father to take such tepid action at every turn? Was it he?"

The sneer returned. "He was not alone. Itkar Moline was a great general and greater man, as was your father the king. Long had he taken the general's counsel which maintained the stability of his kingdom.

I learned all I know from both." He straightened for the first time in minutes. "That is all I will say, Queen Talis Darmon."

Her arms extended and touched his temples, and he recoiled as far as his restraints would allow. I expected her aura to flare again, but instead, it extinguished like a dying candle, the power of her words replacing the energy.

"You are a contemptible creature, Marviel Lanconin."

She released him.

"I command you to tell all to the investigators. There will be a trial, and the arbiters will decide your fate."

She rose, but before she left, she spun to look down at him.

"And if you plead for mercy, you may be allowed to take the walk north. But it would be more pleasing if you save your remorse and choose a cell."

All parted way for her to join me. She was serene and beautiful, the razor edges of her blade again in its scabbard. "First Shield, please continue. What he has admitted under my suggestion may be challenged in his arbitration, so you will need him to repeat all for your record to be presented at his trial. I sense that he has greater knowledge about the incompetence with which all served my father during the crisis. I ask that you wring him dry."

"It will be done, Queen Talis Darmon." He saluted and left.

I gave a quick head tilt telling everyone to give her and me some privacy. "Did you sense anything about, you know, the others?" I didn't want to name them. That an ancient evil awakened was still known to only a select few. I'd strained my own senses but didn't feel the tingle deep within.

"No. Their evil is not present in Marviel Lanconin or these other fools. They may be the tools of others so possessed, but I think more likely their deeds arise from the rot of their nepotism and ineptitude. But it will soon be exposed in public and their essence cleansed from Shansara." She made a wry smile. "This is the character of my life with you, Benjamin Colt. One moment I despair that I am in the jaws of my demise. Then as abruptly, you put the beast on its back."

"You're very welcome, Talis Darmon. I wish I could take credit that it was all part of some elaborate plan on my part, but it was just another example of my stepping in godahl droppings and coming up smelling like perfume." I'd made the best approximation I could for the idiom that most commonly applied to my life.

She frowned. "My coarse soldier, as always. Come home now, and let us scrub the ordeal from your body." She whiffed. "And this uniform. Can we let Beraal burn it at last? It stinks of an evil all its own."

✳ ✳ ✳

For the first time in many weeks, I dreamed of my former teammate, Brandon Bryant. His silver helmet of hair, his sour voice, and his many injuries against me. I saw Chuck's melted face. I heard Mark's screams from within the pit of the soul-eater. Domeel Doreen abused a Tarn maiden as a child clung to her legs with all four arms. I saw an armada of air ships, their decks crowded with Yellow warriors, flying over the great rift that separated our kingdoms. And I saw a city on a black ocean, and a dreaming malevolence awakening from its watery slumber. Jawn Kurz's voice snapped me awake.

"Come find me, Warlord."

Talis Darmon's warmth was near and Apache snored softly close by. I lay awake until morning when I silently began packing.

"Benjamin Colt, I do not understand. I thought that we were over our distress. We have not had time to repair, but we will. I swear, I had no idea it would harm you so to not know I had been married before. It was never my intention to withhold anything from you. It is simply that our circumstances have been tumultuous. Always, time is against us. Do not leave."

My own hands seemed alien to me as I looked at their actions. Why was I packing? Where was I going?

"It's not that, my princess."

"Then, pray tell, what?"

A hazy memory was just out of my reach. The forgotten part of a dream. I had only a feeling. There was something I had to do. But what?

"Do you believe I'm a man of honor?"

"Of course. You needn't ask. There is no man more honorable."

I felt a pull to fly over the desert, and that at the end of the journey would be something I must find. The eroded fortifications of a once great citadel teased my thoughts with a compulsion to stand on them. I sank onto the bed. "Do you think I'm competent? Mentally?"

She raised an eyebrow. "What are you asking, Benjamin Colt? This is not about our relationship, is it? What distresses you?"

I told her of my visions, and how Jawn Kurz was telling me to find him. And rather than scoff or tell me I'd been deluded by the stress of my ordeal, she became one of the many other Talis Darmons I knew. Her inquisitiveness piqued, she was the woman who was the learned mistress of many arts.

"And now you feel this strange urge to find—what? Jawn Kurz is long vanished."

I'd experienced a lot of things on Mars that I'd previously thought impossible. What this was, I wasn't sure, but it wasn't just a dream.

"I don't know."

"Would you lay, Benjamin Colt?" She said it as a request, but was firm in her invitation.

I stared up into her eyes as she placed hands on my head. "I'll talk, Princess. No need to zap me like you did Marviel Lanconin."

"Shh. Think of your visions. Picture the Warlord Jawn Kurz."

With my head in her lap, I stared into her eyes and fell deep into them as everything else faded away.

After some time, she removed her hands and I sat up, feeling refreshed.

"I feel like a million bucks. Thanks. We should do that more often."

She ignored my flippancy as she paced around the room, Apache staring and wagging his stubby tail nervously. I watched, knowing she was in deep concentration, and kept my tongue. Finally, she shook her head as if she was dismissing a bad idea.

"Benjamin Colt, what calls comes from a place that springs forth from other than your internal environment. I see as you do—a ruin. Is this where you feel pulled to seek?"

I collected my thoughts. "It's like a fuzzy transmission where I only understand half of the words. I don't know where it is, so unless I start dreaming about a map and some grid coordinates, I'd just be wandering around the desert."

"I have firmed your mind against these intrusions. They should not distract you again. So strange. It is a matter beyond my understanding."

"Is there someone who would?"

She grimaced. "Benjamin Colt, I do not know. But will you promise me you will not leave? Go and do a Warlord's work. But return or let it be known to me where you are, and I will wear one of the wristlets. And do not go off alone. Take Apache with you as you promised."

"Yes, my princess. What do you think's happening? Is it the same kind of thing like the dreams that tortured Avril Mysteen?"

"No. Yes. Perhaps. Whatever it is, I am not going to let this proceed without the light of the Sylah dynasty on it."

12

In the next weeks, my singular compulsion to fly into the desert wasn't the result of some nebulous dream. My drive was accompanied by a firm destination attached, and at last it was in my sight.

Pyreenia.

"Warlord, our army is ready."

"Proceed, Khraal Kahlees. Good hunting."

"We send all our enemies to sail the Blix today, Warlord." His cloud extinguished.

The twin moons had yet risen. Beyond the open deck of my flitter, the night air took on the same crisp chill that should have put me in mind of other battles in the dark. Where was the sense of dread anticipation I'd so often felt at this same moment? Where was the gnawing apprehension of looming disaster? The consuming doubt that I'd overlooked something and my error would be all our undoing?

It was never until the first shots were fired that my doubts quelled, replaced by the need for action. But this time was different. This time I knew.

We would destroy them.

A siege, this was not. Pyreenia was *our* city. We were taking it back. We hovered over the desert, the glow of the city the expanse of my horizon. Brigades of mounted troops spread in a wide front, aimed at Pyreenia. Soon our river would rise to spill over the banks, lick the edges of the city, then pierce its borders and flood it with our might.

The sound of M134s and K-maxes told me our slaughter had begun. Reconnaissance confirmed what Avril Mysteen told us: the bulk of the Mydreen were west of the city. Sorties of up-gunned flitters flew stealthily to come at them from the west to commence our shock and awe. But just as the gun runs began, they faded. Much too quickly.

Dave's face appeared. He was on the ground with the cavalry, driving into Pyreenia from the east. "Ben, we're crossing phase line Mulholland. Why's the air attack stalled out?" I wondered the same thing. Double-K should be wiping out the Mydreen garrisons camped in the western desert. Then he'd pull back. Our push into Pyreenia should give the rats a place to run, and our air power would return to mow them down at will, the desert west of Pyreenia their highway of death. Then, mopping up any remaining resistance in the city would start. Street by street, building by building, room by room.

The answer as to why the shooting had stopped came to us both with Khraal Kahlees's frown. "Warlord, the San Sheel plains are all but empty. Only a token force remained. Many arkall, few troops. They can only be in one place."

Dave grimaced. "They're in the city. Sharks among the fish."

Our forward patrols had silenced many bands of pilgrims still answering the call of Domeel Doreen, but it was not possible to assemble our thousands in the desert without the enemy knowing our intent. Our design to expel them hadn't had the effect to make them flee nor to build a fortified defense against our advance.

"This was their intention all along. To make us destroy Pyreenia around them. Gentlemen, accommodate them."

"Yes, sir." Dave signed off.

"The air assets remain on station, ready to respond. I move to join our ground forces, Warlord."

"As do I, Khraal Kahlees. Out."

I nudged my pilot. "Take us down."

The last surviving GMV on all of Mars made it easy to find. Doug waited beside it. "Not what we wanted, Ben."

"Not at all. I better report in before we get too deep." I raised the wristlet and Talis Darmon appeared with Karlo and Cynar close behind in the cloud view. I gave them the bad news. The queen winced.

"The contingency that this would be necessary was well anticipated, Warlord. I know you will use all means to protect the lives of those held trapped."

"Thank you. Karlo, any last-minute ideas?"

My friend gave me his best look of support. "I wish I did. Laying siege to starve out the Mydreen would surely kill all the Pyreenians first. They're already barely surviving. Whatever you may think of my squeamishness about war these days, Ben, I won't be second-guessing you when this is all over. I know you'll do your best to avoid civilian casualties. Their deaths are on the hands of others."

"Thank you, Karlo. No secret ways beneath the city you've recently remembered, Cynar?"

For once, the old hermit didn't use the opportunity to berate my intellect. "No such passages exist, Benjamin Colt. The aqueduct disappears into the aquifers of deep groundwater far from her borders."

"Just thought I'd ask one last time. I'll report in when I have something worth reporting. Out."

I climbed up through the gunner hatch and took in the view through my thermal. "We might as well roll on, Doug. We can't leave Dave out there alone."

"He ain't alone, Ben. He's got a thousand green arms with him, all holding K-specs, and twice that many animal legs pounding the ground with him."

"You know what I mean." A flitter whirred over the desert to intercept the cavalry. "Looks like Double-K made it down to join the party. Let's roll."

There was a silence to our army's movement. Not that arkall didn't make noise. And the GMV rumbled above that. But there wasn't the buzz in my ear of constant radio squelch nor the light of blue force trackers to overwhelm the senses with information. Order of movement had been set and once in action, nothing else need be communicated to my army. We caught up to the rear of the formation and trailed along.

Doug drove with his NODS down, the smooth ride of the GMV a long forgotten luxury to me. "Won't be long now, Ben."

A half-klick ahead, the leading edge of our front dressed their line. At the transition from the rolling dunes onto the plain, the bellow of a horn pierced the night, unleashing the Korund's rage. The ground vibrated with thousands of hooves as the charge engaged.

"Double-K was adamant about this, wasn't he, Ben?"

We'd halted and Doug stood beside our gun truck, his NODs still lowered. He was so tall that his head almost reached to my height standing in the gunner hole.

"You have to pick your battles, Doug, and a mounted charge is their thing. But he didn't put up too much of a fight about integrating the Kardans into their formations." Doug had single-handedly directed the improvement program to armor the ground-hovers and arm them with K-maxes. There was one for every company. Kardan were a hard-shelled scrounging varmint, kind of like a cross between an armadillo and an eight-legged turtle. I'd never seen one, but when we'd tried to name the new gun truck and described our own hard-backed critters, the engineers in the Golden Hub immediately offered the Vistaran equivalent.

"Rhino was a better name," Doug said with some regret. With the muzzle of the ray gun protruding up front, the one-horned analogy wasn't wrong, but still didn't exactly fit.

"Lucky they don't have unicorns, Dougie, 'cause that's what I was going to suggest before they offered up Kardan."

"Ugh. Never figured you for that type, dude. A brony maybe, but never a unicorn lover."

We resumed our silence to witness the stampede slow. I zoomed up the Elcan on my M4 to look through the clip-on night vision device sitting on the rail in front of it. I aimed high above the thoroughfare I thought Avril Mysteen had described, expecting a firefight to break out any second. I scanned left and right, waiting to see the first break into battle snap to life as our mounted troops broke the barrier between without and within. How much longer? Hadn't we touched the spider's web with the sound to charge? Hadn't we crossed the imaginary line where hell should've unleashed? Hadn't we sprung the tripwire?

I couldn't hold off. "Dave, gimme a sitrep."

His voice came back. "I'm in the middle of our line. Dead quiet. We're just clear of the first buildings of phase line Howard and are pushing deeper."

As he finished, first through his voice comm, then lagging a second behind traveling across the sands from Pyreenia, came the sound of fizzle fire.

"Troops in contact. Out."

Flashes spilled up and between spires, up and down the line.

"Waiting's over," Doug said. "I was beginning to wonder if they'd all bugged out, but I guess nothing on Mars is ever that easy."

With distinctive cracks of lightning, K-maxes on the Kardans joined the mix, along with K-specs and the occasional M4.

"Guess that's probably some of the guns the Mydreen had from our first run, Ben-dog. Only other M4 up there is Dave's."

I'd had enough. "Screw guessing. Let's get up there and see for ourselves."

Doug sucked through his teeth.

"If you get hurt worse than what it takes a Band-Aid to fix, it better be straight to a body bag for both of us, Ben-dog. I heard the queen lay down the law about you playing army."

"Don't sass the Warlord. Do I have to drive this pig?"

"Yes. Switch. I'll be in the gunner's hatch. I couldn't fit much armor around the K-max squeezed in so close next to the fifty. You get down here where I can at least tell her I *tried* to keep you where you had another layer around you."

"Humph. Fair enough."

Once we hit the flats, I gunned it. I hadn't driven anything with wheels in a very long time, and though a GMV isn't a sports car, compared to the anemic response of a flitter, its meaty rumble and acceleration made it as muscled as an F1 racer to my reset sensibilities. I didn't slow until we hit the road into the central thoroughfare, the way blocked by herds of mounted riders.

"What's the holdup?" Doug asked a rider whose arkall sidestepped out of our way to let us idle alongside.

"We wait in reserve to be called forward."

"Where's the White general?"

"I do not know general David Masamuni's location. Khraal Kahlees is somewhere in that direction." He pointed with a lower hand and I eased ahead. The street narrowed and took a radius to weave off through a maze of staggering dark towers of differing heights. Violet flashes of gunfire reflected off the smooth surfaces like lightning off distant clouds. A narrow clearing showed the next nearest tower was the focus of many K-specs, blasts aimed on it from many points on the ground. Despite the fire peppering it from different directions, fizzle fire rained down from several windows around its midpoint.

"Doug, you got a clear shot? There must not be a Kardan on hand. Lay some hate on that tower."

"Roger."

The architecture and materials of Pyreenia differed from elsewhere in Mihdradahl. Shansara was built from quarried stone and concrete. Whatever these towers and helical buildings were constructed from, the K-spec fire wasn't doing much damage. I wondered what effect the K-max would have. In short succession, Doug sent one burst, a second, then a third whizzing above me. The impacts were solid and like metal striking metal, blossoming showers of sparks were flying from each hit like airburst fireworks.

Fire from both directions—ours and theirs—ceased.

"On target, Dougie. Give it a sec."

The illuminated glow that radiated from the surface of the building faded above the impact zone, like a bad bulb in a string of Christmas lights causing all after it to short out.

"That did something," Doug said with pride. "Let's roll on, Ben-dog. They ain't pinning anyone down no more."

I was about to put us in drive when Dougie barked, "Ben! Look!"

The dark tower twisted, tilted, and as the grind of failing materials shrieked, Doug screamed with it, "TIMBER! LOOK OUT BELOW!"

A thousand tons of severed spire careened off and crashed with all the ugliness of a dump truck hitting a bridge abutment. I hit my wristlet for all local recipients. "That was us. We knocked down a tower with a K-max. Be warned."

Dave answered, "I just found out the same thing." He was farther south of us. "I gave the order to hold off using them unless it's a last option. No idea if we caused any civilian casualties; we're still clearing our way forward."

A cloud materialized. It was Khraal Kahlees.

"Benjamin Colt, I am forward of your location. We are pushing through heavy resistance, building by building. I have just received a report that in the first of the residences cleared, civilians have been found dead."

I grimaced. "Were they executed?"

"It is unclear. We have encountered only Mydreen as of yet. They are using edged weapons for close quarters fighting. I believe our assessments correct that their armament reserve is limited."

"Keep the tempo. We're moving to your location. Out."

I touched the accelerator a little too abruptly and bumped a riderless arkall on a hind quarter, the animal bellowing, then giving a disgusted snort before moving aside. If anything, the animal had done more damage to our fender than I'd done to it.

"Sorry, boy," I said out the window as we passed. We didn't get far before the giant beasts had the arteries of travel clogged. "Time for us to go on foot, Doug."

"This place is like a forest, Ben. Clearings here and there, but everywhere else, it's thick."

Along the way, Korundi worked. They forced their way through doors, sometimes with tools as we'd show them, sometimes with the sheer force of muscled shoulders. Once I saw an arkall coaxed to back into a door, bulging it in like an aluminum can before the troops kicked it open.

Fizzle fire from higher vantages was sporadic—the higher it came from, the less a threat the weak discharges were to those below. I got a tickle from just such an impact scattered up from the ground where I was about to step when it forced me abruptly back. Several Tarns joined Doug and me in returning fire at its source. Across a short patch of open ground, two Tarn breached a door to one of the shorter, helical buildings.

"Doug, c'mon. I want to see inside one of these." I sprinted after them, yelling as I reached the folded back door, "Coming in behind you!"

Doug glided in with me.

"Dang it, Ben."

"Yeah, yeah. Check it out."

I aimed my IR illuminator up. Like a medieval castle, a circular stairway coursed along the perimeter as it rose to disappear through the next level. The Korundi assaulters awaited.

"Join us, Warlord."

Doug pushed ahead of me onto the stairs. "You stay behind me, dude."

I didn't argue, and simply followed. The two Tarns rushed up to the next level, the first struck by a burst of fizzle through the opening. His partner stepped in and answered with the more powerful K-spec, then vaulted in, sword drawn with upper arm.

Doug chased after him. "Shit," he complained as he made an unbalanced vault off the Tarn stunned on the stairs. I bounced over the body and sprang up through the door after him.

The Korundi was engaged with two Mydreen, black sashes across their elongated frames, swords and daggers swinging in every hand. I slid to one side with Doug to join him in hammering the pair to the ground with our M4s. The head of a Tarn was a very large target at these distances, moving or no. Brains on the wall behind them and limp bodies were death check enough.

A quick flourish with his curved sword, a wet spatter of Mydreen blood sprayed from his blade, and our Tarn companion sheathed. "Many thanks, but not necessary."

"Save it, and go check on your buddy," Doug said. "There's about a thousand more of these to clear." He looked around. "Curiosity satisfied, Ben-dog?"

The Korundi helped his stunned partner down the stairs and we left. Outside, the first humans we'd seen besides ourselves were being ushered past in the direction of the outskirts. Dressed in black from head to toe, a bent woman huddled two small children under her as behind them, a man and woman hobbled to keep up.

"Benjamin Colt!" Khraal Kahlees strode up to meet us. "I was told you'd made it into the fray. We hold this section and the next tier of the shell, but the city is dense with Mydreen. They infest every structure, harass from above, and force us to root them out of every hole, one by one."

"Are those the first civilians?"

"The first found alive. I have seen many dead. They appear starved. We have not yet reached the dense areas of residences. I predict we will find harsh conditions as we do."

I gave orders to anticipate receiving evacuees and took a sitrep from Dave and the subordinate commanders. We had a foothold almost uniformly across this side of the city, like a slow-moving brushfire trying to build from a smolder into a blaze. The sky hinted the end of night, and I broke my NODS off their mount and stowed them.

"If there are thousands of Mydreen sprinkled like this throughout Pyreenia, we'll be at this for weeks. Even if they're about out of fizzle guns, our attrition's going to be high. We need to break them. Where're the Joker and Queen of Spades going to be?"

Dave was with us by cloud. "Chuck and his witch?"

He understood me perfectly.

"Yeah. Time to drop right into the middle of their ant nest."

Khraal Kahlees growled, "And with them, the vile Domeel Doreen shall be."

"First and Second Battalion, stay on mission," I ordered. "I'm moving back to take the Third for an air mobile assault on the governance quarter."

Dave raised his eyebrows. "Third battalion? The Reds? They're ninety percent recruits."

I nodded. "You heard me right. The Korundi aren't going to bear the burden of leading this fight the whole way. The two-armed troops are gonna to prove to themselves and to their four-armed brothers that they know how to lay hate, too. Their trigger time has arrived."

13

"My participation is essential, Benjamin Colt."

Leaving Double-K behind when there was a good chance we'd be dropping into Domeel Doreen's front yard was as futile as house painting in a rainstorm. A wise man would know it was a bad idea beforehand. I'm rarely wise, but in this case, I surrendered quickly to the inevitability. No matter how many coats I might lay down, when the sun came out, they'd all be washed off. After one attempt to keep him out of it, I folded.

"Besides, Warlord, are you not always recommending the development of subordinates by entrusting them to cope with the dynamic haze of combat operations? The cohort commanders and sub-unit leaders are conducting the clearing operations with velocity and appropriate fervor. My presence should be where I can effect critical decisions, and that will be at the nexus to our next disruptive action."

Dave's jaw dropped. "Did you graduate from the Command and General Staff College in the last week, Double-K? You just dropped enough bullet points to get selected for the joint chief's, brah."

It was time to move along. "Then you're staying, Dave."

"No argument. No one on Vistara's run an air op this complex, and it looks like I'm the man for the job. Dougie, how about organizing a mobile reaction force, brah? A half dozen Kardans on call to barrel through for relief of any air assault element bogged down?"

Doug was tracing a route over the glowing scroll of Pyreenia. "This place is a maze. You need more ass on the target area, bros. Close air support is going to be cocked up if not impossible in that damn pincushion forest of spires and towers. It's no kind of rescue if we're lost or halted in some kind of big tussle on the way to reach a unit pinned down in contact. I don't do shit a day late and a dollar short. We're taking off as soon as I get us mustered."

I liked it. "I leave it to you, Dougie." I pointed to each of three potential LZs around the governance quarter. A stadium's parade field that looked big enough to land at least six flitters at a time, and two smaller plazas would accommodate the same. The sun crested the horizon and grew with every second I wasted watching it.

"Dave, you and I'll make the aerial recon. Khraal Kahlees, marshal the troops, and when we return, it'll be a bare bones op order and we launch."

Nearby stood Jodal Jark and Sarkan Sell. Dave pointed at them. "You two, with us. And so I don't have to say it again, don't let him go *anywhere* without both of you stuck to him like the hide on an arkall, understood?"

The Tarns crossed arms over chests. The older Sarkan Sell answered, "It is understood, David Masamuni."

I had the flitter fired up by the time the last foot hit the deck, and we were off.

Dave had his tablet in hand. "I'll get some images I can brief the pilots with. It'll be better than the strip maps."

I took us high and flew a general bearing into the urban sprawl. The governance quarter was striking, surrounded by a ring of the highest towers. In its center stood the opulent architecture of what was essentially a palace in residence for the royal family. In that quarter were the other structures of administration and the city's bureaucracy, equal parts art and functional space.

"We could never pull this off in the dark. Hell, I'm not sure we can do this thing in daylight, brah." He knife-handed me to bear left. "That trio of twisted high-rises that join at the top. That's a waypoint for sure."

I pushed us faster and higher until I was sure we were over our target and made a slow right-hand racetrack so I could easily look down on everything. Dave leaned over the gunwale with his tablet. There was troop movement below.

Dave switched to his binos. "Humans, brah. I think that's confirmation he's there. Chucky's got his best closest to him."

I was only a novice pilot, but I felt sure the LZs would work and that we could navigate the flights onto them. "We know what we need to know. Time to hightail it back. See anything else on the images?"

Dave examined the screen, enlarging the shots. "Digital reconnaissance this is not, brah. But there are definitely a lot of black uniforms down there. I don't see any T-90 Russkie battle tanks or artillery, if that's what you mean."

"They wish. I've got something for their asses."

In no time, we were back over the plains outside the city. Dougie waved at me from the top of the GMV as his armored rat patrol floated after him into the maze of Pyreenia. The battalion was gathered, and two dozen grounded flitters were being attended by Red and Green crews. Dave gathered the pilots, company commanders, and platoon leaders tightly.

"I'll bring you each up one at a time for a better look, but this is the concept of operation. Landing zone Parade Ground. LZ Fountain Plaza. LZ Green Plaza. I kept the names simple so there's no confusion. You'll be assigned an LZ by me. Because there are so few wristlets, once we launch, it'll get chaotic. There'll be a gunship on station near each LZ for you to guide on to for the first run, then after that, the terrain and routes will be familiar. Get your troops disembarked and get the hell back here for your next load. You don't stop until we have the last rifleman on the ground.

"Ground commanders, follow my marshal's commands. Load your troops efficiently and be ready to fight as soon as you hit the ground. Anticipate the LZs will have to be fought to secure even after the gunships have had their turns. I'll be assigning primary and alternate objectives for you to assault after the LZs are secured. We have the same difficulty—not enough wristlets to go around. Use your initiative. Keep your men doing what they know how to do—shoot, move, communicate. You have superior firepower and are better trained than our enemy.

"Be flexible. No plan survives first contact with an opponent. We have close air support and light armor nearby ready to respond. Special weapons teams should be utilized freely, but cautiously. Fratricide is a significant risk in this environment."

Dave turned to me.

"Your rules of engagement are simple," I said. "All Mydreen are to be eliminated. They do not surrender, and we do not have the ability to take prisoners. Wounded Red soldiers incapable of fighting will be given quarter. Otherwise, you see a black uniform—if they have any fight in them, finish them. Avoid civilian casualties."

Khraal Kahlees grinned approval. A SOCOM lawyer would've stroked at my ROE. There was nothing more I needed to add, so I handed it back to Dave.

"I'll call you up by flight and company for individual assignment."

I stepped to put my back to the troops and mumbled, "Not one 'brah' or 'da kine' in your entire brief, Davey-Dave. When you're in the spotlight, you really do know actual English."

He shot me a one-finger salute.

"I'm going back to work, Warlord. I'll give you a heads-up when the first sortie is loaded. I can't talk you out of staying back and letting me lead them in, brah?"

"Not a chance. Where're my gunships?"

✳ ✳ ✳

Standing next to the gunner, I guided us in from the bow. In trail on either side were our two other gunships. I chose the funny melded towers Dave had used as our initial point, and touched my wristlet. The gunship pilots each had one of our precious comm devices, but I looked forward to the day when everyone had one.

"First run on LZ Parade Ground," I said.

With M134s on the noses and a pair of K-maxes on each waist, our gunships were as capable as the Apaches I'd named my puppy after. My namesake wagged his tail happily, drool splattering the front of the console, but my pilot was too engaged to care. I had a magazine of tracers in my M4 to mark targets with and was eager to raise the curtains on this production.

We were about eight hundred feet off the deck and dropping to thread between two towers as the stadium rim came into view. Two hundred yards was about the max effective range of the high-powered fizzles that were normally deck mounted on air cars. If they'd repurposed any of them—which I was sure Chuck had done—any lower than this, they were the only real threat. If they hadn't, we could loiter at this altitude with virtual impunity and hammer them until we got bored. Fizzle fire erupted from below and from the towers, but it wasn't until a deck gun mounted on the back of an arkall sent a shot across our bow that I cringed. On the concourse outside the stadium, a crew of black-uniformed Reds scurried around the eight-legged beast that was their version of a self-propelled.

"Light 'em up."

The air defense artillery crew fought to turn the animal to track us. I sent a few crimson tracers at them, but my gunner was already proving he understood where I wanted him to send the heat.

The M134 came to life like a revving engine. Dave had worked with the Red gunners and was confident they'd make us proud. The kid's first burst turned the eight-legged elephant into red paste while the waist guns pasted more troops in the open and the towers above us. Even at our anemic velocity, we were past the stadium in seconds, the trailing birds adding to the destruction below until our pilot weaved us through the forest of spires, headed for the fountain plaza.

"Fountains coming up," I said into the silver band. I tapped the gunner on the shoulder. "Give short bursts to everything you can cover. Spread it around."

There were scattered human and Mydreen troops below and the fizzle fire opened up. Our gunship flattened most of them, and the trailing birds found few targets worth wasting charges or rounds on.

"LZ Green, then move to your guidon points. Good luck."

As tight a bank as the flitters could make put us on course. We weaved through forests of thick and thin towers, leveling out as we broke out over the last LZ. A haven for what Mars might once have been, it was a botanical garden of red and purple vegetation. And like any army would, it was treated as just another piece of dirt. Fighting positions and berms were excavated throughout, trees felled, and barriers formed. We raked the rectangular field on its longest axis with the minigun and the K-maxes on a single pass, and broke off to head back to the stadium.

"Dave, our first pass is complete. Tell the pilots we've made our runs and we're waiting to guide them in. Expect there will still be light resistance, copy?"

"Good copy. Lifting now, Ben. Out."

I leaned over the port side to send a few tracers onto a squad-size element on the run through a narrow street toward the parade ground. The waist gunner opened up, some of the blasts glancing off the polished surfaces of the surrounding buildings to scatter ineffectively. One blast made it through the screen of structures and a pair of black-uniformed Reds dropped, their uniforms catching fire. I bet even NOMEX would burn if you hit it with a K-max.

We swung around the palace before dropping to make another run on the stadium LZ, a new direction of attack. The Reds might've been under some kind of mind control, but it hadn't made them stupid or fearless. Troops that had filtered back in to the open now scattered underneath concourse bridges and into tunnels, sending a few defiant bursts of fizzle fire up in random directions. I let the waist guns send some suppressive fire into the defilades and the narrow streets outside the stadium. I ignited my wristlet to talk to the other gunship pilots.

"Sorties sighted inbound."

Three clusters of air cars were spreading out as they neared, and at the edge of the city another flight was just gaining altitude before flying over the city. We rose to a thousand feet and waited. A few blasts aimed from nearby towers came at us, and I let the waist guns answer them with restraint.

"No more than one good impact per story, boys. Let's not drop any towers unless we need to. There are civilians somewhere in all that maze."

Our first sortie was near and dropping altitude. Soon they'd spill their troops, and empty flitters would be lifting off to bring back decks crowded with more meat for the grinder. In an hour, we should have the entire battalion moving like an army bent on total domination of the entire quarter.

Jodal Jark was still the excitable young warrior. "Warlord, when will we join on the ground?"

"After the first sortie has some time to clean up the ground resistance. Here they come."

The six flitters bound for LZ Parade Ground passed below us. From above, the decks reminded me of cartons of red sketching pencils, their gold helmets the eraser heads, packed so tightly, not one more could be fit in between.

Man, I hated those uniforms.

I motioned the pilot to follow them down. "Let the gunners on the landing sorties have the priority of fire. Anything outside the stadium is fair game."

It was easy to get sucked into your sights and forget that there was a whole world of people and things between you and any target.

"Warlord! What is that?"

I sprang to the bow and squinted where the gunner pointed. Rising to meet the descending flitters, a swirling cloud of black dots spewed from out of a tunnel mouth beneath the reviewing dais. The cloud spread as it rose and grew thicker to envelope the lead flitter. Shrieks punctuated the screams of the injured on the deck as desperate men pitched themselves over the sides, flailing and fighting as they fell.

The engulfed air car veered off in an acute bank and dived over the stadium crest before a loud crash and fireball rose. The cloud had split and reached the next ships. The trailing two aircraft peeled off, saving themselves as the rest were consumed in the same way. I pounded the shoulder of the minigunner.

"Lay it on that tunnel. THERE!"

The cloud came from deep within the shadows of the tunnel. When he failed to respond, I pushed him aside. I took the spade grip and wheeled the muzzle over, hit the laser, and let the green beacon show me the way. Dragon fire from six spinning barrels spit out 4000 rounds per minute. I walked the rounds in and around the mouth of the dark portal, chewing up concrete, stone, and whatever else. The starboard waist gun joined in, and in seconds, the passage collapsed on itself. I got on the horn.

"Any inbound sortie, proceed to LZ Parade Ground immediately."

Only a few of the flights had wristlets. I prayed at least one of them responded and the rest would follow. I repeated the call several times until a flight assumed a track for the stadium.

Dave appeared. "Warlord is moving to ground. Continue mission and launch all sorties."

"What happened?"

"Black death clouds took out most of the first sortie. The same kind of magic we've seen before."

"LZ Greenspace is having the same issue. LZ Fountain's first sortie is on the ground intact, and they're returning for the next. I'm coming on the next wave."

"Stick with the plan, Dave. You be on the last bird of troops."

"I'll buzz when I'm inbound, Ben. Out."

I took a quick look toward LZ Greenspace. Smoke and debris filled the air. Above it, the gunship sat as guidon, and a new sortie of three birds was on a descent course to the LZ.

"What happened?" I asked.

"A wispy black smoke gushed forth from one of the towers. It was like nothing I've ever seen, Warlord. It consumed the aircraft. I violated your order and brought the tower down."

"You did right. Shoot and don't stop shooting until the threat changes shape or catches fire. Good work."

Below me, the last of six flitters took off from the parade ground, Red troops spreading out into the stands and onto the concourses, white blasts of K-specs flaring as they advanced.

"Take me down!" I yelled to the pilot.

There was a green hand on my shoulder. "Do not spring off, Warlord." It was Sarkan Sell. "You often take to the air without your shield arms beside you. I urge restraint, lord."

"Together then. Let's go."

The flitter had not quite touched down when I leaped. My two bodyguards and Apache were just over the deck when the pilot spun up and was gone. Beneath a grand arch at the far end of the field, a perimeter of Red soldiers was proned out and a Tarn officer stood in their center. I indicated to head there and kept to a trot to let my escort keep pace. As soon as we got into a fight, the fiction of my holding back would be as ancient history as the Amethyst Sea.

The Tarn crossed arms to chest at my approach. "We hold this intersection until the last sortie is down, Warlord."

Squads climbed over dead black uniforms and up stadium risers to reach the rim. At the far end, an assistant gunner laid out a tripod then helped his gunner heft the K-max onto it. There was a hundred meters of high-speed avenue of approach visible outside the stadium from that point. The heavy gun was perfectly placed to chew up anything that came from that direction. A few fizzles and a heavier blast threatened from a higher elevation, and dozens of K-specs responded in kind. I stepped back into the bowl to see where the shots had come from. Impacts into the nearest tower overlooking the grounds answered my question.

The Tarn platoon leader was beside me. "I have two squads on that building as we speak, Warlord."

"Good work, son. What's your name?"

"Kel Rez, Warlord."

"Where's the company commander?"

"I believe he rides the Blix. He was on the first aircraft."

"Keep it up, Lieutenant. We're going to have more help soon."

The whizz of inbound flitters broke over the rim of the stadium, and in the lead bird was Washington crossing the Delaware. Khraal Kahlees stood with one foot on the gunwale. He was first on the ground as streams of Red soldiers piled off both sides, their Tarn NCOs pushing them from behind.

Double-K placed lower hands on hips as he assessed the stadium and the positions of the anchoring forces. A bolt passed over his shoulder from behind to scorch the ground. He turned in annoyance and pointed.

"Warriors, do work."

Red recruits scrambled as a Tarn NCO barked and his troop's return fire started, slowly, then in earnest. These were the first shots by men in their first war. Soon enough, they would be veterans. If they lived. Satisfied, the general marched over.

"I will have words with David Masamuni when next I see him, Benjamin Colt. He sent me on an urgent errand to retrieve a box of grid squares from his rucksack, and whilst I searched, he launched the first sortie. I *told* him I would be first on the ground. Such a devious man may have Mydreen in his ancestry."

"I know you don't mean that. You'll be thanking him." I described what happened.

He growled. "So I heard over wristlet. Three of the black witches were seen here, and two of our LZs met with their sorcery. If one was killed in the Spectral Hall, my calculation leads me to think two are the number we seek to destroy along with their black army."

"Don't forget the one who tried to kill Talis Darmon."

"No matter the sums then. If witchery produced the evil vortices, that which loosed them must be found and exterminated."

He pointed to the destroyed dais and the cave-in we'd caused below it.

"If one of the black sorceresses was not crushed in the passage, then I believe it is where the tunnel leads that she will be found."

From above the stadium rim, the palace towers waited invitingly.

"Her and any of her ilk. And most importantly, Domeel Doreen. And along the way, these recruits will become blooded and experienced warriors."

He transferred his rifle lower and drew his sword with a sky hand.

"This is a great day, Warlord."

14

"URBAN ASSAULT'S SLOW WORK, BRAH. WHAT I WOULDN'T GIVE TO HAVE our Stryker again." Dave had found his way to our forward position. I'd just sent a Tarn sergeant and his squad out to secure a blind avenue.

"Next time we fly through a QST, I'm bringing an Abrams, dude."

"I've got Karlo's next project for Baby Blue, brah."

A flash erupted ahead, and with it, a dozen screams. A red-caped soldier engulfed in jade green fire took faltering steps out of the alley before he dropped, the crackle of his burning body the only remnant of sound.

"What the hell was that?" Dave said what I thought. The chug of a fifty came from deep to our right. Blasts from a K-max followed along with it, then the bloop of a 40mm grenade launching. It exploded deep within the chasm where the squad had been set ablaze by some unknown weapon. There was only one combination of these weapons collected in one place in all known existence.

"Doug, what you got?" I asked.

Doug and his crews were spread thin, roaming ahead of foot patrols and chewing up black army fighters by the dozen. I didn't know he was in our vicinity. I told him where we were in relation to his position, still out of our line of sight down the narrow winding street.

"They've got some kind of nasty flamethrowers. That's the second one we've run into, Ben. We're coming out. Tell your guys," Dave yelled, and in a second the GMV rolled into sight from one of the labyrinths of streets, past smooth walls reflecting green flames. A Red soldier drove the gun truck with another on the 240 from the passenger side. Doug acknowledged my wave from the gunner turret and the GMV motored to us.

Past another twisting block of buildings and towers was the palace. Troops were filtering up slowly, and Dave picked out a weapons team carrying a Carl Gustave and gave them the sign hustle to him. "Take your team and send a beehive and an HE down that street and hold the intersection." He slapped the young section leaders' shoulders and sent them off, and rejoined me at the GMV.

"We're having the same problems everywhere, brah. The Tarn want to charge at everything, and the Red troops aren't aggressive enough. We're losing a lot of troops for both reasons."

Doug wiped his face with his shemagh. "Haven't run into any Mydreen for a few blocks." He tossed down a bronze badge. It was a stamping of a lapel-size gazraal—a mountain lion.

"I ran into a platoon of them holding a crossroads. They stayed shoulder to shoulder while we chopped them up. Never seen Reds so committed. Chuck ran the show here. He turned his army into a suicide cult—that's a new trick."

The Goose fired one, then a second round down the road winding gradually lower to the palace grounds.

It had taken a day to get this far. From our three LZs, patrols built in strength and worked street by street, through the black army barricaded at so many points to delay our progress to the palace grounds. They ambushed us from the high rises and from concealed bunkers. Though they hadn't been equal in firepower, they were deadly enough we couldn't make a breakout run to the ultimate objective.

"Doug, hammer all these towers with fifty. It's so dense, the gunships weren't able to get much penetration. Soon as we get a full company up here, we're clearing down this street and then the push is on for the palace. Let me see where Double-K is."

Dave bumped me. "I'm going back. We should have a company's worth filled in here by now." He took off running.

The cloud appeared with Khraal Kahlees.

"Warlord, we advance. I am in sight of the prize."

He panned his wrist to show me the wide street and a view of one side of the palace beyond. He was somewhere ahead and to our left.

"Well done, General," I told him. "Collect troops and get ready to join our push from your right. I'll comm when we're ready, but you'll damn well know it because we'll be bringing hell with us. Do you have Kardans?"

"Two."

"Use them. I don't hear weapons teams sending ordnance. Get them employed. Out." I yelled the last over the hammer of Doug's fifty peppering the towers looming over the path ahead. Dave was back, leading a dense mass of bodies.

I brought him close. "It'll take a day to get through this section if we insist on clearing every building before we proceed. Ground floors and first stories, and we keep rolling through." I patted Doug's side. "We'll follow you. Go."

Sarkan Sell and Jodal Jark were ever close, Apache leashed to one of them at all times. Now they could trail the gun truck. The GMV rolled and I walked alongside as we creeped to the intersection. Squads pushed out on both sides and a Tarn sergeant stood in front of the hood, yelling encouragement to each, though they needed none. Doors were breached, windows raked, and grenades tossed. Frag and spall rained out into the street, troops firing madly as they entered. CQB it was not. Battle Drill number five's what it was: knock out a bunker. I couldn't have been prouder. I was surprised we had any grenades left. Well before we finished this street, the satchels would be empty. At least, it would make travel lighter for the fight to come, up those steep palace steps I'd spied from the air.

We rolled forward like this, hitting a set of opposing structures at a time. Fizzle fire from balconies was quickly answered by K-specs and Doug's assortment of GMV arms. A spout of flaming green liquid aimed its way at us from a corner window several stories up, and dozens of white flashes and 240 fire met the flamer, the odd bladder on his back that contained the fuel igniting in a blinding splash as he fell to the street. Had the anxious flamer been patient, he would've cooked our front column and me with it. Such was combat luck. We had it. He didn't. The thick liquid coated the street and walls and still smoldered by the time we reached the soldier, skin charred to a black as deep as his uniform had been moments before, now reduced to ash.

At the end of the block, the path dipped and expanded out to the rectangular bowl of the complex of the governance seat. Beyond the cover of the last few buildings waited the wide expanse of stonework and statues of the palace grounds. The whir of a flitter overhead caught my attention, and between spires, I caught a glimpse of a gunship circling. They'd made many runs, and I hoped anyone between us and the palace was well perforated.

"Gunships, pull off the palace," I ordered. "We're beginning the ground assault."

Dave had been running a marathon, to the rear and back up front, again and again, covering a hundred steps for each one that I travelled in a single direction beside the GMV. "We're up, Ben."

Crowded thickly on both sides of the streets were helmeted heads above red capes, none of them clean or unblemished but instead, scuffed and dented, stained with blood and grime, the faces below them grim and calloused. Hands gripped rifles with the care of prized possessions.

It struck me that Khraal Kahlees had been right. This was a great day.

I drew my sword. Doug needed no further prompt and from behind the K-max, hammered a fist against the roof of the gun truck. It lurched ahead, Doug running the K-max to announce our entrance into the wide kill zone as I raised my sword and screamed, "With me!"

Troops fanned out to form the line I set for us as the fifty and K-max took turns singing over our heads. Fire teams broke into rushes to take brief cover behind monstrous piles of destruction and send furious fire into the dark spaces of the palace. The wild game of bounding overwatch, so precise and clean on a whiteboard, became a deformed but living thing as we brought the cure to attack the disease wherever it festered.

From the towers and tops of the buildings, the defenders fought to keep us away. Green arcs of jellied flames rained in gushes, and deck guns sent powerful bursts into our front with horrifying effect. From our flank, Khraal Kahlees led his men as they encroached into the bowl in the same short charges we made. Tsunamis of men spread and rushed to find cover behind the ample remains of what had been, now less than the rough stuff from which dead artisans had crafted a life's work. When a redoubt piled full, the flood sent men down new avenues, ever forward. The terraced stairs surrounding the palace were bathed in the late afternoon light and called us to mount them.

I had my rifle again and sent one 40mm after another arcing onto the rooftops and terraces as Dave did the same from my left. Angular and precise where all else in Pyreenia was built as twisted radiuses, the stairs led to more terraces stacked like boxes, and atop its ultimate plateau, a single grand dome. From our flank, a pair of Goose gunners joined ours to send rounds into the open architecture of the mezzanine level meant to coax entry by all who ascended the pyramid of stairs.

The designers never envisioned us accepting the invitation.

A charge takes on a life all its own. It's a colony-type life-form composed of organisms commensal in their exhaustion and murderous intent, each fueled by the individual desire to reach the summit, to stand over the bodies of a vanquished defender, to rest if only for a moment before the next bloody clash. These men saw the peak and, like me, thought the view from it was the only thing that mattered.

Up the stairs we moved. The GMV climbed with us until felled columns and ruined statues blocked its ascent. Doug leaped from his perch, rifle in hand, a mad grin frozen across his face. "Let's do this!"

Halfway up, the returning fire dropped off, and without thought, I sprang. Because a warlord is always at the front.

Jawn Kurz charged in the open. Not me. While not a three-second rush, I had my own version of individual movement techniques on Mars. I zigzagged as I bounced, landed on the summit, and jagged. I slid over to the opposite side of the pillar I landed behind and sent a 40mm blindly ahead.

Dave was on my left, Doug to my right, both screaming in mantras set on repeat about the consanguinity of my parents and resulting lack of intelligence, so loud I heard every word in each ear above their firing. Behind us, a swell of Tarn howls and human screams rose and propelled us to ride the power of the voices like surf. Only butchered remains and wrecking ball detritus stood between us and the stairs up to the gallery. At the landing, I paused and drew my sword again to thrust its tip upward.

"Take it all."

Fevered soldiers sprinted around me, and Apache had broken free to be near me in the fight. There was no time to corral him. Khraal Kahlees leaped from the other ascent and with him, another wave of men gripped by the same lust to see the thing finished. There was no time for talk, no moment for method or tactic. It was time for blood. The mountain of stairs opened to what I expected, a long hall where a throne awaited with nothing and no one in sight. Soldiers in the grip of bloodlust gushed in and spread throughout, toppling statues, pulling tapestries off walls, not content to rest until the last enemy was found and rendered to lifeless meat. Finding none, a mass realization spread. The field of battle was theirs alone. And just as has happened since the first dirt-caked savages took up clubs of animal femurs to bludgeon their enemies into bloody pulp, animalistic howls of victory filled the air.

Dave sidled to me. Doug and Khraal Kahlees filtered through the sea of celebrating hordes to our island.

"This whole place is empty, brah. Why the hell would the HVTs even be here?"

"And why'd they defend it to the death? There must be something here," I said.

Double-K growled, "Then we must not stop until we have searched every corner."

I was about to order a reorganization to do just that when a shadow fell. A black cloud rolled over us and I was not alone in being drawn to look up for the cause. The curved dome of the rotunda was a void of space, so black it sucked all the light into it. Even our baffled gasps seemed to be drawn upward into the nothingness. A chill filled the room. I gave warning, but it was as though I screamed from a mute throat into deaf air. Then *they* dropped from the nothingness into our midst.

The creatures from Avril Mysteen's nightmares.

Clawed limbs and barbed tentacles attached to hideous chimeras of beasts tore into us silently, rasped tongues tearing off the skin of the fallen with bloody licks. I fired up into them as they continued to fall from the void above, the flashes of M4s and K-specs joining mine in a silence as unsettling as the monsters themselves. Apache had a mouthful of a tentacled three-legged beast and shook it wildly until he threw its limp body away. Khraal Kahlees with sword and dagger hacked at the madly formed creatures—and suddenly Tarn hands grasped me from both sides and I was lifted off my feet. The waters of our conquering flood of soldiers receded out and down the stairs. Carried by a force not under my control, I was swept along in the wave.

"Let go of me!" My voice made sound again as I struggled free of the grasp of my two bodyguards. I seated a fresh magazine and rotated the happy switch on my M4 all the way back. If ever there were a time when full-auto was appropriate, I'd found it. My comrades were with me at the base of the stairs as we fired above the heads of our men into the maw of the descending darkness. At the peak of the dome was an orb. A green globe. It wasn't until it blinked that I understood. It was an eye. A giant pupiled eye.

Doug sent a grenade and I shot to bolt lock. Then hands grasped me, and once more I lost the battle and was swept away with the stampede.

Dave was on his wristlet as we ran. "All gunships respond, fire on the palace. Do it now." We flooded down the terraced stairs into the fading red light of day. Doug leaped up to the deck of the GMV as Dave gained the driver's seat.

The gun truck reversed and bounced backward as Doug fired from the turret. I bounded down the last rise, Apache a mountain of muscle keeping pace with me. I turned to witness men spilling from the mezzanine in all directions as the darkness welled out in a liquid stream to meet the last of daylight. The black overtook and engulfed the last few trying to escape. They screamed as they disappeared into the growing void.

As abruptly, the black swell halted.

The gun truck careened backward off the last rise and down onto the plaza and skidded to a stop. I landed beside it, opened the door, and swung the 240 out. Crouched to raise the barrel as high as it would go, I turned loose. Kardans ringing the sunken plaza fired above our heads. The angels of our gunships appeared, first one, then all three. The confusion of what they saw paused them no longer and joined our fusillade. Hell showered without restraint onto the dome and the high terraces as minigun brass fell onto us like searing hail. Soldiers came from behind their shelter to stand their ground, firing until their guns discharged their last, then drew swords and waited.

Dave had a Javelin—our last. He checked behind and launched. The rocket screamed for a brief second before it struck. Suddenly, what had been only cracks in the dome became the dam giving way, a cataclysm collapsing onto itself. With the billow of debris, the darkness from within evaporated. Thin rays of the last sun pierced the clouds of dust as we watched the settling of the destruction, expecting something to rise again.

There were no words as we waited. Then a lone green figure appeared. Khraal Kahlees strode defiantly before the destruction, blade held overhead.

"Do you see this great building? One stone set upon another to stand for eons. Not one remains that has not been thrown down. Do any doubt what we shape by the Warlord's will? Now we will finish ridding Pyreenia of its sickness."

Cheers rose as men drew closer to claim victory over the dropped colossus.

I fed a new belt into the machine gun and slapped the feed tray cover closed. Doug tended his guns and reported. "This K-max is cooked.

And we're out of fifty." Dave walked around the truck and handed me a bottle of water.

"Well, we know the kid wasn't talking bullshit," he said.

Double-K descended to meet us. "Clansmen, it is time. The work continues. Is it not so, Warlord?"

Doug patted the resting fifty with affection, like the well-serving companion it was. "What *was* all that?"

Khraal Kahlees grinned. "It is good to give name to our enemy. I name it—dead."

15

DOUBLE-K HAD A WAY OF CLARIFYING THINGS IN THE MOMENT—THERE was still work to be done. We searched the rubble. If there were bodies to be found from the alien creatures, they were sealed deep in the same tomb that held our sacred dead. There was no remaining foulness to be tasted in the tonic of the clean night air.

The rest of the mission may have been rolling along like a greased bowling ball or stalled out like a mower full of bad gas—I didn't know. I believed in trusting subordinates. But you can only delegate authority. The responsibility for this whole thing was mine, and I had to get back to being the big picture kind of Warlord.

One task I could not delegate—it was time to update the queen. Waiting was a burden all its own and as I retold the events to her, I could see the weight increasing rather than lifting from her shoulders.

"I must see for myself."

"Absolutely not, Talis Darmon. There are Mydreen infesting every building and who knows what else." I let that hang. "We have weeks of hard, deadly work left."

But she anticipated where I was leading.

"The works of the Golden Hub are on the way, Benjamin Colt. Karlo Columbo and his able direction have amassed a city's worth of supplies."

"They'll be needed, but I can't say how many civilians are even alive. It doesn't look good."

"All the more reason their queen be there to direct the relief of the refugees."

"When it is safe, Talis Darmon. Not before. As both your Warlord and your betrothed, I insist."

Her fury stoked and I readied for the scalding steam, but what she released was tepid mist.

"Just because you are correct doesn't mean I must like it, Benjamin Colt."

"You're a natural soldier, my love. Thank you."

A minor battle won for her to stay where she was—safe—sent a wave of exhaustion through me. I leaned back into the seat of the gun truck. In the rearview mirror, Dave paced as he talked to Karlo by cloud. If not for the need for privacy, I'd be on my feet doing the same. No doubt in addition to discussing our logistics, he was filling Karlo in on the unnamed things we fought from the nightmare realm. That was Double-K's name for it. But unlike that point of agreement, whatever the giant green eye was attached to, I didn't think it dead.

As if she saw it in my face, she asked, "It was truly the manifestation of the evil Avril Mysteen described? Not vision? Not dream? Not delusion?"

Every other trace of the dark monsters might be gone, but Khraal Kahlees had two blades dripping black goo and Apache had similar stains that he rolled in the dirt to remove.

"It was all real. We lost men. We didn't imagine it."

Her countenance grew steely. "The Karnak may have touched this plane again, but you have defeated them. If there is a way for them to appear as anything other than shadowy apparitions, they now know they use such means at great risk to themselves. Perhaps you have already sealed them in their realm for good."

The pesky scratches at my spine were gone for now, but like the memory of any pain, I knew it waited to inflict itself upon me again at any time. "I wish that were true."

"I do not give hollow encouragement when I say I sense a quiet in Pyreenia, Benjamin Colt. Even before you told me of the victory, I felt the emanations diminish to almost nothing. You know my ability in this way."

She was right. I'd never seen an electron whizzing around an atom, but I knew they existed, just like there were things as real that she could touch but I'd never understand.

"That's the best news I've had in a while."

"And lest you think I have been idle during your campaign, I must inform you that I have been in disciplined study. I ask, have you felt the call again?"

The voice of Jawn Kurz had not spoken to me since I left Shansara.

"No. If the old boy's trying to tell me something, he's gone mute. Or maybe it's that when I do get a single hour of shut-eye, I crash so hard, not even a ghost can reach my subconscious. Ugh, let's not talk about sleep, Talis Darmon."

If I had any snuff, right now I'd have a double mouthful and be chasing it with an IV of black coffee. Apache snored on the ground beside the GMV. If I didn't have to lead an army just then, I'd have lain down next to him.

"When you return to Shansara with victory secured, we will continue to investigate this thing. I have found a guide to aid us. Until then, give it no more thought."

"That's the easiest promise I've ever made to you, my princess. I don't even remember who Jawn Kurz is. Was. Whatever."

Her soulful eyes shined wetly. "It is your betrothed who now orders *you*, Benjamin Colt. Warlord. My love. You must rest. I beseech your presence, but instead await your next communication." Her tears fell, and she extinguished the cloud before I could answer.

Dave took the seat next to me.

"The queen good, brah?"

"Itching to be here and take charge."

"I bet. Karlo shipped us out a freight-ton of ammo and guns days ago. Should be here tomorrow. Everything else is coming soon, too. C'mon. I got you a TOC fit for a Warlord."

"Where's Dougie?"

"He's walking the lines with Double-K. C'mon."

He led us on foot back to one of the adjoining streets where a checkpoint of three soldiers stood guard. Fatigued, filthy, but fueled by duty—just like us—they snapped tall and saluted.

"Well fought, men," I said. "Where are you from, trooper?"

The nearest man lowered his arm.

"Clymaira, Warlord."

"And you men?"

"We both come from Thoria, Warlord."

I didn't need to ask if they were new to the army. Without even a single brass button on their cloaks, they were all fresh from training. "You're veterans now. Proven fierce as the Korundi, fit as a gadron, and twice as smart."

They laughed, which is what I intended. Apache gave a short bark as if on cue.

The man from Clymaira stayed at braced attention. "Warlord, if I may ask? What—" he stumbled. "What came through that darkness? We've all talked. They were no manner of life from Vistara."

One of the Thorians added, "My Nan told stories about the things that once lived at the bottom of the Amethyst Sea. They reminded me of the bad dreams her tales gave me when I was a hatchling."

He wasn't wrong.

"They're a new enemy," I answered. "We think they're responsible for what happened here in Pyreenia, and maybe elsewhere."

The man next to him broke attention and grimaced, as if he couldn't hold back. "And Thoria, Warlord? It was Mydreen and Thulians who invaded our home, not those things." The man cast a furtive glance at Dave, then stiffened again as if waiting for my rebuke. His fellow Thorian nudged him.

"As you were! The Warlord and his Thulian brothers were first into the fray! They stood their ground firm against that foulness whilst we fled. They are the only reason we draw breath now!"

Whatever I said next I knew would travel through the army faster than if said over wristlet cloud.

"Whether against Mydreen, creatures from the nightmare place, or the other Thulians—any and all who are our enemies—our only choice is to fight together or die separately. It's only united that we will make things right on Vistara."

It may not have been the best answer, but it sufficed to turn the cagey Thorian away from an insubordinate path and return him to discipline—all without my having to act like a martinet. The man warmed and stood proud at attention.

"Yes, Warlord. I beg forgiveness for my undisciplined words. Victory for all comes with us at your side."

Dave waited until we'd departed. "Nice job, Ben-dog. Before the sun's up, that scuttlebutt will've spread to every grunt in Pyreenia. If there are other Thorians like him still pissed off, I think today sucked out most of the poison. Here." He pointed to an arch. Inside a small courtyard, my two Tarn bodyguards had a place cleared and a fire burning, sticks of broken furniture stacked nearby.

"I think you're sending me for riser grease or canopy lights, Davey-Dave."

"I'm out to check on a few things. Get some shut-eye and I'll be back in a couple of hours, brah. I'll roust you sooner if anything needs a warlord's attention."

✳ ✳ ✳

I awoke to someone saying my name.

"Benjamin Colt, Khraal Kahlees sends for you."

The sun was rising and with it, the hazy realization that I must've slept for several hours. I lay propped against Apache, who slowly stirred. A familiar Tarn towered over me.

"Garlak Ranz?"

"Yes, Warlord. Khraal Kahlees begs you join him."

"Where is he?"

"He gathers us at LZ Parade Ground. It is Domeel Doreen. He has been found."

We floated in a Kardan with Apache ambling beside us. The road that had taken a lifetime to travel and cost many lives in toll, we made in reverse route in fifteen minutes. I'd live to be as old as a Vistaran if each day of the rest of my life were as long as the last twenty-four hours.

Dave and Doug were there to meet me at the entrance to the ground that was our beachhead. Green and Red sentries mingled on the stadium rim. On the field, arkall mounted Korundi formed a shell for the central sight—Khraal Kahlees and the massive Tarn at his feet.

Domeel Doreen.

Doug explained quickly as we picked up the pace. "I was on a patrol with Garlak Ranz when we found him. He was in an unguarded cell, covered in his own filth like some kind of mental patient. There's something wrong with him, Ben, if it's even him. He's the right size."

Even in his current state, I was certain it was the Mydreen chieftain. I'd suffered his hospitality and verbally fenced with him for weeks before ending up in his dungeon.

Double-K grinned as only a Tarn can, tusks thrust forward and nostrils flared. "Warlord, now that you and my Thulian brothers are here, I fulfill the blood oath to which you were witness. I regret only that there is not an audience of Mydreen vermin to also attest to its fulfillment."

Dave whispered, "Oh boy."

I alone knew why he'd made the oath that day on the sands of Thoria with the first K-spec in his hands, a new means with which to serve a bloody end to all our enemies. I'd set into motion what was about to transpire. And I had no right to stop it.

"Khraal Kahlees, is there no information we can rend from him first?"

Garlak Ranz stepped forward. "Warlord, we have tried. There is something wrong with his mind."

Garlak Ranz was not only Korundi, he was related to Khraal Kahlees, from the same band and village. Khraal Kahlees had entrusted

Garlak Ranz to me for service and he'd proven an able warrior and an adept learner. In turn, he'd ascended as one of the warmasters for the training of the reconstituted army. And just as he now aided Khraal Kahlees to complete his revenge, he'd also been there for me and mine as I'd sent Mark to his end.

Crouched in a catatonic haze and stripped down to a loincloth, Domeel Doreen stared glassily. Drool coated his bare green chest. He seemed unaware he was the guest of honor at his own execution. Khraal Kahlees drew.

"Warlord, I would gladly spend a year torturing from him all the lies his tongue would tell, but there are no valued words to bring from him. There is only the oath. And clansman, you above all know its inception."

There was nothing else to be done. I dipped my head for him to continue.

"Ben-dog—"

Before Dave could go on, I held up a hand.

"I'll tell you later."

To stand a Tarn on his feet to kill him allowed him to pass with honor intact to the Vistaran afterworld shared by both Red and Green. Garlak Ranz assisted, moving as though part of a well-rehearsed ritual. He brought Domeel Doreen to his knees and with a flourish produced a coil of looped cord from his side. In a practiced fashion, he bound the prisoner's hands behind to join the cords around his bent ankles before stepping away in martial perfection.

Khraal Kahlees bent to raise the Tarn's chin, and where I expected a fury, instead my friend spoke with pity.

"You go on to nothingness, fool."

A swing, the head severed cleanly, the body stayed in place. Garlak Ranz in the same ritualistic perfection retrieved the fallen head and with sky hands, held it aloft for all to see. "You have borne witness. A blood oath has been fulfilled." He placed the head next to the body, preserved in kneeling humiliation.

The Tarns in attendance did not howl, did not cheer, did not hoot. No fizzle fire rent the air. Instead, they grasped forearms with each other, mumbled words of congratulations and blessings for the future.

"Honor done, clansman."

"Prosperity for our clan, Korundi."

Dave whispered, "It's like a wedding toast, brah."

Doug whispered back, "No, man, check it out—it's like they all found the true spirit of Christmas or something. Don't know what I expected, but it wasn't that. Just when I thought I knew a little about Tarns."

Khraal Kahlees stepped to place hands on his second's shoulders. "Garlak Ranz, in honor of your virtue on the battlefield, I name you captain. Recall this day to your hatchlings and the lesson within. No revenge is ever perfect. A warrior takes what is offered."

"Thank you, General. To act as second to see blood oath fulfilled—there is no higher honor."

Khraal Kahlees strode to clasp forearms with each of us. "Thank you for bearing witness. Were there not a war to wage, a week of celebrations would have us feast around the fire and share memories of great warriors gone to walk with honor. But there are more enemies to send to Temple Farnest or oblivion as they would choose. We have another prisoner, Warlord. Come."

16

"Is it Chuck?" Dave blurted.

"No, David Masamuni. He has not been found, nor the black witches."

He was about to step off when he double-clutched to a halt. "And lest you think I have forgotten your deception, I have not. Douglas Knoblock has educated me. Grid squares, indeed."

Dave shrugged. "Sorry, Double-K. We can barely afford one guy who always tries to go first." He thumbed at me. "I don't want your job. I'm happy as second-in-command. And you're welcome, by the way."

Khraal Kahlees ground his tusks side to side as he considered. "Very well. The outcome was acceptable, I will give you that. But be warned. We Korundi have our own way of repaying such trickery in kind. Brah!"

It was the first Red captured alive. Dried blood from a lacerated scalp caked his hair and black tunic. A Red and Green soldier stood just behind the chair he was lashed to.

"He was found alive but unconscious, Warlord. Orders were followed that any be given quarter if conditions were met." Double-K gestured like inviting us to dance. "Here he is, Benjamin Colt. This one speaks, unlike our last prisoner." He made the violent hack of a Tarn laugh.

The black uniformed Red was sullen but insubmissive, angrily testing his bonds as if to return to the fight when a weakness had been found. The only device on his uniform was the small silver emblem, the mountain lion. Dave nudged me and thumbed his own chest, indicating he wanted to take the lead.

"Give him some water."

The Tarn soldier guarding him placed a container to the man's lips, who resisted like a toddler in a high chair offered pureed peas.

"He will take none, General."

"Suit yourself. We'll get your injuries treated."

Now the man's eyes flared. "This body will be remade greater and more powerful in his service. No such transformation awaits you. Where you go, your agony will be the song of his delight for eternity."

Like a cornered animal, he snapped to bite at Dave.

The Red soldier jostled the prisoner with the butt of his rifle. "I've warned you once. Try that with the general again and you'll shit those teeth as you ride the Blix."

The prisoner flared with all his might against his restraints, shrieking, "The Blix! Temple Farnest! All lies! The sleeping god awakes."

In a blur he was on his feet, the chair attached. The soldiers made to grasp but, too late. The prisoner accelerated head-on into the wall, his collision the snap of a green branch. His body jerked once and he was still, a wild-eyed smile his death mask.

Dave—mystified—exploded, "I didn't even have to dodge. He wasn't aiming for me."

Doug gave a golf clap. "Masterful tactical questioning, bro-man. Top notch."

It'd been a while since Dave compounded that many expletives and physical impossibilities into one string. Doug roared with amusement.

"What's it matter? You know how you beat a suicide cult? Help 'em achieve their goal. I'm just sayin'."

Khraal Kahlees slapped Doug's shoulder. "Benjamin Colt, not only is this one as large as a Tarn, he's the only Thulian I know visited by our wisdom spirit. Douglas Knoblock has the truth of it. Let us not taint my joyous day with trifles such as this. We send the rest to their reward, whatever delusion they be so warped to believe."

I drew my knife and bent over the corpse.

"Whatcha doing, Ben?"

"Just curious, Doug."

A few draw strokes cut the dead man's bonds. Doug helped by discarding the chair and tossing it at the feet of the soldiers, still frozen in witness of the suicide.

"Say, boys," Doug drawled, "I don't suppose I have to tell you that's not how you secure a prisoner?"

I ignored Doug's sarcastic rebuke to the embarrassed soldiers as I split the tunic down the middle.

Between the shoulder blades was the same raised scar Avril Mysteen bore.

"They've got a secret brand that lets 'em into the members-only bar. Creepy, but so what? Don't mean nothing, Ben-dog."

Dave groaned, "Hell it doesn't, brah. You haven't seen everything we've seen."

"What? You mean something worse than a big black butthole dropping furry squid monsters on us, dude? Everything they threw at us, we gave back to them, handed 'em their hats, and booted them in the ass on the way out the door."

"Enough." I wiped my hands and stood.

Khraal Kahlees looked approvingly at Doug. He had a new friend.

Dave just shook his head and yawned as he mumbled, "I picked the wrong week to stop sniffing glue."

Doug sidebarred Double-K. "*Airplane*. Classic. Wish you could see it."

"If you're all ready?" I asked.

Two of us were still riding a combat high, one of us was crashing, and as the one with the most sleep, I was the closest to level. Which is why the guy at the top sometimes had to get his head right with some sleep while others kept watch, like Dave had engineered for me. Though he'd hoodwinked me into it like he had Khraal Kahlees.

"Order of march. Security, resupply, refit. As soon as I get a status on operations, we focus on coalescing cleared zones and moving displaced civilians into the safe areas."

"Anyone sees any clouds of magic bees, I want to know," Doug said. "I want a witch scalp to hang off my M4."

"You'll be first to know, Dougie. Let's go, brah. There's a city the size of Charlotte needs clearing."

On the morning of the twenty-first day after our violent penetration of dark Pyreenia, the city was wholly ours.

✳ ✳ ✳

I was moving to check on the next shipment from Shansara when my wristlet warned me and Dave's cloud appeared.

"Ben, Talis Darmon's here."

"You've gotta be kidding me!"

"Nope. She just showed up with the supply flight, brah."

I bounced and Apache broke into a run to keep up. The field outside the city was a Lego village of crates and tents, air cars and ground-hovers, and volunteers from the capital trying to sort through it all. Dave had just reached her retinue when I bounced in. My landing brought a shock that parted the entourage, capes billowing as they made startled retreat, leaving the queen the center of my attention. I made a grand bow.

"Queen Talis Darmon, this is an unexpected pleasure."

She held her statuesque pose for an instant before dipping her head, one corner of her mouth tilting in wry amusement at my entrance and the cause for it. She'd been a bad girl and she knew it.

"Warlord Benjamin Colt."

I winked at Beraal who raised an eyebrow in disapproval. Always the big sister. Some in the crowd huffed and composed themselves. I enjoyed showing off, though I shouldn't have. I recognized a few of the stuffed shirts from the council. If the queen corralled them here, it was most likely because she'd shamed them into coming. It was time to show more of the noble than the barbarian they thought me to be.

"Welcome to Pyreenia, gentle visitors. We have little to offer, but my staff will endeavor to make your stay comfortable as you work to assist in the rebuilding effort."

I received a few polite bows, a few curt head dips, and some frowns. I returned a salute from Kleeve Hartus, who'd not moved an inch, other than to place hand on pistol like a pro.

"General David Masamuni was about to take us through the effort, Warlord. Would you be so kind as to lead?"

She accepted my arm and direction. As soon as we had a little distance, I made prison yard talk.

"Talis Darmon, I'm not sure whether I should kiss you or paddle you. Good thing for you we're in public."

"A kiss would be more welcome first, Benjamin Colt. Later, the second."

"Sweetheart, why didn't you tell me you were coming?"

"You know why. You would have postured that it was not yet safe. A queen goes where she pleases, betrothed."

"Yes, ma'am. Duly noted. You've been days flying, would you prefer to rest?"

"No. It's important that we begin. I cannot remain for long. I will have ample time for rest on the return journey."

"Who's got the keys to the kingdom in your place?"

"I have appointed Karlo Columbo as first administrator in my absence."

"I bet he liked that."

"He fought most diplomatically, but surrendered due to his sense of duty."

"Did you threaten him with dismemberment to keep him from warning me you were coming?"

"Ritual castration." She winked. "He is a trusted confidant. I may return to find he will have inspired more progress than I. His logic is unassailable, and his ability to sway others almost makes me think he has Sylah blood in his veins. I wish to see as much as I can in a single day and make my return."

"It's safe here in the rear area, but most of the city's a disaster zone. It's better that we take a flitter to tour it, if that's your desire?"

"Please. Unless I can appreciate the scope of the problem, I cannot properly petition for the assistance necessary from the rest of the kingdom."

I paused to trade grips with Kleeve Hartus, who said, "A good entrance, Warlord. They may wear armor, but it is costume. They fear they may be enmeshed in combat at any second. I dare say none of them have left the splendor of the capital in many annuals."

"I'm glad you're here, First Shield."

"I've brought a small detachment of Guards. As soon as your soldiers can get them acclimated, they will be ready to assume the restoration of civil order to lawless Pyreenia."

"That's a tall order, my friend. We'll be leaving the army here for as long as we can, but that's not going to be very long. We have to get back to Shansara and ready for whatever's building against us in the south."

"Ever a sword above our heads, is there not?"

We flew high at first to show the area of largest devastation, the governance section. Talis Darmon and Beraal were with Dave at the bow as Kleeve Hartus kept me apart.

"Was it as dire as the queen relayed?" he asked. "The foul evil that was met there?"

"It was as bad as Avril Mysteen described, only it wasn't a dream. It was real."

The first shield's face darkened. "I bear ill news, Benjamin Colt. Avril Mysteen did not recover. He succumbed to his injuries and has passed to life in the underworld."

It was icy water in my face. "He was well! Karlo said he was on the mend."

"It was by his own hand, my friend. Found by the healer shortly after he drew razor across his own throat, the terror frozen in his lifeless eyes. He could not persevere against what haunted him."

I crossed my arms and bowed. "A warrior now walks with his glorious ancestors in the underworld. I'm truly sorry, Kleeve Hartus. I know he was a little brother to you, as he was to me. Had we known what waited for him here—"

"Those who are culpable have not yet begun to pay for their crimes."

"No, they have not."

"None of your former team nor the black witches have been captured?"

"No. Chuck was here. Bryant? He hadn't been seen for some time. He's in the Yellow Kingdom, I'm positive, trying to stir up some poison against us."

The queen joined us. "I see other evidence of the war's aftermath. Many towers and buildings brought down. I wish to visit the survivors. They must know that their queen sees their tribulations and mobilizes the might of the kingdom to aid them."

I directed us to the largest of the intact boroughs where the bulk of the survivors had been relocated. Tarns are efficient at many things. Coping with refugees is not one of them. A food riot was brought to an abrupt but bloody halt when a Korundi took the initiative to quell the disturbance by removing the head of its leader.

Soldiers aren't cops. Especially Tarns. Even in the Korund, order was maintained at the village level by tribal law, same as with the Mydreen. There were no police. Minor crimes and major crimes were settled in the same way. By duel.

As aid and workers arrived from Shansara, we threw them into the fray and withdrew as many of the Green troops as fast as was feasible. Our Red veterans soon went from frontline infantry to Guards, human faces more easily accepted than the Korundi, who to the civilians were no different from the Mydreen who'd ruled them.

Adults left doors and tents to line the street as we passed. Every day more clothing arrived with the relief. Pyreenians dressed modestly to begin with, and rather than show skin, those who did not yet have adequate replacement still wore the dark robes, but left their heads uncovered in regained freedom. Children played in the streets—a healthy sign that people were being fed and the oppressive restrictions of the city's imprisonment was officially over.

A little blonde girl dashed into the street in front of us, tripped, and as she recovered to catch up to her pack, came to startled notice of the visitors on her playground. Her eyes rested on Talis Darmon and her tiny jaw dropped open. She curtsied in the Vistaran manner—dipping low to rest one hand over the other as both hands touched the ground—before running off to join her playmates.

"Don't expect me to bow to the likes of you," sneered a woman from the crowd. At first, she was the only one who did not lower her eyes, but others quickly joined her, glaring and scowling. Guards gripped their hilts and shifted forward.

"No," Talis Darmon whispered. She took a gliding step forward… and then bowed.

"You have suffered greatly, grandmother," the queen said. "I come with the wealth of my kingdom to ease your privation and restore your well-being."

A man cried, "Your brother and his cabal made us prisoners in our own homes. Then they starved us. Where was Shansara then? Your father abandoned us to his bastard."

A gaunt woman stepped around the man. "You destroy our Pyreenia in a war you started and claim to bring help but refuse us our basic freedoms."

"We have the right to return to our homes."

"Pyreenia isn't yours. We don't want you here."

"Sylah, go home!"

"Take your brazen lustfulness with you, whore, and your White defilers, and all your Green puppets with you!"

The crowd grew larger and louder. Red troopers moved to push the crowd back and Dave was on his wristlet calling the cavalry.

I took her by the elbow. "This is going to get out of hand, Talis Darmon. We have to get you out of here while we still can. If this mob turns violent, blood's going to flow—theirs."

"No, Benjamin Colt," the queen firmly said. Then she parted us all with wide arms and stepped farther ahead, the calm at the center of a swirling storm. She closed her eyes and began to sing.

"Ashen and paled and colored in sorrow
Frail and fell low, not meant for the morrow
Hunger, deep pain, extinguished true light
Halls of kind welcome, removed from delight

"Mean in estate, cast out, then made blind
Sight stolen, forsaken, reduced in kind
Forgive, forgive them, made ugly and cruel
Neither cowed in defeat nor hatred askew

"Save souls, all to bear
Great calumny spared
So harkened, so fair
Hail, Desudun Cahlair."

The woman who'd refused to bow took slowly to both knees. More in the crowd joined her to take to knee as well, shushing and motioning down the younger ones—who, though confused, reluctantly obeyed.

"She knows the 'Song of Sorrow,'" someone whispered, as if that explained everything.

Tension eased, the crowd quieted, their lemming march turned from the precipice of bloodshed. Talis Darmon crossed hands over herself.

"Pyreenia sprang from the tears of those who anguished in guilt over the persecution of Desudun Cahlair. Their water filled the sands beneath. It was by her forgiveness that they wept. I cannot bring forth the tears to match what has been shed for her affliction. I can only weep with you at the defilement of the sacred ground over her well."

The woman choked back tears of her own. "We do not seek to be as you. We are hatched in a different soil. We toil under a different sun. We wet lips from different springs. We sleep under the shelter of different moons. The Sylah Dynasty remembers this?"

"I do, grandmother. And I ask of you the chance to aid in healing Pyreenia and restoring her as you would have her, not as others would. First are the needs of her body, then can her spirit be restored and have a home."

The woman rose. "Her spirit and body are one." Then she bowed deeply. "Queen Talis Darmon Sylah."

The crowd dissipated. "No better time to make our exit," I murmured, and turned us back towards the flitters. "Talis Darmon, what defused them? I didn't understand any of what you said. And that song! What was it?"

She was neither hurried nor harried. "The young do not even know why they hold Mihdradahl in disdain. It was a gamble that even the old would understand the bridge I sought to build.

"Pyreenia does not hold belief common with the rest of the kingdom. Their ways and their culture are molded by events thousands of years past. The ancient people of this land were more brutal and cruel than all the races of Vistara, save the Karnak. They hold connection to one who brought them from that barbarity, one who suffered at the hands of their cruelty, who taught them compassion."

"A prophet? A holy figure?"

"A teacher, and one largely forgotten, but the essence of her influence remains strong. I was taught of it, taught how it defines the people here, and my mother was correct—scratch the surface of Pyreenia, and the ancient color remains. Pyreenia has long been a reluctant part of the kingdom, which is why there has always been a royal presence here. If it is possible to repair these feelings of disaffection, I may be able to sustain her within the fold. If not, then we have yet another wound that will tear at us."

17

SHE DID NOT ORDER ME, BUT MADE THE CASE WHY I MUST LEAVE WITH her today for Shansara. "Your return to the capital will communicate that Pyreenia is no longer held by the enemy. It will also send warning to our enemies that the Warlord's sword arm is again near his queen."

"Didn't me clapping the last plotters in irons muffle the noises of their fellow elites?"

"It has been calm since you captured Marviel Lanconin and the others. Only a handful of minor supporters have been further identified. If there are more on the council in conspiracy against me, fear of joining the traitors has driven them to demonstrate loyalty most convincingly. Which will suffice. In politics, false fealty is practically as good as true. The trial will begin soon, and you are needed to publicly bear witness of their crimes."

Every holiday has an end.

"Someone's coming back with me today," I told the boys. "But don't worry, you won't be alone for long. As soon as the Guards can stand enough men, the army's pulling out. Pyreenia is in the hands of the civilians now. It's their problem."

"It should be me, brah," Dave said. "I've about worked myself out of a job. The logistics are being run by the civvies. I'll get things ready back on the receiving end so we can hit the ground running. New tactics and methods to be practiced, new boom sticks and war machines to be trained, new strategies for improved capabilities."

"Karlo have more R-and-D to be T-and-E'd?"

"He's a busy man, our brother Karlo."

Doug said, "We've already worked it out, Ben-dog. I'll stay back and interface with the Guards a while longer, Double-K will lead off with the first two battalions."

"Departing with all Korundi will aid the atmosphere of Pyreenia's resurrection, Warlord. We will be weeks on the return campaign. It will provide an opportunity to interdict any Mydreen who may yet be mistakenly seeking to join their chieftain. I will oblige them. If I may ask, would you entrust your MK 22 to me for the march?"

"You're welcome to her, brother. But I want her back."

"I will protect her as if she were your first hatchling."

There'd been another ceremony this morning, and at Beraal's side I was the only other in attendance. Her father presented her with the head of Domeel Doreen. What may sound gruesome was, in fact, more touching than any rite I'd been a part of. Brief and to the point, father offered daughter the proof of his virtue.

"Dosenie Beraal, accept this as a token of my apology. I make amends to you and to your mother, Lassa Laloo."

She took the head from him. "I accept, Khraal Kahlees."

"Accepting this, would you also accept my paternity for all to know?"

"I do, Father. With this mark erased, it is with honor I bear the name."

"With witness then, it is done. It will be chiseled in stone in the Korund for all time, Beraal Kahlees."

But even with the lump in my throat, I couldn't help but fantasize about offering Brandon Bryant's head to my betrothed in like manner.

Somehow, I didn't think it would be received with the same effect it had on Beraal.

The father and daughter touched foreheads and parted, and she and I walked together for the queen's yacht.

"Sister, will you ever tell Talis Darmon the whole story?"

"It seems unimportant now. To dwell in what is past would go against the purpose of the ceremony. But I give you dispensation, brother, to share with her such if the need ever arises. But hold concern no longer for my happiness. My father has made me whole."

As we neared the three ships of our armada, she held me back.

"Brother, I say to you with respect—there is a rift you need mend. There may be no better time for you to do so than presently. I know it is her wish. Please consider my words."

The queen's yacht was quite the air car. Where all our flitters were bare deck and utilitarian, this had cushioned couches and all the comforts duly befitting a queen. Our armada departed for the capital, and I sat beside the queen as we flew home. It wasn't until that night as we shared the fur of some great beast and we coasted beneath the clear Martian night, that I found the courage.

"Talis Darmon, do you wish to talk?"

"You wish to speak of all the things left unsaid, betrothed?"

"Only if you do."

"I've wanted nothing since."

My butterflies were few. I was fully recovered from the shock at learning that with her long life, she'd had many of the full experiences of such. I even felt slightly foolish for my reaction, and already decided that whatever she told me, it couldn't change how I felt about her.

"To understand, I need tell you of my life as it once was. My father was not born to ascend the throne. The Darmon line, while of royal blood, was not in court. The paternal dynasty of Partell held the seat of Mihdradahl's rule. The tragedy that befell them was swift. The Great Forlorn struck him and his line, and one by one, they traveled to the Blix, inconsolable as to its necessity."

"You're going to have to explain that."

She sighed. "I have spoken with Karlo Columbo. He has been a valued councilor and confidant. He has explained much to aid my understanding regarding your perplexity concerning our world. As you know of such, there is not disease on Vistara. We do not succumb to the ravages of the infirmities he described to me as common on Thulia. I did not know. It pains me to think of how your race lives, knowing such predators hunt you throughout your lives.

"As you so inadvertently learned in manner to my regret, that our lives are long. Unless by great injury or accident, it is by choice to join the underworld that we leave this world. Many grow tired and indolent of purpose after so many revolutions through the ether, longing for a change and to reunite with those departed."

"Depression and suicide? But your healing arts do so much for the mind!"

"When one hears the call to ride the Blix, it is more than melancholy which drives them. I would talk of that later if you wish, but what I mean to describe is that there does exist an ailment here that affects us. The Great Forlorn. It has taken many score to the underworld before their choosing, and when it appears, it often strikes the whole of a lineage at a time. It had not happened in ages to one who held the throne, but it struck in the time of my youth.

"I was a scholar. I had been tutored since birth in the arts and sciences, and it was without other responsibility that I gladly chose my path.

"Serin Lasell was from a common line. A family of scholars and artisans. We grew up together. We were young and happy and ensconced in the joy of our learning. He was kind and intelligent, funny and tender. It was only natural that we fell in love. With our parents' blessings, we wed. We were happy.

"And then the Partell dynasty fell. You cannot imagine the chaos it caused. I can still feel the pall that fell over the kingdom when the Spectral Throne was rendered bare. The day that the council called my father to court was as unexpected as the tragedy itself.

"My father was thrust from his life as a soldier to become regent. He taught me duty from the earliest age, and with my mother and my brother, we became the first family of Mihdradahl. I was named princess. It was an abrupt end to our way of life.

"To my husband, it was a burden. One that Serin Lasell could not bear. He was unable to adapt to life at court. Thrust into training for the inevitability that he may someday be consort to the future ruler and no longer able to dedicate himself to his studies, we grew apart.

He became resentful and distant. I thought with time he would find happiness again, but it was he who asked to be set apart from me, that our marriage be dissolved.

"I learned that he had fallen in love with another. Another scholar became the subject of his affections. It was a bitter blow to me after all that had happened to disrupt my own life, and I felt abandoned and alone. If not for the love of my family and Beraal, I too may have crossed to Temple Farnest from my despondency, such is the weakness of youth."

I gripped her hand tightly. "I'm so sorry."

"With time and renewed dedication to my role as princess, I healed. But it was also my responsibility to build our line. Eventually, my mother chose a suitor for me.

"Kilvan Tollus was of aristocratic line and a soldier. One who understood duty as necessary in all parts of the life of one who served Mihdradahl. He was handsome and strong. Where Serin Lasell was thoughtful and retiring, he was brash and bold. He made me hopeful that one who was so disciplined would fulfill an oath to me for a lifetime and not succumb to the strife and weight of our offices as my selfish scholar had. But he did not love me. And even knowing this, I let the match go forward and became his wife."

"Why, sweetheart? What would you accept the proposal of someone who didn't make you happy?"

"It was not even a true proposal. It was more contract than betrothal. Many years had passed in the time since I had been set apart from Serin Lasell. In that time, I had matured. The thoughts of romantic love and all it meant dwindled in importance to me. I had grown colder, ensconced in responsibilities. I was now ambassador in my father's service. My new husband was gone much of the time, serving in many parts of the kingdom as was his desire. My father supported this, proud that his new son carried on in martial tradition when his own son chose otherwise. But I had a newfound hope for happiness.

"Our egg was in its honored place and my anticipation at meeting the life that grew within gave me new hope for happiness. Therein was a soul with whom to share my life, whom I could show all my love and care. I glimpsed a new kind of love that I did not previously know existed. My husband visited, stayed for short times, always anxious to leave and be on arkall or in the air, headed for some anticipated glory or adventure.

"His death was not glorious or proud. It was nothing more than an accident. He left one day in his air car and never returned. He was found in the crash after many days searching. No cause of the failure was discovered. It was an ignominious end to a man who deserved better. I had hoped that with our hatchling, the child would've made his desire for the hunt dwindle in importance, and that he might've grown closer to me as he would his offspring."

There was a silence hanging in the night air that constrained me with bonds firmer than those that had held me in the chill waters of my abduction.

She sobbed quietly. "Some eggs do not hatch, I was told."

My chin quivered and eyes blurred with hot tears, the wind unable to dry them.

"A hundred revolutions around the sun have I traveled since then, Benjamin Colt. Do you believe me when I say that though the pain of those occurrences has never fully healed, that over so much time, they do not consume me? I do not dwell on them nor oft think of them. It was not by design that I did not share with you those things. They are simply days and joys and disappointments and injuries long past."

"I do understand, Talis Darmon."

"It brings me great relief for you to say such. You have suffered much loss and hurt for one so young. Because you are so capable and always ready to thrust yourself so surely into whatever tempest assails, it was a similar shock to learn *your* true age. I've told you before that I would release you from—"

"Shh." I put my finger to her lips. "You're stuck with me. Sorry. *You're* going to have to be the one to put *me* aside. But I do have a question. Did you sorceress me into loving you? Because you didn't have to." It was a joke between us, one I hadn't used in a long time. It made her sniffle a laugh.

"You know the answer. By touching your animus, it made our connection strong and personal—for a time. But I do not have the ability to cloud a mind in such a manner as to make you act against your will."

I feigned my best hypnotic drone. "Yes, mistress. I hear and obey."

She elbowed me.

"Ow. Just kidding."

I put an arm around her, and she snuggled close.

"I bare all to you, Benjamin Colt—the night you asked me to be yours, I could never have wished for such happiness for myself. For more than a hundred years—nay, in all my life—I have not felt what I feel for you. I need you."

"And I need you."

We stayed like that for a while.

"Sweetheart, was this part of your plan? To come to Pyreenia against my wishes in order to get me alone for the trip back?"

"A queen sees the complexities of many courses and influences them from twain divergencies to steer them aright toward a more harmonious path."

"Hmm. More sorcery, eh? Marviel Lanconin thought you used magic to bring us here from Thulia. Is that one possible?"

"Pah. Please do not mention that idiot."

But there was a pause that followed. And in it, I sensed her struggle to compose her answer. Was she about to tell me there was truth to the conspiracy theory? Or was there something else that influenced the astronomically improbable roll of the dice that led to a dumb ground-pounder rescuing a princess from another world?

"But if I could have, when in my most dire hour in Domeel Doreen's cage, as I prayed for a savior, if I had a spell to reach across the ether of our worlds to summon you, what say you if I did?"

"I'd say, lucky for me."

18

THE DAY STARTED EARLY AND BADLY. FROM THE BEDSIDE TABLE, MY wristlet flashed. We'd arrived late. The sun had not risen which by itself was a bad sign. Kleeve Hartus in the cloud was just as bad. I anticipated with the same dread as if he were the highway patrolman popping up in my rearview mirror.

"These little reunions make me long for the days when bad news traveled slower. What is it?"

"Warlord, I return only to discover betrayal within my ranks. The conspirators are gone from the detention center, as are the air wizards."

"WHAT!"

Talis Darmon and Apache snorted awake together, my outburst also precipitating a knock at our door and a guard entering. Apache was in tow as Kleeve Hartus took us to the cells where blankets were pulled away to reveal carefully positioned cushions and false heads complete with wigs.

Dave blew out in disgust. "Someone saw *Escape from Alcatraz*."

My curses were a poor imitation of Dave's masterful combinations, motel art compared to Rembrandt. "Seven men don't make it out of a jail without inside help, First Shield. What happened?"

"Before retiring, I came to receive report from the officer of the watch, arriving just as the alert sounded from this finding. The facility is completely locked down. The entirety of the Guard is mobilized and search is underway."

"Dave, let's get as many troops as we can in the air. They've got to be trying for an escape from Shansara."

"Warlord, it is no coincidence this occurred during my absence in Pyreenia. It may take days, but my investigators will find a discrepancy, some variation in conduct to implicate whoever participated. We will discover who betrayed their vows of integrity. I am tempted by the example of Khraal Kahlees to encourage revelation. Treason by a member of the Guard carries the sentence of execution. It is the highest of crimes."

Dave stepped back into our tête-à-tête. "The only squadron still in the capital is joining the search, First Shield. The detachment commander is contacting your men now."

"Thank you, David Masamuni. Warlord, I will not rest until this is seen through, or I will offer my sword and journey north. I take my leave."

Dave looked concerned. "You're not going to let him do something like that, are you, Ben?"

"Of course not, dude."

"All this palace intrigue and backstabbing runs deep. He's beating himself up about something he's not responsible for. I'll help kick-start this dirt bike and be at the garrison if you need me. You may as well get some sleep, brah."

"Fat chance I'll sleep. Got plenty on the long flight back."

"You guys work things out on the way?"

There'd been many nights on the campaign when I'd talked to Dave about my private life and all the implications that came with the revelations I'd come into possession of so unexpectedly.

"There was nothing to work out, brother. I just had to come to terms with being a self-centered prick."

"Brah, go easy on yourself. That was a lot to take in all at once. Makes me wonder what other big shockers are waiting to drop on us about life on Mars?"

"As a grunt, I try not to think about it. As the Big Kahuna, I need to. And somewhere in there is just me, the guy in love with a woman who's going to outlive him by who knows how long. I'm trying to be more like you and just roll with it."

"It's all you can do. *Shaka*, brah."

"I never have asked. What does that mean?"

"Huh? You don't know? I say it all the time. Hang loose."

"I wasn't far off then. Always how I took it."

"Maybe what I should be telling you is, *o ka pono ke hana 'ia a iho mai nā lani.*"

All I could do was raise my eyebrows and wait for the translation from Hawaiian.

"Something my tutu used to say. It means like, 'continue to do good, and the heavens will come down to you.'"

"I don't know if I'm doing that, bro."

"Huh? We just saved a lot of people, Ben-dog. And if there's still haters in the kingdom, that's life. Mihdradahl wasn't built in a day. These douche nozzles getting loose? Big deal. Go home and tell Talis Darmon not to worry. It's little stuff."

"We've got a saying where I come from, Dave. 'Preciate ya."

"Thanks, brah. Go home. You do the big stuff, you got us to handle the rest."

"C'mon, Apache. At least one of us'll get some sleep."

I didn't want to spoil the moment by telling Dave that the big stuff was a dark place where a giant green eye was waiting to do us harm.

✳ ✳ ✳

Karlo finished his report to the queen and the council.

"With your permission, ma'am, I would like to return to my previous duties."

"With thanks, Karlo Columbo. I have many accolades to bestow upon the body of the Golden Hub as well as the members of this council, and upon the many volunteers who have left comfort to aid others in need. As tragic as these times may be, I see in our kingdom a spirit of vigor that I have not before witnessed."

The chief auditor spoke up. "It is demonstrably true. Optimism throughout the kingdom is on the rise. Employment and vitality metrics increase together. There is an increase in the number of families expecting hatchlings. These indicators have not grown at such rates since before your father reigned. It is also true that pilgrimages north have dropped to an immeasurable number. It is as if the turmoil and its recovery have sparked new purpose and life, figuratively and literally."

Talis Darmon exuded warmth, as everyone in the room seemed to feel a similar sense of well-being. "I believe the worst is behind us. Mihdradahl is on the way to her greatest days. And it is to all of you that your regent bows, such a gesture inadequate to recognize the service you have done for your people and a grateful kingdom." She rose grandly and dipped, not as low as one would to her, but quite low. In turn, all were on their feet to return the gesture.

All but one.

Cynar was withdrawn, suspended within his own thoughts. The nobility I'd felt in the moment, the fleeting feeling I'd allowed myself that all was as she'd said, fled from me like smoke through my fingers.

The hermit's paralysis did not escape attention. Talis Darmon took her seat as did we all, the shrunken and ancient man looking dry and feeble, as though with a breeze, he would become dust before our eyes.

With kindness, she said, "Cynar the Magnificent, what troubles you? You need not bear any ill alone. Pray tell us what ails you."

He remained silent and averted his gaze downward. Talis Darmon gave me the look to proceed.

"Cynar—"

He mumbled, "Call me Magnificent no more. I can find no way."

"No way to what?"

"The atmosphere works elude my understanding!" he exclaimed. Then his shoulders shook and he sobbed.

"Cynar, you just need more time, buddy. You've only been at it a short while."

"No."

"No what?"

The sobs were gone, his fire returned.

"Do you hear the word so infrequently that you no longer understand its meaning, Warlord? No, the works do not yet produce. No, I have not secured a solution. No, I do not understand why. I am at the end of my wits."

She dismissed the group until it was only us and Karlo with the water priest.

Calm now and with Karlo at his side, he explained, "I have toiled until the more I pull at the thread of problem, the firmer the tangle becomes. What fails, how it once functioned, I have no science with which to unravel the puzzle."

Karlo quietly said, "Cynar's been at it without a break. He's been working harder than any of us and I haven't had a moment to assist him. With you here again, ma'am, I can turn my full attention to helping him with the problem."

Cynar was still distraught but seemed to accept the suggestion.

"There is an essence that should bind all the processes that are depleted or missing. If you can so name what I cannot, Karlo Columbo, then I hope I live to see it. My time on Vistara soon comes to a close."

Pleading, Talis Darmon said, "Cynar, dear friend, do not leave to go north to travel the Blix. You must resist the call for the good of us all."

Cynar looked at her with pity. "I do not hold to that belief, Queen. It is no Forlorn as you would call it that grips me. It is the failing of this body. All life ends, Talis Darmon Sylah... But I now sadly presage, my departure heralds the following of all with me."

We watched him go as Karlo led our friend away.

"It is Cynar's great fatigue that has overwhelmed him to produce such despair and frustration. We have depended on him for so much, and he has delivered miracles at each beck and call. Surely, Karlo Columbo will provide clarity where Cynar's strain has rendered his faculties weakened. Do you remember a time in the Korund when in my own frail state, I was unable to form even drops of water to sustain us?

It is with memory of that duress and my own sense of helplessness that I believe he is afflicted."

"Where's Dureen Zell? He could use a little tender loving care about now." The old seamstress had been keeping company with Cynar, but I'd lost track of their status together.

"She has been entrusted with an errand. I told you I have not been idle during your campaign. Dureen Zell investigates a medium to explain that which has touched you from the past."

I hadn't thought of Jawn Kurz in some time. "That compulsion's gone. We don't need to waste time on that stuff."

Her brow crinkled.

"I am not so sure. She should be returning soon. When she does, I will send her to Cynar with haste."

My wristlet warmed and it was Dave.

"Ben-dog. Get your spurs on and let's ride. Best lead we've had so far. A patrol saw a flitter headed out of the capital late last night."

"Great. I'm on the way. Where're we going?"

"If they were hightailing it and not worried about being followed, my best guess—their azimuth shoots a beeline for Maleska Mal."

✳ ✳ ✳

The Tarn all touched hilts, checked that collimators were tightly mounted on their K-specs, and crowded the rails, the heights assuming insignificance in comparison to what they hoped awaited. The electric anticipation of action that supercharged them arced across the deck to me.

Kleeve Hartus joined Dave and I in our trio of flitters, one piled with Guards and two of the Korundi who'd been left behind to man the garrison when we marched for Pyreenia. The lieutenant caught me in contemplation.

"To be the tip of the spear is a great distinction, Warlord. We are eager to meet the Mydreen in their nest."

This was a difference with the Tarn. In my old army, the barriers between ranks meant a junior would never do what Calus Gree did now. Could I have ever walked up to the Chairman of the Joint Chiefs of Staff and initiate a conversation? Not without lightning striking me dead or the silicon chip implanted in my brain causing paralysis. The Tarn were brave, fierce, and it goes without saying—disciplined. But they did not hold that a warrior was constrained from speaking his mind to another, rank be damned. Which sometimes led to duels.

You take the bad with the good.

I enjoyed the fraternization. It was a lot like SF. What was wrong with SF was the same stuff that was wrong with the rest of the army. What was right with SF the rest of the army had never heard of. But there was no more Special Forces, or U.S. Army, or United States. Reflecting on the past was a perpetual habit of mine, but the longer I was here, the more those reflections seemed like memories stolen from some old book and not my own life.

"Had the capital been attacked in my absence, Lieutenant, you would have been more than the tip. Songs of your company's bravery would be sung in the Korund for a thousand years. You were chosen to protect Shansara for a reason."

"Thank you, Warlord. It did not come to pass, and it is with regret of all that we did not accompany you to Pyreenia, but if we regain dignity now, praise the fates."

I didn't give him the spiel about how every mission was important, how every soldier should take honor no matter the task. I knew what it was like to be left behind when everyone else went to war.

It was not a good feeling.

"Calus Gree, you have nothing to prove to me nor to any, least of all yourselves. But, do not fear. Even if there is not a fight waiting at the end of this journey, there are more battles to come. This I know."

"It is a good life, Warlord."

It was on the second morning that Dave tapped me awake. "Come look." He pointed over the side as we passed high over the wreck of the C-17. The drifting sands had removed much of the evidence of the struggles that played out around it.

"We should go give it a once-over sometime. We did leave some stuff on her, though it's probably been picked over good by now by any passing Mydreen."

"If there was anything Karlo needed, he'd have gotten it already. Mike and the captain got burned down right there." I pointed to a trio of dunes. "I've got no desire to walk down the memory lane of that shit show."

"Sorry. I know what you mean. Just didn't want you to miss it. Besides, we're almost there."

On the horizon were those same towers and domes that had teased us from the site of our crash. The dilapidated city that was once the seat of the Mydreen, and many ages before that one of the grand Red cities of Mihdradahl, grew closer.

"We've left it alone for a long time. What are we going to find?"

"One way to find out, brah. Recon by occupation."

A pass over the city drew little attention and no defensive response mounted to repel our intrusion. What few Tarn were on the streets below fled for cover. Kleeve Hartus piloted, and we swung high above the columns of the atmosphere works. In the courtyard behind the impenetrable walls sat an air car.

Dave and I were first over the side, dropping ten meters onto one of the featureless buildings as the first shield veered away to deposit Calus Gree and his Tarn outside the walls. The other flitters hovered nearby, deck guns ready to respond.

"All quiet. Bring 'em down, Dave."

He waved the birds into the courtyard as I continued to cover the towers and narrow grounds. There wasn't enough room in the tiny space for another air car to touch down, so one at a time they hovered low enough to drop Green and Red until the space could hold no more.

We hopped a cascading path down, bouncing off the few flats and the curving surfaces of the works to land in the courtyard. Dave was already pulling out a strip charge.

"There's a portal, just like at the Clymaira works," he said.

The vault door cracked inward a sliver, and both our rifles came up.

"Please, Warlord. Do not fire. I beg of you." The voice through it held a contrition I'd never heard before.

"Come out, Tyreen Sorell. Keep your hands up where I can see them. Anyone else in there, do the same and you won't get hurt."

One by one, three purple-robed, henna-bearded wizards appeared and behind them, four other familiar faces. Moments later, we had them searched, cuffed, and splayed out on their stomachs. I stayed behind as Dave supervised clearing the works.

"I admire your resilience and the execution of your plan, but you're going back," I told them. "I'm glad you weren't so desperate as to make us bust our way in."

Marviel Lanconin flopped like a fish on dry land to look back at me. "Are you not curious why we came to Filestra? Let Master Tyreen Sorell speak."

"Tell me why I shouldn't shoot you on the spot, General. I haven't turned the other cheek about you trying to murder me."

"I was left little choice. It was that or allow all Vistara to die. I am a patriot. The life of one misguided and powerful despot brought to end would save us all. I do not expect you to forget my actions, but listen to him. You must."

Abusing prisoners was unacceptable. That's what I told myself as I fought the urge to kick him.

"Now someone wants to explain? All right, let's hear it."

The wizard rolled to his side at my command, grimacing in discomfort.

"Spill it, beardy. I'll give you one chance. I want you to act like what you say next is the most important thing you're ever going to say, and I'm only going to give you one sentence in which to tell me before I gag you all for the ride back to your neck-tie party. Big breath in—ready? And, go."

In one breath, he blurted it out.

"I know what ails the atmosphere works and it is here in Maleska Mal that the answer lies to correct all."

19

"You're actually considering it, brah?"

"Tyreen Sorell makes a case for forgiveness in which I find little merit," Kleeve Hartus said. "Warlord, I am in a position of grave responsibility. Below the queen, your word is supreme. But I am the custodian of the law. If that is your decision, know it is not out of disloyalty to you that I must make petition to the queen for assurance."

"I respect that, First Shield. I truly do. I hate to see you troubled. You're a man of great conscience and duty. That will never affect our bond." He lightened considerably.

"Benjamin Colt, I offer this. I am given authority to offer concessions for cooperation. These conspirators have been as firm and cold as the peaks of the Sharpa Mountains. I did not think them so capable of hardy resolve against our questioning. If I am to recommend to the queen this course of action, I will have this settled once and for all, here and now. A full accounting of their deeds and names of those who participated. And if there is rot within my ranks, they will reveal it. I tire of wasting time hunting conspirators when there are other threats that the efforts of the Guard should be undistracted from investigating."

Dave scrunched his face. "You mean a plea bargain?"

Kleeve Hartus considered. "An interesting phrase. In our law, it is called the favor of admission."

"How do you want to proceed, First Shield?"

"Allow me to leverage their proposal against a complete accounting of their full conspiracy. I will appeal to the patriotism they claim to represent."

Back in the room with the prisoners, Kleeve Hartus gave them his ultimatum. The three men who'd participated in my abduction looked to Marviel Lanconin for permission. He nodded to Terran Dullmar.

"My nephew. He serves under me in the works. He used the labyrinth of accesses to enter the stockade to free us."

Kleeve Hartus's shock was a block of C-4 going high order. "Of what do you speak?"

Again, Marviel Lanconin nodded in permission.

"There are many secret passages throughout Shansara known only to my family. Do not judge my nephew as you judge us. He has many weaknesses and is indebted to me from gambling debts. His participation was coerced by my hold over him. You have no conspirators within the Guard that I know of."

"How did you communicate with your nephew to coordinate this complex task?"

Marviel Lanconin answered, "Our legal counselor."

The first shield looked at me with mouth askew. "A curse on all lawyers. You will reveal all details of these secrets, fully, and to my satisfaction when we return to Shansara. Name all others in support of your cabal and I will recommend lenience to the arbiters. I will put this in document binding both the Kingdom and your party. Is it agreed?"

Affirmatives passed from all lips.

"Who else participated in the plot to murder the Warlord?"

The head of their scheme spoke. "None. I procured the medicament that subdued him without the knowledge of the owner."

"You will name its source and we will determine the innocence of the owner. And the air car used in your escape?"

The former minister of works said, "The works have a fleet, secreted and unrevealed."

Kleeve Hartus shook his head. "So, in addition to your other crimes, you ignored the call to give all support to the kingdom when ordered by the queen? Pathetic. And what of the air wizards? What knew they of the murder plot?"

Tyreen Sorell burst out, "Absolutely nothing! We were incarcerated when that occurred. No indignity or threat could make this soul which has been dedicated to sustaining life conjure such thought or act."

"It is true, lords," Marviel Lanconin said. "I swear it is so."

Kleeve Hartus drummed his fingers on a bicep. "There will be more you must account for, but if you continue to produce without evasion, I will continue to honor the pact of favor. Warlord?"

"Almost. If I'm going to release the wizards to remain in Maleska Mal to man the air factory, I want to know why. Why didn't you tell the queen you had a solution? Why didn't you put it into play a long time ago? And you, Marviel Lanconin. Why did you want me dead?"

With not a whit of contrition, but instead with pure candor, he said, "You forced our hand. When the queen jailed the wizards, I knew it marked the peril of Vistara. The supreme guild master assured me that your water priest could not succeed. And with an unstoppable White Ape at her side, there would be no recourse or petition to the queen by which to return them to their rightful seats."

"Unstoppable is right, huh?" Dave taunted. To that the general swallowed bitterly.

My exasperation meter was pegging. "Tyreen Sorell, I am mystified by the constant intransigence that has led us to where we are now. This could've all been solved so easily. Why?"

His scornful aloof gone, he said, "I have had much time to consider my failure, Warlord. Fear, is my answer. Fear that if the true nature of the predicament were known, we would lose position. Fear that we would not be able to address the challenge. Fear that the asphyxiation of Vistara is unavoidable. I regret my selfish omission and commissions. I repent."

"I know there's an ancient enmity between your guild and the water priests, but you fought Cynar's help at every step."

Now the man recovered some backbone. "And tell me, Warlord, has your hermit brought our salvation?"

"No."

Dave took up. "So, what's changed? Why do you think you have the answer now? Especially if he's failed, too?"

"I may have been blinded by the hatred of my guild for his, and especially by their reigning buffoon, but it has a history and one that explains why he fails. He is as much bound by his prejudices as are we by ours. His sect is willfully ignorant to the existence of the full spectrum of rays. The tenth, eleventh, and twelfth rays are thought heresy by his discipline. And it is the eleventh ray which fails, which is why the works have dwindled so."

"Ben-dog, didn't one of the air wizards say something about how they communicated over long distance by the tenth ray? Cynar had a conniption about it, said it was nonsense."

Tyreen Sorell seemed placated. "See? As I told you."

"What's the issue? You can't generate the eleventh ray anymore? What makes you think you can do it now?"

"The Filestra works, I believe, may hold hope." He used the older Mihdra name for Maleska Mal. "When it was closed by the vile Domeel Doreen and our brethren tortured and expelled, it was my counsel to tread lightly. If King Harsan Partell exercised force that drove the Mydreen to harm the works in retaliation, it would be far worse than if it had been left asleep. Two hundred cycles ago, the plants were all still functioning adequately. Not at true capacity, but far better than now. It was as the situation worsened that I petitioned King Osric Darmon to try for reconciliation."

"And we all know what happened from there," Dave interjected. "Talis Darmon ended up a hostage."

"Were you one of those advising against a retaliation to rescue her?"

"The Mydreen are childish and contrary. They have always acted in a manner to turn every hand against them. It was more vital than ever the plant not be harmed. But then to compound tragedy—your monstrous compatriots destroyed the plant in Califex! The situation could hardly have been made worse. The constriction of my predicament grew."

"What's the way forward?"

"The essence that produces the eleventh ray is rare. So much so, that when my ancestors built the works across Vistara, it required many generations laboring to gather enough of the essence to power the processes of the works. The manner of extracting that essence is lost. Wars and calamities and time have removed the knowledge. We have tried for many lifetimes to rediscover it, and have failed. We are shadows of the great intellects who came before us.

"For two hundred years, these works have sat silent. I faced choices that have tortured me long and dreadfully, so awful they are that they have left me impotent in the face of them. The easiest path is to restart the works of Filestra. The production would prolong the life of Vistara for a time while another solution may yet be found. We have perhaps another two hundred years until it too fades."

"But another solution doesn't seem likely, does it?"

"It does not."

"And the other option?"

"The material is highly toxic. The chamber here has been at rest for perhaps long enough to have calmed the furor of its power if exposed. I do not know if it is possible, but if it can be extracted safely, I hold hope that with examination it would lead to a way to locate other of its like. To recreate its refinement and concentration."

My heart skipped a beat. "To copy it?"

Dave nearly swallowed his tongue as he struggled to regain control. "Ben-dog, do you mean—Baby Blue?"

"We know who to ask."

✳ ✳ ✳

Kleeve Hartus spoke to himself as I removed the cuffs from the wizards. "So many secrets have combined to undermine this kingdom for so long, I wonder if we have truly reached the floor of their depths."

With the wizards behind me, I discussed all with the queen and Karlo. She yielded to our engineer.

"Baby Blue has a mass spectrometer and quantum state analyzer. If it's any form of matter, I suppose it's possible. Can it reproduce whatever this stuff is? How can I say? But I have another plan I've been working on."

"What?"

"Electrolysis. We do exactly what Cynar's railed against. We build plants to electrolyze the oxygen out of the water. I also got Cynar to admit there's ice at the poles we could mine. It would require projects on several grand scales. But even if we split every water molecule from every source, it won't be enough to replenish an atmosphere. So, we concentrate the oxygen in the domed cities we'll build. In the decades that requires, we'll be wearing oxygen masks. The new cities will be even more of a closed biosphere than we are now, and we'll have to go to strict population control. But I think we can maintain a balance between water production and electrolysis that will sustain life."

"Doesn't sound like much of a future, Karlo."

"But it is a future, Ben."

If ever I'd seen Talis Darmon in turmoil, it was now. With eyes closed, she placed a hand on her chest and took a slow, rising breath as if willing the air dense again. Sighing in exhale, she opened her eyes again, composed.

"Tyreen Sorell, step forward. I make the decision for you. With all your gifts and powers, with all responsibility and dedication to life, I commission you to extract this essence for examination. I forgive any and all crimes, revealed or yet concealed by you and your guild, and restore you to the confidence of your queen."

The three wizards bowed deeply.

"Leave us. I would have words alone with the Warlord."

"For what it's worth, Talis Darmon, I agree with your decision, not that we conferred."

"Some things a regent cannot ask another to bear with her. They could have fled to Annameria or elsewhere to live out their lives in safety. They chose to go to Maleska Mal with intent to act in good faith, though it has all been done in a way frightfully distorted and vain. Are you prepared that the arbiters may grant more than mere lenience for Marviel Lanconin and his conspirators? They may be found to have acted reasonably and released?"

"Such is life."

"Do you return now?"

"Yes. I want to investigate the goings on here before we do. This place is a ghost town."

"Then make haste, my love. More than ever, I wish to live in the moments we have. Before another crisis looms, we must return to the subject of our wedding."

"Powder-blue tuxedos and top hats it is, my princess."

✖ ✖ ✖

The streets were desolate. "Haven't seen a rat yet, Ben. Detectives call that a clue." The Mydreen caged vereen and raised them for food, and the vermin were common sights in the streets, feasting off the refuse.

"I guess Domeel Doreen's call to Pyreenia was well heeded."

Calus Gree hailed me from down a street, "Warlord. We have located a household of Mydreen to question."

They were in poor shape. The old man had two broken tusks. One of the women was missing an arm. Scrawny children hid in the next room.

"Tell the Warlord what you told us," Calus Gree urged.

The old man blindly squinted in the big Tarn's direction.

"Little to tell. All those able followed the call, left. It was promised that those who stayed would be rewarded when Domeel Doreen returned, and the wealth raided from the Red cities shared with all. But after you Korundi came, there was little reason for the young to stay, and they too left to answer the call. Those of us who have grown too weak to ride remain."

I was missing something. "What do you mean, grandfather? When did the Korundi come?"

He covered head with all hands. The women brayed their sorrow. One angrily answered me, "The nesting grounds." She hid her face and spoke no more.

"I want to see."

The lieutenant gestured a trooper forward. "This Korundi will show you."

I piloted us and followed the trooper's directions. "You've been here before?"

"Yes, Warlord. I came to Shansara late as part of the reinforcements sent by Chieftain Parkus Laan in support of his friend the queen. But I was not a hatchling in your ranks when I arrived, Warlord. I was already blooded, honored to be selected for the war party that avenged the Korund."

I put us down near the barren foothills. With Sarkan Sell and Jodal Jark ever ready at our flanks, Dave and I followed the soldier into a pass. At a sure-footed pace, he led us to the bowl that was the nesting grounds of the Mydreen.

"Before he was made chieftain, Parkus Laan commanded us to see our house avenged. We traveled many days beneath the Korund Range to reach our assignment. While we missed the glory of joining your great battles in Clymaira and Shansara, we returned to Califex with honor, Warlord. We left not one egg intact."

Shattered shells lay in their graves, more than I could count. Tiny skeletons rendered to pieces littered the bowl.

"There are two more I can show you to confirm the debt to our offspring was well settled, Warlord."

I thought about another egg. Not shattered, but grown cold and bathed in Talis Darmon's tears.

"No, trooper. I believe you."

✳ ✳ ✳

Dave removed his wristlet and presented it to Tyreen Sorell. "Don't lose it."

"Someone will check in with you daily so that you can keep us appraised of your progress. I assume you can get your own communications working to contact your people in the other works?"

"I conceal nothing, Warlord. Yes."

"If talking to your people in Annameria or elsewhere aids your work, do so. But do not betray the confidence of the queen. Any knowledge you transmit may provide help to those who seek to harm us, you understand? I'm placing great trust in you by not smashing your console as was done in Thoria."

"Thank you. Warlord. So that you are aware, that one is again functioning."

"Then on behalf of us all, I wish you success, Supreme Guild Master Tyreen Sorell."

With everyone loaded, including our prisoners, we lifted.

"I don't even know what to think about that scene, brah. I remember Double-K swearing to exterminate all the Mydreen. I kind of thought it was a grandiose statement, but I guess the Korundi always mean what they say."

"The Mydreen brought it down on themselves by what they did to the nesting grounds in Califex. I wonder if Khraal Kahlees knew?"

"He knows how we react to this kind of stuff. He just kept it to himself. Still, I'll tell him what we saw and pretend he didn't know. Might buy me a little goodwill and take some of the heat out of whatever revenge he has planned for the grid square thing."

I laughed weakly. "Brother, I don't want to joke about this. We can't condone genocide. Not by the Mydreen, not by the Korundi. I just don't know that there's anything we can do about it."

"Tarn gonna Tarn, brah."

20

Talis Darmon would not be in attendance.

"I cannot be seen to bear influence, Benjamin Colt."

By any design, it would be recognizable as a courtroom. A panel of three sat high behind an onyx black bench. I was given a crash course in Vistaran judicial proceedings by the first shield. "The woman in the center wearing the gold robe is the chief arbiter. Just follow her instructions and speak to her as if she were the only person in the room." We sat on one side opposite the four accused. There were sniffles and weeping from behind us where the families sat as a herald read the long statement contained in the favor of admission.

It was a brief affair from there. After Kleeve Hartus, I was called to stand and give an account of my abduction and what followed.

"Warlord, is it your testimony that the accused were not coerced by physical means nor threat of reprisal made against their families to secure their admissions?"

"I do so swear, Chief Arbiter."

"You may be seated."

The counselor was on his feet. "Chief Arbiter, the Thulian Benjamin Colt is a being of supernatural strength and deadly reputation—nay, one who has been proven unstoppable in his homicidal ability and cruelty. He has committed acts of deadly violence with his bare hands even against his own soldiers! It can be implied that by his mere presence, the threat of great physical harm would be communicated to my clients if they refused to cooperate."

Kleeve Hartus was on his feet. "The incident so referred to was one of self-defense against a craven attack on the Warlord's person by deranged Thorian insurgents, come to Shansara with the sole purpose of assassinating the Warlord. Benjamin Colt's integrity is not on trial here."

The judge nodded. "Agreed, First Shield. We do not countenance any slur against his character."

While the audience chattered, I whispered to the first shield, "How is that guy still practicing? He was part of the conspiracy to bust those guys out of jail."

Muttering, Kleeve Hartus seethed, "The arbiters have held in abeyance the accusation against him until they conclude their own investigation. They tread carefully against their own kind because all hold ransom over each other, curse them. There are no honest lawyers, only the rare honest man who practices law."

The chief arbiter touched a chime calling for quiet. "The accused have waived their right to offer further defense, having fully admitted their acts and the collective beliefs by which they formed their decisions. We rule the admission valid. Our panel now departs to consider a just edict. If the accused feel there are additional facts not contained in the document that may further mitigate their actions, or additional statements of remorse that may further influence our sentence, they may make them at this time."

Marviel Lanconin stood. "I have been asked by my fellow accused to speak for us all."

The judge nodded.

"We unanimously ask that we be allowed to take the journey north, to travel the Blix, and pass through Temple Farnest to join our ancestors in the underworld." More sobs broke out behind us.

"I anticipated this," Kleeve Hartus whispered to me. "Hearing their own admission read in open court, they correctly judge that the air is against the panel finding them justified and would release them. If sentenced to imprisonment, they could not then petition to take the journey. With execution removed from possibility by their bargain, it is their last chance to avoid a cell rather than gamble."

The chime sounded again.

"The request has been made properly before sentencing. The court suspends further deliberation until a priest renders the request pious or false. The declarers will be escorted to the temple."

We got up as the arbiters left, and bailiffs escorted the four men from the courtroom. In Kleeve Hartus's office, the first shield poured thimbles of green syrup for each of us. Dave drained his in one shot and held for another.

"Someone's got to explain this to me. I've heard about the Blix and Farnest and the underworld for so long, they don't even register as something I don't understand. Are these real places?"

Kleeve Hartus propped his feet on his desk. "They are, David Masamuni."

"Dave's right. I'm in the dark on this, too. I've just always thought it's some kind of allegory for dying, or committing suicide, or something like that. But these things don't make it clear." I pointed to my decipher.

Dave took another shot. "The few times I've ever asked about it, I've gotten looks like I had a dick growing outta my forehead. It's cool to talk about sex at the dinner table, but ask a question about this stuff, and you get treated like you pooped in the punch bowl."

Kleeve Hartus choked amid laughter, wiping thick green droplets from the desktop. "That translated well enough, my friend."

It was time to go for it. I downed mine. "Kleeve Hartus, can a couple of displaced Thulians ask you about the afterlife without giving offense?"

"Yes. We've been through much together. To us!"

We all drank to his toast, and he began.

"I am not given to piety, but our afterlife transcends such. The underworld is where all Vistarans travel once they leave the surface. The Temple Farnest lies deep beneath the Sharpa Mountains in the farthest north, reached by riding the sacred river of the Blix. Celeste Hom is the portal temple, from whence the Blix forms from springs sent from the underworld. It is guarded by the servants of the White Lords, the Hortha.

"Some reach Celeste Hom by the pilgrimage of expiation—a difficult foot journey north to reach the portal temple. But most choose to travel to Celest Hom by the Iridium Path from the greater temple of Transspellum.

"At Celest Hom, the pious are admitted by the Hortha to ride on crystal craft over the coursing waters of the Blix until arriving at Temple Farnest. There the White Lords review each person's record of life and admit the traveler to pass through Farnest, and finally join their ancestors to live in the center of Vistara in the eternal underworld."

He wiped misty eyes. "For those that die without making such pilgrimage, the soul awakens from slumber in a revitalized and perfect form to be joined to one's ancestors in joyous reunion."

I downed another and let the burn incinerate my astonished skepticism.

Not Dave.

"Do people just skip all the extra steps and kill themselves to get to the underworld? Seems a lot easier."

The look Dave had previously described came over our friend's face.

"Did you not understand what I said? What derangement would cause one to choose such a path? To miss the resplendent journey that is the birthright of every Vistaran? I am no adherent, and I have surely failed to describe with due reverence the beauty of such an experience and how it prepares one for the eternal underworld. Are you not touched by what I share with you? You too are now Vistarans. It is the afterlife you also have awaiting you."

I tried to calm the waters of respect Dave agitated.

"It is an amazing picture you paint, brother. Thank you for sharing something so personal and sacred. But what happens now with the four defendants?"

"It is formality. The priest will find them dedicated and consecrate their departure. They'll travel from the city temple to Transspellum in the Hah Shur Valley and travel the Iridium Path north."

I asked him to tell us about that. I cringed as Dave summarized. "So, it's a high-speed underground train. Why didn't someone mention that earlier? We could've used that to infil from the Korund instead of the aqueduct."

Kleeve Hartus was on his feet. "You test the bonds of our brotherhood by such irreverence, David Masamuni!"

Sex, politics, religion. On Vistara, I guess it was just religion you didn't mix with booze. I intervened.

"Davey-Dave! Apologize, bro."

He meekly tilted his thimble to show it was empty.

"Too much to drink, brother. It's my Japanese blood, Kleeve Hartus. When you see this face turn red, I'm not responsible for anything I say. I didn't mean to be rude. Honest."

The first shield's posture said the sting of Dave's desecration was still felt. "I forgive the insult. I too have imbibed. It is perhaps not the proper atmosphere in which to discuss such matters. The fault is mine."

Dave slurred, "Let's all forgive and forget. We're all we've got, brothers."

Kleeve Hartus relaxed. "It is so." He was sullen for a time. "I judge you both harshly and unfairly. All on Vistara are educated in these truths from hatching. Perhaps there will come a time when you would desire to speak to the city priest and receive instruction?"

"Maybe," I offered and left it at that. I didn't want to stir the waters muddy again. Religion didn't seem to be a big deal here. The single building in each city that I'd been told was a temple were all uniformly conspicuous only by their small footprint and plain design. I'd rarely even seen one of the white-robed priests that occupied them. From all that, I'd assumed religion was of minor importance.

If Kleeve Hartus didn't think himself much of an adherent, yet had such a visceral response to his beliefs being challenged, then I'd blown it again. If I'd fouled up at cross-cultural communication this badly on Robin Sage, my Q-course instructors would've sent me back to the 82nd the same day.

"If it would help your faith, do you wish to see?"

"I've seen the Hortha, Kleeve Hartus. You don't have to prove to me they're real. And Temple Farnest seems a long way. "

"Do not be ridiculous, Benjamin Colt. There is no return once on the Blix. I invite you to see the greater temple and witness the travelers depart on the Iridium Path."

✶ ✶ ✶

We staggered out together, a Guard flying us each home. I dropped onto our bed, my head spinning for reasons more than drink. I stirred when Talis Darmon parted the covers.

"I did not wish to disturb you. You are still dressed and slept through dinner. So, the saying is true that even a single day before the arbiters is a war to tax the strongest soldier."

"I've been drinking."

"Proving the other saying, that a day in court ends in drunkenness, no matter win or loss. And you were not even on trial. The four scoundrels take the ride to Farnest, eh? I think they would take the long way there so the record of life would show them in kinder light."

"I don't know what to think, baby. What's next? I get red pilled and wake up from the Matrix? I find the sunglasses that let me see the real world? Or do green Martians land in a flying saucer and tell me everything I know is wrong? Sorry, not that last one. There really are green Martians." Whatever she said next, I lost as I passed out again.

Kleeve Hartus retrieved Dave and I the next morning. We flew last in the procession over the rolls and dips of the desert in a direction I had not traveled and soon landed where irregular sawtooth peaks formed the palisades of a tiny mountain range protecting a hidden valley. It was not possible to see over the peaks into what lay within.

I'd sworn Dave to silence. "I promise. For once in my life, I ain't sayin' nuttin', I'm so freaked out trying not to imagine what we might see."

There was a well-worn path ahead and we followed at a distance behind the four white-robed travelers and their families. The path wound through the peaks until a short tunnel bored through the rock beckoned with daylight beyond. Instead of a depression formed by the impact of some massive celestial body, it looked as if it had all been formed by something expelled from beneath the surface, like steel plate pierced by a bullet to leave jagged petals as shelter around the deep crater. Even passing overhead, it would be difficult to glimpse what lay inside.

"There is Transspellum, the greater temple of Hah Shur. Magnificent, is it not? Out of respect, we will remain at a great distance from the temple entrance as we are not family."

We traversed the descending corniche to the bottom and remained there as the procession advanced. Much like the lone temple in Shansara, a simple smooth white cuboid waited. At the party's approach, a seamless portal slid open and a white-robed priest appeared. It was some distance away and what lay through the open passage was obscured by the activity—there were hugs and crying with farewells—until all parted to allow the white-robed pilgrims to follow the priest inside.

A gilt carriage awaited them. The four ascended and sat. The priest bowed and the conveyance slid away, followed by the portal sealing slowly to a close. Kleeve Hartus broke me from raptured attention.

"We should depart from Hah Shur ahead of the families. It is only proper."

Dave continued to keep his word to me as we flew back, maintaining perfect silence as though he'd cut out his own tongue to keep the promise. The unflappable master of cool guy toughness looked worried. I thought carefully and several times tested my questions before airing them.

"Does everyone on the planet come here?"

"From east and west, pilgrims travel here. In far Turmallia, there is a similar, greater temple, as there are in the south. Portal temples likewise exist in other places to reach the springs of the Blix. At the southernmost, there is also a final temple by which to meet the White Lords and make passage to the center of Vistara."

He dropped us both off together at the garrison and we bid him thanks and goodbye. Before we entered the gates, I had to hear it.

"Well?"

Permission given, Dave's mouth opened, closed, then opened again.

"To keep what little sanity I have remaining, I beg you, brah—let us never speak of this again."

21

Some days are just good days if for no reason other than no one's trying to kill you, and frankly, I'd been due. Layers of bodyguards and locked doors gave me respite, but it was each day returning to Talis Darmon and a real home—complete with a tail-wagging puppy—that returned my peace. No one can live at condition red all the time without becoming a paranoid mess. And when guys lose the ability to turn the rheostat of situational awareness from high to low and back as needed, that's exactly what happens.

What would make today a *great* day would take more than just an absence of murder aimed at yours truly. I needed a win. When Karlo summoned me, grinning and refusing to reveal the reason, something told me I might get one, and that Christmas was coming early.

Dave was waiting in the warehouse with Karlo as Apache and I strolled past security. Unlike the sailboat hidden in one of those magic eye 3D images—which I could never see, no matter how long I stared at the card and stupidly ranged it back and forth while trying *not* to focus, per the instructions—I knew what these three things were without any coaching. A self-propelled anti-aircraft gun, a mortar, and an honest-to-goodness tank. It wasn't the size of an M-1, but by any name, it was a tank.

Any lingering resentment I still held because Santa never put a GI Joe aircraft carrier or Cobra Commander A-10 under the tree was no more.

"You like, Ben-dog?" Karlo beamed like Clark W. Griswold showing off the light display.

I broke into a Cynar-esque mad cackle.

"Hehehe. Like? I think I'm in love!"

"If you're not thinking about the next war, you're only ready to fight the last one. These are all prototype proofs of concept. But they're in finished enough form that I thought it was finally time to reveal the products of my Golden Hub skunk works."

He patted the four-barreled gun platform. "If Annameria comes, it'll be by air. This is medicine for that snake bite. Modified K-maxes on a floater." Next, he stood in front of the 4.2-inch mortar. "My contractors can produce the tubes, but there's no chemical propellant industry here, so Baby Blue has to make the rounds. I thought about real artillery, but this is the quickest way to improve our ranged warfare capability."

Lastly, he walked over to the grounded monster. "This is the best bang for our buck to deal with ground threats. I've put all small arms production from Baby Blue into making .308 for the miniguns and 240s. No reason to make M4s for the army anymore since K-spec manufacture's humming along. This is a highly mobile armored package that lets us utilize our best anti-personnel weapons."

"Little shiny, isn't it, brah?"

"Don't be a buzzkill, Dave. Prototype means it's a primitive form."

"I was ignoring him, but thank you, Ben."

Dave kept at it. "Speaking of skunk works, looks like it's stealthed with all those angles. Expecting to sneak it in under someone's radar? No even uses that on Mars."

"Don't even bother responding to him, Ben. He's just yanking my chain. He already knows the faceted surfaces are to defeat impacts from kinetic and energy-based weapons. Wish I could tell you that we were ready to produce and field all this, but not quite."

"When do you start testing?"

"Done some. Real trials start when we get the troops back from Pyreenia."

I was riding high. "Karlo, on top of everything else you've accomplished, this is nothing short of stupendous. It couldn't have come at a better time. Lest I let myself get too optimistic, anything substantial to report from Maleska Mal?"

"Maybe. I detailed one of Perrin Halser's senior guys to be the day-to-day contact, but yesterday I spoke to Tyreen Sorell myself. He says the work is very touchy and slow going. I mentioned I'd be at a point soon where I could divert the time to come help if he desired. Know what he said?"

Dave guessed. "Told you to get stuffed because you're a moron?"

"He thanked me and said he'd welcome my input. If he got to a point where he was stuck, he said he'd consult me."

My mouth dropped. "Was he sincere?"

"Pretty sure he was."

"He invite Cynar?"

"That he did not."

"Baby steps. How's Cynar? I haven't seen him in a while."

"His ego's on the mend. His girlfriend's back and he's working again. You should go see him. It'd cheer him up to insult your intelligence."

"Who am I not to facilitate a friend's hobby?"

There was a skip in my step and I was on the sunny side of the street. Apache sensed my joy, panting happily as he waddled with me. It had in fact gone from a good day to a *great* day. I had nothing but stellar news to bring home for supper and afterward, could sit down and plan a wedding without feeling like we were on the deck of the *Titanic*, rushing the padre to hitch us before we sank into freezing waters.

My wristlet hummed mid whistle in my chorus of "Walking on Sunshine," and I opened the cloud to a face that abruptly shuffled the iTunes of my emotional playlist straight to "Raining Blood."

Brandon Bryant.

"This didn't go so well last time, Colt, so before you get all spun up, I have something important to talk to you about. Something important for everyone. So can you be cool?"

✳ ✳ ✳

The best I could manage wasn't very good.

"I'm cool as a refrigerated pear, Bryant."

My lame rejoinder made him smirk in the way I hated so much. Bryant had a wristlet. How? I had a million questions, but he'd ambushed me and the only way out of the kill zone was to close the comm. So even though I'd just dropped through a trap door onto a bed of sharpened spikes—the longest and sharpest one right up my waste ejection port—I had to take it.

"Good for you, Colt. Catch you at a bad time?"

What was I going to say?

"Just a second."

A quick look around for a quiet spot to park it and Apache dropped at my feet. Not exactly a SCIF, but his bulk had the effect of making passersby take a wide detour while I pondered where this was going.

"How did you get—" I pointed at this wrist.

"Not here to talk about that, Colt."

Grrr. We were compromised. I wondered how long he'd had one of our devices and if there was any way he'd been able to use it to eavesdrop on our private comms. It meant he either got one from a source he had here in Shansara or...

"You got it from Pyreenia. We lost one there." We had a very strict count on the devices. The only one I knew to be missing was the one taken from Avril Mysteen. Bryant smiled with the smart-ass expression that was one of the many I wanted to smash off his face.

"I'll throw you a bone. I have a net running there. Surprised? It's not a brag when it's true; I'm twice the operations and intelligence specialist you are."

"Then you know I cleaned house there. If you *had* a net, it's dead now. Every member of your army, both Red and Green, is worm food, and I was there to see your stooge Domeel Doreen's head get separated from his body. You've got nothing left in Mihdradahl to threaten us with."

"I didn't call to make threats, Colt, but it is fun to rattle your cage."

"Get to the point, Bryant. Or piss off, because you're wasting my time. Anything you tell me I'm automatically treating as a hundred percent disinformation."

Bryant considered this.

"Fair 'nuff. Believe it or not, I didn't buzz you just to rile you up, but I understand our history makes it kinda tough. I meant what I said, I have something you want to hear. So, if I give you some background on what I've been up to, maybe it'll let you up my source rating to something more reliable."

"I'm listening."

"Let me ask you, when you were in Pyreenia, did you see Chuckie?"

I'd already blown my cool and given him information I shouldn't have, telling him about losing a wristlet in Pyreenia. Stupid of me. His question about Chuck was a weird one, but I couldn't see how answering and even doing it honestly could come back on me.

"No."

"And did you wonder why?"

"I figured he just ran to his big brother, wherever you are now."

"I'm in Annameria, Colt, and Chuck's not welcome here."

That was a big reveal. Not that Bryant was in the Yellow Kingdom— that I suspected—but that he and Chuck were on the outs.

"Keep going."

"I made inroads with the Yellow Kingdom early on, while Chuck was working the prince and getting Pyreenia set straight to invade Shansara. I like it here. If we'd have crashed here, things would be entirely different now. What do you know about the Yellows, Colt?"

"I know enough."

"They're not a half-ass, third-world nation like Mihdradahl. Shit here is locked down and squared away."

"If that's true, then what did you have to offer them?"

He rolled his eyes.

"Tsk, tsk, Colt. Try not to be an asshole. It's simple." He ticked off fingers. "I brought first-rate intel from the other side of the Grand Canyon on what was happening with their biggest rival. I brought samples of better weapons and a track record of superior tactics utilizing them, all proven by how we took a bunch of desert dwellers and led them to take over Mihdradahl."

"Not quite."

"I'll give you that. But in addition to the tech I brought—which they went gaga over—I made friends the old-fashioned way." He held up a shining bar of gold.

"Where'd that come from? You steal it from some vault in Mihdradahl?"

Gold was rare here. Rarer than on Earth. He chuckled.

"You never knew. The Agency and State Department geeks wanted hard currency on hand in the future. Gold. Platinum. Synthetic diamonds and rubies. Stuff that has value for exchange and for industrial use." My face scrunched in disbelief as I tried to imagine how that could be true when he lit on my puzzlement with a smile. "Only Mike, the captain, and I knew. It was all spread out and concealed in containers with other mundane supplies on the C-17. Me and Marky cached it in the desert before we took the team to Maleska Mal. I recovered all of it and staged it in Pyreenia, that is until it was time for me to take it south and put it to use making new friends."

Bryant and Marky spent a lot of time together out of my sight in those early days on Mars. I believed him.

"Congrats. Glad you've found a new bunch to exploit. But you also know that whatever you've conned them into thinking's a big deal is all a 1970 console TV compared to the flat screen 5K LEDs we've cranked out. If you're trying to tell me you're making the Yellows a peer-level threat to us—you're smoking dope."

"Chill, Colt. If anything, you should be thanking me. I'm the one's calmed the supreme magnate down about trying to jump into your backyard while you all are on your heels."

"I bet."

"It's true. But you're getting us off track. I'm trying to explain why you should take me seriously about what I'm trying to get your help with."

"My help? To do what?"

He put a restraining palm up.

"Bear with me just a little while longer, Colt. Wanna know *why* I'm in Aetheria and Chuck's not?"

I couldn't resist.

"Because we smoked the balls off you and your army and it was the only way to save your own ass?"

"Because what was waiting in Pyreenia for Chuck was something I couldn't control. Convincing Domeel Doreen that our interests were aligned? A newbie out of the Q course could've done it. But in Pyreenia, the tables got turned. I wasn't playing the prince to get what I wanted. He was using us to get what he wanted. What *they* wanted. Chuck was well on the way to being one of them by the time I got there. I played along, deceived them for a while and resisted, until if I didn't want to end up like the rest of them, I had to leave."

It was time for him to give without getting. I shook my head like I didn't understand, but I pictured black witches casting clouds of death, a keloid brand, and a monstrous green eye.

"You haven't figured it out yet, have you, Colt? You think you're sitting pretty. I'm in the lowlands and our atmosphere plants are working fine." He took a deep breath and blew it out with theatrical ecstasy. "You're asphyxiating. But before that'll kill you, underneath your feet is something about to swallow you whole. And someday, it may reach Annameria. So, before that happens, I thought I'd give you a heads-up and get you focused on your real problem. You still don't have a clue, do you?"

He squinted at me in contempt.

"The Yellows figured it out. The Karnak are coming back. And your buddy the hermit and the water guild caused it to happen. When you see him again, ask him why the sands are wet in the Furrow."

22

I CALLED FOR AN EMERGENCY INNER COUNCIL. I WOULD HAVE BROUGHT Double-K in by cloud from wherever he was on the trail from Pyreenia, but I had big questions about our OPSEC. Without explaining why, I collected everyone's wristlet and placed them under guard in the anteroom. Bryant had told me more, and I related the chronology of what happened to our enemy after we took back the capital.

"Bryant and Domeel Doreen were with their army in Shansara while Chuck led the attack on Clymaira. They all escaped to Pyreenia, even half-dead Chuck. Bryant was intent on rebuilding the army to try at us again, but he couldn't stick it out. He lost control of what was going on there. Domeel Doreen became erratic. Chuck had become strange long before the mustard gas attack, but afterward, things got worse.

"The witches went to work repairing Chuck. Domeel Doreen became a babbling incompetent. Black uniforms. Ceremonies and brands. Bryant tried to distance himself from the witches, but one day the head gal cornered him to be 'inducted,' and that straw broke the camel's back. Bryant may be an egotistical shitbag, but he's not stupid. He saw rightly that whatever Chuck had stumbled into in Pyreenia was the kind of influence he couldn't bend to suit his ends, and gave up on Mihdradahl entirely to save himself."

"Fills in some blanks," Dave said. "The cult stuff was too much, even for him. Guess we blew it by not hitting Pyreenia right away."

Karlo shook his head. "We had nothing left. It would've been one massive Gettysburg-style bayonet charge."

Talis Darmon dismissed it with a wave. "That is the past. You have retaken Pyreenia. Wherever the witches hide, I cannot taste their scent on the winds of perception. What concerns me is the stench in the form of Brandon Bryant. Surely, he stirs trouble for us in the south. Benjamin Colt, do you believe that the Thulian now holds influence with the supreme magnate of Annameria?"

"I don't believe the Yellow Kingdom isn't a threat on his say-so, that's what I believe. And I'm worried he knows too much about us. Cynar, could he be using the wristlet to monitor our conversations without us knowing?" The devices were partially telepathic, similar to the deciphers. One simply thought about who to talk to and the link was established.

Cynar was focused and clear.

"I understand your concern, but no. It is more likely that he has a compatriot in our midst with whom he communicates."

"I'm an idiot. I blew it big time by spilling that we lost one in Pyreenia. I haven't been caught so off guard since I answered a knock on my barracks door to find my battalion commander looking at me like murder. Someone told him his daughter was in my room."

"You never told me that one, brah."

"She wasn't, but she was in the barracks."

"Yikes."

Karlo huffed, "I'd have been just as surprised at seeing Bryant, Ben. But if he just rolled with your slip and didn't actually get the wristlet from Pyreenia, then we have to consider there's a Rosenburg among us. Cynar, could there be one that made it out of your shop without you knowing?"

Cynar shook his head solemnly.

"They have all been built by these hands in the secure workspace next to Baby Blue. I believe the most logical explanation is the most obvious. Though Benjamin Colt has the self-control of a rutting godahl, hehehe, the one in Brandon Bryant's possession came from Pyreenia. If you make contact with him again, I may be able to confirm its signature. That is, if you think you can risk doing so without giving away more secrets, hehehe."

Whatever existential crisis he'd suffered for failing to fix the atmosphere works, the sea legs of his deprecating wit were firmed up enough to support his riding the tossing deck of my self-esteem.

"Glad you're back to your old form, Cynar. Kleeve Hartus, this is an internal security problem. We'll get you a list of every device holder, and your investigators can start a counterintelligence operation to look for a possible leak."

"This is a task we will undertake with great relish, Warlord."

That settled, there was the last big reveal to share. When Bryant named them, I nearly swallowed my tongue.

"I have to put you on the spot, Cynar. Bryant said something pretty incredible. And he specifically told me to ask you about it. The Yellows say there's groundwater rising through the sands of the Furrow."

"Eh? Impossible."

"Why?"

"Because—" He clouded over. "Because it cannot be!"

Talis Darmon grasped my arm. "Benjamin Colt! You waited to tell me this?"

"I'm sorry, my love. In the past hour I've had a lot to process. I wanted us all together and as certain as I could be that this tidbit stayed with only us."

She bit her knuckle, the gears turning in her head so loud, I could almost hear them mesh.

Dave was lost. "What?"

"Bryant said the Yellows believe the water bubbling up from the deepest part of the Furrow has something to do with—the Karnak. Cynar, could the products of the Revered Guild of the Life-Giving Waters have become so plentiful, that it's somehow constituted into a subterranean ocean?"

"Aiiiyee!" Talis Darmon shrieked, and my blood turned to ice. "I trust you as no other, but I could not give credence that you had actually fought them in the palace of Pyreenia. It wasn't that I doubted your experience, but the power of the witches to cloud minds is strong. Rather than probe further, I let it go to focus on the material matters of Pyreenia. I see now I was a fool.

"What Avril Mysteen witnessed was not vision cast upon him. He was transported to their realm! Awakened from ancient slumber, the Karnak live again in an ocean of blackness beneath us!"

Cynar gasped. "It cannot be!"

Karlo was mesmerized. "Cynar, the waters from your underground factory—building for so long, filling the bowels of Vistara as they have—when I saw your works, I knew the collective effluence had to be immense. It's risen to such heights to reach the ceiling of the Furrow. If this is true, then somewhere beneath the western plains of Mihdradahl, there's water enough to fill an underground sea."

Talis Darmon hadn't been the only one waiting to lay down their hole card.

"And in it, the leviathan god of the Karnak, Anso-Kylon, rules again."

✻ ✻ ✻

"As I told you," my queen said to me, "I have been in study during your absence, plunged into the delirium of the history of the Karnak and of their last days on Vistara. It is an indecipherable blur of myth mixed with reality, even more so than the rest of our antiquity. The syllables I thought meaningless I found mention of in records so ancient, they crumbled in my hands as I read them. Anso-Kylon was a god of the Karnak in their final days. A giant being that defies imagination. If not for all the small pieces of this puzzle collected before us, I would still discount the description as fable."

I flew us, taking direction from Dureen Zell. Next to Cynar, she was the oldest person I knew on Vistara.

"My lady, mark my words," she put in. "As small steel sharpens the longest sword and shavings kindle an inferno, such efforts can only serve to tease open the lock on things best kept imprisoned."

"And in ignorance lies peril, Dureen Zell."

"I found your witch, my lady. If she will aid you, I cannot say. Locating her was one thing, gaining her cooperation was another. She would not leave her den. If I'd thought it so important that the queen must deign to go to *her*, I would have kidnapped her to drop at your feet."

The old woman was a feisty one. I had the scars to prove it.

"I'm glad you didn't," I told her. "That doesn't yield happy subjects. Ask me how I know." I wiggled my fingers at her and she made a grin that showed her gums. "What do you think she can tell us, Talis Darmon?"

"If anyone living can aid us in understanding, I believe it to be her."

"When you say she's a witch, do you mean like the ones in Pyreenia? I should've brought a whole platoon if that's the case."

Sarkan Sell, who'd been listening, rumbled, "Warlord, Jodal Jark and I will deal with her. We will gladly send another one to whatever afterlife awaits such corruption of flesh."

"She is of a kind far different from the black-robed women," Talis Darmon said. "We must tread lightly, though. And she will demand payment for her help. If I can bargain her price, she may have answers about that which touches us, both dark and light."

"You're the queen. How can she refuse?"

"She cares not for the authority of the Spectral Throne. I prefer to travel the path of ally with her rather than the ground of adversary, but if she refuses to respect the blood of the Sylah, I will instruct her in the folly of her hubris!"

We'd soon be in sight of the Furrow of the Creator's Hand, the enormous fracture in the surface of Vistara that was a Berlin Wall between north and south. I'd seen it from the inside, the walls many miles high and its bed a maze of inhospitable fissures and ridges. By comparison, the Grand Canyon was a tiny, jagged sidewalk crack.

Mesas and buttes dotted the landscape as the plains sank gradually deeper and deeper as we neared the southernmost boundary of Mihdradahl.

Dureen Zell kept her eyes on the horizon. "There, Warlord. The Towers of the Brothers. I hatched beneath their shadow. Never have they left my memory, nor has Dureen Zell left the memory of the Zi-Sahn. Land near the entrance."

What remained of the colossal monuments teased at the grandeur they once held. Carved from the very rock on either side of the valley were the decay of mighty men. Curved swords held in resting salute by hands folded over cross guards, the trunks of the giants long absent and without sign of their remnants below. I could only fantasize about what grand visage would have sat atop wide shoulders and broad chests of the ones who dominated this place, the trunkless forms another of the constant reminders of the glory Vistara left behind. Past the guardians, the way descended into a grand basin and in it a low city—ancient yet living.

A wide gorge fell off behind the city, one that split the remaining wastes as it traveled to a horizon where the sky ruled over an endless space of nothing.

I asked Dureen Zell, "This was once a port, wasn't it?"

"You are correct, Warlord. The Amethyst Sea kissed the shores and the deep haven harbor of Shelasa was a crossroads. The sisterhood remembers when the waters danced with her partners such as Shelasa and all of Oceania. The witch's den is far into the rim. We must walk to reach it. It is best that the Korundi remain here. Tarn are not welcome, and their presence would create much discord. As would your pet."

Apache knew he was being talked about and looked soulfully to me for reassurance.

I assured the Korundi it was fine, and we set off, leaving a distraught Apache to be soothed by Beraal's caresses. The people we saw were sullen and suspicious. Dureen Zell made a sign of recognition to each as we passed, interlacing her fingers and receiving the same in return. Once in the city, the greetings stopped and our presence became

unremarkable, especially as we took a deserted path to the border between habitation and the tall canyon walls that sheltered it.

"Why are Tarn unwelcome? Do the Mydreen raid the city?"

"The Mydreen avoid Shelasa. The Vermeel of the great chasm stay
well away also. My people do not have care for the rest of Vistara, and
Vistara has forgotten them."

"You came from here?"

"My parents took us to Shansara when I was young, and never
looked back. When my lady asked me to make this journey, I could
not even say with confidence that my people remained. But Shelasa
continues, as firm as the stone around her, stubborn in her refusal to
die unlike the ocean that once lapped at her bosom."

We followed the path between the rock face and the city toward
its far arm. Thin dribbles of water trickled from the strata to pool into
a narrow bowl that followed the contours of the wall for many steps.
"Here they value water. I have enduring memories of our long journey
on foot to Shansara. We survived the desert like the Mydreen. None
but the Zi-Sahn are raised to take but a few mouthfuls of water a day.
I remember as clearly as if it were yesterday how I knew I had reached
a fabled land of plenty, when my mother taught me to bathe as the
Mihdra did. It was a glory, the first touch of liquid caressing the skin
everywhere at once, immersing in water and breaking a great taboo.
Such are the memories of an old woman. Come."

We left the city to skirt over empty ground beneath the cliffs.
Perhaps this had once been a beach and beneath our feet were the preserved skeletons of the great aquatic beasts that swam the long dried sea
of Vistara? The images of great silver ships piercing purple waves came
alive as I imagined how it had once been. I wondered if Talis Darmon
was likewise lost in thoughts of the past as we trudged silently along.
Dureen Zell broke me out of my trance.

"Around this bend is her refuge."

A break in the cliffs grew wider, and through it, a collection of
stone huts, and at the head of the small basin sat a squat circular building ringed in spirals, as unlike from the low buildings of the city as

was the ordered form of a tiered wasp nest from a plain brick wall. I wondered at the impossible.

"Is that sculpted stone? It's not, is it?"

The stout cylinder of mottled brown and white stood ten meters tall and nearly as wide in the diameter.

"It was the shell of a creature that lived in the depths beyond," Dureen Zell said.

I no longer had to wonder if a fossil record existed. This was proof.

The eyeful that stepped from the entrance took my breath away. Her face was bronze and her hair a surging mass of waves of the same amethyst the sea had once been. Her skin was painted with a myriad of tattoos in vivid colors and detail. She wore the canvas of her body as clothing, with silver ornamentations piercing her flesh. As quickly as she appeared, she removed herself from our sight—not in retreat, but beckoning us into her audience.

There were internet sites that catered to that very look, but I'd not seen in person such a living work of the artist's needle. Not on Earth, and definitely not on Vistara. Talis Darmon placed a hand on my sword arm.

"She is not what she appears. And she will use her appearance to deceive and allure you. Do not fall prey to her trap. If we are in peril, I will unleash you. But until then, allow me to carry this battle. And, Benjamin Colt. Close your mouth."

23

THE CHAMBER WAS BATHED IN LIGHT FILTERED THROUGH THE TRANS-
lucent walls. Hanging from the ceiling was more of my fossilized evidence, the blanched skeletons of branching corals and ancient marine
creatures.

Facing away from us, unperturbed by our entrance, she spoke, her
voice sonorous and calm, "For many passings of the twin sisters across
the night sky have I heard your footfalls approaching, long before this
exiled child came to seek my presence. What delayed you from bringing the queen to me sooner, Dureen Zell?"

"I serve at her pleasure, not yours, Mother Oceansong."

"You have the fire of the Zi-Sahn, though so young and apart from
us so long."

Dureen Zell, young? She was wrinkled and sinewy like an old cow.
The painted woman turned and it was then I saw her eyes were the
same shade as her hair and the dead sea so named. She locked on Talis
Darmon like a Hellfire missile.

"I know your line, Sylah. The chime and colors of the Spectral
Throne send a proclamation to reach even Shelasa. Why have you
come?"

"I humble myself, Mother, to ask your guidance."

"And humility you should have. You are the last queen of a shriv-
eling land. But I demand further proof that you are worthy to be entrusted with our knowledge." She struck a defiant pose with her palms
toward us, purple emanations rising around her. Talis Darmon told me
to be cool until she said otherwise, and for me, a hand on my pistol still

qualified. It wasn't unless I drew that the line was crossed. I'd killed a black witch; a purple one shouldn't be a problem.

In response, my princess cast her own aura, different from any I'd yet seen. I remembered each of their different colors and energies like sunsets and rises changing with each season. This new glow came in pulses of red and grew in ferocity with her words.

"I have endured and triumphed, Mother Oceansong. I have grown by necessity. The teachers I needed were within me. Do not think to deny me."

The witch's violet radiance grew darker as Talis Darmon's became lighter, both expanding until they met and melded into a mist of shifting colors.

"You are not the minor adept I believed, Queen. You touch the rays. You have not ignored your heritage, but you do not possess the might of the Sylah of old. Enough."

Both auras extinguished, as if by her command.

"I have no need to prolong this. Had you not sought me, I would have soon sent you a herald. It is not out of spite that I did not respond to your invitation. I cannot leave this place, and from here I am unable to turn the tide against that which we once defeated. How did you find me?"

"My scholarship led me to you. Vistara outside your walls has suffered calamities and more, and not all have been explained by things of the world touched and understood. Within the archives of forgotten lore, I searched for knowledge of the Karnak. I found mention of Shelasa, Jawn Kurz, and the Sisterhood of Oceania. The old languages are vague, but it was further proof that my mother's instruction was faithful.

"I knew of but one who had knowledge of Shelasa. I sent my trusted friend Dureen Zell to search the nesting grounds of her birth. If the coven of the Karnak worshippers lived, then I so hoped that their ancient foes remained."

"You show wisdom. Who is this?"

"This is Warlord Benjamin Colt."

She squinted to focus her purple laser beams on me. "You named him Warlord without dispensation of the Sisterhood. A Thulian, even! It is so like the Sylah to presume. But I see it was by desperation that you did so, not knowing if we had retreated into memory as the ocean. I forgive this petulance.

"For you must know it was *our* queen who named Jawn Kurz Warlord. She found him worthy to battle all enemies above and below. I have touched your essence and I find you true. But if I am also to initiate *him* in the knowledge you desire, it is not by your word that I accept him also worthy to receive it. I would touch him and know his essence."

"I do not offer him to you as payment, Mother Oceansong."

"I sense jealousy. I take that as a compliment, Queen. But I do not ask for such a price to be paid. I am beyond such yearning now. I *will* touch him if he is to learn from me what you also wish to know."

The witch sized me up with amusement, as if I were some savory morsel. Talis Darmon spoke in my ear, "I do not command you. If you do not wish her to touch your animus as I have done, we will find another way."

"But you brought me here because there isn't, isn't that so?"

The painted sorceress giggled. "Are you a Warlord or a shy boy?"

"What kind of a test is this, Talis Darmon?"

"I cannot say."

"I follow where you lead, my princess."

"You are brave and dutiful, Benjamin Colt. Remember, she may use her allure against you. Be strong and know that I trust you."

I knew the position and followed the witch's direction to lie down. She raised my head and placed it in her lap. "Look into my eyes and listen."

Her skin was soft and she folded herself above me. Her sparkling eyes were soothing and I fell under her spell as she hummed a soft song. I fell into her mind and found myself in a place where just the two of us floated on clouds of silk. Her body pressed against me and her mouth sought mine. I turned my lips from hers and pushed away. The trance was broken, and suddenly I was looking up into her eyes.

"Hmm. Interesting. Were there time for games, I would try again. Relax, Benjamin Colt, and listen."

She sang and I let myself drift away again. When I settled in this new place, I was alone. But here there was no comfort. I found myself gripped by an old anguish, returned to me as though I'd passed into its maw. I felt the claws against my bones and my breath seized as I was once again in the pit of the soul-eater.

As quickly, the panic left me. I was back in her lap, staring into her eyes.

"Calm yourself now, warrior. You do not have to travel farther into that void for me to understand. Listen." She hummed again and her fingers massaged my temples, then pushed into my skull with no more resistance than a marshmallow. She touched my memories, and as she did, I saw glimpses of hers. I don't know how long I lay in her spell. A minute. A year. But the images faded until I was floating in a purple ocean. Gentle waves crashed against a castle and above their noise I heard his voice.

"Come find me."

She released her touch from my temples and bid me to rise.

"Had you sought my counsel, he would have been found worthy. To have survived the remnant of the Karnak's malevolence is rare and that alone is testament enough to his fitness. But to hear the call of our great son from across the ether is no coincidence. All of this you have correctly interpreted, Talis Darmon Sylah."

She winked at me. "He is strong to resist. He is yours alone, Queen." She moved to leave. "Follow me and I will see you educated. It is all I can do."

✳ ✳ ✳

We followed her outside. The sunlight made me dizzy and Talis Darmon's hands steadied me with a grip of steel beneath velvet. "I've always felt refreshed after you touch my mind, but this is—"

"Like after a battle, yes? If it could have been avoided, I would have so preferred. You did well, Benjamin Colt. We are almost there. Now we take a step closer to understanding the solution to our dilemma."

Without looking to see if we still followed, behind the shell Mother Oceansong entered a tunnel in the side of the basin. Amber stones came to life to shine on a pedestal in the center of the smooth cave.

"Come, gather and see."

She picked up a pitcher and filled the bowl. As the surface settled, the clear water took form. "Do you recognize him?"

A scene played out like those I'd watched before, as Yellow warriors in armor made from the shells of some animal fell to his sword. I'd seen Jawn Kurz many times. "I do. Not just by his face, but because a warlord is always at the front, leading the battle."

"He battled not only foe above, but those below."

The image shifted to a murky view, and denizens of the deep danced before us.

"The name of their race is lost. They were once beings much like the other creatures of the sea. As they matured and gained intelligence, learned science and philosophy, they grew tired of their limited existence. They explored the ether of all creation, traveled to other worlds, and returned with greater knowledge.

"On their travels they met an even older race, an evil and dark force that turned these flawed creatures into the Karnak."

The surface rippled and cleared to show great and terrible empires on the bottom of the ocean, sprawling and teeming with life of all sorts and shapes.

"The Karnak secluded themselves in their realm for an eternity. They experimented and sacrificed all kinds of creatures and even their own race in their quest for immortality. Above them, on a Vistara bathed by sun, our kin were born and thrived. They too eventually gained great science, built magnificent cities, and probed the ether to visit other worlds."

A planet at night twinkled with thousands of lights—civilizations and peoples long absent and their record vanished.

"The Karnak touched the races of the surface, where some even came to worship the denizens of the deep as gods. But it was not until the shallow oceans began to recede that the inevitable conflict would ensue, and the Karnak sought to dominate the world above.

"By this time, the Karnak were few but had achieved the immortality they sought. They left their abyss to establish reign over new kingdoms, subjecting those on the surface that they had ignored for a million years.

"The Amethyst Sea alone remained, and it was in this age that Jawn Kurz led his army to tame the warring states of Oceania. The peace was not yet won when the darkness came for them all from below."

Giant tentacled creatures pulled a ship beneath the waves as smaller chimera of nightmarish combinations overwhelmed and consumed the Red and Yellow sailors on the decks. Black creatures rose from the depths to wade ashore toward a coastal city, glorious and bright, and soon fires burned and battles raged. Energy weapons of great power blazed, aircraft dove at the invaders, some crashing into the invaders in a suicidal frenzy. Nothing stopped the darkness as it engulfed its prey.

"But the Karnak were not alone to have once traveled the ether. Knowledge held by the sisterhood turned the tide. They fashioned weapons infused with the same power that had banished the wellspring of the Karnak from other realms."

Jawn Kurz stood naked with arms wide as the sisters dressed him. The armor shone with the brilliance of the Milky Way. The sword. The rifle and its ruby-red beam. My hands remembered them as if I truly had touched them all.

The Warlord stood alone on a shore of tar, slain creatures piled around him in mounds. He sent crimson thunderbolts to cleave amorphous black blobs off the leviathan until it surrendered and retreated below the waves.

He stood on the bow of an odd craft with no sails, bobbing on the waves, as behind him, spacefaring ships speared out of the waters to escape for the heavens, only to be met by bursts of energy fired from the ground. Each of the massive ships exploded and fell from the stratosphere back into the sea, the wakes of their wrecks all that remained.

The boat coasted into a cove where a castle dominated. I recognized this place as the fullness of the vestige I had dreamed of, the place to which I felt myself pulled. Inside a watery redoubt whose walls reflected the brilliance of the moons outside, Jawn Kurz stepped off the strange craft and into the arms of his queen. Joined, they did not look back as they ascended stairs, and the strange craft sank from sight.

I knew these next images were the turning of the last page.

A convocation of painted sisters wept and tore at their hair while one knelt at the shore and set a golden orb on the waters. It floated away, the women's wails driving it on. It sank and was gone. Tears streamed down a face I recognized, having passed into the depths of those eyes myself.

Sands blew across the ridges of a desolate plain, shadows cast across their depths by the dizzying heights of the walls of the Furrow of the Creator's Hand.

What we witnessed in the waters of the bowl I had also seen in glimpses, viewed from Mother Oceansong's eyes when she touched me. I didn't need to ask. She was as old as the sands that swept the chasm of the Furrow. She'd been the one to send the device into the sea that dried the last waters on Vistara and banished the last of the Karnak beneath an arid world.

Until now.

"Are these the answers you seek, Talis Darmon Sylah?"

"As much as I now know, still I do not have what I need. Where lies the awakened leviathan? How do we reach his realm to do battle? Where are the tools with which you armed Jawn Kurz? You admit you do not desire to prolong this. Speak plainly, Mother Oceansong."

"Then you shall have it plainly."

From an alcove she produced a trunk and inside lay the armor I had only dreamed of. Real. Its surface was a velvet night, and the uncountable spiral galaxies within teased an impossible dimension of depth, as though I could fall into it and float among the stars there. "It is time it passed to one who can wear it. Take it."

I closed the trunk. There would be another time to inspect the items. That time called for reverent solitude.

"The Warlord knows where the chariot awaits that will traverse the medium to where the leviathan gathers strength."

"And the weapons?" Talis Darmon asked.

"I have kept my portion of the trust. The remainder is in the care of my sister across the dried ocean."

I only knew there to be one place on the other side of the Furrow. "Where do we find her?"

"You know it as Aetheria."

24

THE FARTHER WE FLEW FROM SHELASA, THE MORE LUDICROUS IT ALL seemed. "I've got a trunk of armor supposed to be from Jawn Kurz, a magic sword and ray gun to retrieve from the middle of our enemy's capital in Annameria, and a memory of how to locate some ruin. All courtesy of a woman so old she should be petrified dust."

With my princess's arm around my waist, she put her lips to my ear. "Perhaps you are attracted to women even older than me? Or mayhap you prefer your women muralled and adorned in studs and fine chains? Your response made it abundantly apparent that her age did not discourage you."

"Huh? Oh. That. I'm just a man, after all, Talis Darmon. Did you know she was going to try some kind of psychic hanky-panky with me? What if I hadn't resisted her advances, even if it was just in my mind?"

"How have you put such into words before? Ah yes. You'd be dead meat." She laughed and kissed my cheek.

"You're taking this all in stride, Talis Darmon. I'm not seeing much to be amused about."

"I'm not amused, my betrothed. Simply enjoying a small moment of triumph together. By victory in Pyreenia, you have purchased for us time to walk the reward of this new path. We have hope on many fronts."

Khraal Kahlees and Doug were back to take part in the recap of events.

"Who's smoking sparkle dust now, Ben?"

Khraal Kahlees laughed with the wet sound of a wolf rending a kill. "Douglas Knoblock again reaches the heart with the spear of his bold wit. I have seen things of imagination take material form and myths become true, but this is difficult to accept. Am I to believe it was with some bewitched armaments that Jawn Kurz defeated a god? And this painted sorceress used some other contrivance of fable to dry the last of the oceans and seal away the Karnak? And now she sends you to find more trinkets with which to act out a fantasy? If this came from any of my clansman save you, Benjamin Colt, I would send you to the Blix on your feet to release you from your mental aberrancy."

Beraal was quick to speak. "I too have witnessed many things, Father."

"Daughter, did you also witness the display Benjamin Colt and the queen describe?"

"No, Father."

I dropped the trunk on the table and opened it. "See for yourself."

The men were all on their feet to peer into the case, until Dave said, "Is there some kind of face-hugger in there, dude? Or brain parasite that's going to infect us with whatever's gotten to you guys?" Even Double-K took a step back.

"Thanks, Dave. Very helpful, smart-ass."

He snorted. "Just kidding, brah." He reached in and hefted the breast plate, holding it out for inspection.

"Humph. Black velvet paintings and panel vans with airbrushed space scenes went out of style a long time ago, brah. All that's missing is Elvis or a naked lady." He thumped the armor and the stars concentrated and swirled in that spot for an instant, then spread and returned to rest. He returned it to the case. "Cool. But so what?"

Khraal Kahlees scoffed, "I needed no trickery to kill the creatures from the nightmare place. Their claws did not find chinks in my armor, and my blades cleaved their flesh in twain by no other power than their sharpness. If that mockery of a foe appears again, we have the tools to fell them, is it not so, Karlo Columbo?"

Karlo was stroking the helmet's curves, and the same sea of stars swam beneath the velvety blanket of night of its surface. "I'm open to the possibility that the armor and weapons have special properties, but I want to test them. You say you saw Jawn Kurz use all this against more than just the Karnak, Ben?" They knew about the mirror in the library of Shansara.

"He was a busy boy, Karlo. After he won against the Karnak, he fought more wars on Vistara with and against both Yellow and Red."

"So, was it the chicken or the egg, brah? He was warlord because he had this stuff, or he got this stuff because he was warlord? And you need it—why, again? Double-K's right. I trust the stuff from Karlo's arms room more than some Excalibur-ancient-alien-Area-51 kinda nonsense."

Talis Darmon frowned. "Your deprecation is not appreciated, David Masamuni. What we have learned is not just a missing part of our past, but a beacon we must follow to attain similar victory."

From Cynar I expected skepticism. Instead, he spoke with a sobriety that usually preceded one of his dark turns. "The sisterhood acted to save life as they saw fit. I was taught they were villains without understanding why. My order came into existence in the days when the Amethyst Sea was no more than a puddle. The seas were already drying when they hastened the disappearance of the last remaining body of water on Vistara. I must accept that my works have led to the awakening of the Karnak. It cannot be denied."

"No, Cynar," Talis Darmon said, "do not think to bear this weight. The Karnak have long slept. I do not think the waters alone are what awakened them, but it may have given them opportunity. And now we have a choice—allow them to regain strength or carry the fight to them before they can truly rise again."

Doug threw up his hands. "Annameria is our destination? I hear it's like North Korea. And remind me again, but didn't they break off diplomatic relations with us? And they're rattling sabers about invading? Sneaking behind their iron curtain is going to kick off a war we ain't ready to fight. Why not just ask them for help?"

The queen was brusque. "It is unlikely that Annameria is poised to respond to an unconditional request from me for assistance in this matter."

Doug's sarcasm knob turned to eleven. "Then, lucky for us we have an asset there, isn't it? Ben, you wanna give the Chief a holler and say, 'Since you're on the scene, dude, would you mind go finding this stuff for us?'"

Dave twisted his lips. "It sounds even weaker when you say it out loud, Dougie. If that ray gun is some kind of secret weapon, he's the last person we'd want to know about it. But let's not get ahead of ourselves. Say we go snatch these things without kicking off a war with the Yellows—then what, Ben-dog? You find this ruin from your vision? You play dress up on some old, dry-docked boat—and sail where? And how? No ocean, brah."

Folding his arms, Doug made his pronouncement. "I'm with Dave. The whole thing's nuts. No offense, Ben. It's a bad mission."

Double-K joined him.

"I am always ready to fight. But, as general of this army, to commit to such a course of action, a worthy objective should weigh against the risk."

"I did not know that Benjamin Colt inspired such tepid loyalty," Talis Darmon quipped.

Oof. She'd caught them all flatfooted with their chins proud, landing her punch from under their line of sight. The barometer in the room dropped. A storm was about to blow in.

She smiled, but her fury was ill-concealed. Although my friends tried to quickly backpedal, they were still caught in the void of surprise when she launched to deliver her KO.

"Nor did I anticipate that *I* have failed to invigorate your continued fidelity. You who have traveled across the ether from another world. You have seen the revelation of truths hidden from us all. You who have fought and bled, only to arrive at a brief moment of safety and inexplicably underestimate the great danger that still faces us. If this is how you answer our call, then you no longer serve a queen or a

Warlord. You are no better than my father's counselors who cautioned him into impotence and his own demise. If the army is not up to the task, then, Generals—begone from my sight!"

Double-K girded briefly. I gave him, Doug, and Dave as motionless a take-the-hint-and-beat-it look as I could. The sting of their dismissal hung around even after they'd left. I tried my best to explain what'd just happened.

"Talis Darmon, they got a little carried away and said things that would've been appropriate for a team room throw down, not the council chamber. In their own unfortunate way, they were giving the best counsel they knew how."

"This is how your generals speak to you? Even Khraal Kahlees?"

After so long around us, Double-K would fit in at the Green Beret Club or any team room on Smoke Bomb Hill—four arms notwithstanding. SF was a big tent organization, welcoming anyone who met the standards.

"Yes, him too. We didn't get to the next step in the process where, after airing all their complaints and negatives, they figure out the way to accomplish the mission."

"Your generals were insubordinate to you! They said it was a bad mission, and the objectives were not worthy!"

"They did. And it would've been better had those things not been said in front of you, or at least in the way they said them. My love, everything we've asked them to do, they've done with impunity. If doing the impossible has made them a little brusque and informal, it's because they're not automatons. They're warriors. What do you say, Karlo?"

"Ma'am, I've heard it said that Special Forces are their own worst enemy because of incidents just like this. Sometimes what comes across as arrogance or dissent is really just part of our process. Outsiders take for granted that we do the difficult on the spot, and the impossible with but little notice. And sometimes those same observers, when they see how the sausage is made, they take offense. The guys took Ben's presence as the okay to speak freely. They meant no disrespect. I guarantee they're working on a plan as we speak."

"In your language does *special* also imply *odd*? Because this 'Special Forces' you claim as your tribe has made you all so."

"Yes, ma'am. But SF didn't make us special. We make SF special."

Kleeve Hartus coughed into his fist in that subtle way. He'd been a study in poise and reserve.

"You've been a statue, Kleeve Hartus," I observed.

"I do have something to offer for consideration, Warlord. The queen is correct. The army is not best suited to this task."

"Oh?"

"I have seen you and yours accomplish many great things, Benjamin Colt, but be aware—Annameria will not in any way be like the environments you have traversed before. They are a people united by their distrust of any without Yellow skin. The supreme magnate is as a god there, and the matriarchy reinforces her rule. How you would operate in such a place, I cannot conceive. By anything less than full military incursion, I think the army ill-suited to achieve the retrieval of these items."

"Do you have a better idea?"

"A better means of facilitation," he said. "Since becoming the kingdom's first shield, I have attempted for many months to resurrect contact with the spies the Guard once had within the Yellow Kingdom. Yesterday, I received a message carried with the trade caravan. We have a source still active within Aetheria. And we have Guardsmen suitable for a covert incursion into their capital."

"You have men trained as covert operatives?"

"It would be more correct to say—Guardswomen."

✹ ✹ ✹

"Warlord, this is Commander Zaylin Twee, just returned from Thoria."

Her blonde hair pulled into a tight bun, the Guardswoman wore no uniform. None of the women did. Neither were they in the fashion of the capital. Loose fitting tunics and trousers of drab colors worn by workers of the rough trades were their dress.

"What were you doing in Thoria, Commander?" I asked.

"The first shield assigned myself and Guardswoman Tranya Olan to infiltrate the works of illicits being manufactured with destination for the capital, Warlord."

"I wasn't aware sparkle dust was a problem here."

"And it won't be, Benjamin Colt," the first shield said.

I shook hands with the one identified as her partner, a diminutive dark-haired Guardswoman with a fixed scowl. Her grip was firm, and for a second, I thought she was going to try to test mine just before she released.

The next Guard was striking in this way—her color was not the Red I was used to, but an indeterminate mix of races and features. "Shasa Karin is from a long line of Guardians, Warlord. As you may have noticed, she shares Yellow ancestry."

She was quick to defend. "My father died in service to King Osric Darmon, Warlord, as I nearly did. My grandmother is Annamerian."

"I don't question your loyalty based on lineage, Guardswoman."

"Thank you, Warlord."

"And this is Keshin Tellest. You may remember her from Clymaira. She remained behind with the resistance during the Mydreen occupation, then led with the civil defense when the Mydreen tried a second time to invade."

Her hair was cropped close like a recruit's, and she snapped to attention. "The civil defense was unnecessary, Warlord. Thanks to your strategy, we never fired a shot. I was assigned to evaluate the battlefield afterward to gather evidence of the Thulian presence. It was a stunning victory."

"That's one word for it, Guardswoman. First Shield, let's get comfortable before you say more."

Around a table, the women sat stiffly while I put my hands in my pockets and leaned back with the nonchalance of a fry cook on a smoke break. I wanted them at ease. Kleeve Hartus spoke but their eyes were on me. "Guards, it is with confidence I have selected you for a dangerous assignment. I cannot tell you details unless you first accept, and it is no dishonor in rejecting the assignment."

"You'll be working under my direct orders," I told them, "and I'll be with you for the mission."

The Clymairan Keshin Tellest asked, "Will other Thulians be joining, Warlord?"

"Why?"

Reluctantly, she admitted, "The Thulians go through their enemies like a sharp blade through paste. If your kind are with you, Warlord, there would be little opportunity for me to fight, I think."

"That concerns you? Not getting the chance to fight?"

"No, Warlord. I air my thoughts poorly. I mean, only I would be in secure company."

"It will be just me."

She considered briefly. "I volunteer."

"As do I," Zaylin Twee said.

The other women volunteered, as well. Kleeve Hartus smiled with pride. "As I told you, Benjamin Colt. The Guard answers when called."

I told them their task. "Your mission is to locate a woman in Aetheria. She will have sensitive items I must retrieve and return to Mihdradahl."

I hadn't named the items or explained their use; this was all they would know until they had a need.

Shasa Karin grinned. "I will be posing as the matriarch of the group then, as I alone speak like a native. Aetheria should be lovely this time of year."

Keshin Tellest raised an eyebrow. "You've been?"

"On several trade missions. I doubt any know the environment as do I. Plus, as a child, I learned of Aetheria and its culture from my grandmother."

Zaylin Twee drummed her fingers. "Warlord, must it be you who retrieves the items?"

Mother Oceansong had been very clear on this. The priestess in Aetheria would insist on testing me. Jawn Kurz's arm braces would be the evidence I already had his armor. Once I passed the test, the priestess should give me the sword and rifle. Key word, *should*.

"I'm the only one who can take possession of them. I'm part of the necessary bona fides for our source."

The commander tsk-tsked. "Getting you into Aetheria will be the most difficult part, then. The Yellows are paranoid in the extreme sense. As women and in good disguise, we will be able to move about. Foreign men are not allowed to enter the city. Even taking disguise as a porter, it will not aid you to do more than see the outer walls. And a woman's disguise—no offense, Warlord, but you would not fool an Annamerian love-starved after a hundred years' captivity."

"I have a few ideas."

The diminutive Tranya Olan's scowl lifted. "At least it will not be necessary for me to disguise as a pleasure girl again. They do not have such in Annameria, do they, Shasa Karin?"

"They do not."

I wanted to start our reverse timetable planning. There was a sanctioned air train that convoyed to Aetheria weekly, carrying manufactured goods and agricultural, and returning with raw materials like fertilizer for the underground farms. Annameria had arable land and water in its lowlands, but somehow needed Mihdradahl's exports. Though other relations had deteriorated, the limited trade continued for now.

"What do we know about your agent in Aetheria, Kleeve Hartus?"

"She's highly placed, I believe. Of course, we don't know her true name. Her agent identifier is Tourmaline."

"We need to cipher a message to her for tomorrow's convoy."

"Yes. I've selected a primary and alternate meeting location and time windows, recognition codes, and am alerting her to prep a safe house for five people."

Keshin Tellest asked, "The agent knows the location of this source for the items?"

Zaylin Twee replied, "The spy will not know our mission until we have assurance she is not compromised. If she is—" She made the universal sign, tracing a finger across her throat.

"We believe Tourmaline is either within or very close to the kingdom's security service."

"Who would have thought the Yellow Roamak would harbor a traitor?" Shasa Karin said.

Thinking aloud, I said, "The train makes a four-day flight across the Furrow, unloads, takes on new cargo, and returns on day seven. If she sends a message to us on the return train, that's ten days before we get it. Unless we receive a wave off from Tourmaline, the mission launches on that very train for Aetheria."

Zaylin Twee grimaced. "If we receive no return message, then we arrive totally blind."

"And the job's even harder. Time is critical. It is what it is," I said.

Keshin Tellest sighed. "These items are that important?"

She got a stern look from Zaylin Twee as if to say, *You don't ask.* The Clymairan took the chastisement sheepishly.

"You'll have three contact locations and windows of opportunity to meet her," Kleeve Hartus said. "If Tourmaline doesn't make contact, then you proceed without support. I said it was a dangerous mission, Zaylin Twee. You've done others just as difficult."

Kleeve Hartus walked with me to the security desk where our wristlets waited. Until Karlo ran his own tests, we couldn't trust the devices as secure. "I'd rather Bryant had figured out how to tap into our wristlets than have you turn up a leak in our midst."

"We work on that very possibility now, Benjamin Colt. What do you think of the team?"

"Zaylin Twee seems like an experienced leader. Shasa Karin, her native language skill and ground experience makes her essential. The average Yellow doesn't wear a decipher and anyone who doesn't speak in Annamese will stand out like a flashing red light. I remember you once pointed out Keshin Tellest as being one of your best. Tranya Olin, though, what's her story? She looks hard as nails, but she's a tiny thing. I don't judge anyone by their size, but—"

"All her clan are on the short side. She comes from a village in the eastern slopes beyond Maleska Mal where her people mine amber stones. She grew up fighting Mydreen raiders and gazraal. She's the one who infiltrated the criminals taking advantage of the renewed commerce in the kingdom. That comment about pleasure girls? She endured much to accomplish her mission. It was her own hand that captured their leader."

"I get it. She's capable."

My friend handed me my wristlet. "I didn't finish. And it was also her blade that spilled the guts of his bodyguard—a man many times her size. Legal homicide in the commission of her duties, of course. The Guard doesn't operate above the law, but Zaylin Twee told me in confidentiality there were other reasons."

"Got it. Don't piss her off."

"The Guards will see it done, Benjamin Colt. But you have not yet said how you plan to infiltrate the Yellow capital."

"Like I said, I have a few ideas."

Smiling, Kleeve Hartus asked, "Would Douglas Knoblock tell you they are bad ideas?"

"It only matters what Karlo thinks."

26

A CONDENSED WEEK WITH MY GUARDS AND THEY WERE ON THEIR WAY. I heaped my confidence on them at every opportunity—all genuine. And I swallowed my anxiety every moment—also genuine. I suffered a malady I'd thought long cured—plagued by an intrusive phantom I couldn't shake.

As we planned and trained for the mission, my head concentrated criticisms that I heard in his voice. As we grappled and practiced close combat, I saw his face looking over our shoulders. It was worse during the few hours I spent at home. The young man I'd sent not to a hell of imagination—but to one apparently real—sat with me at the dinner table or watched me in the dark as I tossed and turned, evaporating before I could ask his forgiveness.

Avril Mysteen.

I told myself that I was not sending these women to their deaths as I had him. Not bound for a city consumed by dark magic but instead, just an urban landscape of xenophobic control freaks. By comparison, another day at the office for four professionals who assured me they thrived on the thrill of working deep undercover. She rarely spoke, never smiled, but as I fussed over them at their departure, it was the diminutive Tranya Olin who made even Avril Mysteen smile in admiration.

"Warlord, if I found out about this job after someone else had done it, I'd go back to the mines for the rest of my life to hide my jealousy."

I didn't tell Talis Darmon about the new companion I carried with me and my inner conversations with Avril Mysteen. My princess accepted my explanation that my funk was just preoccupation with the mission, but I think she knew it was more than that. And she spared me her own fears, doing a better job supporting me than I did for her. Other than holding her until she fell asleep, I failed to be the man I wanted to be for her.

As it turns out, it's easier being a superhuman killer than it is being a soulmate.

Tonight was our last before my departure. Karlo and the boys had helped me with my preparations, and with nothing left to do but try to pass the hours until dawn, I returned home, resolved to wear a bright face for my princess. Voices came from the kitchen, and I stuck my head in to find Talis Darmon and Beraal hovering around one of the cooks. I'd intruded on something private and ducked back out, but my princess bade me come in again.

"Pasell Idan, please tell the Warlord what you shared with us."

"I beg you, Queen, I am too embarrassed." The woman's face fell into her hands.

Talis Darmon comforted her. "Go home and rest. All will be well."

"I will not sleep. I prefer to work. Please."

"As you wish." I followed them both back into our quarters.

"What's up with Pasell Idan?"

Beraal told me. "She's been most unlike herself for days. She conceals fatigue and moves about without her usual joy. When she admitted the cause of her distress, I asked the queen to hear her complaint. She dreams of dark images and horrors. She is not alone. Many are speaking of nightmares that rob them of sleep. It is similar to what befell Pyreenia."

Had the black witches found a way into Shansara? Were hordes of demons waiting to appear through some portal into our midst? Without running through a list of all the dread possibilities, I asked her what she felt.

"If I felt their presence, I would send our warriors to tear the city apart this instant. It is a current I sense, but it does not flow from above. You know as I do, it is below us. It has been at rest and now recovers."

Talis Darmon gave voice to my own thoughts. "We are out of time."

Resolved to carry through on my promise, I said, "All the more reason to get this show on the road. I'll be back before you know it. And if we're right, just having the full complement of Jawn Kurz's accoutrements will scare the ink out of them. You'll see." I gave her my best hero smile.

"I long for the day when it is not you who does these things."

My mantra was for me alone, but for a lack of anything better in the moment, I acted the dumb private and gave her my new *hoorah*.

"WLFTF, sugar."

"What does that mean?"

"Warlords lead from the front."

It didn't bring the laugh I thought it might. But I'm stupid like that.

"I know what you are trying to do, Benjamin Colt. But right now, your cavalier manner fills me with more dread than if you were simply truthful."

"The truth is, I'm only up against Yellow fanatics, not demons. Easy day. Let's forget about it all and try to enjoy our time together, the three of us."

We managed to eat, but it was difficult to avoid the inevitable topic of the next challenge.

"You have not told me how you will be joining the women of your mission in Aetheria," Talis Darmon said. "They left over a week ago. The generals have avoided the palace, but I know they attend you. Do they go with you to make for stealthy intrusion? I would feel better knowing you were not alone."

I'd painted my plan in big brush strokes but omitted some details, not sure myself if things would play out the way I'd hoped. Karlo'd come through and I'd done a successful test, so it seemed safe to tell her.

When I finished, the blood drained from her face and she left the room in a flurry. The sound of her retching filled me with terrible guilt. She reappeared, woozy and pale, and Beraal moved to comfort her. "Benjamin Colt would not do this if he were not confident of success."

My princess seemed about to be sick again. "Mother Oceansong's proclamations seem more fantastic and improbable with every day. I should have endorsed your friends in their doubts. What you propose is desperate. There must be another way."

"You already said it; we're out of time."

It was very late when we both abandoned the masquerade that we slept. Without turning, she whispered into the dark, "What I did not tell you about my marriage to Kilvan Tollus is that at return from each of his adventures, I craved for his departure and was relieved when it came. Your partings cause me discontent. Each day you are gone, I wonder at the inspiration that made me resurrect the ancient title. Did I truly conceive of such, or was it a seed planted in my mind by powerful forces? When this is over, we will be done with manipulation by all witches, and I swear I will not be parted from you again."

In the morning, we started the trek south. On the second day, our sortie dropped to a few hundred feet above the floor of the Furrow to the altitude from which we'd finish all but the last of our flight. There wasn't more to prepare, so it was easy to get lost in the mesmerizing patterns below. Doug took the spot on the railing beside me.

"There's a kind of Tarn that lives in there?" he asked.

"The Vermeel. I'm told they make the Mydreen look like English gentry by comparison."

"We run into any while we're waiting for your call, and it'll be the worst day of their lives."

Khraal Kahlees joined us from my other side. "They are craven. They only attack when in superior numbers. If we encounter them while grounded in their lands, they will flee and hide. Three armed airships and dozens of soldiers will be too many for their liking."

Dave wandered over. "Pilot says we'll reach the breaks just before dark, then it's a few hours to the mission support site. If you get the signal from your ground party, then we go for it tonight, Ben."

The terrain below changed to wider, deeper crevices, indicating we neared our staging point. Grounded and with patrols out, I pulled the cover off my wristlet and waited. Before we left, Karlo had made what was the equivalent of a Faraday cage for our comms, but had bad news to go along with the new device.

"It's possible the wristlets can be monitored without anyone being aware. How anyone in Annameria figured it out, I don't know, I just know you can never count on the other guy being stupid. Cynar's taking it hard. I don't know whether to believe him anymore about being on the way out, or if he's just doing a Fred Sanford." Karlo clutched his chest. "I'm comin', Elizabeth."

I was going about the business of laying out my gear when a series of hums touched my wrist. A triplet, a pause, followed by another triplet. It was the first quarter after the top of the hour. Perfect.

"I got it! We're good to go. Let's go skids up and we'll finish prepping under oxygen."

At roughly thirty thousand feet, the lights of Aetheria didn't look like much until I dropped my NODS. Even then, they were little more than suggestions about what lay near them. Aetheria had once been Shelasa's complement, the major port for Oceania on the southern coast of the Amethyst Sea. The Yellow Kingdom spread far south across the lowlands, and unlike Mihdradahl, there was water. And with it, open agriculture—the last on Mars.

"You call for dragon fire, we'll come running, Brah."

"If I call for a hot extract, then it's all-out war, Davey-Dave."

"What else is new?"

Khraal Kahlees had watched my one and only test, and admitted it unnerved him. From the middle of the deck, he saluted with lower hands, his oxygen mask somewhat ill-fitting and needing a sky hand dedicated to keep it over his mouth. "For our sake, Benjamin Colt, return safely. The wrath of the queen still burns us. If you make a misstep amongst the Yellows, we have little choice remaining than to take refuge in the Korund." That's when I realized how much I'd learned about Tarns, because I recognized his laugh as forced.

I threw him a hand salute and jumped.

I frogged out, counted to five to make sure I was clear, and opened. The canopy was twice as wide as what I was used to, but in the test had a good turn response and provided me a smooth landing. It had been a long time since I'd skydived, but some things are second nature—just like my drown proofing had been.

When I corralled Karlo with my plan, it turned out that on a lark, he'd already done all the calculations some time ago. I should've known.

"You mentioned it once, and one night when I couldn't sleep, I worked it out," he said. "I've got a static line version that'll handle a Tarn with a full combat load, but I designed a ram-air first, figuring we might need it for some unforeseen occasion."

Karlo was truly our greatest secret weapon. Baby Blue had two parachutes produced in an hour and we tested them that day, first with dead weight, then me.

I turned to put the lights ahead of me, released the toggle extensions, and got my feet in them to steer for the long ride. The twin sisters would be set by the time I got close enough to the edge of the Furrow for anyone to possibly detect me—if sentries even looked to the night sky. All the intel said the Yellows maintained a lock down on air travel to any but state controlled entities, and they did not fly at night. If anyone looked up and saw a shadow block a tiny swathe of stars, what would they even think of it?

I was checking the boxes for a lot of firsts on Mars tonight. If they had a Guinness book of world records, I was a shoo-in.

Being under canopy for so long is tiring. The harness digs into your butt cheeks and the swaying makes for a kind of motion sickness for those so susceptible. I'd never been, but after the first hour, I wish I'd let Karlo give me something preemptively.

Hindsight's a bitch.

I forgot about my nausea as I floated on. I had a chute tear on me when under canopy once. A cell deflated, and I weighed cutting away to my reserve or riding it down. I stuck with it, and I was fine but ever since, I've always had anxieties about stitches giving way and shroud lines snapping. But not tonight. Baby Blue produced a seam-less, monomolecular wonder that couldn't fail. Soon enough, my nau-sea vanished.

The walled city at the top of the cliffs stood out like Mount Olympus above the clouds. There were no steep mountain ranges beyond it, and on the horizon against a blanket of stars, I counted no less than three atmosphere works, distinct in their warped and twisting tubular stalks. I sent a series of triplets over my wristlet and got my answer in the form of an IR beacon. It pulsed like a metronome in 4/4 tempo and stood out in the black expanse that was my LZ, invisible to anyone but me.

I was at ten thousand feet and spilled air in a wide circle to descend over the concentric rings of walls that made up the tiers of Aetheria. It was far from ideal, but the light pollution from the city would work against anyone on the ground getting a good look at what floated in their airspace.

In the green and black tones of night vision, the skyscrapers struck me as forests of resting giants, ready to swat me from the sky like an insect if I got too close. As I descended, the reason for my premonition became clear. The buildings were capped by the profiles of massive stone faces, elongated chins and noses below sunken brows that kept watch over the kingdom and its subjects.

I set a course between two towers and broke out into what had to be a park, the edges ringed with irregular shapes that, if I didn't know better, I'd swear were the long-forgotten shapes of trees. Someone stood in the middle of the LZ, the beacon held overhead. In a few moments, I'd be on the ground. If there were agitated villagers waiting in the shadows, they at least had the discipline to not light torches or wave their pitchforks just yet. Maybe that would come later. First would be the town meeting, then the mob would form to kill the monster who'd dropped into their backyard.

The ground rushed, I flared, and landed as if I'd made a thousand of the same.

The unmistakable shapes of two females trotting to me was com-forting. I popped my harness and soon had hands helping gather my canopy. It was Zaylin Twee's lips at my ear. "We have a vehicle near." Keshin Tellest was at my side and hefted the kit bag with my chute. My LZ was only a few acres in size. There was cushy turf beneath my feet, and for a moment I thought of a golf course. Down a gentle slope, a vehicle waited on the street—unusual in that it was enclosed. Mounted on top was Shasa Karin and on the ground was Tranya Olan, holding open a gull wing door. Still under my NODs, the lights of the city from over the sanctuary wall made everything bright as daylight. The women were all dressed in the same strict high-collared uniform, held tight at the waist by a belt and dagger, then spreading wide to the ankle. Hands guided me into the compartment just as a male voice broke through the dark.

"Ho, Roamak."

"Get in," Zaylin Twee said and moved to cover my passage.

I hesitated and turned to see a man in similar garb as theirs round the rear of the vehicle. I reacted. A short hop and I landed and hooked him with a hard fist. I'd caught him so unsuspecting, his hands never came up. The snap of his neck was audible, as was the displeasure of the women.

In the darkness, Zaylin Twee scolded, "No, Warlord. This is bad. He will be missed." She put a hand on the frozen Keshin Tellest. "Help me get him into the growth. We must strip him."

I easily hefted the dead man up with both hands. "Show me." I followed them to a spot between some saw-toothed leafy shrubs and dropped him. As his clothing was cut off, Tranya Olin appeared, holding a vial. Zaylin Twee pointed at the stripped corpse.

"He's ready. Do it."

The small Guard moved in. "Everyone, step back." A hand on my shoulder coaxed me away. She sprinkled something carefully over the body. It wasn't until I saw the skin shrivel that I understood. "Nothing more to see here. The body will be gone soon, and so must we."

Inside the conveyance, the door closed on the windowless compartment, and we floated off.

"Color me impressed."

What was that stuff that decomposed a body on the spot?

Zaylin Twee adjusted the boxy hat pinned to her hair, but beneath the calm, she simmered. "We would have handled that, Warlord. Such action was ill taken."

Keshin Tellest was flustered too, but not at me. "Lay off, Commander. You cannot float through the air nor kill with a single blow. In the space of a few minutes, we witnessed legend."

Zaylin Twee scoffed, "Enjoy the spectacle, because we're not going to live to tell anyone of it."

"Sorry, friends. Force of habit. Where're we headed? Safe house?"

Zaylin Twee was calm again. "Yes. Tourmaline has provided our disguises and this vehicle of the Yellow Roamak. She is indeed highly placed in the state security service, but we are not insulated from harm. The demons suspect each other as much as their populace, and even she falls under constant scrutiny in their system of accountability. We've ventured out only twice, and on each, Shasa Karin has had to negotiate challenges. To be out at night invites attention. Stupid, stupid, stupid," she cursed to herself.

"Sorry, Commander." I meant it.

"Let us be still and attentive. Warlord, unless Tranya Olan gives signal from the driver's mount that we are in danger, please restrain your impulse for homicide."

"What's the signal?"

"Three sharp blows on the hull."

"And then I'm okay to go wild?"

She groaned like I was a pet who'd made a mess on the kitchen floor. "He said you were as reckless as you were brave, and it made you stupid."

"Who said?"

"The first shield. If we survive this, I will offer an apology for my disbelief. Along with my request for retirement. I turned a hundred last month. I wish to see the next hundred pass less stressfully."

27

THE SAFE HOUSE WAS A FEW ROOMS ABOVE A WAREHOUSE STOCKED with many ignored and dirty machines. Keshin Tellest proctored me in an hour of morning watch as I observed the city come to life.

"Women travel alone or in groups on the streets, but never men. If men are outside the home or the place of work, they're always accompanied by women whom they follow several steps behind. Most men labor in the mines, factories, or on the farms. Except for the Yellow Roamak. They keep a good supply of men in their lower ranks who do the dirty work of intimidation, the constant reminders of the supreme magnate's power. The whole place is as orderly and controlled as a recruit barracks."

Shasa Karin closed the door behind her. She was dressed in a simple robe, her dark hair fashioned to hide her face. Her skin was like mine—we'd both dyed easily to yellow. The effect was less effective on the others but fortunately, in Aetheria little skin was displayed.

"I have moved the stone to the opposite side of the monument pedestal. Tourmaline said she would check twice daily. She could appear at any time."

"Bringing with her the entirety of the Yellow Roamak if she is duplicitous," Tranya Olan said, cradling her K-spec as she peered between the drapes. I appreciated paranoia as a virtue of the professional, like keeping the bolt on an M4 wet with lube.

"I like how you're thinking, but if she's going to do us some kind of treachery, it's her end too. Kleeve Hartus doesn't have her identity locked, but if he gave the Yellows what he knew about her, she'd definitely get swept up in a search for a spy in their organization. It's mutually assured destruction."

Keshin Tellest grinned. "Good enough for me. If we are betrayed, I will awaken in Farnest content that she suffered a slow, painful demise at the hands of her own people. I'll be observing the rear approach corridor." She took her own rifle and disappeared to the back room.

Shasa Karin changed back into the strict uniform of the secret police. "If we have to move, we'll do so in our best cover." She looked at me. "I dare say this is our riskiest moment yet." She purred the words. I knew an adrenaline junkie, being one myself.

Tranya Olan said, "We'll soon know. Her conveyance just passed. She will come again from the opposite direction to look for the signal of the window parted open that it is safe. Then we will see."

Zaylin Twee stood. "I will meet her at the inner gate. Warlord, should you hide?"

"Serves no purpose, Commander. Bring her up."

The trudge of feet ascending stairs broke our silence. Tourmaline was in black up to her neck. She stayed close to the threshold as if she was not sure she would stay. As I surveyed her, she did the same to me. She was the first Annamerian I'd seen up close and in full light. Where Shasa Karin had just the cheek bones and a color that was neither red nor yellow, Tourmaline displayed the full features of her race. Her skin was almost butter-rich in color, her eyes as black as her perfectly swept-back hair. Her lips were thin and cruel, and unlike the rest of the uniforms I'd seen in Aetheria, hers was all but painted on her. Maybe the strange trees they had here leaked sap for natural rubber. Her get-up was the closest thing to latex I'd seen on Vistara.

Her appearance and affect provoked me to consider if she was under the influence of the black witches, but my early warning alarm didn't bring so much as an itch. I was supposed to let her make the first move, and after an interminable silence, she said in Mihdra, "The twin sisters rise late."

I answered in kind. "And remain as the red sun breaks."

After another freeze, she took a few cautious steps in. "Your Mihdra is good. But you're not a Red. You're a Thulian."

If my face could show color through the dye job, it would be gray. "What makes you think that?"

"That's not important. What is important is that you tell me what insanity brings you here. To risk exposing myself, I trusted that it was as my handler communicated—the gravest of matters. It may be to Mihdradahl, but I promise it is not so to me. If I agree to provide further assistance, I warn you my bill will be excessive. I give you a dozen breaths to convince me before I tell you to be on your way back across the Furrow."

"I need your help finding someone."

The corner of her mouth curled. "Unless I miss my guess, you've already found someone. There is a Roamak sentry missing from his post near the conservatory. That was clumsy and will be hard to ignore. My bill is already large. I don't know if I can risk letting it grow larger."

"They won't find a body," Zaylin Twee said.

"Let us hope."

"We used a destabilizer," Tranya Olan said. "I stayed long enough to see bone melt."

"Hmm. Very well. Then he will be assumed to have died in drunken fall into the Furrow. Not unheard of. I can insinuate a report from his fellows that he was unreliable in this way. Whom do you seek?"

"My source couldn't give me an exact location or by what name she uses here, but I was given enough details to identify her and where she should be in the city." I told her.

"I know it. In the oldest part of the antiquity that is Aetheria is where it is found. You wish me to find this place and retrieve what from your contact?"

"I must go there."

"Why?"

"That's my business."

"Difficult. Not impossible. It lies within the corridor reserved for the first caste, where the greatest treasures and arts of the kingdom are kept. Luckily, it is in an area much ignored. Entrance to the palace grounds and residential sanctuary is more tightly controlled than is the citadel around Aetheria itself. My bill grows by order of magnitude, because it will require my participation to see you inside. If you are caught, I will be joining you in the dance of remorse as they carve us down, piece by piece."

"Sounds lovely. So, can you arrange it?"

She let me hang as she considered. "Tonight. I will arrive at dusk. Be ready to immediately depart the city from the inner realm. You will not be coming back here."

***

It was a long day in the flat. Tranya Olan relieved me from watch, and I checked my kit one last time. Zaylin Twee rested fitfully as Keshin Tellest moved carefully to sit next to me. She whispered, so as not to wake her commander, "Benjamin Colt, what is it like to float on the air without rays to provide your flight?"

"It's as close to being a bird as you can get."

"Creatures that fly are fantasy from the wildest stories of imagination. But so are invincible warriors from across the ether. What else will I learn from you?" She stroked my arm. "We have time until we depart."

Without removing her arm from across her eyes, Zaylin Twee spoke from her recumbency. "Keshin Tellest, are you from Clymaira or Thoria? Go relieve Shasa Karin if you cannot sleep. Go."

The young Guard humphed, but winked at me before she left. The commander rose and sighed. "Do not judge her harshly, Warlord. The young are subject to their drives, and constant danger often ignites the full spectrum."

Tranya Olan didn't take her eyes from the street. "Let her play pleasure girl once. She will never suffer such confusion again."

The commander dressed. "When the items are retrieved, Tourmaline intends us to depart by caravan for Hidalla. When we reach the eastern rim of the Furrow, will your recovery party be ready to retrieve us?"

"They're standing by. It'll take them a while, so once we're on our way, I'll release them to make their approach. Then the clock starts running."

"I find it's always the last moments before extraction that are the worst. In deep work, one is surrounded by those who would send you straight to the underworld if you break stride to give the slightest hint that you may be of the Guard. It is fear that there is no rescue coming that makes for the loosest bowels and most vomitus guts."

"We have angels to carry us home, and they're bringing enough death power with them to level Aetheria if need be."

"Is what you seek so important that the Queen would risk thrusting us into a war to see you safely home?"

"It is."

"Then the Guard will see it done."

✳ ✳ ✳

A new vehicle pulled into the warehouse with Tourmaline at the helm.

"You." She pointed at Tranya Olan. "You will drive and you—" she pointed to Shasa Karin, "—sit beside her. Keep your answers brief. Your Annamese is not that good. Just flash them this." She handed her a black gem. "At the checkpoint to the inner citadel, they will inspect the compartment. That is where I will be, befitting my position. You—"

It was my turn to be identified.

"There are few men in the inner citadel, and I could not obtain a permission to get you through, so you go here."

The hidden floor compartment was just big enough for me to curl into. Sealed in my coffin, we were on our way.

The arrested motion of the vehicle at each checkpoint was brief, but I still tensed despite Tourmaline's seniority. As yet I didn't know her real name or position, but it was clear she was a top dog. Just flashing the carved black stone was enough to get us little more than a gliding halt before we were passed through. The fifth deceleration and halt took me to the bottom of my countdown to the innermost ring of Aetheria, and I nervously gripped my K-spec, the stock in my face and the barrel between my legs. This halt was longer than the others and the vibrations of conversation reaching into my crypt meant someone was directly above me. I readied to spring. The gentle pulse of acceleration told me we were through, and a knock-knock warned me my entombment was over. A crack of dim light and fresh air came with Keshin Tellest cautiously peering in before offering her hand.

"Don't kill me. We're in."

Tourmaline gave more clipped instructions. "I'm going up to take over. When we park, wait for me to open up. It will be a short walk to the relics and antiquities section. In the uniform of the Roamak or not, even a male with clearance to be in the inner citadel is of low status, so be in the rear of the group. It is unlikely we will encounter anyone on the street, but let me do all the talking."

As Tourmaline wished, I stayed rearmost. My habit of turning frequently to check behind us as we walked let me take in the environment. It was unlike the Aetherian streets I'd watched from the safehouse. The streets were unlit here, and her course took us on the darkest route. A break after the next colonnade opened into a deep courtyard occupied by a spiral shell the size of a small house. Where Mother Oceansong's redoubt had been a squat cylinder, this was like the conical snail shell of a prized beachcombing, one you couldn't move with a crane. This had to be it.

Zaylin Twee asked, "What happens now?"

"Help me find an entrance." I went one way around the circumference, and soon enough ran into the women coming from the other direction. I threw up my hands. I had the same feeling as being on the receiving end of a one-way gunfight. What was I supposed to do?

Tourmaline stepped aggressively into my personal space and hissed in covert tones. "I am risking much and I trusted you knew what you were doing. We can't wander around here for long. There are roving foot patrols. We must leave if you cannot proceed, fool!"

"There was an entrance to the one in Shelasa. Right on the face of it. And Mother Oceansong was waiting for us."

"You don't know how to reach your contact?" Zaylin Twee said it like an accusation. "I can't help if you don't tell me more. Who's this Mother Shelasa?"

I was looking around at the bare stone walls of the surrounding buildings that sheltered the courtyard when a voice surprised me from above.

"What do the Yellow Roamak want here? This place carries the seal of the supreme magnate as a sacred treasure of the people, or do you not know?"

I couldn't see her face clearly, but from directly above me, she spoke from a portal in the shell. I cupped my hands to my mouth and, in a non-tactical whisper, went for it.

"I'm looking for Sister Wavecrest. I come from Shelasa with a message from Mother Oceansong."

It was eerily silent for a time.

"Wait." The small window she appeared from closed abruptly.

"I don't know what I expected, but it wasn't this," Keshin Tellest said under her breath as she faced away. The grind of stone and the release of amber light drew my attention to the wall. A concealed portal slid farther back and aside, revealing an amethyst-haired beauty— Mother Oceansong's twin. But whereas she had clothed only in bronze skin decorated by ink and jewelry, this goddess was covered from neck to feet in a filmy white gown, the creamy skin of her face and arms the color of melted butter.

"Come in. Quickly. You'll be safe inside."

Crowded into the room, the door slid back under her hand, and the priestess turned to face us. Before she could say anything, I spoke.

"I know you must be Sister Wavecrest. She said I couldn't mistake you." I pulled back my uniform sleeves to show her the arm braces. She gingerly touched the offered one. Even Tranya Olan gasped when the stars within reacted.

The priestess put a hand to her chest. "I know my sister remains. I sense her tides through their pull." Her eyes rested on Tourmaline. "If you are here, then I hold over you as much as you over me. Though we each hold her favor, if our meeting here were revealed to the supreme magnate, it would be perilous, agreed?"

"It is agreed."

"You knew who she was all along?" I blasted Tourmaline.

Sister Wavecrest drew herself up into an even more statue-perfect feminine ideal. "She knows me by another title in the service of the supreme magnate."

Tourmaline smirked. "She is the aedile memorian. She alone occupies this place. But, because you never said you were looking for a purple-haired goddess, I offered nothing more, my friend."

"All will wait here," Sister Wavecrest ordered, and she took my arm. I followed her and the amber stone she carried, through narrow passages, down and up stairs, until the curved walls and marine theme told me we had reached the sanctuary. Like its counterpart in Shelasa. It was a marvel to me, as was the woman.

Asking for no explanation, she said, "Lie down, and I will know all."

I did as told. The experience was different, and she did not exploit our close connection to toy with me as Mother Oceansong had done. I was aware of what she touched in my mind, and I concentrated strongly on thoughts of her sister, the armor, my visions of Jawn Kurz, and the brotherly beckon he called me with. It wasn't long before she released me.

"I have received her message. Thank you for allowing me to touch you so deeply. It is as if I was in her presence again, after so very many years."

There was a great sadness in her eyes that matched what reached me through her touch. Mother Oceansong held a disdain for everything outside her dead cove, her exile self-imposed and satisfying in a kind of necessity for her peace. I sensed the emptiness of a longing in this woman, as though her station were one of an unwanted isolation, like a grave duty or even a sentence.

"I've seen your face before, Sister Wavecrest. You were there, with Mother Oceansong, the day you and your sisters dried the sea to kill the last of the Karnak for good."

"Never for good. We flushed out many and they were destroyed as they attempted to escape into the ether. Those that could not, especially their leviathan, had no recourse but to slumber in deep tombs. But the evil incarnate of the Karnak can never be extinguished. We saved what life we could, but by doing so, we also hastened Vistara's demise. I have lived with the knowledge that that is all we did."

"Now you're helping us to stop them again, before they can do more harm."

Her smile was benevolent.

"I have all the reassurance needed to entrust the gifts to you. Follow. There are things sensed, and things said. I held out hope that rumors of a Warlord were true, just as I dreaded what the discovery of the new waters meant. I know you've risked much to come here. These people are sickly and narrow of mind. Over so many years have I seen them degenerate into this barbarism of conformity and strangled spirit. The Yellows of the Vistara you have come to experience are far different than were those of the peoples of Oceania that were once divided but also joined together the Amethyst Sea."

From beneath a shelf, she produced a long slender shape wrapped in a blue cloth. She lay it down and unrolled the bundle to show me the two objects. The sheathed sword. The rifle. She rolled and tied them together again. "Take them and go. The Karnak swim in a living ocean beneath your kingdom. There they will rise. And if they do, their shadow will eclipse all. This Vistara is a fraction of what once was, and all her people counted together are few compared to the might of the armies that fought the Karnak under Jawn Kurz."

"He fought them alone, though, didn't he?"

"I know what she showed you. You saw the Warlord's goodbye to his beloved *Ashante*, the craft by which he brought his war to the evil in the abyss. We have not the time, so I will tell you. Jawn Kurz was given the tools, but it was with his queen and closest companions at his side that together they carried the battle. The behemoth Anso-Kylon and his offspring are not as strong as they were then, but you too will need the help of those most fit and proven to hold the light and protect you."

"Hold the light? Like a flashlight? I don't understand."

"Your queen knows. Trust her. I trust you know how to find the keep where the *Ashante* awaits her next captain?"

The vision of the ruins pulled me to go to the far western rim of the Furrow.

"But I don't know what to do when I find it," I said.

"Trust, Warlord. Trust that Jawn Kurz will fill you with all you need." She wiped at her eyes.

"Come with us, Sister Wavecrest. I know your loneliness. You could go to Shelasa."

She beamed. "You are kind. Your empathy is strong. It is the mark of a pure warrior. Yes, I am lonely. But, I am ever occupied. If I were gone, it would raise great havoc. I serve the supreme magnate, as I have her ancestors. She alone in Annameria knows who I am. She keeps me to touch the past and ponder the future for her counsel. Such are the means I have to protect this sacred place, nearly the last on this side of the Furrow."

"Does the woman who brought us here know this about you, that you're a witch?"

She laughed. "She suspects. Sophena Pah is ambitious and dangerous. She is the shadowy hand that does the bidding of the supreme magnate. Such is her vileness that many times I have sought for connection between her and the Karnak, but it is her own appetites that make her so. Wait."

She stopped and placed her hands behind her neck and removed a chain from around her neck and handed the dangling silver pendant to me. "This is a gift for your queen. I know my sister well. She will never forgive the Sylah, but it is time long past for such petty squabbles to be healed." She curled my hand around the warmth of the weightless charm. "Now go. Every moment wasted is a moment he grows stronger."

We broke into the waiting area where a heated discussion was underway.

"You're setting us up." Zaylin Twee was in Tourmaline's face.

"Don't be daft. Until you are out of Aetheria, I'm at as much risk as you."

The commander fumed, "Warlord, she wants to go alone to retrieve the conveyance. I don't trust that she's coming back."

"What gives here, Tourmaline?"

"Nothing. It is safest that I go alone. I will come with the conveyance, and we will be off. Back through the rings to the outer circle where the convoy waits take you to Hidalla." She gestured at the package I carried. "If you have what you came for, it is best we go. The hours of darkness pass too quickly for us all. Come with me then, if it makes you feel better."

Zaylin Twee gave her a menacing look, then dropped it. "Agreed. Stay hidden, and I'll come to escort everyone to the vehicle as soon as it's clear. Let us out, please."

Sister Wavecrest opened the portal and the two were gone. We waited, then also stepped into the darkness to prepare for our departure. If we got compromised, we wouldn't hide in the sanctuary. We'd fight, put as much distance between us and this place as quickly as possible, clean the scene as we went, and do our best to shield Sister Wavecrest from discovery.

I searched for something to say to the timeless woman before she returned to her sanctuary, and I lost the chance to tell her something meaningful, maybe forever. To tell her, someday, I would find a way to end the heartache she lived with. She was the lone guardian on a wall, walking an eternity of watch among the unfeeling Yellow robots that were the children of her once noble race.

She was a soldier if ever I knew one.

"I don't have the words to thank you. Maybe someday—"

"It is not necessary. Thank us by what you do."

The portal closed and I caught my last glimpse of her. Shasa Karin reverently said, "She is the most beautiful woman I've ever seen. Who is she, Benjamin Colt?"

"Duty, Guardian!" Tranya Olan snapped. "The conveyance approaches."

I crowded behind her to peer around the radius of the shrine of the ancient shell. The vehicle floated to a rest and the door lifted. Tourmaline was on top and waved us forward.

"Something's off. Where's Zaylin Twee?"

Just then, she leaned out from the compartment and gave a clipped nod.

My senses tingled. "Let's go."

We were padding quickly ahead, the three women around me, when it all came apart. From each direction, a black ground car sped at us. I was about to launch into action when from within the compartment, Zaylin Twee was thrust forward, a gun at her head. The silver mane and sardonic voice of Brandon Bryant mocked me.

"I love moments like this. You should see the look on your face, Colt. Don't do anything stupid, and I promise this will come out just fine. Get in."

28

Bryant was dressed in the uniform of the Yellow Roamak. Zaylin Twee kneeled on the deck between the legs of his billowy trousers as the seated Bryant continued to hold his M17 to her head. As if he read my thoughts, he sank lower behind her. "You're not quick enough to snap my neck before I shoot her, Colt. Relax. I meant what I said—this is going to come out just fine if you keep your cool."

The door closed, leaving just the three of us in the compartment as the car floated into drive. "Your friends are coming too, Colt. We have to get all of you out of here and on your way, and this is a nice chance for us to get caught up on the ride. What you got there?"

I cradled the package beside me. He shifted the barrel underneath her chin. "I like show and tell. Start by showing me. Open it up."

Gritting my teeth, I untied the bundle and flipped back the cloth. He leaned aside to see, and frowned.

"What the hell, Colt? Not what I was expecting. You came a long way for those."

"It's nothing that'll help you, Bryant. That little problem you came to me about? This is to bring the good news to them."

"A sword and an old fizzle gun don't look like much in the way of heavy firepower, Colt."

"And they aren't. To anyone but me."

He shoved Zaylin Twee down onto the deck and turned the gun on me. "If you needed help in Aetheria, you should've asked me. You're causing us a lot of exposure here, Colt. Spill the goods."

"I need these things to fight the Karnak. It's as simple as that."

Bryant lost his smirk. "The Karnak." He sniffed. "I've seen stuff here, Colt. You've traveled in some high level circles. Have you seen the history mirrors? You have, haven't you? I've seen some of their ancient history. I would've thought all this magic stuff was total bullshit if it hadn't been for me being there to see the Harridans myself. Their spells and what they did to Chuck. What they wanted to do to me, to make me like the other drones in their cult."

I knew an involuntary shiver when I saw it.

"The Harridans?" I pressed.

"Pfft. You really are behind the times, Colt. The black witches of the Karnak."

I'd never heard them called by any name. It somehow made the coven seem even more dangerous. Just like Bryant. He knew things even Talis Darmon did not, which sat about as well with me as a stomach full of curdled milk on a steamy summer day at Fort Benning. It was time to try to get Bryant to reveal more. Hard to do with him holding the gun.

"Sophena Pah knew I was a Thulian from you, that right?"

He sneered, "Sophena Pah's the smartest person in the Yellow Kingdom. The supreme magnate's not stupid, but she is a paranoid psycho. Her advisers aren't the bunch of incompetents King Osric Darmon had. The Yellows knew what was going on in Pyreenia right under Osric Darmon's nose, and that it was the first sign that the Karnak were coming back. When their enemies are screwing up by the numbers, they're content to stay out of it and let the dust settle."

"And had you won Mihdradahl, the Yellows would've been dealing with you to do something about the Karnak, is that what would've happened?"

"I would've eventually taken care of the prince and his band of nasty whores. You fouled that up for me. But if wishes were horses, right, Colt? The past is the past. I know Karlo's been doing big stuff. We've got smart boys here, too. Maybe this is the game-changing tech that'll balance the books and let us catapult ahead of you in the arms race."

"But you already know it's not, don't you? You know the Karnak are real. That they're something we can't conceive of, with powers we might not have the weaponry to counter. You admit there's some kind of magic mumbo-jumbo in all this. You came to me to handle this problem before it gets big enough to cause you to have to deal with it. If these antiques are some kind of antidote for the squid monsters, keeping them in Aetheria is a bad move."

He ruminated on this.

"If we'd known this stuff was here, we'd have had the scientists pull it apart to find out to be sure. Still might." He tapped the face of the trigger lightly with his index finger as an obnoxious threat. "Here's what's going to happen. Take your antiques with you, but you're leaving all your fancy new rifles here with me. K-specs? Good name. Sounds like something Dave would come up with. It's time our side got a look at one so we can make our own. It'll put us in good stead with the supreme magnate. Another intel coup."

"Us?"

"You might say I've had the same kind of luck with Sophena Pah that you had with your little cupcake. What can I say? It was love at first sight. I told you she was the smartest person in the Yellow Kingdom."

"Like knows like, eh, Bryant?"

"You know it. So, here's the play for you, Colt. Take your magic doo-dads and your harem and beat it back to Red land. I wish you good luck against the monsters in the black goo under your shitty kingdom. You win? It's good for all of us. I always mean what I say—I hold influence here, and it's growing. I'll keep my word and use that influence, and Sophena Pah and I'll keep Annameria turned inward and keep the cold war cold. I know these people. If they feel less threatened because we have the same weapons as Mihdradahl, it'll make them more likely to stay chill than to use their greater numbers to invade north. Back on Earth, a good deterrent went a long way to preventing a hot war, wouldn't you say? You know, you guys are still pretty on your heels. A million Yellow soldiers is a lot to deal with, even with all your fancy shit."

Boiling rage, I said, "I know you, Bryant. You're running more of a game than just getting some kind of status quo maintained."

He was back to his self-satisfied best. "Sophena Pah told you guys you were going to owe her, right? When the time comes, we're going to ask you to pay that bill. I'm speaking hypothetically now, Colt. There might be a new supreme magnate in Annameria someday soon. And it could be that a little help from our friends to the north would be appreciated. So, can I count on you to be cool for everyone's sake?" He tilted the muzzle up from Zaylin Twee's temple and made a mocking shrug with the question.

The vehicle came to a stop and settled. The door opened and fizzle guns in the hands of Yellow Roamak menaced me. "We're outside the citadel, Colt. There's a convoy waiting to take you all to Hidalla—minus your K-specs. Or, we can make the dungeons of the security service the next stop. You thought the Mydreen played with their prisoners? The dance of remorse thing the Annamese do makes my stomach turn, but it is nothing short of spectacular in the results it brings. Time's about up, Colt."

I swallowed bile. "I agree."

"How'd you get through the citadel security, by the way?"

I wasn't going to tell him about our capability to do freefall insertions here on Mars, and we'd destroyed my chute and the O-2 cylinder in the shop beneath the safe house so completely, they couldn't ever be recognized for what they were.

"I dressed up as a woman," I told him.

"Bullshit. It'd mean death for every guard on a shift if a man sneaked in from the port. You'd be the ugliest broad on two worlds if you tried that. You wouldn't fool anyone."

I stayed mum. He let it go.

"I don't care. What's your exfil look like? Because if you blow it and get rolled up, there's nothing we can do to help you. Before you get returned to Aetheria, Sophena Pah will have you killed trying to escape from custody—to make sure you don't give us up under torture, you understand?"

I gave it to him. "I have exfil aircraft on hold at a mission support site in the Furrow. I call, they'll come fetch us. Usual clandestine LZ and extraction routine, Bryant."

"Humph. Okay. I'll leave you your wristlet and whatever IR beacon you're using for the guys to find you. Everything else except your antiques there, you give up. Good enough?"

"I need my NODS."

"Nice try, Colt. They need to see you; you don't have to see them."

"If we get caught, it's going to screw things up, Bryant. Who's to say the Yellow Roamak don't get an earful of us dropping your names before Tourmaline's people can whack us? Don't think I'd burn you on my way out?"

He narrowed his eyes into slits. "Alright then. Just the K-specs." He twisted his wrist in the air to tease me. "And one of your wristlets. If Sophena Pah and I each had one, it'd help your people out, too. Let you connect to your friends here easier than through those ciphers hidden in the trade shipments."

"What's up? Your people can't copy the tech, or they haven't had the chance because you've kept it hidden all to yourself?"

"I've given all I'm giving, Colt. Get out now and let's do this."

True to his word, the animal-drawn carts loaded with goods from our kingdom were waiting to deliver us east. It was still night and it would take us until the next to reach to Hidalla. The Guards did as I instructed and our K-specs and Keshin Tellest's wristlet were turned over to Tourmaline. The woman in the black spray-on costume gave Bryant a sly, admiring smile that made my stomach turn.

Two jackals, sharing a kill.

She instructed Shasa Karin, "You still have the stone? It should serve to keep any but the most fanatic of state security commander at bay. A junior officer carrying a message wouldn't be suspicious." She handed Shasa Karin a scroll. "But a contingent of five from Aetheria, all unknown to any detachment commander, would be impossible to explain. Keep the others hidden and you should be fine."

The caravan master took the Guards to show them their hiding places, but Bryant held me back. "Colt, I know you think I'm the enemy, but I'm not. I want you to beat these Karnak freaks. I want a stable Mihdradahl. What I'm building here is going to be good for all of us. If not an entente, the Yellows and the Reds can maybe find a détente. Then we can concentrate on things more important than preparing to go to war with one another. Like trading more tech and agriculture, fixing the atmosphere, stuff that'll be good for everyone." He holstered his pistol for the first time.

"Only Nixon can go to China, is that it?"

"History's going to have a mirror showing it's only Brandon Bryant that can save Vistara."

I'd have laughed except it would only prolong the conversation with my derision sparking him to bloviate more.

"I'd like that," I lied.

He snorted.

"Wow. I was trying to goad you and you wouldn't even take the bait. Look who's growing up. Maybe there's hope for you yet, Colt."

I hunkered down in the wagon next to Zaylin Twee. Before the teamsters sealed us behind a layer of crates, my last sight before being sealed in darkness was of Bryant and Tourmaline exchanging smirks.

We lay back to back in the tight space, the snap of the teamster's whip launching us into a lurch, then settling into a swaying roll. I faked sleeping, and I knew Zaylin Twee was doing the same. We stayed like that for some time until she released a loud sigh.

"What have we accomplished, Warlord? We have improved our enemy against us. This nonsense you talked about with the other Thulian. The Karnak? Tales to keep children in their beds at night. We return with nothing more than useless artifacts and our lives. It will be with shame that I report to the first shield."

"No, Commander. We came out ahead in this exchange."

She shook her head in the darkness. "I cannot see how."

I pulled the Faraday cover off my wristlet. "Dave-Dave. You got me? We're rolling."

I received a triplet of three squelches.

"It's okay, you can talk in the clear. Bryant hasn't penetrated our comms."

Dave's face appeared. "How you figure?"

"He more or less told me."

"You trust him?"

"I'd sooner trust a Taco Bell fart."

"Right on, brah. We're hunkered down at the MSS. It'll take us about two hours to reach the border."

"I'll keep you up to date. When we find a good extraction point, we'll lay in and I'll holler."

"Roger-roger, brah. Looking forward to hearing about what our old buddy Bryant is up to."

"I'll spoil the ending. It's not going to surprise you."

I closed the link and stretched out onto my back to give my shoulder a break. The bundle was between us, but she kept her back to me, breathing in a way that betrayed her restlessness.

"Warlord, I am accustomed to never knowing the full scope of what it is I do, but can you please tell me how it is that we are ahead in this exchange? I feel as though I will be returning to defend my Guards against what will be an accusation of espionage after delivering so many of our advances to the enemy."

I snorted in amusement. This was a good soldier, and it was time to let her in on the joke, or at least part of it.

"The collimators on the K-specs we brought with us aren't full strength. When the Yellows back-engineer them, at best it will improve their weapons only modestly. Maybe they can eventually figure how to improve the output, but it'll take time, and they don't have a Karlo Columbo."

She rolled to face me. "You expected the possibility that the Thulian would intervene in our mission! And we were not told of the deception within the weapons we carried in case we were captured. But the wristlets? Surely, we have ceded an even greater advantage to the Yellows!"

I considered telling her that as a result of us believing it was possible for Bryant to passively monitor communications through the wristlets, that Karlo and Cynar had actually figured out how to do it. We'd be able to monitor conversations between Bryant and Tourmaline without their knowledge.

But that was a secret.

"It'll be okay, Commander. Where I come from, we have a saying.

"Once I had a buddy—
A buddy tried and true.
Be sure and screw your buddy
Before he can screw you."

✳ ✳ ✳

After an uneventful day rolling over rough roads behind a team of arkall, Shasa Karin's face appeared through the moonlit crack of crates pulled aside. "See what you think. Perhaps this will suffice."

We'd only had one stop for necessities and my back teeth were floating. Keshin Tellest giggled in the dark at my return to the caravan. "One would mistake you for an arkall at its business."

Tranya Olan's voice held the irritation of a first sergeant on inspection morning. "You are an elite Guard, not a rutting godahl, woman."

I ignored them both. I scanned around us methodically, flipping my NODS up and down several times to compare natural light to night vision—a good way to get the true sense of a new environment and its depth. We'd halted in the curve of a gentle dip that took us below the line of sight in both directions, and the drop-off of the Furrow was perhaps a hundred meters from the road.

"How far to Hidalla, Shasa Karin?"

"The wagon master says we reach the turn in an hour. From there it is another hour's travel inland to Hidalla."

We rolled at about four to five miles per hour, which meant Hidalla was a good distance, far enough to make detection difficult by most any roving eyes watching from the city. "Nice location. This is as good as it's going to get." I got back in the wagon to shield the light of my wristlet.

"Dave-Dave, come to papa." I gave him our location in relation to Hidalla—the lights of which they should be able to navigate by—and dug out the IR strobe.

"We're coasting to you already, Ben. We'll kick it into high gear and be there ASAP, brah. Out."

I handed the beacon to Zaylin Twee. "I'm going up the road to keep an eye peeled. You know how to operate it. I'll signal when they're close."

"How long?"

"Less than an hour."

Galloping hooves percussed the ground from ahead. I dropped my NODS down to see a party of mounted riders crest the road, then slow at the sight of our caravan. From what I'd been led to believe, no one but state security would be out at this time of night. Zaylin Twee moved near, and I whispered, "Baggy trousers. It's Yellow Roamak."

Shasa Karin was already boldly striding ahead to intercept the riders, her confidence displayed as she waved overhead to the lead rider before he could hail her. "Ho, Roamak."

The trio at the head of their formation trotted to her. "Ho, Roamak. Why on the road at this hour?"

"I travel with official caravan, bearing dispatches for the precept in Hidalla, along with the trade disbursement from Aetheria, by the grace of the supreme magnate's benevolent concern."

The mounted woman raised a palm and blandly repeated the benediction. "I am the enforcer of the state's will for Hidalla. Your name, Roamak?"

She gave her cover name.

"I do not know you."

"I have been in service only a year, enforcer."

"There are Roamak with you. Why do they hide?"

Shasa Karin stepped closer and thrust the scroll up. "Perhaps it is a SNAFU that clears this up." She said the word with emphasis, one we'd rehearsed as the action word. It was similar sounding to the word in Mihdra and Annamese for "courtesy." When coming up with a covert phrase for a situation gone to hell, it was too good not to use.

I launched.

By the time I landed, Shasa Karin had used the distraction of the enforcer reaching for the scroll to leap and pull the officer forward by a fistful of tunic, her dagger buried in the off-balance woman's throat. She was weaving around the startled arkall when I landed and sprang again for the nearest seated rider, hammering her off her mount with both feet as I continued past to the ground. Startled riders who paused up the road unslung fizzle guns and started randomly blasting into the wagons and the teamsters as they spread and charged for the caravan.

Without bothering to recover the Roamak's fizzle gun, I launched again, over the mount and landed behind the nearest rider. Standing in stirrups, he whirled his horse and brought his rifle muzzle up as he sought a target. I was about to launch at him when a diminutive body collided into his flank, a pair of reversed daggers stabbing and slicing in ceaseless arcs from all planes. Tranya Olan.

Two of my Guards jumped and dodged from point to point at a full run into the advancing riders. It was combat by echolocation in the pitch black for all save me and my enhanced green vision. Riders came to an abrupt halt and fired wildly at the advancing figures. One good leap and I landed in the middle of them, startling the mounts. I braced with bent knees to drive my shoulder into the nearest horse and with all my power, pushed. The arkall stumbled into the next, toppling both to the ground along with their riders.

I spun and drove a rear cross into, through, and beyond the arkall behind me, and received a shrieking bray of pain, the satisfying crunch of huge ribs fracturing beneath my fist. The horse raised on its rear legs, and I wasted no time in springing onto the fallen rider. On both sides of me, Guards attacked with edged weapons, feet, and fists, the smallest of them dwarfed by two male Roamak.

Tranya Olan was a Tasmanian Devil in full rotation. A slash with two knives across the one to her front blended into a spinning kick to contact the head of the man behind her, caught in indecision between bringing rifle to bear or transferring to blade. Shasa Karin was there, her own blades catching the light of the rising twin sisters in flashing glints as they worked.

The flash of a fizzle gun illuminated the sight of Zaylin Twee falling. Keshin Tellest vaulted off a short staff to close with the Roamak who'd felled the commander. She landed and with both hands brought the staff overhead, finishing in a downward stroke onto the man's head. The crack against the skull was as loud as the discharge of the weapon had been.

I looked around. There were no more mounted riders to launch myself at, and I sprang to the fallen Zaylin Twee. Keshin Tellest looked up as she finished drawing her blade across the throat of the felled Roamak. "Is she okay?"

I helped the commander to her feet as she groaned, "I will recover, Guard. I was grazed and do not have the use of my left arm." She took a step away, then staggered back into my arms as I eased her down.

"Stay with her," I said and made a quick scan around before I sprang to where Shasa Karin and Tranya Olan were finishing the last of the fallen Roamak with single, clean draws of edges across throats.

I brought my wristlet up. "Dave-Dave, we're in trouble."

"We're in sight of the coast, Ben. Where's the beacon?"

"Shit. I'm on it. Get ready to come in hot." I bounced back to the other pair. "Zaylin Twee, where's the beacon?"

The commander groaned as she struggled to produce it from inside her tunic. Shasa Karin tore open the high collar and found the strobe loose over her abdomen. I hit the button and handed it back to her. "Get in the open near the cliff," I said, pointing. "I'll bring her. Run."

I scooped up Zaylin Twee and jogged after our pulsing beacon as it made a bouncing ball over the words to the song of our predicament.

"Ben-dog, we got you. What kind of hornet's nest have you stirred up down there?"

"What you got?"

"There's a dozen riders making for your location."

"Light 'em up, Dave. They ain't friendlies."

I reached the rest of our party. "Here. Take Zaylin Twee and make for Shasa Karin. Rescue's inbound. I'll be right behind you." I lit off for the wagons where the bray of scorched arkall and moans of injured teamsters told me they'd been hit hard. The bundle was where I'd left it. I grabbed it and turned, startled at the appearance of the caravan master.

"Kill us. The dance of remorse awaits us all. Do us this mercy."

"Come with us. Gather all your people and we'll take you with us to Mihdradahl."

The man hesitated.

"It's now or never, buddy." I pointed toward the furrow. "Meet us over there now or you get what you get." I bounded off.

The *brrrt!* of a chain saw and the red spit of a dragon's tongue came from the dark sky, the object of its anger out of sight over the rise. Two dark flitters sped across the blanket of stars, blotting a rapidly widening swathe of the twinkling night sky as they descended on us. Another burst of dragon fire came from on station high above, the majesty of the spectacle inescapably drawing all eyes to its miraculous glory.

I landed next to the four Guards, interrupting their mesmerized gaze at the heavens as the beacon showered us all in its pulsing strobe. "Flitters inbound now. Stay together, and I'll send you out when the birds are down."

Puffs of labored breaths came from behind. Two men assisted two other wounded figures limping for us.

"Don't leave us, I beg you."

"Just in time."

The hum of two flitters filled the night air and their touchdown brought a puff of gritty dust to my lips.

"Go!"

I aimed my Guards at one air car as I guided the four Yellow refugees to the other and hoisted the first over the rails as green arms pulled at the other men.

I yelled, "Take off!" and bounded back and into the flitter with my Guardswomen. A quick head count for the four Guards, and I pounded the pilot on the shoulder. "Dust off, let's go."

We lifted with enough force to throw the four women to the deck and to cause the Korundi to grasp rails with four hands. We shot out over the Furrow, the lights of Hidalla diminishing in the distance until I flipped my NODS up and removed my helmet.

Dave appeared next to me pushing a flask into my hand. "You get what you came for?"

Just then a petite figure brushed past us and stopped at the stern to place cupped hands around her mouth, sending thunder as unknown on cloudless Vistara to crash against the retreating cliffs.

"Urine garglers and fecal lickers! We rode you hard and sweated you dry to the last drop of your breast milk! My grandmother's last egg fell from her with more force than you brought to bear against us! Cross the Furrow at your own peril, Yellow specialists in mating within your hatch! We own you like caged vermin!"

Fury spent, she stepped back from the stern, flashed what was for all I knew the first smile to ever touch Tranya Olan's lips. Her grin was still on her lips when she said, "I hope you have need of me in the future, Warlord. That was fun." She nodded curtly to Dave and headed forward to rejoin her fellow Guards.

Dave's eyes followed her away. Then he gulped loudly and regained the power of speech.

"Dude! Introduce me to your friend."

29

THE SUN WAS WARM AND I FLAKED OUT ON THE DECK, LISTENING TO the women answer queries from Double-K, Dave, and Dougie about their combat. More than anyone else, soldiers learn by stories, and a good storyteller can make you feel as though you were there. Keshin Tellest was that kind. While the men exclaimed admiration, I fell fast asleep. From the deepest peace of my unconsciousness, I awoke to the smiling face of Jawn Kurz looking down on me. He offered a hand and brought me to my feet.

"You have all that you need, Warlord. It is time. Come find me." He placed one hand on my shoulder as though I were a long absent friend, and with the other, pointed to the distant horizon. Beyond the deck of the floating air car were the battlements of the castle I'd seen in my vision, their ruins a dominating bastion over the Furrow. Suddenly, I knew the way there as surely as I knew the road through the hills to the home of my youth, the same feeling of completeness and safety that awaited me in that place so far removed from me forever.

"I wait for you, brother. Come and take up the last mantle of your duty."

My eyes shot open to the red sun above us, and I sat up. "How long until we hit Shansara?"

Doug was behind the console. "Tonight, homie."

"We go straight into council, boys. It's time to finish this."

Talis Darmon sat at the head while I stood to brief. I was too charged up to ground the electricity building in me. I got that way sometimes when I was jumpmaster, the responsibility leaving me unable to relax until the last of us was safe on the ground.

But it would be me and me alone on this jump.

Dave scoffed. "So, his plan's to become Kim Jong Bryant?"

Karlo humphed. "Bryant Jong Un, actually."

My princess frowned. "I do not understand. Please cease with your secret references." She was still mad at my brothers. I was going to fix that tonight.

"They refer to a Thulian dictator, Talis Darmon, and their comparison is apt."

She tapped her lips with a finger. "There have been male rulers over Annameria, but it seems most unlikely Brandon Bryant could achieve such an ascendency. In his short time in the Yellow Kingdom, it appears he has become a dangerous hand, orchestrating the will of the one desirous of the title Supreme Magnate. This Sophena Pah, who is she, First Shield?"

Kleeve Hartus stroked his forehead. "Even I did not suspect our agent was so highly placed. She is the head of state security, the Yellow Roamak. Next to the supreme magnate, her power in the kingdom is greatest, even above that of the khan of their people's army. This brings us significant options.

"I can expose her scheme to the supreme magnate. I have other minor agents in Aetheria, some of them in the elite, even one lower in Sophena Pah's own agency. I can inundate an accusation that she is our agent. By spreading this information across many members of their elite, it will prove difficult for Sophena Pah to compartmentalize and extinguish the accusations, and even more difficult will it be for her to dismiss the information as mere disinformation by us. It will be sure to reach the ears of the supreme magnate. After such a campaign were instituted, a diplomatic communication from yourself would serve to solidify the accusation, Queen. It would most certainly cast great suspicion on the ruler's closest confidante and undermine Sophena Pah's power. The result could even be the rapid but unpleasant end to her and Brandon Bryant."

Talis Darmon continued where the first shield's assessment was leading. "That is, if we think a radical change to the seat of power in Annameria were detrimental to our interests. What say you, Warlord?"

I'd thought long about this very thing on the ride back from Aetheria. "I don't trust any of Bryant's claims to be the broker of a restrained peace between our kingdoms. He wants to be the top dog on Vistara. Period."

Karlo was ready for me. "But there's always the chance, isn't there, Ben? Even if he's sincere he means to keep the Yellows from going to war with us, your history with him makes it impossible for you to trust anything he says. Not that you don't have cause. That's why he's banking that laying himself wide open for you to snitch him out communicates his true intentions better than by words alone. I think it's proof that he's genuine."

I shook my head in reluctant resignation that Karlo was correct. "I came to the same conclusion. Dammit. I'd like nothing better than the sound sleep that would come from him doing the dance of remorse. Shit." I plopped into my seat beside the queen. "How close are you guys to being able to eavesdrop on their comms?"

Cynar cackled. "Hehehe, at will. The wristlets you carried were all loaded with the 'backdoor' Karlo Columbo suggested. The one you surrendered to them will load the means into other in their possession at their first linkage. It will work."

"Then it seems like the best thing to do for now is we gather more information about their intent, and wait. Kleeve Hartus, do you have assets ready to perform such a task?" I knew he did. Kleeve Hartus could have run every three-letter U.S. government agency by himself with time left over.

"Warlord, I am ready to dedicate a section to nothing but. This is work the Guards do best. At your command, I will direct our technical staff to form a cell for this purpose, reporting only to myself, you, and the queen, of course."

"Add the other members of this group to that list because I'm going to be on a mission, and this operation needs to proceed regardless of my availability to analyze the intel."

The first shield raised his eyebrows. "I see."

Flustered, my queen asked, "Of what do you speak, betrothed?"

It was time to put it all out there.

"I must address the issue of the Karnak." I picked up the bundle from beside my chair and laid it on the table. I fully unwrapped the cloth to reveal the sword and the rifle. "I have the last pieces of the Warlord's tools with which he defeated the Karnak. The Sisterhood of Oceania have given me all the help they can. I know the location of the craft that will take me to their realm. Jawn Kurz is telling me to come find him. I must do this."

I looked at their faces. While Sister Wavecrest may have told me that I needed companions and even my queen at my side to fight the Karnak, I knew better. Jawn Kurz filled me with his example, and it had nothing to do with taking the ones he loved most to the nightmare realm.

Talis Darmon paled. "At last, it has come to this," she said, her words a vessel for all our fear and dread.

I placed a hand over hers. "A Warlord must lead."

She burst into tears.

From her other side, Beraal Kahlees laid hands on her. "Their evil grows. The call of the Karnak plague more and more of your people's dreams. Benjamin Colt is the one chosen to fight for us all. Save him, there is no other so bestowed with the confidence of this world's hidden protectors. Their wisdom must be obeyed. You know this to be so."

Dave was on his feet. "You ain't goin' nowhere without me, brah. I don't give a goddamn about any of this occult mumbo-jumbo. We wasted them before, and I'm more than ready to do it again. The op order from some dead guy and a duffel bag of his old duds don't change you needing me to drop bodies with you."

Dougie roared a mad laugh. "Straight up, Ben-dog. I've got something for their ass. You ain't keeping me outta this."

Khraal Kahlees raised sky hands. "David Masamuni! Douglas Knoblock! How dare you best me before I could form profound words with which to mark the history of this momentous undertaking! Bah! The moment is gone." He pounded the desktop then folded his arms as he fumed. "I travel the road of war with you once again, Benjamin Colt. There!"

This was not how I'd thought to restore Talis Darmon's confidence in them all. I'd planned to talk them up and have them renew their pledges to protect and serve her as my closest, most trusted, most capable friends, then leave to find the nightmare realm, alone. The lump in my throat was big enough to choke on. If it had been a secret burden to walk this path alone, they'd lifted it from me. "Okay."

Karlo winked. "I'm coming too, brother."

"No, Karlo, you're not. And neither is Kleeve Hartus. Forgive me, brothers, but that's the way it has to be. You're both critical to the future of the kingdom and the safety of our queen. Your Warlord will entertain no arguments to the contrary. Be the good soldiers you are and tell me you'll both follow orders."

"Yes, Ben."

"Yes, Benjamin Colt."

"Hehehe, I am no soldier!" Cynar cackled until he hacked and had to compose himself before speaking again, still fighting the occasional breakthrough cough. "And I follow no orders save those confirmed as reasonable by my own superior intellect. I go with you to bathe this undertaking with the luminosity of the most brilliant mind on Vistara. You will need such to aid a group of dullards as yourselves. Hehehe."

I gasped. "Cynar—no!" This I never expected.

"Your protests avail you not, oaf. This life is nearly spent. I will not go to oblivion or to whatever awaits with regret. If I have learned anything from my unfortunate association with you, it is that on the other side of fear lies great reward." He sprang to his feet. "I am alive with the prospect of the unknown! And who better to delve into its mysteries than Cynar the Magnificent! The Karnak? Pfff. Against the light of my science, the recluses of some dark swamp cannot prevail. Hehehe."

She wiped at her eyes. "Is this your desire, Warlord? That these of my sworn servants accompany you to do battle on behalf of your queen and her kingdom?"

I rose and bowed. "It is, Queen Talis Darmon."

She choked. "Then, before your departure, I must charge you all to make assurance of unhindered continuance by those who would fulfill your duties in the event—" She sobbed. "In the event you do not return." She ran from the council chambers as Beraal looked to me with mournful eyes.

"Go to her, sister. I'll be along. We're not leaving just yet."

✵ ✵ ✵

She wept.

Didn't I love her more than my own life? Wasn't it my need of her that had made me whole? I questioned these things because I shed not one tear. I don't say that out of some kind of pride. I say it because it perplexed me.

I'd been in the presence of soldiers who'd performed the deadliest of tasks, who on crossing the point of no return had accepted that they would die, and that it didn't matter. The mission was all that mattered. I suppose I'd been there before, but never like this.

She and I both knew that I would not return from the nightmare realm.

I released my hold of her and reached into my pocket. The feather-light silver chain and the woven, coral-like shape of the dangling pendant was in my hand. "This is a gift for you from Sister Wavecrest." I placed it in her palm. It was a relief to us both to have any distraction.

She sniffed.

"What was she like?"

"She was different from Mother Oceansong. Genial. Kind. She told me that even if her sister couldn't, she forgave the feud between the sisterhood and the Sylah dynasty. Here." I fastened it around her neck. "She also said—it was something about the light. I feel stupid that I can't remember exactly how she said it. Anyway, she was very sincere that she wanted you to have this."

Talis Darmon pressed the pendant to her breast. "I feel something of her in it. It sings to me of—hope."

With her in my arms, I dreamed of Jawn Kurz. It wasn't so much what he said to me, it was how he treated me, how he encouraged me. He was fatherly and brotherly at the same time. He reminded me of Mike, my team sergeant who'd given me the greatest boost of self-worth I'd ever experienced by recruiting me to his team. I awoke confident, calm, and alone.

This was a turnabout. It was usually me who slunk away before the sun rose whenever I had to leave Talis Darmon to do my soldier's work. She was not in the apartment nor was Beraal. I respected her desire to not have to part with me again, and maybe I was relieved by her choice. With only the task at hand in mind, I set off for the team room.

The gear layout was well underway by the time I got to the inner sanctum of the vault where Baby Blue and all our native Thulian equipment was stored. Karlo was a mother hen, inspecting the nests of gear with Dave, Dougie, and Double-K.

"Yo, bro." Karlo pointed to a fourth pile. "I got a full load out ready for you." The dark bags under his eyes told me he'd been working all night.

I laid down a kit bag containing Jawn Kurz's armor and the bundle with the sword and rifle, and started to dress.

"You test that thing, brah?" Dave squatted to poke the rifle like it was roadkill.

"I don't need to."

"'Kay." He went back to his own layout.

I stripped the plates out of my carrier, and put it on over Jawn Kurz's armor. By letting out all the straps, it just fit. It was tattered, and on its last legs, but it only needed to last a little longer. I needed all the pouches to hold bangs and frags. A chest rig stuffed with mags went over all that. My war belt rode just fine, like always. My sword scabbard belted over my hips with the pommel at my left side, and a few draws of my M17 proved to my satisfaction the new configuration didn't interfere. I liked to wear the sword on my back, but there'd be no room for it there this time.

To one side of my chest I slung my M4 and its grenade launcher. It wasn't an M203, but a lot of us still used the old nomenclature for the combo. In the inanity and inconsistency of our lingo, some things persisted. A new two-point sling attached to Jawn Kurz's ruby red death-beam followed over my neck to find a place on the other side of my chest. Like a newbie butter bar headed to the field for the first time, I had everything but the kitchen sink on me. I took a few hops. Everything stayed in place.

I stripped it all off save the armor and checked my ruck. Bandoliers of 40mm grenades, more mags, frags, water, and a couple of stripped MREs. I put both Jawn Kurz's helm and my own lid into the ruck and sealed it. Batteries, fresh in all devices and my plastic box of spares. If there was anything else needed, I couldn't fit it.

Dave and Doug were similarly outfitted. Double-K wore a full complement of sharp edges, two K-specs, and at his feet, the drag bag with my MK 22.

"Expecting a chance to get some long shots in?" I teased him.

"Needing and not having is a grave error, as you well know, Benjamin Colt. A missed opportunity would be long felt." He had one of our rucks that, by the look of it—and I have a lot of experience in this—had to hold well over a hundred pounds of deadly wares within. It disappeared behind his wide back.

Cynar stepped in, toting a multicam ruck. It dwarfed him. "I have every tool necessary with which to prove master of this new frontier. Spirits and magic are the stuff of weak minds. My science will dissect and reveal whatever secrets these denizens in their deep hole think the sole property of their twisted use of the rays. Hehehe, I so look forward to proving their exercise of science a paltry imitation of my own, he-hehe!"

"Don't bust a hernia, brah. Better let us crossload some of your kit into our own."

"Nonsense. Fresh from a night bathing in the healing rays, I have the strength of a man many years younger. Hundreds. Nay, a thousand. Let us dally no longer."

Dougie thumbed at Cynar. "Someone's beans are boiling over. I've got the flitter stuffed with about a ton of hardware. We ain't running out of nothing, bros. I'm ready. Let's do it."

Cynar mumbled and even hummed to himself as we walked. If I'd seen him happier, I couldn't recall it. I knew Dave was fine by the curses he made as he shifted the ruck on his back to find the perfection of a temporary position of comfort for the giant leech riding his back. Doug laughed appropriately loud as Double-K boisterously discussed the annual mating rites of the Korund.

"A youngster like yourself would be well suited to a Tarn woman, Douglas Knoblock. You would produce no issue, but the experience, ah, the experience is one that would make you truly Korundi."

We turned the corner and stepped into the bright morning light and I lost my breath. Next to the flitter, a small crowd. Apache strained against Beraal's grip on his collar. Kleeve Hartus stood in the formal dress of the Guard, his gold cloak in contrast to the white-robed priest beside him. They parted to reveal a goddess of war.

Dressed in silver armor and helm, a curved sword on her back crossed by a rifle, a flowing purple robe draped from her shoulders, was Talis Darmon. She stepped forward and placed her hands on her hips.

"Betrothed, it is by foolish insistence on proper ceremony to satisfy the needs of a kingdom rather than considering our own welfare that I have delayed our marriage. Thus, I ask you, in the presence of our closest friends, will you be joined with me now, for all time to come?"

✲ ✲ ✲

The words the priest spoke were a blur until he said, "Then let you be joined together above and below Vistara, until Temple Farnest and the eternal life with our cherished ancestors in the underworld and beyond."

We had to bend so that the little bald man could reach to place his hands on our heads. "You are joined as one—Queen Talis Darmon to Warlord Benjamin Colt."

He stepped back and I again took both of her hands in mine. Her eyes twinkled with joy, but mine were moist.

"Husband."

I choked, "Wife."

Our friends cheered and Apache howled. Hugs and handshakes went all around. My joy at her stunning act was diminished as I struggled to think of the proper words for the parting that had to come next.

My queen—my wife—placed both hands on Beraal's lower shoulders. "You have all my trust in this sacred duty. I depart without concern, sister."

"Wait a minute—" I started.

Ignoring me, she fixed Karlo and Kleeve Hartus with a hand on each of their shoulders. "You as well have my trust, absolute and firm, that you will assist Beraal Kahlees in this task."

Karlo was always serious. Now, he spoke with a gravity that threatened to pull the hurtling towers down around us. "Yes, Queen Talis Darmon. I swear."

Kleeve Hartus placed a hand over his heart. "We have all borne witness in the presence of a priest, and the inviolable oath of this Guard stands in defense to its truthfulness, against any enemy, beyond passage to life in the underworld."

I gasped in disbelief, "You're not going with us!"

She gave a haughty laugh like Streep but with the fierceness of Schwarzenegger. "Benjamin Colt, you forget yourself. A Warlord does not order a queen. I have told you before, you do not yet know all there is to know about your Talis Darmon."

She drew the sword from over her shoulder as she leaped back, completing a diagonal swing and drawing it back across the other diagonal before completing a spinning kick and landing in a deep stance. She raised herself and drove the tip over her shoulder to flawlessly find the scabbard on her back.

"Our destiny awaits. Mount up, warriors."

30

I aimed us west. Destination—the farthest end of the Furrow. I turned the console over to Doug and took a deep breath.

No matter what she thought, Talis Darmon would not be accompanying us.

At least, no farther than the ruins that overlooked the chasm—the stronghold where Jawn Kurz drove me to find him. We had days to reach it and rather than argue, it was easier to play along. For now. By the time we arrived, it would be settled that she'd remain on the Vistara of the surface. To where and by how the rest of us would journey—TBD.

The guys clustered aft to leave the queen alone at the prow. They all avoided my eyes and even each other's, unsure how to broach the subject of the new warrior on our team—clad in shining silver.

"It is a beautiful morning, husband."

The sun reflecting off her polished armor made me pull down my last pair of Oakley's.

"It is. Wife."

I'd already been bonded to her, and she to me. But being made husband and wife—it affected me. Was it words from a priest of a faith I didn't accept? The eyes of our friends on us? Or just the humbling thought that she wanted our union made as permanent as such a thing could be made among impermanent mortals. You can be affected by something and not understand why. And it was in those same ways and with that same feeling of grace and nobility that made me swear, when this day came, that I would rise above and not spoil it with ill words.

Laying down the law wasn't a tactic that worked for anyone but a drill sergeant, and then, only with your recruits—I learned that lesson. Even elsewhere in the military, a reasoned approach got better results. With someone you love, no matter the intent, words spoken harshly harm rather than help. I settled on a more diplomatic approach, maybe even one I learned from watching Talis Darmon at work.

"Baby, can we talk about this, please?"

She reached for my hand and said, "We can. But the decision has been made. As queen, I need no consensus."

"How about as my wife?"

She squeezed. "On both counts, I seek no concurrence. It is my decision that if I lose you, husband, then there is no life I want to live."

"But if you fall, what happens to the kingdom?"

"If I fall, the kingdom remains. If the Karnak are not defeated, the kingdom falls."

"That's why I'm going. To prevent that from happening."

"And you need my help. I was present when Mother Oceansong revealed history. I too witnessed that Jawn Kurz had a queen at his side." I remembered Jawn Kurz stepping off his ship and into the arms of his waiting queen.

"Sister Wavecrest told me that was *after* the Karnak had been defeated, but, yeah, she did say that—" I stopped myself.

"She showed you that it was not alone that Jawn Kurz went to battle the Karnak, didn't she?"

Me and my big mouth. That's why I never played cards. But how did she know?

"Sister Wavecrest didn't have time to do the whole mirror-bowl thing, she just told me Jawn Kurz wasn't alone at the end to fight the Karnak. How did you know?"

"I didn't. Not exactly. In my research of the ancient records, the poems and songs referred to his company—not his singleness—that battled the Karnak. What you take for chivalry, Warlord, I assess as conspiracy to hide from your queen relevant information. But I forgive you."

"Baby, I'm not even sure how we're going to get there, or even how we're going to fight. But I know it's going to be bloody. I've fought these things and I've fought with these men. If we can't protect Cynar, he's accepted that. We can't be distracted trying to be your personal security detail. It's not our mission."

"And you will not. Though you have no reason to believe me, I am a capable fighter."

I suppressed a groan. "I liked your kung-fu display back there, but that's not fighting."

She frowned. "I trained under my father's tutelage and that of his warmasters, both Red and Green, for decades."

"Sure, baby. But what have you done lately?"

Her frown deepened. "You know that I train my body. Beraal and I."

"I figured you were doing jazzercise or something."

"I do not know what that is, but I know you are being deprecating, husband. It does not become you. I *choose* to allow others to defend me. It is not by necessity that I do so."

"And I love you for it. But it's not the same thing as war."

"This war will demand many skills to achieve victory. You know that it is those skills which only I possess that may turn the tide of our battle."

My skull hurt from the inability to force the gears in my head to mesh and grind out a suitable counter.

"Enough for now, my love. My husband. My warlord. My king. We have a long journey ahead of us. We all need rest and to be at our strongest and in good spirits when we arrive. To be disjointed in any way will only serve to harm the realization of our purpose. Let us make a meal and serve our companions and enjoy this time together. It is what comrades do."

"This is a heck of a way to spend a honeymoon, that's for sure."

"Honeymoon? What is this word?"

"It's a Thulian custom for a newly married couple. They go away, alone. Usually to some kind of beach resort. Anyway, that's how all the movies make it look. It's a time for them to get to know each other, to block out the distraction of the rest of the world, and just be in love."

"We have a similar custom, Benjamin Colt. The Blissitude of Three. Three days of absolute privacy. We have never had time for anything like that, have we, my love? Nor will we. But I do not regret it. You provide me all the bliss I need, in the cold of the Korund or the maelstrom of combat. As long as we are together, I am whole."

I wrapped my arms around her, the vanishing point of the horizon reeling both of us to the Furrow the Creator's Hand, the dizzying drop into the rent that scarred this land, always somewhere just beyond sight. Reaching it was inevitable, as inevitable as the snare of our duty that pulled at us to go ever forward.

"It is settled then, Benjamin Colt. Promise that we will not waste another moment in conflict. Let us enjoy this time together with our friends and celebrate this life. For that is why we fight."

She was right. I didn't have to like it. I just had to accept it. As I pictured the referee hoisting her silvered arm high while announcing the winner, if there was a sting to my loss, it was dissipated by the feel of her next to me.

"I promise. C'mon. Let me introduce you to the wonders of chili mac with tabasco. No sense in saving them for later. After all, it's our wedding day."

✳ ✳ ✳

"Brah, how the hell did you pass the criminal background check?"

Dougie grinned evilly. "I was two days shy of my eighteenth birthday, bro. In California, a minor's record gets wiped. But I never got convicted of anything. They couldn't put together the evidence to make it stick, but the judge wasn't going to let me off."

I didn't know a lot about the civilian legal system, but it sounded like clear-cut grand theft. "A storage locker full of stolen art wasn't enough evidence?"

"I just had a key. The locker wasn't in my name, and they never got prints, vids, or anything that proved I was on any of the jobs."

Double-K was in rapt attention. "But you were."

"Hells yeah, I was!"

"How'd you get caught, brah?"

"The cops had been onto my brother's crew for a while. It was a couple months after that job when he sent me to retrieve a couple of pieces to take to our fence. They had a bogus warrant, but it got everyone picked up, and that was the end of us. My brother and his crew all went down for it. Oh, not like basketball numbers, not even football numbers. It was like soccer numbers. We had a good lawyer. They were back at it in no time."

I'd never heard any of this before. "So, it was the Army or jail for you, something like that?"

"The judge said I had to join the Marines. The Marine recruiter was cool and everything, but hanging out on a ship with the Navy for months and months was not my idea of a good time. I'd bumped my head in all the floating museums I visited in school. Ships are cramped, yo! I was already six-six by the time I was sixteen. No thanks. The Army recruiter had been a grunt. He sized me up and said, 'I got just the thing for you. Do you wanna machine-gun dudes without going to prison?' Sounded good to me. The judge was cool with me taking a Ranger contract, and off I went."

Dave chuckled. "My recruiter said the same thing. Guess they teach 'em that."

Talis Darmon gave Dougie a beatific smile as only she could. "And here you are, Douglas Knoblock. Risen from petty circumstances to become a noble warrior."

"I don't know about that, Talis Darmon. But I've got no regrets about how I grew up. Long Beach was da bomb. I cut class to surf every day. There were babes aplenty. Maybe my family didn't raise me right, but I found my true family. S'all good."

My princess clapped. "How well said. David Masamuni, Benjamin Colt has told me you came from a splendorous place of lush green lands with clear waters, colorful swimming creatures, and mild temperatures. Is it so?"

"Brah, you said you never been closer to Hawaii than watching *Magnum P.I.*?"

"Dude, we trudged through the Korund for months. I told every TV show and movie plot I could remember. Would you rather I'd have described Hawaii from *Dog the Bounty Hunter*?"

"True dat. Stupid haole."

Talis Darmon was enthralled. "He has said that you lived surrounded in all directions by the beauty of the moving waters, and that you too rode on its waves. No tale of such a feat exists on Vistara. I can scarce even picture what that must look like, much less imagine myself doing something so incredible. When I rode in a craft floating on the water it was—unnerving. Was surfing a rite of passage for all warriors near the waters?"

"Ha!" Dave coughed a laugh. "Sorry, Talis Darmon. I wasn't laughing at your question. It's just that, most of the guys I surfed with, they couldn't even hold a job. Most of them were low-level criminals and druggies. Yeah, there were some real badass soul surfers and dudes who were fearless beyond belief. And I bet a lot of them thought of themselves as warriors, but they'd have been wrong. Being a warrior isn't about taking risks when it suits you, or doing dangerous stuff just for the thrill of it. The thought of serving was the last thing on their minds. They didn't care about the future. *Aloha, 'ohana, pono*—all the things I learned from my tutu—they were just words to those guys. Being selfish is what they knew best."

Talis Darmon softly said, "Don't judge the tribe of your youth so harshly, David Masamuni. Not all are inspired to live in a noble way so early in life, like you and the tribe you chose to join. The young need time to find their proper place in the world. Perhaps those you were hatched with were someday inspired, and with maturity became responsible people."

Dave got a sad look. "Maybe."

My princess understood. "Forgive me. I know there is much pain over what occurred on Thulia."

"There are days I don't even think about it," Doug said. "And when I do, I've learned to be grateful. I remember all the good things. When I can share those memories, it keeps home alive. And reminds me that I'm not alone."

The mood had grown somber. What Talis Darmon did next was more impressive than sorcery.

"Could I have learned to surf?"

I couldn't have been alone to imagine her in a bikini and long sleeve T-shirt, riding the waves with a white smile.

Dougie laughed. "Whaddaya say, broski? Could we have gotten her up on a board? Maybe start her out by clamdragging."

"Brah! Re-speck!"

Doug turtled down into his peaked traps with a grimace. "Oh, sorry! Yes, ma'am. We'd have you shredding in no time. And you, Double-K! There was a stick in my grandpa's garage—an old wooden long board that was so heavy—it could've held you for a ride."

Khraal Kahlees   considered it, then dismissed the idea. "Bah! If it does not serve to deliver a warrior into battle, then what purpose could it have? Instead, I consider the example of Benjamin Colt and his taking flight to arrive so unexpectedly in the midst of his enemies. Wizard Cynar, tell us if you would put effort into producing such things so that I too can arrive violently from the heavens to meet our foes, rather than us ponder recreation on a sea that does not exist?"

Cynar had been quietly taking a hand at the console. It needed very little attention by a pilot as we skimmed along at the same height as the lip of the coast off to our right. He frequently maneuvered small crystals around another pad laid nearby and scribbled with a stylus on a lighted scroll.

"A sea that does not exist," he repeated mesmerically. "That we course above the floor of a dead sea to where I have inadvertently given life for it to arise anew, it is an irony not lost on me. My calculations have led me to an inevitable conclusion.

"Instead of life to Vistara, I have brought death."

Avril Mysteen was there, arms folded, shaking his head in displeasure. His eyes welled with tears and I alone heard his accusation.

"What have you done?"

✱ ✱ ✱

"There it is," I said over the hot wind searing our faces. Dominating from the point of a narrow but deep channel were the ruins of a castle.

"And check it out," Dougie yelled. It was obvious what had his interest. For miles, the mirage rising from the floor of the chasm below the breaks of the Furrow had stood out as a peculiarity. The sheen of it reflected the sun like a mirror. It was standing water in the abyss. "Bendog, worth a look before we dig through some ruins?"

Cynar said, "Yes, Benjamin Colt. I should like to inspect."

"Down we go." I dropped us the many thousands of feet to the floor of the canyon to rest on the sand a cautious distance from the edge of the stagnate pool. It covered many acres to form a large pond. As we approached, small desert dwellers scattered from the water's edge and scurried back to their hiding places in dens tunneled in the undulating surface of the canyon floor.

Khraal Kahlees pointed. "Those are gazraal tracks. This one is small, even smaller than those of the desert below the Korund. I did not know they ranged in this place."

My wife surveyed the shore created by the pool. "I did not doubt, but it is something different to see for oneself. Water in the Furrow. Amazing."

Cynar was on a knee next to the edge, a finger testing the surface. He produced a slate and let the glow of the many colored crystals speak to him in a way I couldn't interpret. Dave picked up a rock and tossed it overhand into the pool. I cringed.

"Hey! Don't be a hobbit, Dave."

But the shallow *plunk* had already served to transmit that the waters were at most a thin veneer over the sands. Doug was already brashly testing the depths by striding into the pond, his dark glasses unable to hide his trepidation as he disturbed the surface, rifle in hand just in case. His boots disturbed the surface like it was a puddle on an asphalt parking lot, the top of his soles still visible.

"It's pretty firm under this puddle, Ben-dog. Ain't gonna need much of a hydrographic reconnaissance."

I walked out to stand next to him in the pool. "I'll go over that way."

"What're we looking for, brah?" Dave said as he strode out into the mercurial water. "You think there's some kinda well or something gonna give us a way to dive down to wherever? We got no scuba gear."

Double-K looked on from the shore with suspicion as he fingered his K-spec.

Cynar cursed us. "Imbeciles!" Talis Darmon remained by Cynar as he did his thing and the three of us sloshed around in different directions. I wasn't sure what we were achieving, other than to make sure there was in fact no drop-off from where an octopus-looking thing would leap out at us. Cynar's insults traveled at the speed of light over the water and reflected back off the canyon wall, adding grand effect to his Don Rickles-quality lambasting of our activities.

"Clots. It is water. Nothing more, nor less. It seeps up from the ground. Sully it no further, nitwits."

I sloshed around in a big cloverleaf pattern, finding nothing. He was right.

"The water tests pure," he said. "There is nothing remarkable about it, other than its location."

We collectively ended our recon and headed back to the flitter.

"Can you tell where it came from?" Dave asked.

"It did not fall from the sky, dunce."

"I mean, is it from your river, brah?"

Cynar groaned. "It is water. It doesn't have a maker's mark. Water is water."

Dougie waved a hand over the small lake. "I thought you'd Cynar this and be able to tell where it came from."

"Thulians," Cynar rolled his eyes. "Do not use my name as a verb. Dipshit." He'd picked that one up from us—probably from me. At least he used it correctly, unlike some of his other attempts when hijacking our slang.

Talis Darmon shielded her eyes to block the sun as she sought the ruins far above us. "To the bastion now, Benjamin Colt?"

"Onward and upward," I replied.

I let the engine's rays lift us straight up. Climbing up the face of the canyon, the channel leading to the redoubt revealed itself as we rose. I lifted high above the rim and flew us around the site so I could clearly survey the place I'd only seen in dreamy vision. The remains of battlements and battery positions lined both sides of the cove, and at its peak, the sprawl and collapse of the castle.

"It was some kind of military harbor," Dave said. "I can imagine what it looked like. Under the ruins, there's still some kind of span making a sheltered cove, like a submarine pen for a German U-boat. Not gonna be anything floating in there, if that's what you were hoping for, brah."

On the inland face of the ruins, the collapse of ancient columns marked the remnants of a grand promenade.

"I'm setting us down."

Dougie was first over the side with his MK 48 aimed into the ruins and the dark depths calling for us to explore into the wide tunneled entrance.

Deadly serious, he said, "I've seen this shit in that mummy movie."

I laughed, then said, "Don't think that's what we're going to find, bro-man. We can go in light. No need to take the whole arms room. We won't be taking off just yet, I don't think."

"What we looking for, brah?"

"Dunno. The Sisters of Oceania said I'd know it. Time to play Indiana Jones."

I gave Talis Darmon the flashlight off my side and clicked on the one mounted on my M4. With the muzzle aimed high, the spill of the beam interlocked with the others to bathe everything in a sterile light such as had never touched the stone blocks of the dark passage beneath this once mighty bastion.

We searched together, taking one path, then another. Some ended in collapse. Others led outside. None of them touched me in any way to indicate *something* was supposed to happen. One of the collapsed passages aimed straight into the center of the castle, and I was about to suggest we set up camp and then tackle excavating our way deeper, when Talis Darmon called out, "Benjamin Colt, see here."

Her light was directed at a spot, obvious as a passage, angled in such a way that from the other direction, we missed it.

Always look back, if for no reason other than to make sure you know what the way looks like for the return.

"It is quite intact."

The floor sloped downward and was without the rubble present everywhere else. Not a footprint or a scuff mark disturbed the sediment caked on all the surfaces from the ages.

Cynar had one of his handheld devices thrust ahead of him. "Warlord, there is something down there."

"What do you mean, Cynar?"

"Rays of many variations emanate from that direction. Faintly, but in combination, and in quantity more than could be merely radiating naturally from the surroundings."

"From what, then?"

"I cannot determine from here."

Dougie thrust ahead. "Me and Dave lead, dude." Dave was beside him with his M4.

"How it is, brah," he told me. "Warlords don't always lead." They set off on line and I came to a high carry, my light splashing across the ceiling. The passage turned ninety degrees. The guys popped the corner, paused briefly, then resumed the same pace, indicating there was no reason not to follow behind. Guys popping corners and saying "Clear" is the stuff of terrible movies.

Another one of the same sharp jogs turned left, and the passage ended cleanly.

"Bupkis," Dougie said as he relaxed and let his big gun drop, producing his handheld flashlight to look around.

"Benjamin Colt, we are under the notice of a focused emanation," Cynar said, holding up a single crystal. It glowed weakly in a pulsing rhythm. He returned it to the folds of his garment and produced the slate once more. We all remained silent as the wizard worked. He turned in place, left and right, as he fine-tuned the projected stones of the device, then pointed.

"Behind that wall is a space."

Dougie laid hands as if to test the solidity of the stones. "I got plenty of demo. We should do a test on another part of the ruins. I can come up with something to get us to the other side of this without bringing the roof down. Probably."

Talis Darmon said, "I have sense of it as well, Wizard Cynar. It is time, Benjamin Colt. It is time to use the gifts given to you by the sisterhood. Demonstrate to whatever awaits that you have their confidence."

"Oh, boy," Dave mumbled. "Shit's about to get weird."

"What the hell, man," Doug nudged him. "Ain't you ready to see something trippy? I am."

"Let's head back to the flitter, everyone. I don't know what's going to happen, but I think we should bring up everything we plan on taking with us."

"I agree, husband. My sense of things is that we have arrived where you are intended to be."

Using my flashlight, Cynar led us back with our full loads to crowd into the dead-end passage. I was not alone in my puzzlement as we all looked about, straining to register for a clue that something—anything—cared about our presence.

"Brah, maybe you gotta do some big thing. *By the Power of Grayskull* or something."

My wife spoke in my ear. "Benjamin Colt, you are not dressed as the Warlord Jawn Kurz. Your many accoutrements of dress are foreign. And you do not wear his helm."

I sighed.

"You're right. Give me a little space to work, guys."

I dropped my ruck, unslung my rifles, and pulled off my chest rig and the flimsy plate carrier. Off came my helmet, on went the helm of the same alluring dark metallic with the mystique of the other items I wore. Everything else stowed in my ruck, my 203 slung at my side and the ancient rifle in hand, I was ready.

"Take a step back, gang. Maybe this'll do it."

I turned in place, trying to let whatever might be there see that I was now fully dressed in the armor of the Warlord. After a slow spin around, I stopped to face the wall Cynar had indicated.

Nothing.

I couldn't think of anything else to do but ask.

"Warlord Jawn Kurz, I heard your call and I have answered. I stand ready to follow your example and lead. If the time is not now, Jawn Kurz, then when?"

A green light filled the air from behind me. The crystal in Cynar's hand glowed brightly. "It answers!" The entirety of the wall slid aside to reveal the passage continued. Beside me, Cynar held the crystal and kept pace to light the way as I moved ahead.

"I got your kit," Dave said, but I already knew he would.

Near the end of the passage, amber stones warmed in answer to our presence. A short wall blocked travel ahead, but the passage split in both directions to give way to whatever lay behind the wall. I chose left and stepped into a low ceilinged room that spread wide. From the other direction came Doug, the light of his weapon penetrating the last dark corners. His light reflected off a squared column in the middle of the room. A mirrored column.

"Kill your light, Dougie."

I ignored the many pedestals, art, statues, and things along the periphery and strode to stand in front of the central pillar. I walked around it, all sides mirrored to form a four-sided block reflecting our images. Talis Darmon moved beside me as we stared back at ourselves in one of the wide facets. We were quite a pair.

"We remind me of another couple," I said.

It was then that the mists formed across the surface, and as our reflections disappeared, in their place were another man and woman.

She was the image of my love, but with amethyst hair and golden skin. He was dressed as I was, in armor surfaced with the night sky of Vistara.

"At last we meet, Benjamin Colt, my brother from across time and the ether. With your queen proud at your side and with your most fit companions, we give hail of glad welcome. My queen and I greet you all."

31

IT'S A SHAMEFUL TESTAMENT TO MY EGO THAT AT THIS MOMENT, I FELT justified. Because my doubting-Thomas friends were here to witness this miracle. But it wasn't time for an "I told you so."

That could come later.

Talis Darmon gasped, "You speak to us from Farnest!"

Her twin complement smiled back. I knew Jawn Kurz's voice as well as my own. What I had previously only seen of her, I now heard. The voice was as sweet and soothing as a light spring rain.

"No, Queen Talis Darmon Sylah. You speak with the remnants of the consciousness we once were."

Behind me, Khraal Kahlees drew his sword. "Sorcery!"

Doug was beside him and reverently said, "Calm, Double-K. This is why we came."

Cynar's face was buried behind his slate, the information it shared with only him more interesting than the wonder in front of us. Dave was relaxed, hands on his M4, but taking in the surroundings with his usual unfocused interest when in a new space. He was looking for another exit.

Bowing deeply, Talis Darmon exclaimed recognition. "Queen Sumera Tashara Calypsis!"

The golden queen smiled as beatifically and regally as I'd only before seen from Talis Darmon. She begged her to rise with palm uplifted. "You do me sweet courtesy, but it is not necessary, Queen."

Jawn Kurz—or the ghost of him—looked ready to pass through the mirror to join us. "Warlord, there is but one final gift I have to share with you. I loved her second only to the one more beautiful and capable than her." If the woman next to him were also a ghost, she was one who still wilted to flattery. "The *Ashante* will serve you, Warlord, as she served me."

He gestured with a sweep of his arm, and at the far end of the room, another wall slid aside. I stepped around to see, and on the next face of the mirrored pillar, Jawn Kurz and his queen were already waiting.

A light grew from the next chamber, and in it sat the craft I had witnessed the Warlord ride upon.

"She never failed to deliver me to battle, nor to bring me home safely. If she is able, she will see the same done for you."

She was the color of rose gold, her lines sleek, slick, and fast. Fins and surfaces to lift or dive flowed from her swollen curves.

"Jawn Kurz, you must help me understand. The seas of Vistara are long dried. Your ship has no waves to carry her, and I don't know to where I must sail."

The queen looked at me with the understanding of a goddess heavy with wisdom, guiding a blind beggar. "The *Ashante* knows the way. The Warlord has already tasked her. She will not lose her way."

A seam split apart and beneath the widening portal a ramp descended, amber light within the *Ashante* offering welcome.

"My sisters built her for one purpose—to serve the one who would protect this land. From the stars came the secrets that my sisterhood guarded for so long. The powers held by the evil in the deep came from the ether as well, but from a realm dark and twisted. The sisterhood had no choice but to risk tainting Vistara with the knowledge they protected, lest this world and others fall to the darkness."

Jawn Kurz transferred the rifle from his back and held it at port arms. "Kesta is also of great and secret power." He lowered the rifle to place a hand on his chest. "Helest is the shell of a mother's protection as no other." The stars swirled around his hand.

I copied him and the same spinning galaxy of lights responded on my chest.

Jawn Kurz turned grim. "Along with great heart and courage, these will provide such means as can be bestowed to counter the vile power that seeks to consume this land."

I placed a hand on the pommel above my hip. "Your sword, Jawn Kurz? Does it hold special powers as well?"

That brought a smile back to him.

"Lady Vivimus balances well, does she not?"

The queen said, "The battle will be fierce, but it is one that you must win. Be not resolute that tragedy and sacrifice are your reward. The Karnak and their rising god are foul, but not invincible. It will be a great calamity to the enemy when you appear in their lair. They are not yet teaming in numbers, nor is Anso-Kylon as strong as when Jawn Kurz banished the leviathan to hide and slumber, waiting to recover and one day rise again."

She made it sound simple. But wasn't there something more I needed to know?

"Warlord, how did you defeat them?"

The Warlord laughed. "Fight until the battle is won."

Talis Darmon crossed her hands over her breast and bowed. "We will see it done."

Jawn Kurz knife-handed towards the *Ashante*. "Take all companions and armaments, your warship awaits. The time is now, Warlord."

"Will we speak again, Jawn Kurz?"

"When the *Ashante* returns you victorious."

Now both he and his queen dipped their heads, the mists covered the glass, and returned us to our reflections.

As abruptly, Dave doused our wonderment in the proverbial lighter fluid of his pragmatism, and tossed the match.

"Charge that hill and don't stop until we get to the top. Not exactly a new tactical strategy. I expected a little more, brah."

I was inclined to agree, but before I could say anything, the flood gates opened.

Khraal Kahlees shook his massive head. "The words of a ghost do not satisfy."

Dougie looked skeptical, too.

"Pretty shitty op order is right, Double-K. How do we know all this isn't some deception by the enemy, Ben-dog? Some kinda interactive Disney trick that's delivering us right to the enemy? We just gonna jump in this bird and drop whenever the green light pops? Wherever the hell that'll be."

Talis Darmon squawked, "What discouragements are these that you voice? In this last place of safety, do you find your courage lacking and formulate reasons to give up?"

Khraal Kahlees roared, "I have taken insult from you before, Talis Darmon. Sworn to your service or no, you will not insult my honor again!"

Hands up, not in surrender but to pour out my aura as if I were a sorcerer myself, I stepped between them. My torrent of colorful language was a mix of Appalachian, U.S. Army, and Vistaran that came out of me like the music of Talis Darmon's incantations—but in the vilest punk-rock-death-metal-rap ever blasted on Mars. My performance would win the Grammy for most revolting combinations. Spent and out of breath, I dropped my arms.

"Just—stop."

There was a lot of foot inspecting going on in the new silence, Talis Darmon included. I'd achieved a result, but not a good one. Me and mouth. I never learn.

Penitent, I said, "Sweetheart, we've talked about this. It's just part of a process."

Without meeting my eyes, she nodded.

Cynar had been locked on his slate the entire time.

"Anything to say, Cynar?" I asked.

For the first time, he seemed to register that there were other people in the room.

"Yes. I studied the mists as you participated in what seemed a genuine exchange with the apparitions. The device exhibited energies not unlike the mists of history, but what we witnessed was not a similar type of vision. There was much more occurring. The projections you interacted with were not powered by construct alone. There was signature unique to the ray of life from both the Warlord and his queen. And something else. During the interaction, I also detected a flux in time itself. It was as if the ones within the mirrors spoke to us from the past, we being in their future. Part of what I detected resembles what is known about the science behind the mists of time."

Talis Darmon puzzled. "The mists of time are rare. I also know of them. One such exists in Clymaira. But, always I was counseled that it is a false science—unreliable and a reflection of one's delusional wishes. But one could not use such to pierce time to communicate into the future, could it? We did not talk to them from the past, did we?"

Cynar humphed. "No. And what I said was that in the signature of its rays, what I examined *resembled* the mists of time, not that this was the same. But, you are correct in what you were taught about such, Talis Darmon. Yet, Benjamin Colt has witnessed the mists as at least somewhat accurate. Tell her."

I'd never told anyone but Cynar about the vision in the mirror where I watched myself crowned Warlord, long before I even knew it was a thing. I tried to push us past this. "Never mind that. Cynar, were what we interacted with real people?"

He stroked his long beard, which he did only when confronted with a genuine challenge. "The first queen of Oceania said that they were remnants of a consciousness. It would require greater study to understand the means by which it is accomplished that such ineffable a thing is captured, stored, and accessed. Yet, because of the many peculiarities I witnessed, I can posit that what we saw was much more than an elaborate deception created by the Karnak. I think they were inadequate in their guidance because they are as they said—remnants. A sort of incomplete life, connected through time to the root of their essence, but capable of little more than what they gave."

"A mystery for another day, then. I didn't sense the Karnak in any of this, did you, Talis Darmon?"

"No. The opposite. I sensed only goodness and hope from a place I associate with Farnest."

DOC SPEARS

Dougie shrugged. "Spoke to us from heaven, huh? Good enough for me."

Dave hoisted his ruck and then picked mine up. "Yeah, yeah. Sorry to spoil the mood. Let's rock."

I caught my wife's eye and tilted my head toward Double-K. She understood.

"Khraal Kahlees, please forgive my words. Your honor and courage are above reproach. You always have my complete trust."

Khraal Kahlees thrust tusks forward, and bowed. "Thank you, Queen. Between warriors, words in haste are forgotten." He rose. "What to expect, Benjamin Colt? That we arrive violently by this craft to surprise our enemies? That we fling ourselves into mad battle on the parting of its gates? What ground do we expect to land upon?"

None of the others had seen what I had, whether vision visited upon me or my own nightmares inspired by Avril Mysteen's tale. "It was a vast underground dominion, dark and bleak. Black waters lapped at tarry sands, and a ruined city pokes up from a stagnate sea. The creatures—you've seen them. The leviathan—I think we saw him, too. At least, one of his giant eyes. That's all I've got."

Dave was his old laid-back self. "Easy day then, brahs. So long as we don't come out underwater, then we just start bringing the hate to them and don't stop until the big guy goes down from AT-4 and Goose rounds. Prolly easier than taking a hill, when you get right down to it."

Talis Darmon was also herself again, serene and wise. "I trust that we are not sent merely to drown, friends."

Doug hefted his massive ruck. "Yeah. Makes sense. And don't forget we got whatever big ka-pow Ben-dog's carrying. I'm ready to see what all the fuss is about. Must be pretty special, even if it doesn't look like much."

"Brah, it's gonna be something friggin' sweet. Purple lady in the mirror made it sound like the sea witches were enforcing some kinda ITAR to keep anyone from getting a hold of whatever super-advanced space-magic they had squirreled away."

The International Traffic in Arms Regulations was meant to keep defense-related items from falling into the hands of America's enemies. And what Queen Sumera Tashara had said sounded exactly like what her sisterhood of Oceania had tried for. Maybe theirs had worked better than ours had.

Dave grinned. "We won't see it in action if we don't get rolling." He set off and the others fell in behind him.

Talis Darmon was at my ear. "I'm sorry I interfered, my love. These men are the bravest of all. As are you."

"You're braver than us all, dear." I had to try a last time. "Wife, will you please—"

"No."

And suddenly, a Warlord found himself not leading, but the last up the ramp.

✳ ✳ ✳

The *Ashante* was thirty feet long and half as wide, leaving little space around it in the room that berthed the ship. If we were to fly, float, or go anywhere, some other portal had to appear. The domed cabin at the top of the ramp was the singular crew space. There were no seats, no obvious controls, and with the six of us and our gear, it was tight. The ramp retracted and the doors sealed, all without sound or command by one of us to get underway.

The *Ashante* was unlike anything on Vistara, proof enough to me the technology was alien. More alien than the alien world I'd adapted to. Karlo would feel the same excitement I did, I was sure. As much as I tried to mimic Dave's aloof disinterest, my physiology thought differently. Skipped beats fluttered in my chest, then my heart resumed its usual rhythm. Cardiac arrest wouldn't be very warlord-ish.

"Auto-pilot or what, brah?"

"Guess we'll find out."

Cynar was buried behind his slate again. "Perhaps I am not interpreting correctly, but—witness along with me!" The curvature of the entire cabin became transparent and the room enclosing the *Ashante* appeared. "A wave builds in intensity."

A glow emanated from the skin of the craft, and its haze clouded our external view. I felt a moment of disorientation until I could figure out what I saw and felt. The room was rising because we were sinking. The force of a down acceleration like an elevator was in my stomach. We sank and dropped below the level of the floor. The light outside dimmed and vanished but before it did, earth and rocks crawled upward around us. The interior of the dome became rose gold again.

Talis Darmon slipped her arms around me. "Wizard Cynar, what is happening?"

He spoke with awe into the face of his slate. "We have left our normal state of presence and we pass through the very solidity of Vistara around us."

"Dematerialized? Cool beans," Doug said. "Now we know how this bad boy works. Wonder how long the ride'll be?" He dug in his ruck and produced a belt of 7.62 to drape around his neck. "Might not be a long one, you know? I say we be ready to go hot."

Amazement broken, I did the same, redressing in the items from my ruck in the reverse order I'd taken them off. The last thing I did was drop a 40mm in the tube and slide it closed.

Dave checked his M4's aiming laser against the curved wall, tapped the button again to extinguish it, and did the rucksack flop. "Might be awhile. Let's switch off being on the door every ten or so, what say you, brah?"

Khraal Kahlees stepped beside me and menaced with his pair of K-specs in the direction outside. "I believe it was here that the portal appeared, was it not, Warlord?" The invisible seam of the closed doors made everything just curved wall.

"Yeah, I was last in, and it was right behind me. Should be it... Talis Darmon, Cynar, I want the both of you out of the view of the doors when they open. When we move out, don't come out until I call you, and when you do, stay to the rear of us at all times."

The rising of my stomach continued, almost like I was in a slow freefall.

Cynar said, "The wave changes. We are far below the surface we left, I cannot say how deeply we have already trav—"

The *Ashante* shook violently, then calmed. The dropping elevator feeling was gone.

"I think we're there! Get ready!"

The dome slowly faded to invisibility and a strange pink light filtered in. Of its own accord, the seam of the portal split and the ramp came to life, allowing more of the sickly rose tint to enter and with it, a nausea.

Double-K growled, "What madness is this?"

A pink sky blanketed an endless vista of rolling pasture, covered in a fur of pastels from illustrations out of a Doctor Seuss book.

"Something approaches!" Khraal Kahlees said, his Tarn eyes sharp. I followed the direction of his rifles. "It has just dropped below the horizon. It was moving in this direction. It will appear again. There!"

Cresting over a hill appeared a hideously shaped head, followed by shoulders too narrow for what sat atop them, elongated arms, and a stretched trunk. Whatever powered the creature's elongated strides and obtuse bounce was hidden beneath the ruffled gown of a tattered wedding dress, its hem dragging along the ground.

"Yoo-hoo!" yelled a tiny shrill voice. It dropped into the next dip and I lost sight of it.

"Shall I kill it?"

"Yoo-hoo," a disembodied voice teased again from out of sight in the valley, louder and closer, and closing still. The creature popped up again. My sense of scale was off, but for all its grotesqueness, I wished it nearer so I could capture the size of it. It was taller than Double-K.

"Not yet, let it get nearer. See anything else?"

"Just that, Ben." Doug was between us. "I thought we were going somewhere dark. This isn't it. Where are we?"

I didn't bother to answer. I didn't know.

Meanwhile, the creature was only a hundred yards away, waving its stick-like arms overhead. "Come out, come out. I must meet you, silly things. Thought you to spoil my feeding? Naughty, naughty. I surprised you, bringing you here. Such a delight, such a delight. Come out, come out!"

"Enough!" Khraal Kahlees fired both rifles. The path of the blasts converged on the creature, turned to nothing, and with a flurry of the thing's arms, the giant Tarn beside me was pulled violently out of the *Ashante*. Doug opened up as did Dave, filled into Double-K's spot. I joined in churning out death at the thing.

Another sweep of its arms and I was snatched into midair like a sliver of steel by a magnet. I met the ground with a crushing thud. My breath gushed from me with great force and all my bones cried like trees twisted by a tornado.

"You cannot harm me here. Don't be so quick to prove yourselves ready for a hasty death; it ruins my pleasure."

Like a marionette, I was flipped onto my back and invisibly pinned to the ground by the weight of an elephant on my chest. The others were positioned as I was and even Khraal Kahlees groaned from the pressure crushing him into the fuzzy turf.

The giantess towered over us, her spiked red hair wild, her skin whiter than that of a painted mime. She smiled with narrow lips whose corners reached her ears, her teeth thin and pointed. Rows of them flashed from her gape as she said, "I have savored you before, little Benny. But you bring many new pleasures with you. So very kind."

She laughed and her head toppled back along the split of her smile. A dozen forked tongues sprouted from her neck to tickle the air as she cackled, then retracted like a window shade pulled to its limit. The head snapped down like a lid to form a face again.

"Did you think I would allow you to squelch the dark harvesters growing beneath your world? How arrogant of those righteous fools to think they could send you without my notice. I would never permit such a thing to happen again, which is why my eye has been on you all."

The weight of a thousand worlds pulled me down, but I fought with all my might until I gathered the strength to croak, "Who are you?"

"Don't you know?" She clapped her hands, and in the sky above her, conveyor after winding conveyor appeared, cubes on their surface moving to the syncopated tick of a second hand.

"I am the Harridan. Welcome home."

32

"Cease your attack," Talis Darmon ordered from the *Ashante*. I strained to tell her to flee, but nothing came out.

The Harridan looked past me toward the voice commanding her and made the hurling motion with which she'd flung us about. She repeated it and then, frustrated, said, "Of course." A yellow radiance burst over me to fight back the pink hue engulfing all around us. The new light's intensity advanced and as it did, the Harridan retreated a step at a time in response. The force restraining me eased, and I rose.

"Stay within my aura," Talis Darmon said as she placed herself between us and our tormentor. Cynar was there to pull me the last few inches to my feet then moved to Doug and Dave to do the same. I was weak, but it was more than that. The superior strength I'd enjoyed on Vistara was gone. Khraal Kahlees was crouched, swords drawn and ready to pounce.

"Allow the queen to carry the contest forward, lord Tarn," Cynar said. "It is her rays we must hide within for now."

The Harridan ceased her retreat just beyond the perimeter of the golden sphere.

"So futile," she hissed, "but this delay only sweetens the anticipation that builds. I long to taste your pain."

The Harridan was held at bay by Talis Darmon's outstretched hands and the fierce and flawless aura that outshined the diseased pigments outside her sphere.

"Let us take our leave," Talis Darmon said without taking her eyes off the Harridan. "We return to our craft to depart your realm."

The Harridan laughed. "I will not permit you to leave. And even if I did, where would you go? No borrowed power in your possession will see you steered from this place. Your craft is useless unless I direct it on its course."

Cynar was deep in concentration over his slate, intent on whatever readings it fed him as he turned in place. "Warlord, we are not beneath Vistara."

"No kidding." Dougie had his gun leveled at the Harridan.

"We are in no time or place I can name, Benjamin Colt. She may speak truth."

Dave's green laser painted a dot on the Harridan's chest.

The Harridan dipped her forehead. "Acceptance is the first step on the path of the inevitable. Woman, your feeble ward only chafes me. It would not deter me should I choose to ignore it. How long can you maintain such a posture? Hmm? Cease your efforts and let us converse so we may learn of each other. It is the polite thing to do. I know you have many questions."

"I am content, sorceress. If you wish to come closer, do so at your own peril."

The Harridan snarled again, but made no move.

I sidled close to our sorceress. "How long can you keep this up?"

"Not long. Benjamin Colt, bring your gift to bear."

The ancient rifle was in my hands. The Harridan's attention snapped to it and she crooked a willowy finger at me.

"You may think to harm me, but doing so will be costly."

The plains of thick cotton candy came alive. The carpet of pale pink, green, and purple fur became an ocean of goose pimples—cats, sprouting from beneath blankets. From blankness, the mounds of raised fur opened their maws. They widened hideously to menace sharp teeth, and millions of rows of tiny daggers grated the air in unison.

She smiled her too-wide smile and folded her arms in an appeal, her hostility transmuted to syrupy request. "I know what you seek. You will never reach your destination unless I permit it. But I am not without pity. I am not without generosity. I always exchange value for value.

There is something you want, and so do I. Rather than battle—and you *will* lose here—isn't fair exchange preferable? Hmm?"

Strained, Talis Darmon quietly said, "I will tire soon. I know not what else to do other than to treat with her. If I cannot secure a solution, then we will go down together to fight her to our last. Do you have another action for us to take, Benjamin Colt?"

I checked the guys. Eyes steeled and weapons ready, their auras were cast as surely as if they were also sorcerers, conjuring the pending violence and malevolence of the war they would bring. "We'll back your play, Talis Darmon. We're ready anytime."

She relaxed and her glow dimmed. The goose flesh and maws of teeth that were the landscape in all directions settled, flattened, and returned to the furry pastures of ill colors. The Harridan clapped with delight. "After a poor start—thanks to your four-armed pet—now we may speak without malice. We come to trading favor for favor. Kindness for kindness."

My queen showed no fear. "You have diverted us from our destination. Why are we here, Harridan?"

The sky was filled with the looping railways of intertwined conveyors and the cubes that moved on them to the time of a slow metronome. The boxes were the same spoiled colors of everything, chains of colored blocks that pulsed along, propelled by the beat of some unseen heart. Cynar's attention was skyward, panning with his slate held out, a vacuum he used to suck in all information unseen about the world around him. To all else, he was oblivious.

The gangly giant stepped closer. Even Khraal Kahlees was but a toddler in contrast as she bent to address us. "I don't know you all, but sweet Benjamin I do. Sweet, sweet Benjamin. Oh, how I missed the flavor of your pain!"

She stretched her full frame to the sky and spread her hands.

"In all of my collection, your empty box did I grieve the most."

A track of a conveyor descended behind her, the parade of boxes never ceasing as they ticked ahead on the line. It came to a rest and for the first time, the line halted.

"Don't you miss it? Tell me you do, sweet little Benjy."

The Harridan stepped aside and the lid of a bile-colored box opened. "Don't you long to come home?"

✳ ✳ ✳

Talis Darmon gasped, "You are the eater of souls!"

The Harridan laughed. "I am not the harvester; I am the founder of the feast! Don't you miss serving at my table, Benjamin?"

It was just a box. Big enough to lie in only if scrunched into a ball. I had no memory of her from my time of inquisition inside the soul-eater. But the feeling of being curled into a constricting, painful cage, that I had memory of.

"It wouldn't work on me again," I told her. "Everything I experienced in the soul-eater was a lie. I wouldn't bring anything sweet for you to feast on. I know its secret and I've been taught how to fight it."

She grinned. "I'm willing to try, if you are. Because if you wish to travel to where the slumbering god Anso-Kylon awakens, that is my price. In exchange for you returning to your proper place in my box, I will see your party transported to his risen city to play your crude games.

"All those marked by my daughters for Anso-Kylon are only temporarily in his service. Every one of those branded that you destroyed, their souls have awoken below your world in the body of one of his minions. But from that place, all will end up in my collection. Every one of them that you destroy there will come to one of my boxes to spend all eternity here. I collect my tax even unto the end of all things!"

I understood. All the Green and Red soldiers of Chuck's dark army we killed—weren't dead. By some evil magic, they became the twisted creatures of Anso-Kylon's army. And when we killed them on the tarry soils of the subterranean lair, she would have their souls in the boxes that danced above us. Just as I once had been.

"So dull, so flavorless, so bland has existence been since Anso-Kylon's desires to rule the surface of that world caused his own subjugation at the hands of the frail creatures who were its masters. It has been a long, hungry time since. The simple beasts who wandered into my snares are unsatisfying in their fear and pain. Few intelligent creatures fell into my traps, and so rarely, each sating me for only a short time until their pain becomes… predictable. No matter the number or type of them, they all are driven by the same base and witless fears. Bland, bland, bland." Her serpent tongue spat the words.

"Then there was you! When you escaped, it hurt me, it hurt me. Your betrayal was diminished by the new soul you sent me to tend. He continues to provide new flavors and textures, and I thank you for it."

More tongues joined the first to caress the spikes of her teeth as she savored whatever trace of flavor was to be found on them.

"Mark Wayne remains in your pit?" I asked.

"He is a delight." She cackled again. "Surprised? You destroyed the path to the snare, not the vessel that captures. Naughty, naughty." She stroked one index finger over the other at me. "Shame, shame. Here is my bargain. I know there is more to squeeze from you, new and lovely pain to discover. I enjoyed you so much that I swear, if you return to my collection, I will see your friends on their way."

Talis Darmon's aura flared. "He will not do so, Harridan. We will fight you to prevent it, and you will have nothing."

Cowed, the thing retreated and shielded her eyes with an arm. "Oh, we can do just that, feeble witch. And in our war, I would rend joy from your suffering at the hands of my domain. But allow me to make my bargain a thousandfold more attractive. Hope is so important to all you mewlings of the outer plane. It is hope that my first offer lacked. Hope of triumph. Hope of love. Hope of fulfillment and all its empty promises. Dim your ward and let me tease you, please—it will bring me such joy."

Talis Darmon let her radiance diminish slightly. "I will give you brief reprieve before your greatest pain comes at our hands, Harridan. Speak."

The Harridan lowered her arm. "If little Benny takes his place again in my box, I will send you to Anso-Kylon's realm. If you defeat him—bring him to me. For him alone will I exchange Benjamin and let you return to your plane to live your silly, pointless lives beneath the veils of your self-deceptions.

"Anso-Kylon contains the sweet pains of all the souls he has consumed since the stars were born. He would never venture close to my realm, no, no, no. My daughters use him to create on your world a place of pain from which I can feed, as does he. But in him already is enough luscious torment to satisfy my hunger until all the stars grow cold."

Her head split across the mouth and flopped back, the many tongues shooting out of the neck like a hundred raspy Jacks-in-the-box to flutter and twitch. They recoiled back like a retracting tape measure and the head snapped closed over them.

"How's that for an irresistible offer?"

I did not hesitate. "I'll do it."

The Harridan grinned. "I knew you would."

"No!" The gold aura flared brighter. "I will not permit it."

I stepped in front of her. "Talis Darmon, there is no other way. If I do this, you have the way to save Vistara. I must."

"It is a trick, Benjamin Colt. She is the mistress of deception. Only you can wield the weapon with which to defeat Anso-Kylon. She knows this. If we surrender to her ploy, she wins all."

The Harridan clucked. "I did not countenance you capable of such perception. To have become so learned an intellect, you must hold much pain, much pain."

Talis Darmon fiercely said, "I will take his place then, Harridan. Does that suffice to alter the bargain and still see you fulfill your end of it?"

Every nerve in me fired. "NO!"

The Harridan danced and sang, the folds of her long dress swaying as she waltzed. "So sweet, so sweet—oh, the suffering!"

"Talis Darmon, you can't. You don't know what it's like, it—"

"I do know, Benjamin Colt. And better than you, I can resist her tortures. It must be you who kills Anso-Kylon and saves Vistara. And when you are victorious, you will return here and exchange him for my freedom, and we will depart this place once and for all." She fixed the dancing monster with her glare. "Is that your bargain, Harridan?"

"It is, it is! Do *you* accept?"

"I do!" My queen extinguished the golden light. "I am ready."

I screamed. Khraal Kahlees was at my side, urging. "Benjamin Colt. Listen to your queen. She makes the way for us. We will see this thing done and return. You must be dutiful, even here. You must be the Warlord. Lead us to victory, Benjamin Colt."

"I come, Harridan," Talis Darmon spat. "Leave me to speak with my husband."

The Harridan's eyes grew wide. "Husband? Oh, yes, yes! Tell him all, tell him all. I will feast on this parting." The monster trembled with anticipation.

Talis Darmon took my face in her hands. "Listen to me, my love. If you do not do this thing, it cannot be done. You must win the day, not only for our entire world, but for another that now grows there."

I heard, but didn't understand. "We'll fight, right now, we'll fight her."

"No. Listen to me, husband. I maneuvered to join us in marriage for all reasons, but most of all because while you slept, I willed a new life to form. The issue of our love is in the care of our own dear sister. A tiny, frail thing it is, safe in the chamber where it will grow. Our child will hatch in the light of Vistara and carry on our line to rule Mihdradahl. Beraal protects our egg with her life, with our other chosen friends sworn to see our progeny safely raised. My life matters not. All that matters is that you win the day and save the world for our child, to see Vistara thrive in peace and safety, with our line seated on the Spectral Throne for the good of all."

My eyes washed blurry with tears. The Harridan moaned and quaked in orgasmic tremors.

"Ohhhh, ohhhh. Such pain, such suffering, such loss. So much more, so much more than I had ever thought within any of you. Yes! Yes! Come, make me wait no longer. Take your place in my box so I can taste this greatest torment!"

Talis Darmon kissed me. "Be swift, husband. Swift not to return for me, but to return to Vistara and watch over our child. If you do this, I will have all the strength I need to resist for all eternity." She broke away and moved to the monster, who draped my tiny love in a gangly arm to escort her to the open container.

Grips like vises held me in place. Dave's hand was on my chest. "We have to back her play, Ben. She knows what she's doing."

I cried her name again and again as she stepped into the box, never looking up as she folded herself down. The Harridan lowered the lid, sealing it with a gentle pat. The syncopated rhythm of the line resumed, and I watched as the box meant for me pulsed away. The conveyor lifted, and I lost sight of her tomb as the moving belt joined the helical collection of cloverleafs and turns, millions of tiny boxes marching in time with my sobs.

33

"Come. I always keep to the obligation of my contract. This way." The Harridan set off.

Doug urged me. "We gotta go, Ben. Come on."

The box holding the crouched and suffering Talis Darmon was gone. I was not alone to be transfixed on the racetracks above us. Cynar was captured by the movements, slate held at his side, mumbling while the colored boxes traveled their paths.

"Get it on, guys." Dave hoisted Cynar's ruck at him. "The Harridan's getting away. Ben! Snap to, brah! Forget everything except what we gotta do. Ranger up, NOW!"

I tore my tear-filled eyes away from the sky, choked back a sob, and grabbed my gear. It was all I could do. Dave's verbal kick to our seats hadn't stirred Cynar yet. He was frozen, all but his head, which tracked his eyes across a selected conveyor, then snapped back to follow another section of the train as it passed. Whatever he was doing, it was to the exclusion of everything that had happened. I touched his shoulder.

"We have to go."

He tore his eyes away, still mumbling to himself, but returned to awareness. He complied and readied.

Khraal Kahlees waited on the rise ahead and yelled, "She is in my sight—follow quickly."

We trotted to where he disappeared over the hill. Over more rolling hills we hurried, the soft falls of my boots igniting in me a dread that at any moment maws of rasping teeth would spring up to gouge at us. The Harridan waited at the bottom of a gentle dip, Khraal Kahlees halted out of her reach. At the sight of us, he turned his full attention back to her.

Fingers steepled, she waited.

"About time. I have other matters to attend to."

"Not so fast," I said as I came to a stop and tilted my head as far backward as it could go to meet the black eyes aimed down at me. "You want Anso-Kylon. How do I bring him to you?"

She stroked her chin. "A fair question of me, if you are to properly meet the terms of your agreement. Wound him gravely enough, in his belly is the essence of him. That is all you need bring to me to satisfy your end."

She clapped her hands and behind her a black vortex swirled and grew, a void of roiling nothingness. "There is your path."

Khraal Kahlees raised rifles in lower hands and drew swords with upper. "How do we return, Harridan?"

The slice of her smile grew to its widest. "I'll be watching. If you succeed, I will send a portal. Ta-ta for now, my precious souls. When you fall there, it is in my collection you shall arrive. Have no worry— no matter the outcome, I'll see you all again."

Khraal Kahlees laughed defiantly. "You will regret the day you brought us here, Harridan!" He strode to the portal. "I lead off, brothers. Once again to war we go." He stepped through. Dave and Doug moved to the edge of the murky churn of the gate. I pulled Cynar beside me.

"We go together. Three, two, one." We stepped off as one and came to a halt in a world of darkness, the sticky ground resisting my pull as I tugged my feet out of their mired fall.

We spread and turned outward into our instinctive perimeter, ready to slay whatever appeared. My vision adjusted to the purple light that coated everything. The grandest expanse of a vaulted underground world surrounded us and, in the distance, came the faint song of the things I'd heard in nightmares. The ceiling was a mile above, the walls as far to either side of where we'd landed.

Khraal Kahlees pointed. "It is this way from which the creatures call." In the far distance was a bend and around it, the source of light and sound.

Cynar had his slate in hand. "We are no longer in the realm of an immaterial plane. We are beneath Vistara. There is no doubt of it." The wizard struggled to pull his feet free, grasping a knee with both hands to assist. He lost balance and fell into the muck. "Curse this!"

I bent to help him up, but he waved me off. "I have a solution." He dug into the pack on his lap to thrust a crystal out to me. "Throw this on the path ahead. Far ahead. I do not know how far the effect will travel."

"What is it?"

"Trust that I know my science, dolt. Do it."

"Make a hole," I said. Double-K took a sticky step aside. I cocked and threw. My Vistaran strength had returned to me. The stone sailed and peaked its trajectory a hundred meters away before coasting down in a long descent, hitting with a moist impact out of my sight.

Dave crouched slightly. "Should we duck? What's supposed to happen?"

"Wait," is all Cynar said.

"Hear that?" Doug said. He ignited his white light and far ahead, cracks in the black surface spread in the spiderwebs of a dried lakebed. It continued reaching toward us, stopping mere steps away.

"Hehehe. I knew it would work. All of you, take all you can carry. Here." He doled out the rocks to us. "Careful not to let them contact the surface. They will firm and solidify and likely encase whatever is mired in the slurry it dries."

Doug stuck his hand out for another. "You mean, if we throw these into a formation of the squid-things, it'll put cement galoshes on them?"

"I speak to you succinctly and you question me in gibberish, oaf."

"That's exactly what he means, Dougie," Dave said, reaching for another and placing it in his dump pouch. "How many do you have for us?"

"Ten for each of us. Hmm." He handed more of them out. "I cannot deliver them as far as any of you. Best I keep none for myself." Now he let me pull him up and steady him. He and I trudged out of the last of the muck to where the rest of our party were already on firm ground. Dave took Cynar's hand and pulled him the last step.

"Big improvement, Cynar. Thanks, brah."

"Let us drive on," Khraal Kahlees said. "It is many steps to reach the bend and the risen city beyond. I have seen the nightmare land in my sleep and yearned to fight more of the creatures that dared tread the surface of Vistara. We meet them in their nest at last."

He surprised me with the revelation. "You never said you'd been touched by visions of the nightmare realm, Khraal Kahlees."

"A few times as of late, Benjamin Colt. I believe the beasts tired of my mocking their oddities as I taunted them to stand before me again. They must be vain, as they visited me no more."

We each took turns tossing a crystal to firm our path, then trotted over the concrete to the edge of the next expanse of tar. We covered a couple of klicks like this, the noises beyond staying the same low boil of babble and a new sound, distinct to me as we drew nearer: falling waters. The next toss would bring us to the radius of the bend, and it was my turn to throw again. I cocked back and at the last second, recovered, halted by Khraal Kahlees's stay.

"They grow louder. Do you smell the stench of them? They come." He pulled out a crystal. "Let us test the wizard's pitfall against them."

I marked a spot where I judged I could reach by my best throw. "You land yours left; I'll take right."

Stepped between us, Dave cocked his grenade launcher and shouldered as Doug brought up his machine gun. The screeches reached a peak, and with it broke a horde of slinking, limping, vaulting monsters. Barbs and quills, fangs and tongues—an inky black flood of them spread across the floor, aimed for us.

"Throw!" We launched. I brought my own rifle up and fired. The MK 48 chopped to life beside me, the *bloop* of a 40mm grenade with it. Two K-specs fired into the stampede, and I launched a grenade of my own as deeply into their ranks as I could, loaded another, and returned to shooting individual shapes as they lumbered nearer.

The crackling of the firming ground broke through the fervor, then the wailing of desperate creatures, captured by the solidifying substance they fought to free themselves of. As the effect spread behind those first trapped, traffic jams formed and more became stuck behind them.

"Keep working the front rows!" I yelled.

We each worked our sectors, easily interlocking fields of fire to overcome the monsters still free at the lead of the advancing effect. The cracked and dried tar stopped a hundred yards away, just in time for the last of the creatures to escape the concrete and fall to our fire. I changed mags and lowered my weapon. Dark stirrings appeared from behind the snared dead and dying beasts.

Doug said, "Over they come. Get ready for the next wave."

Spilling over top of the many beasts captured in the hardened mess sprang a new horde, advancing to find firm ground by which to catapult at us with new velocity.

I sent another grenade arcing shallowly into their midst. They were too near for me to load another, and I started pulling the trigger again. The spoon of a hand grenade pinged, followed by another as Dave pulled and threw in quick succession. Doug's 7.62 chatter continued as did the buzz of K-specs. I went through two more mags until I was out of targets. More dark chimeras writhed and gurgled in death. If there were another wave to come, it wasn't yet building to crash onto our shore.

"We must press ahead," Double-K urged. "I will protect the advance from here. Cross this filth. Go."

"No," I countermanded. "Double-K, carry Cynar across. Guys, bound with me." I took a few steps rearward, broke into a sprint, and jumped. I sailed over the muck, landing only slightly short of the next hard surface. Dave landed just behind to my left. Doug landed onto the concrete ahead on my right and guarded as Dave and I took the last steps out of the quagmire to join him on line.

"Beat you," Dougie teased as I came into his peripheral.

"I am not some bundle to be jostled, lord Tarn. Careful with these old bones."

I stole a quick glance back to see Double-K high-stepping through the muck, Cynar held over a shoulder like an infant. He deposited the old man gently behind me.

"Forgive me, great wizard. I sought only to protect you by making haste."

"It is fine, my son," Cynar said, dropping his ruck and massaging his neck. "If only to be even a hundred annuals younger."

The stink of rotting flesh filled the air. The writhing of trapped creatures and their wails of effort to pull free called to us.

"Don't waste a bullet if you can help it," I said, drawing my sword. "Let's make a path through them."

Double-K gripped his blades. "With pleasure." He came to the first struggling beast and sliced horizontally with two edges to split its soft head like a rotten melon, spattering black goo from its interior. We spread out, hacking and stabbing our way through the monsters. I ignored the ones with all appendages trapped, their only danger to us that our ear drums would burst from their piercing screams. Now, here was one with a single barbed tentacle still free. It used its lone weapon like a whip to lash in me into its oval mouth filled with raspy spikes. I pulled my M17 and put two in the spot central to its three eyes. It fell limp.

"Check it out—this one's gnawing off its legs to get at me," Doug said. "Go for it, dude, then whatcha gonna do? Roll at me?"

He thrust his blade tip into a monster's open mouth as it lunged at him, and withdrew. It too fell limp.

Through many yards of black meat, we hacked. The curve of the bend lessened and beyond, a larger opening beckoned. At the edge of our firm shore, Khraal Kahlees tossed a crystal while keeping his rifles pointed ahead in lower hands.

"Let us be ready to rush. A new wave constitutes in the distance."

The cracks raced to us, dwindling to a stop to leave only a tiny gap between us and our next lily pad.

With a grunt of satisfaction, he said, "I impress myself. We move."

I took off. Doug sprinted up beside me. "Ben-Ben, ain't it time you try out your magic rifle? Could save us a lot of time and ammo."

"We have to save it for the big guy, Dougie. We don't know how much juice it's got."

Clearing the bend, many new bits of information struck me at once. The only one that mattered was the black flow of creatures advancing at us from the next tarry bog. I slowed and reached into my dump pouch for a stone.

"Here we go!" Dave yelled as he passed me, taking a triple jump build-up, landing his last hop on the edge of the firm ground, and unleashed his cocked arm. Doug landed beside him, having matched the technique and finishing a moment behind. Another wouldn't hurt, and I threw. Chimeric creatures made of parts marine and terrestrial engaged in the same sequence of tactics we'd already fought. For our part, we stuck with what worked. There's a special sexiness to boringly reliable firepower. It was another one-sided victory. I took the momentary pause to redistribute my ammo load from my ruck onto my body.

Dave sent a 40mm grenade off. It landed in the midst of the mired beasts, its welcome *WHUMP* and shock wave detonation silencing a wide radius in the middle of our planned path. "I got plenty of forty, and I'm gonna use it."

"I'm halfway through my load, guys," Doug said as he slapped a belt into place. "That wave was bigger than the first. Another one like that, I'm dry. It'll be my K-spec from there. When that goes dry, I got blades and spit left." He'd been responsible for the most damage to the waves of snarling attackers, Double-K a close second.

The Tarn discarded both rifles with unceremonious release and drew another pair off his back with his upper hands. "I have these to work with, then other tools not as producing of mass casualties." He squinted at the horizon. "No matter. I think us at our destination soon."

From the darkness ahead came a new roar—not that of more monsters, but of something much more magical and yet mundane. The rough cascades of water falling from a great height.

Cynar cried, "My works! Their end made known at last!"

From the periphery of a cavern so vast and tall I couldn't find its ceiling, towering waterfalls gushed from the walls. The violent cascades frothed and sent swells of dark waves rippling into the great black sea before lapping at the shore of an island. Protruding from the tar and shallows were the first of many giant pillars and structures of abnormal geometries and acute angles. All graven with symbols and characters of no language. With our own eyes, we saw what Avril Mysteen's words could only fail to describe with proper horror.

The island disrupting the waters was capped by more of the repellent architecture. From it, a symphonic chant grew.

"Anso-Kylon, Anso-Kylon...!"

34

I RAGED. HOW WE WOULD GET TO THE RISEN CITY WAS NOT APPARENT. Rounding the shoreline we stood on, creatures piled ahead and over each other to reach us. Frustrated, I did a split-second consultation with no one and hurled a stone into the waters.

Scolding me, Cynar said, "It will not produce effect, Benjamin Colt. It is pointless, we must instead—"

The water erupted in one geyser, then another, and another. The jets of water fell in a spray, revealing black columns above the surface like a disorganized checkerboard. Dave shouted a single obscenity and then grunted with effort as he hurled. Kerplunks and more geysers erupted.

Dave leaped onto the first stone, tested it, then sprang diagonally onto another, then another. He paused to turn. "There's enough to hopscotch on. C'mon." He set off, choosing a course as he landed on the next column.

"I cannot follow you," Cynar said.

I sent a grenade lobbing at the curving shore and the distant horde. "I won't leave you, Cynar."

"I will not be left behind, dullard." In his hands he unrolled a ball of burlap. He held firmly to one end and with a sudden throw, the limp mass snapped into the shape of a flat crescent dish. It was one of his canoes. "It was all I could manage to bring. I thought to shuttle us, but I will use it for myself. Go."

Before I could speak, he spread it on the water, stepped in and pushed off with one foot to propel onto the black ocean, almost losing his balance and toppling in to the drink with the effort. It would have been comical at any other time and place.

"Do you have a rope to throw me? I can pull you along."

"Take care of yourself. I have prepared. Go." He fiddled with something from his backpack, and I set off after Double-K, taking the spot he had just unoccupied. Leap after leap, I followed until the train came to a stop. With no more places to leap, Dave was the lead car of the pileup.

"I need more stones," Dave yelled.

We were far into the expanse of the water. Behind us, the first of the beasts left the shore to start on the new path we'd created. I shot it in mid-air, disturbing its landing to miss and splash into the water.

"Slide over," Doug yelled. He leaped and landed on the flat beside Dave, almost toppling off before being steadied by Dave's grasp. The huge man tossed another of Cynar's stones, then another, until we could resume our movement, mimicking an accordion as our party expanded and contracted across the waters.

"Go quickly, Benjamin Colt."

I almost fell into the water from the surprise of Cynar floating off to my side. His craft motored slowly ahead, propelled by some churn, its wake disturbing the water behind it. The water ahead of him bubbled and some dark, oily monster rose. Without thinking, I grabbed a grenade, pulled the pin, and tossed. The spoon pinged away and my M67 iron baseball plunked into the waters near the rising beast. With a muffled *ka-WOOM*, the water exploded. Tentacles flailed and a screeching mouth surfaced, teeth flashing, shrieking its last to sink beneath the ripples with a final gurgle.

"I take back all of my insults," Cynar yelled back over his shoulder as he sped by.

I tossed another frag much farther along Cynar's course, threw another behind me, and sprang a double distance to land onto the rock just emptied of Double-K's mass. The far shore of the city was close. Dave was halted. Doug landed on an angled pedestal just a few yards aside of him to also freeze. More irregular pillars dotted the surface of the water ahead, almost reaching the pitch-black shallows of the beach. Why weren't they moving?

"Black clouds! Black clouds! There's a swarm of them building!" Dave shouted.

Khraal Kahlees bellowed, "Witches!"

I checked behind us. Writhing, clumsy fur-squids pursued, the faster ones knocking the slower off the stones and into the water to begin a snakelike writhing swim across the rippling surface. I threw more grenades into wherever a mass of them churned the water, the explosion from my last grenade drenching me like a theme park ride. On the waters floated and bobbed many parts, but none of them swam. I vaulted ahead.

Doug was working, raking staccato bursts on the shore ahead where more beasts awaited. Dave fired slowly, carefully, locked to his optic as he chose his targets. I landed on a rounded, rough monolith just to Dave's left. With a disappointed tone, he said, "I saw two witches, clear as day, doing witchy shit on that flat roof by the leaning tower of pizza thing." I didn't correct him. I zoomed up my Elcan and searched. The black cloud of bees hovering above the shore was spread out and thin, but not gone. It was like a swarm of bees, undecided where to go next.

"I didn't drop either of them, brah, but one of them flinched like I parted her hair with a bullet. They stopped what they were doing and beat feet."

Khraal Kahlees was far off to my right. "Keep all behind us occupied, brothers, and leave me unharried. It is time." Double-K sat cross-legged. In his hands was the MK 22, an arm snaking through the loop of the sling. "They will appear again, and when they do, I will greet them with my kiss."

I spun rearward to oblige. They were fewer in number, but more of the pack gathered on the shore, still intent on following. They were slow learners. I launched another 40mm grenade into the center of their herd, then took a few deep breaths to settle in. I chose a spot where the base of a thick horse-like neck met a scaled back. I pressed the trigger without moving another fiber of my being and concentrated. My discipline was rewarded with the gift of seeing a tiny muddy splotch erupt from the very spot I'd chosen. The nightmare dropped. I'd found its off switch. Nothing to do but what it said on the bottle...

Lather, rinse, and repeat.

From their spots on the pedestals of our 3-D chessboard, Doug and Dave joined in, the blast of their muzzles and the whiz of bullets breaking the sound barrier from my left.

"I have them now," Double-D mumbled, his mantra spoken in a language of deadly concentration I understood.

A muffled crack, and the smooth racking of the bolt followed.

Another dull cough, a pause, followed by the soft metallic glide of a bolt sliding forward and down into its resting place. Khraal Kahlees gave a contended grunt.

I spun to see the tar-black swarm of bees had taken a bearing for where we were poised on the columns like figurines atop a trophy but, as if sprayed by poison, the black bees faltered and crashed into the water, and the air ahead cleared.

"It is done. The black witches have absorbed my lesson. Their magic is a fool's folly against the sorcery of a sniper's precise violence."

Doug raked the shore with controlled bursts of 7.62 until, after a final long chug, he stopped, the barrel smoking and red. It sizzled as he dropped the MK 48 into the waters beside him, a brief squeak of the quench making it out over the splash. "Goodbye, baby." A K-spec was immediately in his hands to fire at the last of the monsters on the new shore. Dave sent another 40 mm grenade arcing off before copying Doug's watery burial ritual.

"I miss you already, baby," Dave said as hands found the K-spec on his back.

"Bound, bound, let's go," I yelled.

We leapfrogged until there was nowhere to go but into what I hoped was the littoral slope of a shallow shore. With all my strength, I exploded. High and up, until gravity's pull overcame my effort and I descended to land with a great splash. My feet came to rest on a sinking bottom, just a few inches deep. I slogged ahead. From avenues between the pyramids and obelisks at the top of the grade came more of the beasts down onto the narrow shore.

We plodded ahead in a skirmish line, this fresh pack of nightmares dropping to our fire no differently from those we'd left butchered behind. My feet found firmer purchase and soon we tromped through black bodies and dark slime onto the cobblestones of the city.

"Where're we going?" Dave asked as he pointed with his K-spec left then right. Ahead of us, a dozen paths twisted through forests of bent stone pedicles, sprouted high like a New York skyline of heated wax candles, grown cold and holding their melted shapes. The glyphs and sick totems raised on the colossal wrecks cursed us in their secret babble.

"Through it." That's all I had.

A screech filled the air and became sharp ice picks that pierced my eardrums and whose tips met in the center of my skull. I mashed palms hard over my ears, but the shriek found new paths to my brain. I staggered and dropped to my knees, the white hot pain melting my will. It stopped, leaving behind a high-pitch ringing, many decibels louder than the one that sang to me when I closed my eyes each night.

The ground vibrated in the drumbeat of a mastodon stampeding through the dining room, wood floors creaking under the strain, place settings shifting with each bounce. My bones became the china, vibrating and cracking inside their cabinet.

Between two bent towers at the far end of a winding path, the source of the earthquake appeared. Pouncing into view with a decisive arrest, it announced its presence with an explosive impact that rocked the city. Its entrance should have been slow and lumbering. Its sudden emergence should not have been possible given the beast was greater than the largest dinosaur assembled in any museum.

Legs as thick as redwoods lofted a squat trunk the size of a battleship. From it sprouted many arms and a neckless head that rocked side to side, its entire body twisting to aim its eyes to search for the source of its irritation. The face was discordant and wrong, even for a nightmare built of mismatched parts. The eyes were rounded and intelligent beneath a brow ridge. The nose and ears were almost human. Thick scars warped the rest.

I froze, thinking I was too miniscule and insignificant for it to notice.

The movies were wrong.

It found me and, like a sinkhole giving way, a twisted mouth of crooked teeth materialized and it growled a warning. With a wet snort, it launched.

I brought my rifle up and fired. White blasts joined my puny bullets to pelt it. K-spec blasts glanced off the slick sheen of its hide, and I knew my tiny bullets were mosquito bites to a rhino. So, when it took a jag to disappear down some unseen alley to escape the fusillade as if we'd hurt it, I was amazed.

The ground shook, the tremors it made along its new course not fading. It was out of sight, but not retreating. Where it would appear from next from out of the maze, I couldn't guess. But I didn't want to remain in the only place it knew us to be.

Dave shouted after it, "How are you here? What are you now, you unholy mess? Noooo!"

Doug was at my side. "It was him!"

"That's not Anso-Kylon," I yelled, correcting them. Even shouting, I could barely hear myself above the deafening ring in my skull.

"Didn't you see? Didn't you see the face?" Dave screamed, insistent.

Doug leaned in, staring at me with wide eyes. "That. Was. Chuck."

✖ ✖ ✖

Thunder shook the ground, warning of proximity. It was time. I dropped my primitive bullet launcher and unslung—The Rifle. The chosen arm of Jawn Kurz. Kesta, he'd called her. I stood my ground, aimed at the avenue where it seemed was the epicenter of the approaching quakes and waited.

Doug appeared beside me. An AT-4 was on his shoulder, resting another at his feet.

"No, Ben, let me," he said.

I could hear again. On my other side, protruding ahead like a cannon from a ship's hull, eased the long barrel of the Goose. Khraal Kahlees was beneath it, Dave at his side, pulling Cynar next to him.

"Don't be behind us. This is going to hurt."

A low rumble of a thousand locomotives growled warning, and there he was. The melding of mastodon and whale, walking tank and warship. The monster's arms pumped as it built speed. The AT-4 fired, the instantaneous blast and pressure that pushed at my back and neck the answer to a child's wish for the omnipotent power of a hero who wielded fury with a single hand. The red rocket streaked ahead and hit with a magnificent blast. The behemoth absorbed the blow, staggered, then paused to raise its head in an angry roar. It was then I recognized him. The burned and melted side of his face. His eye sockets—one covered by a thick, bushy brow, the other smooth. It was Chuck, mutated and grown, mocked by some sick artist's hand to be a cruel reminder that this had once been human.

He charged.

The Goose unleashed, joined by the last AT-4.

One impact, two.

Chunks of blubberous flesh fell from the body, the largest of these departing the trunk and taking with it one of the front legs. It toppled forward and was driven to its chest.

"Hit it again!" Dave yelled. "Backblast area clear."

The recoilless rifle roared another thunderous war cry and with it, took away the fetid air we sucked, the vacuum and acrid burn a welcome change from the sour smell of rotting decay. But the real pleasure evaded us. Monster Chuck sprang ahead, tripped, colliding into a tower. The inadvertently chaotic evasion worked, the Goose round just missing and impacting to detonate just behind him in a cloud of rocky spall. Dusty but otherwise not further injured, the monster gained its legs again.

I raised Kesta, ready to finally bathe in the glow of the ruby-red bolt I'd seen played for me as a history lesson.

"Hold!" Cynar cried, thrusting forward a large prickly emerald the size of a bowling ball. "Send this forth. Hurry!"

Double-K palmed the rock the way only Shaq could a basketball. It seemed tiny in his hand. He cocked and hurled. It arced away, following the will of my wishes as it coursed down and intersected the path of the hurtling onslaught, landing squarely on Chuck's chest. Green liquid burst from the crystal like a paint-filled balloon dropped from the tallest skyscraper. It spread across the giant's broad chest and, at last, found the fuel it lacked when it united with oxygen and burst into flame.

The monster halted, its many arms flailing and slapping anywhere it could reach, its purpose to crush our tiny frames into paste no longer important. With each attempt to extinguish the flames, the green and yellow fire splashed and landed elsewhere in sticky globs, the futile slaps billowing air to cause the flames to burn brighter.

The beast spun, rolled, and bucked. It threw its head back and wailed a terrible shriek of agony. It took a few more frenzied steps before it collapsed. Flames creeped over its shoulders to flow down its sloping back, until the last uncovered area between its haunches glowed brightly in the thick green napalm fire. Fat spewed out in pressurized geysers from the burst sausage casing of its scorched and shrinking skin. The drizzle caught fire, burning a brighter yellow as the streams sizzled loudly. It moved no more.

Cynar breathed a sigh of relief. "A fine throw, lord of the Korund. There are times that I too impress myself. The rate of combustion and spread was better than I had hoped."

Double-K gurgled in a dumbfounded way. "Had that cracked open inside your satchel during our journey, would it have ignited so?"

"Most certainly. Which is why I was its keeper, not one of you clumsy children."

"We would have roasted like skinned meat ourselves, wizard!"

"Ingratitude is my eternal thanks, it seems. My genius and foresight allowed us to save Benjamin Colt's weapon for the purpose intended, not squander its resource on a lesser danger. To kill what awaits, even I can only imagine what will be required."

Dave pulled off his helmet, waving away the fumes wafting over us from the well-done giant. "What else you got for us in that bag of tricks, old man?"

Cynar did not take umbrage. "I have no more surprises, my friend. The bottom of my bottomless container of miracles has been reached."

A familiar, low chant returned. The syllables of the refrain, I didn't need to hear. It was in a cadence I knew.

"*Anso-Kylon. Anso-Kylon. Anso-Kylon.*"

Then, all noise ceased.

I spoke, but no sound came out. Contracting every muscle with which to propel my words by the last breath squeezed from the bottom of my lungs, nothing came out.

Mouths moved in panic, but no sound came from them. It was not me that was deaf. A hand was on my shoulder, shaking me like a rat. Dave pointed, his eyes wide and white. Rising from above the city was the darkest of all the black things in this black place. Through gaps and spaces between the mansions of the dead city's denizens, something as wide as the horizon itself grew.

No sound could exist in his presence.

And all paths led to a final audience with a god.

I bounded and flew, unable to hear the labor of my breaths or the beat of my heart. The way ahead widened and I broke into a vacuous plain in the middle of the sick city. In the heart of it was a trapped sea and from it, the one that was so large, so unbelievable in scale, I knew it for what it was. The cause of Avril Mysteen's shattered psyche. The thing that made him question his place in the universe. And like him, I was nothing but a tiny speck of sand.

Anso-Kylon.

From the depths, it rose. Awful in its malevolent glare, its tentacles waving as if conducting some silent orchestra of pain, its lobed skull throbbing in expansions and contractions as if breathing in a harvest of fear through those awful eyes.

But this god would get none from me.

I raised the rifle and pressed the trigger. A ruby rod grew from Kesta's tip and crossed the distance, not in a flash, not in a scream, but in a flight retarded as if traveling through oil. I continued to hold the trigger back until the line from my barrel stretched across the distance to finally touch the mountain with a microscopically thin red ray. I released the trigger and the break of nothing trailed along the path of the rod and the beam extinguished, like the last car of a train vanishing into a tunnel.

Sound returned.

My friends were with me, firing blast after blast at Anso-Kylon. Their lungs screamed with furious hatred as they fired. I fired again. This time, the ruby rod carried with it a siren that spoke of true power as it again stretched toward the leviathan. A thousand tentacled beasts boiled from the waters and set for us, jaws and beaks snapping and grinding in anticipation of tasting our flesh.

Kesta's beam no sooner reached the blackness of its body when a new energy, more powerful than that which caused creation itself, boomed and vibrated through every molecule in existence. It was the voice of Anso-Kylon.

"*Doom,*" my cells translated as they tore asunder.

I was flung backward as if blown by the wind of a nuclear explosion. I retched as I struggled for air. The moans, wet gasps, and agonized breaths of my companions intertwined with mine. I struggled up to stand. I was alone on my feet. Tentacles as massive as mountain chains raised from the pool. Pupils as large as moons rolled in the depths of the green eyes.

Both fixed on the miniscule container of my shrinking soul.

In each black pupil, a chaos of whorls and eddies beat to a fervor. A staticky shaft holding the power of anti-life shot out, too wide to evade—all of it for me. I shut my eyes.

"Thank you for this life, my love. Forgive me for failing."

I ceased to exist.

35

I WAS REBORN.

A new life energy filled me. Grew from me. Built to a peak and then burst from me. Swathes of stars spun out from my chest in rotating spiral galaxies, batting away the crackling static assault aimed at me.

The advancing waves of foul aquatic monstrosities were flung asunder, struck by hurricane-force winds created with the power of the awakening galaxies from my center, and all were blown away. I raised my rifle and fired. The ruby rod traveled as true light should, reaching across the gap to strike the so-called god with instant fury. Anso-Kylon trembled. Its arms palsied in seizure. Its pupils rolled back in its head.

I kept the trigger mashed and looped an ever-widening spiral as the ruby-red beam flayed its flesh.

I had my own aura. The blue-white purity of a thousand million stars coalesced around me to make me a celestial body to rival all other galaxies in the universe. The leviathan shrank. It lost its barely shaped form to melt into an even more amorphous blob of black nothing. Its expanse wilted over the pool it sprang from. I continued to paint every available inch of it with Kesta's red beam, the jellied mass desiccating and crinkling in massive waves of crisp and shrinking plastic.

"The squids are all dying, too." It was Doug, on his feet, hands on his knees, gritting his teeth in pain as he strained to speak. Wherever the tiny black things lay, they twitched as they shriveled until forming odd angles, and ceased to be.

I released the trigger.

"The stars!" Dave was on his feet. I knew what he meant. The glow of creation emanating from me dimmed, and the constellations were sucked into the velvet of my armor, the stars settling to twinkle and swim in the pools of purple ether between them.

Khraal Kahlees scooped Cynar into his arms. "The wizard is badly injured."

"I am fine. Do not cradle me as if I were an invalid," he croaked out. "Nor shed tears, nor kiss me. Help me to stand if you wish to render service." On his feet with Double-K supplying lower arms for support, the old wizard coughed. "Is it dead?"

"I'm off to make sure," I replied and bounded.

It felt good to fly. With new vigor, I sprang at racing speed. The stench of vile corruption grew stronger as I closed on the mountain of flesh. I touched down firmly on top of it, but a twitch beneath my feet threatened to unbalance my landing, forcing me to take a hop to avoid disappearing into the canyon formed by folds of its loose skin.

Anso-Kylon was not dead. It shuddered across its bulk then erupted into a rolling slither. It was trying to crawl away. I fired steadily into it, the beam drilling into its bowels. Something deep within burbled and a stream of sickness gushed out from the wound. I was perforating more of it when two men landed near and opened up with K-specs.

"Keep it up until there's nothing left, Ben," Dougie hollered. "We'll join you."

"Don't know if we're doing any good," Dave said. "And we'll be out of juice soon." The gun did not respond to his next trigger pull. "Dang it." He threw it down. "What's the thing the Harridan needs?"

I didn't know. "His essence? She said it was in his belly."

"That could be anywhere," Doug said, spreading his arms wide.

Khraal Kahlees carried Cynar like a baby over the black terrain. Rather than protest, Cynar's slate was in his hands and he directed his nurse like a taxi driver. "Turn to your left. Slowly. Move ahead. Farther. Continue on this bearing. Come, Benjamin Colt. This way we must go."

Cynar made more adjustments to the course, and after we'd traveled farther and were surrounded by the vileness leaking from Kesta's deepest cuts, he asked to be put down. "It lives yet. It regains strength. Here you must burrow. Be quick."

I fired and let go of the trigger as a bucking wave of skin, so tall it could capsize a battleship, crashed at us. Everyone was flung in a different direction, save me. I jumped straight up, chose my spot, and fired again. I kept the trigger pulled back as I landed, fixed to the same spot. The next wave was just a tiny swell we easily rode, then a soft release of tension came across its skin. I bored deeper and deeper, Kesta's beam slicing and cooking away its protoplasm, the smoke rising from it acrid and gagging.

I worked to deepen the ever-widening hole. Dave grabbed my belt. "Don't fall in, brah." He coughed, then vomited, but didn't release his grasp.

Doug spat wet words. "Ben, hold up."

I released the trigger.

He retched, then drew a gagging breath. "Floating—up—is that something?"

A glowing amber cube, no bigger than a footstool, floated in a pond of black muck.

"You gotta be shitting me," Dave coughed. "What the hell?"

"Put me down again," Cynar said with curiosity. Steadying him, Khraal Kahlees eased forward to let Cynar peer in. "In my bag is a coil of cord. Use it. The nightmare god is dead now. The essence of it is within that container." He lowered his slate again. "It is surely so."

We fiddled with roping the glowing cube for what seemed an eternity, only succeeding in bringing it closer until, by all of us holding Double-K's legs, he was able to grasp it with outstretched upper arms.

"Ahhh!" he screamed. "It burns! Quickly. Quickly."

We pulled him back, and he dropped the object of our surgical dredging, the amber cube shedding goo and beneath it, the pulsing glow of whatever energy it encased.

Double-K assessed himself. "I seem to be fine."

Doug inspected him carefully. "Dude, I nearly died when you screamed. Holy shit. I don't see any burns or anything. You sure you're okay?"

"I am, Douglas Knoblock. But do not touch it. It is most unpleasant."

I tossed an overhand loop around it, risked kicking it over, then ran another slip around it. I did that another time, then cinched down a knot. It wasn't pretty. I'd never get work as a long shoreman. But it was done. "I'll drag the damn box out of here."

Dave dry heaved, then wiped his dry mouth. "Where? All the way back to where we landed?"

A black vortex swirled into existence in front of us.

"The Harridan keeps her promise!" Khraal Kahlees exclaimed. "I bring the wizard. Let us take our leave."

I crowded behind them all, the cube trailing behind me. "Three, two, one. Go."

We stood on a carpet of lime-green fur, the sickly pink light of an invisible sun making me squint. The Harridan was there waiting.

"All returned to me. Success, success!" she cried. "Oh, what diversion, oh what amusement. So much more than that last fool who faced Anso-Kylon."

"Why didn't Jawn Kurz kill it?"

She crowed with delight. "He did not have *me* to disclose how it could be done. I waited an eternity for the sleeping god to regain strength. Now you have brought him to me, to live in my box forever. The infinite souls he has swallowed and stolen from me now mine, all mine!"

She swung on Khraal Kahlees. "You killed my daughters."

Double-K shrugged. "You could have warned them to stay clear of us, but you did not."

"Bah!"

She was already over the loss. She clapped and danced her way to the smoking cube. The fur it sat on smoldered. The thick carpet raised in lumps that scurried away to escape the singe of the hot iron pressed to their nylon blanket. With a raw and scratchy throat I swallowed my revulsion. The air stank sourly, but it was cleaner than where we'd been. I dropped the rope and dodged the sickening vermin fleeing under my feet. She bent low to run fingers along an amber corner. A single forked tongue caressed her lips.

"I will summon your carriage, unless you've changed your minds and would like to stay? I have a box for you, and you, and you—so many empty boxes. All are welcome!"

"Not so fast, Harridan. Talis. Darmon." Kesta was at my side, begging me to use her.

"Testy, testy." The Harridan was wary, as though she sensed the weapon at my side whispering to me. "I only tease. The bargain was made and you have fulfilled your end of it." She swept a hand across the pink sky and the system of conveyors materialized from nothing. Box after Easter-pastel-colored box traveled the skinny highways, winding and turning, loop after loop.

"Pick out yours and I'll open it."

My stomach seized. "That wasn't the bargain."

"I cannot be expected to remember where you lost your toy!" She laughed. "Don't *you* remember where you misplaced it?" She waved a hand down and a single conveyor lowered, the boxes steadily ticking along on it. "Surely, you can't have forgotten? I watched as you sent her to take your place, how your longing and guilt would not let your eyes be torn from it. Pick it out, and I will open it."

Kesta was in my hands.

"I've already killed one god today," I informed her.

All guns came up with mine.

"Open her box. Now."

The Harridan's teeth sprouted, as did she, stretching and growing to tower even higher over us. "You do not command here!" The pink sky turned dark and purple bolts of lightning crashed around us. "If you prefer to die, so be it."

Helest came to life. The spiral galaxy expanded from my chest, the intensities of a trillion tiny suns of blue-white energy repelling the darkness. The Harridan retreated, averting her eyes. We stayed like this for but a moment. Suddenly, the lightning stopped, the winds died, the skies cleared. The Harridan shrank back to being a mere giant.

I relaxed and with me, the spinning arms of stars retreated to swim across my armor.

"You would not win. Even if I were wounded, you would not win. You will die and I will recover. You may borrow powers come to you by accident's hand, but you do not ken the way of the cosmos. I am eternal."

"Open her box, Harridan."

"I will. Choose."

Cynar had been in rapt attention, fixed to the motions of the intricate clockworks above. "Hehehe." His finger tracked far above us. "We choose that one, Harridan."

The Harridan's eyes shot wide.

"I will allow only one to be opened. Only one. Are so sure that is your selection?"

The Harridan did not sound confident. I wasn't, either.

"Cynar, are you sure?"

He ignored me.

"Harridan, bring down that track. Do not try to distract me. A day, a week, nay a hundred years will I wait to choose correctly if that is how long it takes. You have lost. Are you not anxious to be rid of us and turn full attention to the prize we have brought you? Waste no more time."

She gnashed sharp teeth and turned her back on us. She flung arms to direct the near conveyor to lift up and away through the weave of many others, while another bent and lowered to take its place.

"Cynar, how can you know?"

He placed a finger to his lips without taking eyes off his target. "STOP."

The line came to a halt. He marched to the row of boxes, pointed to a faded green one, and smiled at the Harridan. "We choose this one. Open it, please."

Could it be?

"Cynar! You have to be sure!" I cried. The color looked right, but there were thousands like this one. More. How could he know?

"Cynar, you haven't even used your device. You're—you're just eye-balling this."

The Harridan stood beside the box. "Your friend seems sure. Are *you* sure, little Benjy? One choice. One choice only once, precious child."

"I am certain, Benjamin Colt," Cynar folded his arms. "Your trust in me will be rewarded. You have my oath."

I took the leap. "Open it."

The Harridan tapped the lid, and it responded with a slow rise. I raced to it and there, curled in a ball, was my Talis Darmon.

Words spilled from me.

"Oh, baby, I'm here. Wake up. It's over." I reached for her. She did not stir to my voice or my gentle touch. "Wake up, baby, wake up." I lifted her limp body out of the cramped container and cradled her to the ground. Her breath blew lightly on my face. Her chest held her beating heart. She remained asleep.

"Harridan! What have you done to her?"

She interlaced her fingers. "You know what happens in there, little Benjy. But not all are as resilient as you. I cannot be held responsible for any damage done to an item you abandoned." Her narrow chest expanded as her arms flung wide, her head tilted back on its hinge, and the snakes shot to the sky, licking and quivering in joy.

Like a gunshot, she recovered. "Your carriage awaits. Go." She snapped her fingers.

Next to us appeared the *Ashante*. The doors split and the ramp descended.

"Leave. While I still allow it."

Khraal Kahlees and Dave were there to lift me. "Come, Benjamin Colt. We must leave. We will not help her by remaining longer. We take her to safety, far from here." At the base of the ramp, I held her up to Khraal Kahlees.

"Take her."

"I have her," he rumbled, "and will not release her but into your arms again, Warlord."

I turned back to the Harridan, still standing next to the empty box.

"Dougie, did you do it?" I asked him, but I already saw that he had. Tucked beneath the ropes of the cube that held the essence of Anso-Kylon, a Claymore mine sat like a cherry on a cake. From one detonator well was an electric blasting cap, wires twisted together and taped to a cold strobe light. From the other well, a small coppery tube I didn't recognize.

"You haven't kept good faith," I told the Harridan. "I want something else from you. Avril Mysteen. Release his soul from your box before we go."

She did not laugh. "There was no bargain for that. Go, little Benjy. I grow irritable."

"Harridan," Doug spoke wearily. "See this?" He held a clacker up. No wire came from it. It was attached to nothing. "One squeeze, and a pound and a half of C-4 and seven hundred steel ball bearings destroy your prize. I hauled that Claymore mine around in the bottom of my ruck this entire time, but the opportunity to use it never came up. I was going to use it to get you to turn Talis Darmon over to us, but Cynar had that locked down. Seems a shame to waste my work."

She sneered, but there was puzzlement in her voice. "I would destroy you all. What hubris would tempt you to threaten the destroyer of the universe?"

Doug grinned. "We're dumb like that. Spite is my hobby."

She spat and where it landed, the bushy carpet melted brown. A finger crooked several times in beckon over her shoulder. From off a high conveyor, a box rose and floated down, coming to rest between us. A quick wave of her hand and the lid opened. I made to move to it when a cloud of glitter levitated from its opening. It hovered, then condensed. Slowly, it took the shape of a man. It grew denser and more refined until the sparkling ghost of Avril Mysteen was formed. He looked at me with shimmering eyes, smiled, then faded and was gone.

"One tiny soul released on its way, in exchange for millions. But no more! I will not tell you again. Go!"

Doug trotted with me up the ramp, then turned back to hold up a small keypad. He thumbed it with a flourish and the white strobe on top of the cube flashed brightly to life. "So's you know, lady, in case you're thinking about double-crossing us, I can detonate that at any time. It's on a quantum tunneling frequency. The wizard set it up."

"Across time and through the ether of the universe, my science penetrates all," Cynar said with dead seriousness.

Doug smirked. "Any funny business and we don't end up back home, ker-blooey. Oh, and it's on a mercury switch. It'll go off if you touch it. We get where we're going, I'll deactivate it. Promise."

She hissed malevolence with a thin black tongue until the sealing of the doors left us in the tiny cabin of the *Ashante*. The cabin was transparent and as we lifted, the sky darkened and lightning struck. Thunder outside shook the *Ashante*. We lost sight of the fury as the dome clouded to feminine gold again. I kneeled to take the curled Talis Darmon from the Tarn warrior, who'd been cradling her with loving care. I pressed her head to my chest as we shook even more violently.

Khraal Kahlees placed a protective arm around us both. "She does not stir, my friend, but she knows she is safe. I feel it in her."

The shaking stopped. Cynar's slate was in hand. "We are returned to the depths of Vistara. We rise. It is certain."

Doug raised an arm, the clacker in his hand an afterthought, and tossed it away.

Dave's eyes scrunched. "What was that all about, Dougie? That clacker wasn't connected to anything. And that strobe? What the heck was that? You couldn't have detonated that Claymore if you wanted to."

"That bitch don't know that. Thanks for playing along with my *Star Trek* gobbledygook, Cynar."

"Humph. I played at nothing, Douglas Knoblock. What I said was truth. My science is supreme."

Dougie scratched at his stubble. "Of course, she's going to be in for a surprise in about five minutes."

"Wha', brah?"

"I crushed a time pencil in the other detonator well. That bad boy's going high-order, come hell or high water."

"Where'd you get a time pencil? Those things are ancient, Dougie."

Doug grinned. "When I ran Baby Blue in Thoria, I found it in the library. She was on the fritz, but a time pencil's pretty simple. I made a bunch of 'em. I never liked that bullshit regulation about no unobserved detonations of ordnance. No regulations on Mars, baby."

The thin copper tube contained a vial of acid. When crushed, the acid would slowly eat through the wire restraining the spring detonator. It was indeed simple, old, and very useful.

"Always heard about the mobile guerilla force guys in Vietnam arming Claymores with a time pencil and leaving them on a trail for pursuit deterrence. First time I've ever used one. Wish I could see it in action."

"We are on the surface," Cynar announced, lowering his pad. The dome cleared. We'd returned to the bay of the *Ashante*'s home.

"Baby, wake up, we're back on Vistara." I expected Talis Darmon to open her eyes at the news. She did not. "What do I do?"

The way parted and through the bay, the wall slid aside. Dave thumbed at Jawn Kurz and his queen waiting in two-dimensional form.

"Ben-dog, if there's anyone who might know what to do, it's them."

36

As carefully as I could, I cushioned the porcelain masterpiece in my arms as I raced down the ramp to the chamber where the pair of phantoms waited with a serene presence.

"Is the thing done, Warlord?" Jawn Kurz asked.

"It is. Anso-Kylon is dead."

"He cannot be killed," the queen said. "You may have gravely injured him to take slumber again, but he cannot be killed, I am sorry to say."

"I removed his essence. His body turned to corruption and all the dark things there died with him."

Jawn Kurz's mouth dropped.

"To where did you carry his essence?"

"I delivered it to another who wanted it. The Harridan."

The remnant of Queen Sumera Tashara Calypsis grew pale. "Impossible! How was it you encountered the profaneness of all creation and escaped?"

Cynar stepped up. "The *Ashante* cannot travel through states immaterial again, Warlord Jawn Kurz. It was in the flux between states of existence where the Harridan waylaid us to her realm. She most certainly lies in ambush to ensnare any who enter that medium again. We did not leave her well disposed toward us."

The amethyst-framed face recovered poise.

"What ails your queen, Benjamin Colt?"

"She was in the box of a soul-eater. She did it so we could fight Anso-Kylon. She—she's not waking up. Can you help her?"

The queen was anguished. "I am but a shadow, Warlord. Take her to my sisters. If any can reach her and provide beacon from which to find her way from slumber, it will be they."

"Wait." Jawn Kurz held up a restraining hand. "Brother Warlord, you may not leave my bastion with the gifts." A drawer slid open from the face of a wall. "Place all pieces of Helest's protection there and lay my dear Kesta beside. They must be protected and hidden anew, awaiting the day when needed again by a true Warlord to defend the light. Would you desire to keep Lady Vivimus? She may live at your side as a token of our eternal bond. May she serve you well."

I allowed Khraal Kahlees to take my beloved and quickly threw off all my gear. I did as he instructed and watched the wall seal again. I wore only my war belt and the sword dangling at my side. Dave and Doug gathered my things as I returned to stand in front of the mirror.

"You have accomplished what I could not. Fare thee well, Warlord Benjamin Colt." He and his queen bowed deeply. The mists returned, the mirror cleared, leaving me to stare at our reflections.

Double-K snarled. "Such magic be damned! Take flight, Benjamin Colt. I will bring your queen."

We raced from the chamber, through the wreck of the castle and out into the sunlight where the flitter waited. "Hang on," I yelled as I brought the craft to life and drove us high, then spun us to aim its nose into the Furrow before I aligned the rays to rocket us away. The glimmer of the waters far below the keep were left behind. "Someone take the helm," I said over the hot wind pelting my face. The beautiful warm sun of Vistara was high, and not a shadow was cast on the empty chasm. Neither above nor below our world was there left a darkness to fear.

Dave was beside me. "Where to?"

"Keep us pointed up the Furrow. We'll find Shelasa along the rim. Don't know how long it'll take."

"I'll run this sucker all out, Ben-dog. I got it."

With his back to the winds, Khraal Kahlees held her in his lap, his wide chest and all arms wrapped around her like a green muscled shroud.

I dropped to her sweet face. "We're on our way, baby. Hang on. We're taking you to help. It's going to be alright."

She was perfect in her stillness.

Doug thrust a bottle at me. He spread out a soft blanket and balled another for a pillow. Double-K laid her down and I wet her lips with my moistened fingers. Propped against the gunwale, I drew her into my lap.

"Drink, Benjamin Colt." A bottle was thrust at me, but I couldn't release her to take it.

Doug dropped to both knees. "Where we headed, Ben?"

"The queen said her sisters could help. There are only two. One's in Aetheria. The other's on this side of the Furrow. It's the only city along the rim. You'll know it when you see it."

I cradled her all day and through the night. I talked to her without end. "Remember when that gazraal stalked us in the Korund? And how Apache dived in to save me? How did I get so lucky to have another friend who'd fight for me? For all of us. I know you love him, even if he is a stink factory sometimes. He loves you, my wife. We all do."

Sometime late in the night, when the air cooled and with skins piled over us, all I knew to do was softly repeat her name. "Talis Darmon. Talis Darmon, come back to me." She'd called to me when I was trapped in the soul-eater. I'd heard her. It was her voice that had brought me from the pit of despair.

It was dawn when Cynar brought me from my trance. "I see it. Shelasa lies ahead."

"Let me take over." I flew us closer to the canyon rim and the city nestled into the cliffs. Below, hands stretched to brows and fingers pointed skyward at the sight of us, then scattered as I dived to buzz over their heads. The dry cove around the cliffs was there and in the middle of it, the great squat shell. I spiraled down to a landing, the hum of the flitter bringing Mother Oceansong from her reclusive home.

Khraal Kahlees was the first out.

"Tarn! Hold! You are not welcome here," the bronzed and painted woman warned with raised hands.

"Silence your bleating, witch. We have one who needs you."

I passed Talis Darmon to him and vaulted over the side. Together we descended on the tattooed woman and her astonishment grew.

"I felt the lifting of the darkness," she said. "It has been done!"

"Talis Darmon's hurt, Mother Oceansong. Queen Sumera Tashara Calypsis told me to bring her to you."

Her eyes settled on the tiny body wrapped in the massive Tarn's arms like a sleeping infant.

"Bring her."

We followed her in, explaining as we went. She absorbed it all without question. Mother Oceansong sat on a bed of pillows, the earthen floor and dangling skeletons of marine life touched by the dim light passing through the translucent shell around us.

"Place her here so that I may touch her." I eased Talis Darmon's head into the lap of crossed legs and brushed her hair back. Tan fingers parted the cloth over the resting chest to reveal the silver chain and pendant that lay between her breasts. Mother Oceansong lifted the branched coral with tenderness and touched the life preserved in metallic perfection with a fingertip.

"My sister." She lowered the necklace then drew her hands to find the gentle depression of Talis Darmon's temples. She hummed deep, sonorous strains, closed her eyes, and a purple aura grew around them both. As I watched, her fingers melted into my queen, just as I had envisioned when she'd held my head in her lap.

"She is protected in a deep, deep place. A citadel of her own construction. Many, many layers of protection around her. Call to her, Benjamin Colt. Call your queen from her redoubt."

I knelt down to whisper. "Come back, Talis Darmon. Come back to me."

"Again. Do not cease."

313

I said her name over and over. Mother Oceansong's voice became gentle waves kissing a pure shore. Talis Darmon's eyes moved beneath her closed lids. Once. Twice. Slowly. Then darted rapidly. The song stopped.

"Talis Darmon. Awake from your slumber."

The lids opened and the most beautiful eyes in the universe met mine. Brown hands pulled away and I replaced them with mine as I scooped her head into my hands.

"Benjamin Colt. I heard you call to me from so very far away."

"Just as you did for me, my love. My wife. My queen." My eyes flooded in tears and blended with hers as I kissed her. I drew her fully into my embrace and squeezed my world so it couldn't escape.

She raised her head from chest. "Am I truly here in your arms, Benjamin Colt, or is this yet another trick of the Harridan?"

The purple witch stood over us. "You are returned and made whole, Talis Darmon. I see now that all I have held against the dynasty of Sylah has been calumny. I bow to the true queen." She dipped deeply.

Between sobs and gushing tears, my love sniffled to draw air with which to speak. "Husband, take me home. I desire only for us to lay hands together on the egg that bears our child. Your great duty is completed. Let us never be parted again."

She kissed me, then placed her fingers on my lips.

"Born of another world, you were brought to life for no purpose save to find me. You are of Vistara and Vistara is of you. Our world is more than we will ever know."

"It is, my love."

The wet snort of a Tarn filled the room. "Curse the smoke in here. In the Korund, we know how to ventilate a domicile. I take my leave outside." He departed brusquely, moist sniffles quickening his race to depart.

Even Cynar wiped at his eyes.

Talis Darmon grasped my neck and I scooped her up.

"Let's go home, baby," I said.

✴ ✴ ✴

"We gather to honor our Warlord on the night before his wedding ceremony. Along with those gathered here, the entirety of the kingdom celebrates its arrival." Khraal Kahlees stood tall. The table was crowded with friends and fellow warriors of all colors. The night sky was bright and fires crackled around us.

"I also take the opportunity to recognize another Thulian brother, my most able second-in-command, General David Masamuni. Clansman, I have for you a special delicacy brought from the Korund, served to honor only the bravest of warriors. For you, my friend."

A servant brought a covered dish and placed it in front of Dave, removing the cover as she stepped away.

Khraal Kahlees raised a cup. "To you, Warlord. And to you, General David Masamuni. Let us eat to provide strength for our bodies to serve in future battles and glory to come."

I tossed my drink back with everyone else and dug in. Roasted godahl leg was a specialty of the Korund. I carved a piece while the Tarns attacked the meat, tearing at the charred flesh with tusks and teeth. Double-K held his, but leered above the cover of the haunch. He cast poorly hidden glances in Dave's direction, who was busy slicing into the meat on his plate. A few of the other Tarns looked over too. Something was up.

Dave speared a piece and chewed it noisily.

Double-K's pleasure was never so apparent. "How do you like your meal, David Masamuni?"

"S'good, thanks, brah. What kinda meat is it?"

"It is the male organ of the gazraal!"

Tarns collapsed with riotous abandon at the revelation. Double-K roared, slurped, and coughed in succession. Chieftain Parkus Laan pounded on Double-K's shoulders, both in hysterical laughter until they turned lime green from hypoxia.

Dave didn't stop eating. Without looking up, he carved yet another large piece, popped it in his mouth, and continued his open mouthed chewing, smacking loudly with each bite.

"Not as rubbery as I mighta thought. Needs salt."

The table fell to stunned silence. Parkus Laan's roar broke the night. "He bests you, Khraal Kahlees! The Thulian bests you at your sport! He doesn't recoil! He thrives!"

The chieftain led the Tarns in more uproarious laughter, green fists pounding, shaking the table so bad, I had to grab my plate to keep it from taking a ride off the table and to the ground.

Double-K fumed. "Grid squares, indeed. I shall yet see justice served, David Masamuni."

Dave swallowed and took a big slurpy drink before making the single loud smack in the most annoying sound in the world. "Ahhh! If your next serving of justice is as bland as this lion schlong, then I won't be losing any sleep, brah. Bring it on." He dug in for more.

Double-K marveled, "He is a thing of legend, like the stone men of the Korund."

I snorted. "They're real, brother. Remember?"

"And he shares ancestry with them." He laughed like a diesel cranking to life. "How dull my life was, absent Thulians in it."

✳ ✳ ✳

I was alone to dress. A knock came at my door and it opened a crack. Karlo's head stuck through.

"Got a minute for us, Ben?"

"Karlo! Cynar! Is Kleeve Hartus with you? He was going to give me the once-over before I have to trot out in front of the whole damn world. I don't care what anyone else thinks, but I don't want to look like a goof for Talis Darmon."

Karlo closed the door behind him. "He said he'd be along. Ben, there's something I wanted you to hear. I think sooner is better than later."

"Shoot. Whatever it is, nothing's going to spoil today."

"Ben, I've had Cynar working on something."

"New gadget?"

"No, Ben. It's a question I've had him trying to answer."

"'Kay. Lay it on me."

Cynar stroked at his long scraggly beard. "Karlo Columbo has allowed me to instruct him in my science. He is an adept learner, certainly the only one of you Thulians even capable of understanding—"

"Please, Cynar. My big wedding day is happening. Can you cut to the chase?"

"Bah! A deeper explanation would be wasted on you, anyway. Oaf. We've come to tell you that you need not fret over your great concern."

I frowned. "What concern would that be? We beat the monsters. The air wizards think they have the thingamajig that runs the atmosphere works figured out. The Yellows are quiet. What concern do I have?"

"Ben, Cynar thinks that we aren't going to die here."

"Huh?"

Cynar groaned. "He is the densest of all. Benjamin Colt, the rays that permeate Vistara are responsible for the long lives of all who are born here. And their effects will be conferred upon any, even a stranded Thulian. No life is infinite, but as far as the length of your pitiful ones, they are not subject to the constraints you were once bound by."

Amazement never ceased on Vistara.

"Ben, it means you don't have to worry about the age thing between you and Talis Darmon. You're going to have long and happy lives together. For hundreds of years, at least. Thought you'd want to know. Happy wedding day, brother."

Alone again, I fumbled with the clasp of my cloak. What good was hundreds of years just now? I had about five minutes before I had to leave. My wristlet hummed and I figured it was Kleeve Hartus telling me not to worry, he was on his way to fix my costume. I brought the cloud to life, only to have Brandon Bryant's smug face appear.

"Going to a costume party, Colt?"

Of all days. "Eat it, Bryant. Not even you can piss me off today."

"Hey, hey, settle down. I called to say your purple-haired Playboy bunny pulled me aside on the QT to tell me you did it. Used your little Buck Rogers crap to kill the big squid. That so?"

I rolled my eyes. "Yes, we did. It's done."

"Glad I could help."

I fumed. "Help? You—"

"So predictable. Always the racoon in the shaken cage."

I shook it off. "How is Sister Wavecrest?"

"She's like all of us, living two lives under the shining beneficence of the supreme magnate."

"Help her if you can, Bryant. Be good to her. You'll never understand how much she's done for us all."

"I gotta take care of myself, Colt. But if I can, and it doesn't hurt me or Sophena Pah, I'll see what I can do."

"Good enough."

"And remember, Colt, you owe her. Big time. You left a hell of a mess for us to clean up. We'll be in touch."

I killed the cloud, and another knock was there.

"Interrupting?" Kleeve Hartus came through. "Apologies, Warlord. Are you well? You look pale, even for you." He fiddled with the clasp of my cloak as he prattled. "After so many wars, the trifle of this pageantry is no cause for a Warlord to be anxious. Trust me. I have been married thrice before. In a way, this is your second. You already know your part. This is mere formality for benefit of the kingdom. See? Your color improves. You've absorbed the Vistaran sun for so long now, you are almost red, my friend. Let me look at you. Perfect."

He left with me, and we walked in silence through the palace to reach the outer doors of the spectral hall. I had a lot to think about along the way.

Our world was more than I would ever know.

"Take your time, Warlord. I'll see you inside."

From this last cover and concealment, it was so quiet, a church mouse would've made a ruckus. Through those doors waited hundreds, a veritable army. And my Talis Darmon. I hadn't seen her in two days, hidden away from me to attain perfection at the hands of a dozen attendants. I couldn't image her being any more beautiful than she already was.

I was wrong.

My queen waited next to the short priest. I gulped and started my walk. As instructed, I did not hurry, pausing along the way to accept curtsies, bows, and hands of congratulations. Some had been enemies, wishing my demise. Only a few were friends. Talis Darmon had once said that in politics, fake loyalty was damn near as good as the real thing. It was the noblesse oblige that often swayed the fakers into leaving their daggers at home. I had a lot to learn. They may have been all smiles today, but I still half expected a knife in the back.

That would never change for me.

At the front rank finally, I moved down the line to accept the blessings of the only people I gave a damn about. Beraal wrapped me in her arms for the first public hug she'd ever dared give me. "Brother, this is the beginning of all good things."

"It is, sister."

Next to her was Dave, and at his side, a beautiful diminutive woman I'd never seen him with before, dressed in high fashion. It suddenly struck me. "Tranya Olan! I almost didn't recognize you."

She curtsied and grinned.

"Next time we go on a mission, it won't be looking like this, Warlord."

Kleeve Hartus was accompanied by another woman also dolled up to the nines in scanty Mihdradahl fashion. Never in my imagination did I place her with the first shield.

"Zaylin Twee! Neither of you two ever mentioned that you were—"

Kleeve Hartus winked. "I told you I was sending you my finest, Benjamin Colt."

Doug was there with his three lady friends, and even Cynar stood with Dureen Zell. It was only Karlo and Khraal Kahlees who were stag.

"Gotta get you guys fixed up."

"Leading an army allows no such time, Warlord."

"I've got my hands full, Ben-dog. Someday. Life is long and good."

I ascended at last to face my queen. How do you describe Venus Rising, the face that launched a thousand ships, or Aphrodite and all the Greek goddesses? I won't even try. The little bald priest spoke his words. They were just as much a blur this time while I stared into her radiant eyes. He laid hands on us.

"You are joined as one—Queen Talis Darmon to Warlord Benjamin Colt."

Facing each other, she beamed. "Husband."

This time my eyes were dry, my voice strong, my smile not forced to disguise the dread of our impending doom. "Wife."

The white-robed munchkin backed away, and the queen accepted my hand in escort. She sat on her throne, and I took my place at her side. With perfect poise, she broke into that wordless song of dulcet tones. The crystal ceiling parted and the light of all spectrums radiated to fill the sky over Shansara.

"The line of Colt-Sylah is now established. My successor follows. The chain will be unbroken. Mihdradahl and all Vistara will prosper by this dynasty."

A herald stepped forth. "Long live the Queen! Long live her Warlord!"

The cheer repeated in deafening refrains.

"Are you happy, my love?"

"The happiest, my princess."

If our world was more than this, then I need never know it.

My name is Deacon Benjamin Colt.

I am Warlord of Mars.

ABOUT THE AUTHOR

Doc Spears is a veteran of the United States Army and works as a consultant and trainer in the defense industry. Writing has been the worst vice he's found yet and doubts he'll be able to stop even with help, which he refuses to seek. When not offending the sensibilities of all decent peoples everywhere, he can be found with Nick Cole and Jason Anspach plotting to infiltrate all realms of sci-fiction.

To be notified about Doc's upcoming books, including the sequel to this title, visit www.WarGateBooks.com

www.ingramcontent.com/pod-product-compliance
Lightning Source LLC
Chambersburg PA
CBHW020842020726
47497CB00005B/1218